Cougar Attack

By: F. Edward Jersey

ALSO BY F. EDWARD JERSEY

(non-fiction)

Softwhere

(fiction)

Paines Creek Mystery

ObitUCrime

Cougar Attack

A Cape Cod Mystery/Thriller

By F. Edward Jersey

Copyright © 2010 by F. Edward Jersey
First Edition February 2010

Cover © 2010 by Penny Turton
Edited by Diane Kelley and Wendy H. Jersey

ISBN: 1448618975
EAN-13: 9781448618972

This book is dedicated to all the folks who work at Sundancers in West Dennis, MA. Thanks for contributing to the story.

Cougar Attack

Chapter 1

The call came into the Dennis Police Station at 9:45 pm. The dispatcher on duty was Sergeant Lou Grimes. Sergeant Grimes was sitting in for Officer Connally who was taking a short break from dispatch. "911 Operator, please state your emergency."

"My name is Donald Fields. I live up near the aqua-farm on Dr. Bottero Road. A little while ago, my wife Barbara and I were taking a walk on Chapin Beach when we heard a person moaning. When we went to investigate, we found a woman unconscious on the dunes behind Chapin Beach near the off-road access. Can you send someone out right away to help the woman?"

"I'll dispatch an officer and paramedics to your location."

"Thank you. Barbara and I will stay with the woman until help arrives."

Sergeant Grimes called the fire department and dispatched the paramedic crew on duty to the location provided by Mr. Fields. He then contacted Officer Trudy who was observing traffic from the Players Shopping Plaza at the intersection of Route 134 and 6A.

"Officer Trudy, this is Sergeant Grimes at dispatch, come in."

"Trudy here, what's up?"

"Trudy, break off your current observation post and go to the Chapin Beach parking lot immediately. There's a woman unconscious on the dunes behind the parking lot. A

Mr. Fields will meet you at the town landing and show you where the victim is located."

"Will do. Trudy out."

The day had been sunny with temperatures reaching eighty degrees, which is pretty hot for Cape Cod. After the sun had set, it cooled down a little although the night was very humid. There were a few clouds in the sky but for the most part, the full moon provided enough light for a walk along the beach.

Off in the distance, the Fields could hear sirens. After a few minutes, they could see the flashing lights of the cruiser and the ambulance coming down the road. Mr. Fields went to the parking lot to meet the paramedics and officer. Both vehicles came to a stop in the parking lot. Officer Trudy asked Mr. Fields where the victim was located and he pointed to the dunes behind the beach and just to the left of the off-road access point. Officer Trudy quickly went over to where Mrs. Fields was bent over trying to help the victim. The paramedics got equipment packs out of their ambulance and then joined Officer Trudy.

As Officer Trudy approached Mrs. Fields, she said, "We'll take it from here." Then the paramedics went to work on the victim. One paramedic took out a tube of something and waived it under the victim's nose. She responded with a shake of the head. While they were doing that, Officer Trudy turned to the Fields and asked, "Can you tell me what happened?"

Mrs. Fields said, "At about nine o'clock, my husband and I were taking a walk on the moon-lit beach when we heard a person moaning. It wasn't far from where we were walking so we went right to where we thought the sound came from but didn't see anyone. When we started to turn away, my husband thought he heard someone moan over here by the dunes. When we looked further, we found this woman laying

2

here. She was breathing but unconscious. When we tried to wake her, we discovered blood on her head. It looked like she had been hit with something, because there are no rocks over there, just sand."

"Did you see anyone else?"

"No, and my husband ran back up to the parking lot to see if anyone else was there. He didn't find anyone and then called 911."

Looking at Mr. Fields, Officer Trudy asked, "Did you see anyone else in the parking lot or any other car?"

Mr. Fields said, "No, no one."

"Ok. Can you and Mrs. Fields stand-by for a few minutes while I see how the paramedics are doing?"

"Sure."

The paramedics were able to awaken the victim and as they shined their lights on her, they could see she had cuts, scrapes and bruises on her face and the back of her arms. The woman was dressed in a pair of white capri slacks and a dark blue tank top. Her clothes were soiled and had some blood on them. She had on one dark blue flip-flop and the other was lying in the middle of the off-road path. On the back of her head she had a cut that while covered in sand was bleeding. Paramedic Mike Jones was applying a gauze pad to the back of the victim's head, and she turned her gaze to his face. "Can you tell us your name?"

"Ann Benard."

"Ms. Benard. I'm paramedic Mike Jones and this is my partner Tom Donovan. We're here to help you. Can you tell us what happened?"

"I came down to the beach to take a walk. After I got out of my car and started down the access path there by the dunes, someone pushed me from behind and I fell down. I think I hit my head and I must have been knocked out because that is all I can remember."

Jones looked over to Donovan, "Tom, get Officer Trudy for me if you would."

3

"Will do."

Donovan went and got Officer Trudy who had been looking around the access path with her flashlight. Officer Trudy had just made a note in her pad of the sign at the beach. It read:

GEORGE H CHAPIN MEMORIAL BEACH
    ENTRANCE AND EXIT
FOR VEHICLES WITH VALID 4 WHEEL STICKERS
MAXIMUM SPEED 15 MPH
MAXIMUM TIRE PRESSURE 15 PSI
KEEP OFF VEGETATION AND DUNES
NO OPEN FIRES OR LITTERING
OVERNIGHT STAYS NOT ALLOWED
$100 FINE PER VIOLATION
    DENNIS CONSERVATION COMMISSION

Trudy said, "What do you have?"

"The victim is a Ms. Ann Benard. She said someone jumped her from behind and pushed her down. She thinks she hit her head on something or was hit in the head as that was the last thing she remembered."

Officer Trudy walked to where the victim was, and bent over next to her.

"Ms. Benard, my name is Officer Trudy of the Dennis Police. Is there anything more you can tell me about the attack?"

"Nothing. I didn't see or hear anyone. The next thing I know was I was being knocked down and everything went black."

"Start from the beginning Ms. Benard. Where had you been before coming to Chapin Beach?"

"I had gone to Gina's By the Sea Restaurant for dinner around five. I had met my friend Katherine Sterns there. We ate and then at around seven-thirty, we went down to Chapin's Restaurant for a drink before heading home. When we were

4

leaving Chapin's, Katherine headed home and I decided to take a walk on the beach since it was such a nice night."

"Did you talk to anyone at the restaurant?"

"Yes. Kat and I knew a few of the people at the bar."

"Do you remember their names?"

"One was Bobby Jones and another was Ken Brown, there might have been a few others we talked to but those are the only names I can remember."

"Do you think any of them could have followed you from the restaurant and done this to you?"

"Why would any of them have attacked me?"

"Not sure, but someone did, right? Ok. I'll make a note of what you've told me and we'll follow-up on these people. Anything else you can tell me?"

"No, that's about all I can remember."

The paramedics continued to clean Ms. Benard up so Officer Trudy turned her attentions to looking for any visual clues in the area.

Officer Trudy shined her flashlight around the ground to see if there were any other prints in the soft sandy soil. There were tracks on the ground, some tire, some people and some animal. Officer Trudy thought it might be difficult to determine anything from the tracks as the parking lot is utilized quite a bit as it is the off-road path leading out on to the beach heading west. One set of tracks looked like they came from a large paw print. One problem with sandy soil is that tracks don't hold their shape very well and this was the case as Officer Trudy surmised. She looked down the off-road path but didn't see anything out of the ordinary.

While she was looking around, the paramedics were cleaning up the cuts and scratches on Ms. Benard when Jones said, "It looks like something scratched you on the back of your arms with a claw or something."

Donovan added, "Yeah, look here, these are definitely scratch marks. It looks like a cat got you or you fell into a briar bush."

Officer Trudy said, "There aren't any briars in this area so I don't think it was that."

Donovan said, "Well, it definitely looks like something scratched her."

Officer Trudy made a note of the comments in a notepad she had taken out. Then, Jones said, "I have some blood on this rock over here. That's weird. There aren't a lot of stones and rocks in this area."

He pointed at a rock that was a little bigger than a softball.

"Do you think she hit her head on it when she fell?" Trudy asked Jones.

Jones responded, "There are some footprints over here that look like they could be Ms. Benard's plus there are other prints here, some human, some animal."

Office Trudy shined her light on the tracks and then made another note in her pad.

Jones added, "But I'm not sure these tracks mean anything. I mean this path gets used quite a bit both day and night by people coming and going to the beach."

"You make a good point," said Officer Trudy. "I'll have someone come back in the morning and see if there are any other clues."

Paramedic Donovan then said Ms. Benard had been checked out and cleaned up. He said she was ready for transport to the hospital, as the cut on her head would require stitches. Officer Trudy went back over to Ms. Benard and asked if there was anything other than the cuts and bruises she wanted to report.

"Not that I can think of."

"Why do you think you were attacked?" pressed Officer Trudy.

"I don't know."

Jones then added, "Maybe the attacker got scared off when the Fields showed up?"

"Could be," said Trudy.

Jones looking to Officer Trudy then added, "Do you think this was going to be a sexual attack?"

Trudy said, "I don't know if we'll ever know. It all happened so fast and whoever or whatever attacked Ms. Benard didn't stay around to be identified."

Jones took one end of the stretcher and Donovan took the other and they took Ms. Benard back to their ambulance. The Fields followed them to the parking lot.

Officer Trudy told the paramedics she would follow them to Cape Cod Hospital and continue the investigation there. Officer Trudy took down the name, address and phone number of the Fields. She said she or someone from the police department would probably call them again. The Fields said to call anytime.

"How will I get my car?" Asked Ms. Benard.

"You can ride back with the paramedics after you are looked at in the hospital as long as the doctor gives you the ok," said Officer Trudy. "If that's not tonight, I'll make sure the overnight officers patrol the lot periodically to ensure the car isn't targeted by vandals, and to not issue any overnight parking citation on it."

"We'll hang around the hospital until you see the doctor unless we get called back out, then an officer can be called to transport you back," added Donovan.

The paramedics put Ms. Benard into the ambulance and then headed to the hospital. Officer Trudy followed. The Fields walked back to the beach and turned east heading back to their cottage overlooking Cape Cod Bay on Dr. Bottero Road.

In the Emergency Room, Dr. Thomas Warren, the doctor on duty said it looked to him like a large cat had attacked Ms. Benard. The scratches had the characteristics of

7

feline scratches. It didn't make sense to Officer Trudy. After all, how could a cat knock a woman down and render her unconscious, unless the cat was a very big cat. He asked Officer Trudy to give him a few minutes to stitch up the cut on Ms. Benard's head and then he would be available to speak with the Officer.

Officer Trudy having observed Dr. Warren conduct his examination said, "Doc, do you think there was any sexual assault here?"

"I checked for that possibility, but there wasn't any semen or any trauma to her body that would indicate a sex attack."

"Do you have an opinion of what happened to her?"

"I can't be sure as the cut on her head looks like it came from a blunt force strike. The bruises look like they are the result of falling in the dunes, but those scratches on the back of her arms; they came from something sharp like claws."

"So would you say that she was mugged from behind and then scratched?"

"From what Ms. Benard said, I would think that's a pretty good description."

"Could those scratches have come from fingernails?"

"If they did, they would have to be pointed, almost sharpened, and as opposed to rounded."

"Or they could have come from an animal."

"I'd think scratches like that could have come from a raccoon, bob-cat or cougar."

"A cougar; we don't have anything like that around here."

"Not in the wild, but I think they have at least one over at the ZooQuarium in Yarmouth. I don't think a raccoon or bob-cat could have rendered an adult person unconscious."

"I wouldn't think so either, but a cougar?"

"Officer Trudy, I think anything is possible in today's world. Maybe someone has a pet mountain lion or something and it got loose. You might want to have someone check with

8

the folks at the ZooQuarium just in case one of their animals got out."

"I guess you have a point. I'll make a note in my report and let the department follow-up tomorrow. I'll also check to see if anyone has reported an exotic pet missing."

Dr. Warren told Ms. Benard she was free to go whenever she wanted. He instructed her in how to attend to her injuries and then walked her to the door. Officer Trudy asked Ms. Benard to wait for her in the waiting room, as she wanted to talk with the doctor for another minute.

After Ms. Benard left, Dr. Warren said to Officer Trudy, "What would a woman who looks like her be doing walking the beach at night?"

"I don't know. Chapin Beach is so isolated from everything else. If those people hadn't heard her moaning, she might be dead right now. Maybe not from her injuries, but from whoever, or whatever, knocked her down."

"Makes you wonder."

Officer Trudy thanked Dr. Warren for his assistance and indicated someone from the department might be calling on him for a report. Dr. Warren said his medical report would be in Ms. Benard's file. Officer Trudy found Ms. Benard in the waiting room and the two left in her cruiser to go back to Chapin Beach to retrieve Ms. Benard's car as the paramedics had been called out to a car accident. On the way Officer Trudy told Ms. Benard someone would contact her in the morning from the Police Department. Ms. Benard thanked Officer Trudy for her help.

Chapter 2

Most summer nights on Cape Cod tend to have a breeze, as the Cape is a thin peninsula surrounded by the Atlantic Ocean on three sides. The normal air currents just naturally cause this. Occasionally, the air would be still, but that only seems to happen one or two nights per month. While the breeze is appreciated during the summer, the water surrounding the Cape is also responsible for high levels of humidity during the days. When the air is still and the humidity is high, most everyone stays indoors. Sticky air with no breeze tends to bring out the little bugs, which locals commonly refer to as no-see-ems. These little buggers are all bite, and for a little bug, they tend to leave a pretty big welt.

Being the first Friday night in July, one of the busiest months of the summer on the Cape, the hot-spot bars were all at or exceeding capacity. In addition to the regular young crowd, Sundancers had a few cougars lurking in the crowd. Harry Adams, whose family owns the restaurant and bar, has worked hard to bring in good entertainment, good food and beverage to the mid-Cape area. For the mid-Cape, Sundancers is the place to be during spring, summer and fall. Darlene Crowe, better known as Dee, Margarita Ortiz and Ron Jessup were tending bar. The band M-Sound was setting up on the stage preparing for their ten o'clock start. A little after nine o'clock Katherine Sterns entered the bar and took up a stool nearest to the stage. Dee looked at Ron, "looks like another cougar."

"Looks like it," said Ron.

Dee looked around and asked, "How many does that make?"

Ron scanned the room. "Looks like four to me."

"Should be an interesting night."

Ron extended his hand to Dee, "Want to make a bet as to who scores first?"

Dee glanced at Margarita and then turned back to Ron, "Why? Do you think you know something?"

"Not really, but it would make our evening more interesting."

Margarita whispered in Dee's ear, "be careful."

Dee turned back to Ron with a smile, "Ok. You're on. What will the bet be?"

"How about dinner next Tuesday night at Alberto's? Looser buys," Ron confidently responded.

Dee looked back, "Ok. I put my money on the one who just came in. Her name is Kat."

"I know who she is. She's been here before," Ron said as he took a beer over to one of the patrons on the other side of the bar.

Ron looked at Katherine. She was very good looking. She had a nice figure, nice clothes and was attractive. It was a hot, sticky night on the Cape, and Katherine, like most of the other women, was wearing hot weather clothes. For Katherine, that was a white halter tied at her neck, a pair of black and white checkered shorts that hit mid-thigh, black flip-flops, and hair piled high with tendrils framing her face. Ron had talked to her in the past and knew she was in her forties. He looked at who he thought the other three cougars were. He said to Dee, "I'll take easy Sue over there."

"Picking a ringer are you?" Margarita said.

Then Ron added, "She's a pretty sure thing to bet on don't you think?"

Margarita said, "Ron, taking a ringer doesn't give Dee much of a chance."

"Dee can have her pick of anyone else here."

11

Margarita added, "Dee should get two picks if you get Sue."

"That's alright Margarita; I can compete with Ron heads up."

"I like a woman with confidence," said Ron.

Dee asked, "So how do we know who wins?"

Ron said, "First one that leaves with her prey signifies the end of contest. Margarita can be the judge."

Dee said, "Ok. You have Sue, I have Kat."

"Oh, look. It looks like Ed Phillips is attempting to get Sue's attention."

"Ron, Ed doesn't have a chance in hell hooking up with Sue."

"Why do you say that?"

"Look at him. He's five foot four and looks like a geek."

"Maybe so, but I think he's working Sue. You might be an early winner, Ron."

Dee looked in Margarita's direction and rolled her eyes.

Ed had walked over to Sue and asked if she wanted a drink. Sue told him no and then went ahead and ordered one for herself. Ed tried to take up the stool next to her when she said, "I'm waiting for someone if you don't mind."

Ed turned and went and sat in the back corner of the bar over by the waitress station just watching what was going on. After about a half hour, he paid his tab and left.

Margarita had been working the waitress service section of the bar when she came over to Dee, "What was that all about?"

"Ed was trying to work easy Sue, but she didn't go for him."

"That would have ended the contest right there."

"Could have."

"Why do you play these games with Ron?"

"It helps pass the time."

"Better watch out Dee, Sue is probably a sure bet. What is the bet anyway?"

"Dinner."

"Sure. What else?"

"One never knows."

"Let me guess."

Then Margarita went back to making drinks for the waitresses at the service area.

Frank Jenkins came into the bar and surveyed the room. Right away, Ron signaled to Dee with his head pointing towards the door. She looked that way and shook her head indicating she agreed. Frank Jenkins looked to be in his early forties. With his good looks and clean-cut appearance, he was definitely cougar bait. Dee said to Ron, "want to make a side bet as to whose predator goes after him first?"

"You're on. Breakfast tomorrow by the loser."

"Ok. I'll take that bet."

Frank Jenkins caught Kat's attention and she got up and went right over to him. She shook his hand and they talked for a moment. Then the two want back to where Kat had been sitting.

"Want to have a drink and something to eat?" asked Kat.

"Just a drink, and make it a diet coke. Let's have one and get out of here?"

"Sure, but Chef Antonio makes one of the best shrimp and sausage sauté around," Kat said with a smile.

"Another time."

"Ok by me. I'm not really hungry for food right now anyway."

They had a drink and paid the tab. Then the two left together.

"Looks like you win Dee" said Margarita.

"Looks that way. Ron, I'll make dinner reservations at Alberto's for next week. You can come by my place say nine tomorrow and you make me breakfast."

"I could do that, but how about I go home with you tonight and we can negotiate breakfast later?"

"Even after a long night here?"

"Yeah, I think that would have been a better bet anyway."

"Why Ron, if I didn't know better, I'd say you were acting like a cougar now."

"Why do you say that Dee? Because you are a few years younger than me?"

"A few. More like ten."

"Let's see. I'm forty-one and you're what, thirty?"

"Twenty-nine."

"Dee, what do you think they call a forty-ish man who hits on a much younger woman?"

"A male cougar?"

"No, a guy."

"So what you're saying is the term only applies to a woman?"

"Yeah. That's about it."

"I'd say you call him a horny old man."

"Let's see how you feel in the morning."

"You're on. Old man."

"I'll show you what this old man can do."

"You'll be hurting all over when I'm done with you."

"Bring it on."

"Later Ron, later."

The two went back to their respective customers at the bar. From time to time, Dee caught Ron looking in her direction. When their eyes met, Ron just smiled.

Margarita watched the two as the night went on. At one point, she said to Dee, "You two need to get a room."

"In due time Margarita. Ron's coming over to make me breakfast."

"Like I said, and what else?"

The two went back to waiting on the patrons in the packed bar.

14

Kat and Frank Jenkins left the bar and got into their vehicles. Jenkins pulled out first with Katherine following. They went left on Route 28 and headed to Kat's house. When they got to her place, he parked in the street and she pulled into the driveway.

"Why didn't you park in the driveway?"
"I didn't want to block you in."
"I'm not planning on going out again tonight, and we could have moved the cars in the morning."
"I don't think it will take all night for us to talk."
"I wasn't thinking about talking."
"Then exactly what did you have in mind?"
"You'll see. Let's go inside."

Frank Jenkins was a Sergeant in the Dennis Police Department when he first met Katherine Sterns. When her husband, Sam, died in a freak fishing accident some time ago, Jenkins was the police officer on the scene when her husband's body was recovered. Jenkins along with Detective Tomlinson had a theory that her husband's death might not have been an accident but they didn't have sufficient evidence to pursue their theory.

After that case, Jenkins was again involved with Katherine investigating a case where a man had robbed a number of widows of significant sums of money. In the latter case, Jenkins was the lead detective heading up the investigation. A few days ago when Detective Jenkins went to the Sterns residence to talk to Katherine about the theory he and Tomlinson had developed regarding her husband's death, he had interrupted Katherine and a young male companion when he knocked on her door. Katherine had indicated to Jenkins that it could have been him coming down her stairs instead of her young male companion for the night, but Jenkins indicated he was there on business. Katherine had suggested he come back another night to continue the discussion. When Jenkins had called earlier in the day, she asked him to meet her at Sundancers bar and they could begin their discussion there.

Entering the Sterns residence, the home was filled with the smell of scented candles. Katherine had lit them before she went to meet her friend Ann Benard for dinner. Even now a few hours later, the fragrances lingered and were easily detected upon entering the home.

"Detective, there's a bottle of red wine in the wine rack. Can you get it and open it for us?"

"I can, but I'm on duty so I'll have to pass on the drink."

"You're staying for a night cap aren't you?"

"Sure, but make mine coffee, black. I guess that wouldn't hurt."

"And after drinks, why don't you plan on staying the night?"

"I hadn't planned on staying the night, but if that's how long it takes for us to discuss our business, then that might happen."

"Oh, I think it will take at least that long for us to discuss business."

While Jenkins was opening the bottle of wine, Katherine went into her bedroom and changed. When she came back out, she had on a pair of silk pajamas. The bottoms were a pair of shorts and the top a loose fitting camisole trimmed in lace. The color, bordeaux red, was the same color as the wine. Jenkins handed her a glass.

"Thanks. Are you sure you won't join me?"

"I'm sure."

Katherine asked him to take a seat at her kitchen bar while she got the coffee ready. At one point, she put pastry rolls on to a pan and put them into the oven. As she did so, she leaned over and made sure that Jenkins had a clear vision of her loose fitting top. Leaning over to put the pan in the oven, her breasts almost came right out of the pajama top. She could see Jenkins reflection off of the oven glass and he was definitely looking down her pajamas. He had a smile on his face. As Katherine was turning around, the phone rang. She just waved at the white wall phone, "Let the call go to voice mail. I'm not sure who would be calling at this time anyway."

"They look nice don't they?"
"Sure do."
"I'll bet you can't wait to get your teeth into them."
"With a little butter I'm sure they will be just delicious."
"Nothing like anticipation."
"Nothing like it."

A few minutes later, she took the pastries out of the oven and put them on the table. The aroma from the freshly baked pastries spread a sweet smell in the air.

Jenkins said, "Those look delicious."
"Looks like we're ready to eat. I love a late dessert."
"It sure smells good."
The two sat there and enjoyed their drinks and pastries.
"So what is it you wanted to talk to me about Detective?"
"Why is it whenever I'm talking official business with you, you call me Detective? Please call me Frank."
"Ok, Frank. What is it you wanted to talk about?"

"Captain Tomlinson and I were going back over the case where your husband died and we aren't so sure things happened the way your husband's fishing partner Tom Bowman said they happened."
"Why do you say that?"
"Well, if you remember when you lost your baby last year, the department asked about taking a DNA sample from the fetus?"

"Yes, I remember you asking, but I thought that was only to dispel the thought the child was Andrew Dunn's."

"That's true. Mr. Dunn had thought the child was his and he had requested the test be performed."

"I never heard anything of the results, only that the question had been satisfactorily resolved."

"Well, it was resolved for Mr. Dunn. The DNA of the baby did not match his DNA. So he was not the father and that ended the issue for him."

"As I had said at the time the baby had been my husband's."

"Yes you did. However, when the lab performed the DNA test against your deceased husband's DNA, it came back no match."

"So what exactly are you saying?"

"Just that the baby did not belong to Mr. Dunn or your deceased husband. After knocking on your door the other day, it looks like you might continue to have had other suitors."

"I know who the baby's father was."

"We think we know who the father was too."

"So?"

"So, Captain Tomlinson contacted the Virginia State Police department to get a DNA sample from Mr. Tom Bowman. He cooperated with our request and when the lab performed the test, it came back a match."

"I did sleep with Mr. Bowman once. I guess the baby could have been his."

"It most certainly was and when Captain Tomlinson and I got to looking at the facts, there might be something more to your husband's death than what had been told."

"What do you mean?"

"Well, maybe events out on the ice were other than as described by Mr. Bowman."

"Do you think Sam might have died in some other manner?"

Just then she sat back and had a confused expression on her face.

"What do you think? Tom killed Sam?"

"We don't know what to think right now. It's just that some developments have given rise for us to consider other possibilities."

"I just know Sam didn't die the way Tom Bowman said he did. Are the police going to do something about it?"

"We're looking into it."

She thought about how Tom Bowman acted after being rescued. The more she considered Tom's actions the angrier she got. She looked at Frank. He could tell she was getting pretty upset. "He's guilty. I don't know why he is being allowed to get away with what he did."

"If he committed a crime we'll get him."

"Just how will you get him?"

"He'll slip up somewhere and when he does, we'll get him."

"If the police don't, I'll have to take care of him myself."

"You have to be patient. I know the police seem to work at a slow pace. We have our ways. If he is guilty, we'll get him."

"I have my ways as well."

"Please be patient."

Katherine thought about it for a few minutes. She realized the line of questioning wasn't going to solve anything. She decided to change the subject.

"This conversation is making me very upset. Do you mind if we talk about something else for a while?"

"No I don't mind, but I'll have to talk about this further before we can put the theory to bed."

"Thank you."

She rose and asked that Jenkins follow her. They walked out of the kitchen and when she got to the end of the hall, she asked him to continue following her.

"I'd like you to see something I've saved from when my husband died."

"What is it you want me to see?"

"Mr. Bowman left something for me the night I went to the Coast Guard Station. He gave me a card and a necklace. He told me they were from Sam, but Sam didn't sign the card so I really don't know whom they came from. Maybe you could have the card checked for finger prints or something and see if Sam's prints are on it."

"We could check, but what would that tell you?"

"If Sam's prints are on the card, then he might very well have gotten me the card, but if only Tom's prints are on the card, then I'm pretty sure it came from him."

"If he did leave the card and necklace for you I would expect his prints to be on the card."

"True, but if only Tom's prints are there, then there might be some truth to your theory. Maybe Tom was trying to get Sam out of the way to have me. Maybe he was more attached than I was, or that I thought he was."

"That's one theory."

"Isn't that the one you're pursuing?"

"It's one of theories we have."

"You have others?"

"We do, and I'll get to them later."

Katherine took this as her cue. She took the card and necklace from Jenkins and put it on the dresser. Then, she took off her camisole and turned to Jenkins. She reached for his arm and turned him to be directly in front of her. He just looked at her. She reached for the top button on his shirt and undid it. Then she continued down until all of the buttons were undone. She put both of her hands inside his shirt and ran them across his chest. As she did so, she pushed the shirt up and off of his shoulders. As the shirt fell back, she put her arms around him and kissed him. When Jenkins returned the kiss, she brought her hands around to the front and undid his belt. Then she unhooked his pants, unzipped his fly and pushed his pants down. She reached down. Jenkins had grown to full size. Katherine slowly lowered herself, kissing his chest and lower mid-section as she descended. She took hold of the sides of his underwear and slowly lowered them.

"I'm still on duty."

She stopped for a moment and looked up. "When duty calls, you have to be ready."

Then she went back to what she was doing. When he sighed, she stopped. Then she removed the rest of her clothing and led him to the bed. She opened the drawer of the nightstand and took out a condom. She opened it and handed it to him. They made passionate love for the next half hour. When done and lying next to each other, Jenkins said, "This shouldn't have happened."

"Maybe not, but wasn't it good?"

"Sex is usually good, but I'm working on a case and can't get involved. It'll compromise my ability to be objective."

"What case? You said you had a theory. It might not even be valid."

"That's true, and if things happened the way Mr. Bowman said they happened, then the additional investigating was for nothing."

"I wouldn't say for nothing," and she took him in her hand.

"I see what you mean."

"If you hadn't been looking into your suspicions, then we might not have gotten together."

"You have something there."

"Frank, I'd like to see more of you."

"Our investigation isn't over. So you'll be seeing more of me."

"I don't mean like that. I mean like this."

"I have to be discrete, but I think this can work."

Katherine felt secure in her relationship with Frank Jenkins. She wasn't sure about the theories he and Captain Tomlinson had about Sam's death. She thought she could stay on top of things as long as she took care of business. She planned on seeing Frank Jenkins often.

Jenkins got out of bed and got dressed. As he was doing so, he said, "Katherine, we can put off the rest of the discussion and my theories until another time."

"That's fine with me."

"I'm not sure anything will come from our investigation but there are some loose ends that need follow up. When we have the answers to those things, I'm sure this whole thing will be settled."

"I sure hope so. Sam is gone and there really isn't anything that can be done about that and I have moved on with my life."

"Do you mind if I ask you if you are seeing other men?"

"I don't mind. Yes, I do see other men from time to time. I'm a single woman now and I have my needs."

"As I recall, you and Sam's partner Andrew Dunn seem to be good friends. Isn't that so?"

"Andrew and I were business partners after Sam's death. I used my skills to keep tabs on my interests there."

"Did you have a relationship with Mr. Dunn before your husband's death?"

"I did not have any relationship with Mr. Dunn at any time prior to the time Sam went missing on the trip where he eventually died."

"But you did have an affair with your husband's friend Tom Bowman. Isn't that right?"

"I wouldn't call it an affair. I slept with him just one time."

"Anyone else?"

"There were a few men from time to time."

"Did your husband know about any of them?"

"I don't think so. At least if he did, he didn't ever say anything. Why are you asking?"

"I'm just gathering information in the ongoing investigation."

"You don't think any of the men I slept with had anything to do with Sam's death do you?"

"Right now, only Mr. Bowman is a suspect."

"A suspect! Then you have already formed an opinion about him and Sam's death."

"I wouldn't call it an opinion, but we do have questions."

"Why don't you just interrogate or polygraph him?"

"In due time."

"Do you think I will have to be involved with your interrogation of Mr. Bowman?"

"We'll try to keep you out of it. What's your concern?"

"I just know guys and if he sees me again, he might think he can have me again and I don't want him around."

"I guess I can understand that. We'll do what we can."

"Thank you."

Jenkins was standing next to the bureau in the bedroom when he picked up a pill bottle that was on the bureau. "What are these for?"

"Since Sam died, I have trouble sleeping and those pills knock me out."

"I know what you mean. Sometimes I have insomnia myself."

"You can take a few if you want."

"No thanks, I'll pass."

"Have it your way."

"Listen, I have to get going. It's getting late and I'll need to file my report."

"Will you have to report everything?"

"I'll report that which is pertinent to the investigation."

"Is our sleeping together pertinent?"

"Not at this time."

Katherine got out of bed and came around to Jenkins. She put her arms around him and kissed him.

"Thanks for keeping that part out of your report."

"I'll have more questions after Captain Tomlinson and I review my report. Do you mind if I call on you again to discuss the matter?"

"Not at all. In fact, I'm counting on you coming again," Katherine said with a smile.

"Then I'll call you in a couple of days and set up another time."

"Next time, plan on staying the night."

"I'll consider it."

Detective Jenkins kissed her and then left the house. Katherine walked him to the door, and as the door was closing, she could see her neighbor peeking out a window. Katherine, standing there nude, just waved.

She went back into the bedroom and retrieved the condom from the trashcan. She put it into a zip-lock bag, wrote "F. Jenkins" on the bag and put it into her freezer.

Chapter 3

When Officer Trudy returned to the Dennis Police Station at the end of her shift patrol, she wrote out her report regarding the incident involving Ms. Benard. Trudy had documented where Ms. Benard had been and listed the names of the people Ms. Benard had contact with that day. When she finished her report, she brought it to Captain Tomlinson.

"Captain, here's my report documenting the incident that happened out at Chapin Beach today."

"Let me take a look at it and the desk Sergeant will address it during tomorrow morning's shift briefing."

"Ok Captain. If you have any questions, I can come see you before I begin my patrol tomorrow."

"See you tomorrow. Have a good night."

Officer Trudy went back to the patrol office. She secured her work area and went home for the night. Captain Tomlinson sat back at his desk and read her report. When he came across Katherine Sterns' name, his eyebrows went up. He remembered her from his detective days when he and Jenkins worked the case where her husband died. "This lady seems to always be in the wrong place at the wrong time."

Sergeant Grimes, who had been assisting with dispatch, stuck his head into the office. "I'm going off duty now Captain. Is there anything you need me to do before I go?"

"Grimes, do you remember the case last year involving the guys who got stranded on the ice?"

"Yeah, didn't one of the guys end up dying?"

"Yes. Sam Sterns died. The other man survived."

"Do you remember the wife of the man who died?"

"Sure do. She was a real looker. I think Jenkins has had contact with her recently."

"Why would Jenkins have contact with her?"

"If you remember, she was also one of the widows who were swindled out of some money by the guy who robbed a number of wealthy widows in the area."

"Yeah, I remember that case, too. What was the guy's name?"

"Chamberlin."

"That's it. Charles Chamberlin."

"So Jenkins has maintained contact with the widow?"

"I think it's more than contact. I think he's seeing her?"

"You're kidding?"

"No, but it really isn't any of my business."

"Well, her name has come up with another situation we're looking into."

"What one is that?"

"The call that came in a little while ago that Trudy followed-up on."

"The one where the lady was attacked out at Chapin Beach?"

"That's the one. Well, the lady who was attacked listed Katherine Sterns as one of the people she had contact with shortly before being attacked."

"Do you think the Sterns woman is involved?"

"I don't know, but I don't like coincidences."

"You'll have to talk with Jenkins for any more information. That's about all I know."

"Well, you have a good night and I'll see you tomorrow."

"Good night Captain. See you tomorrow."

Officer Grimes left the station to go home for the night. As he was getting into his car outside the station, Detective Jenkins was just getting out of his car. Grimes said to him, "Detective, I think Captain Tomlinson might want to see you for a few minutes."

"Do you know what it's about?"

"Something to do with an incident that took place up at Chapin Beach today."

"Ok, I'll stop in and see him."

"The Captain said one of the names mentioned in Officer Trudy's report was Katherine Sterns. You know her pretty well, don't you Detective?"

"Why would you say that Grimes?"

"I have taken a few calls from a Katherine over the past few months for you, so I thought it was one and the same."

"What did you tell the Captain?"

"I told him he would have to speak with you regarding Ms. Sterns."

Jenkins shot Grimes an unpleasant look, but didn't say anything else.

Grimes got into his car and started it up. He rolled down his window on the driver's side, "Isn't the Sterns woman the same one involved in the computer money theft scheme earlier this year."

Jenkins turned back to Grimes, "Yeah, I know her." Then he turned and continued walking.

Detective Jenkins thought for a minute and recalled the two situations where he had the first contact with Ms. Katherine Sterns. In the first situation, her husband and another man had gone missing on a fishing trip. Her husband ended up dying. The other man survived. In the other situation, Mrs. Sterns had been robbed electronically of a few million dollars she had inherited. Since those incidents, Jenkins had called on Ms. Katherine Sterns a few times. He thought he was being discrete.

Entering the station, Detective Jenkins poked his head into Captain Tomlinson's office.

"Want to see me Captain?"

Tomlinson waved him in without looking up from his papers. Jenkins sat down and waited for Captain Tomlinson to finish reading whatever it was he had in his hands.

Tomlinson said, "I have Trudy's report here where she investigated a situation that happened today up at Chapin Beach."

"Grimes mentioned it to me. What happened?"

"We don't really know all the details yet, but it looks to me like this Ms. Benard was assaulted and for some reason Ms. Katherine Sterns' name is in the report."

"How was she involved?"

"Ms. Benard indicated she had a few drinks with Ms. Sterns at Gina's by the Sea and Chapin's Restaurants before she was attacked at the beach."

"Was Ms. Sterns with her at the beach?"

"No, the two had gone their separate ways after leaving the restaurant. You know me, I don't like coincidences."

"What would you like me to do Captain?"

"I'd like you to follow-up on Trudy's report and see if you can get to the bottom of this situation."

"Will do Captain. I'll get back to you as soon as I know something."

"Call the Cape Cod Times and get an abbreviated story put into tomorrow's paper. Don't spell out any of the specifics of the case, just say a person was hurt at Chapin Beach tonight around nine and ask that anyone with any information contact you at the Dennis Police Station."

"Do you want me to say anything about the assault?"

"Not yet. You'll need to do some investigating before drawing any conclusions. And Jenkins? Don't let any personal involvement get in the way of your investigation."

"What do you mean?"

28

"Rumor has it you have had a relationship with Ms. Sterns. So, just don't let your personal feelings get involved."

"You don't have to worry about me Captain."

"Make sure it stays that way."

"I'll get back to you."

Jenkins took Officer Trudy's report from the Captain and went back to his office. He read the report and wondered who might have attacked a woman walking on Chapin Beach. That beach gets a lot of traffic. It has an off road access point with fisherman coming and going all the time, even at night.

He called the Cape Cod Times and asked to speak with the editor.

The paper editor, Bill Williams, took the call. "How can I help you Detective Jenkins?"

"Mr. Williams, we want to put a police report in tomorrow's paper about a woman who was hurt up at Chapin Beach earlier tonight."

"Let me see. I think I can still get into tomorrow's paper. How much information do you want in the article?"

"Not much. We want to see if we can get any leads from the article."

"What happened?"

"I'll tell you what I know, and I'll tell you what I want printed."

"Fine with me Detective."

"A middle aged woman was hurt tonight at Chapin Beach. She said she was taking a walk on the beach and was hit on the head. She was knocked unconscious. When she woke up, she didn't know what had happened to her."

"Was she sexually assaulted?"

"Why do you want to know that?"

"Well, sex sells newspapers and if the story has some juice to it, then it's better for the paper."

"We don't know if she was sexually assaulted. When the woman was examined at the ER, the doctor could not find any signs of a sexual assault."

"So you don't know if she was raped?"

"I don't know. For now, I only want to report that a woman was hurt up at the beach."

"Ok. What exactly do you want me to print?"

"Print that a woman was injured tonight between eight and nine. Don't indicate how or what the nature of the injuries were and don't make any mention of a sex crime. Just ask that anyone having any information contact Detective Frank Jenkins at the Dennis Police Station."

"I can do that. Listen Detective, can I have one of my reporters follow-up with you about the case?"

"Sure. Have your reporter call the station and I'll arrange a meeting as things unfold."

"Thanks Detective. We're happy to help."

"You're welcome Bill. I'll look in tomorrow's paper for the article."

Chapter 4

On any given Friday night at Sundancers, there are a number of cougars prowling and tonight was no exception. Over on the right, by the waitress station was Susan Kent. At forty-four, she was a regular and had come to earn the nickname of Easy Sue. Whenever she came in by herself, someone was going to get lucky. She had dressed in her battle costume, low cut blouse revealing her generous breasts that had been supported by a push-up bra all above a pair of black capris. She had on a pair of five-inch Stiletto heels bringing her to a height of six feet. When a man entered the bar, Sue would look down at his feet. Sue believed in the old adage about a man's shoe size and she was looking for someone with big shoes.

The next cougar sitting by the entrance to the kitchen was Linda Sage. Linda was in her late thirties and was a rather petite woman. At five feet one-quarter inch and displaying size Ds, Linda was a sight to behold. Her breasts were her focal point and most men who looked at her became captivated with them. Partially concealed about half way down the inside of her left breast, Linda had a tattoo in the image of a black rose. Linda wore a tight v-neck shirt that looked to be made of spandex because all you could see was the clear definition of her breasts, short denim shorts and gold sandals with two-inch heels. Definitely the cougar look. Additionally, Linda had her hair pulled back into a high ponytail.

A third cougar, Tina Fletcher sat on the far side of the bar nearest to the dance floor. Tina always wanted to be close to the action. Tina dressed nicely in a white button down blouse over jeans. She wore simple flats in order to bring her six foot one frame down to the smallest height possible. She used quite a bit of makeup in order to take away as much of the forty-eight year look that showed on her face. Tina had a slender figure that at one time represented a very attractive woman. The years, and the bar, had taken a toll on her looks but it was not easy to dissuade Tina. While Tina didn't really look like a woman on the prowl, she had history and was definitely on the prowl.

Bobby Jones came into the bar around 9:45 and took up the stool next to Sue Kent. Bobby fancied himself as somewhat of a ladies man. He said hello or waived to all the cougars and gave a high-five to the guys he knew. Bobby was a pretty good dresser. He had on black slacks with a teal Ralph Lauren polo. It looked good against his summer tan. Overall, he was well groomed. If he had any shortfall, he used too much cologne.

Dee came over to him, "What will you have Bobby?"

"Get me a Bud draft Dee."

"Sure."

Bobby turned to Sue, "Didn't we just have drinks at Chapin's?

"What's your point Bobby?"

"We have to stop meeting like this. You got any plans?"

"Nothing yet, I'm looking for a man with big shoes. What did you have in mind?"

"I have size fourteen shoes. Is that big enough?"

"I don't need to know your shoe size Bobby. We already know each other remember?

"I was just thinking, maybe you and I could do something together."

"Like what?"

32

"Take a walk on the beach or something?"

"You're only saying that because Ann said it when we saw her up at Chapin's. You might think your creative, but I know better."

"It did sound kind of romantic didn't it?"

"Bobby, skip the romantic stuff. You want to get laid or not?"

"Sue, you have a way with words. No sense beating around the bush."

"You finally see my point. I don't believe it."

"I just thought we might do something a little different besides just jumping in the sack."

"But isn't your goal the same? Why do those other things when all we both want is the same thing?"

"Ok. I see your point."

"Then you want to get out of here or what?"

"Let me finish my beer and then let's go."

"I'm ready when you are."

"Give me a few minutes."

Bobby motioned to Dee to get him his check and Sue's. She did and when she put them on the bar she said, "Do you want me to keep yours open?"

"No, I don't think I'll be back tonight."

"Ok."

Bobby paid the tabs and went back to finishing his beer.

Linda Sage had taken a seat next to Tommy Anderson and Paul Bremmer. Tommy and Paul were both in their early twenties. Paul was a big guy, around 6'4" and about 270lbs. Tommy was a slender 6'2" and maybe 170lbs. The two had been playing in a baseball game and had come into the bar after the game for a few cold ones. They still had their Sundancers team uniforms on. After about a half hour and two beers, Paul got up and left. This gave Linda the chance she was waiting for.

"So you and your friend played in a ball game today?"

Tommy turned to face her, "Yeah, we won six to three." He couldn't help looking. His eyes kept dropping down to stare at her tattoo.

"What position do you play?"

"I pitched today."

"And gave up three?"

"They got lucky and my third baseman made an error."

"So do you make any errors?"

"Not usually."

"Then you might get lucky as well."

"Are you here with anyone?" asked Tommy.

"I wasn't when I came in, but I could be now."

Glancing down, again, Tommy said, "Then let me buy you a drink."

"That sounds good to me. Later, I'll see what I can come up with to repay your generosity. Maybe you'll even get a better look at my tattoo."

She put her palms on the outside of her breasts and pressed inwards.

"I'll hold you to it."

"Oh you don't have to worry about me. I always hold it."

Ron got the signal from Tommy and came over for their order.

"What'll it be Tommy?"

"I'll have another beer and get Linda here whatever she's having."

Ron looked at Linda, "Another martini?"

"Please."

Ron looked back to Tommy, "How did you do today?"

"Great. We won. Six to three."

"So you out doing a little celebrating?"

"Just having a few beers."

Linda chimed in, "Oh, I'll see to it he gets the appropriate rewards."

"I'm sure you will Linda," Ron said as he turned away from her to get their drinks. Tommy could see Ron's face and

Ron was raising his eyebrows and had a smile on his face for only Tommy to see as he turned away. Tommy just gave him thumbs up.

Margarita, the other bartenders, came over to Ron, "I saw that. Watch it or I'll tell Dee about your devious mind."

"She already knows about my devious mind."

"I'll bet she does."

Tina had been on her cell phone around 10:30pm and when she hung up, she motioned to Dee.

"Dee, I just got off the phone with Ann Benard. She was down at the hospital. She was assaulted earlier tonight up at Chapin Beach."

"No way. Did they catch the person who did it?"

"Not yet."

"Who was she up there with?"

"She said she went there by herself after having dinner with Katherine Sterns at Gina's and then having a few drinks at Chapin's bar."

"Kat was in here earlier and left with that Detective Jenkins."

"Yeah, she kind of has a thing going with him."

"Oh, I didn't think she was a one man woman."

"Oh, she isn't."

"I overheard Sue over there talking to Bobby. He said they had a few drinks with Kat and Ann earlier tonight at Chapin's. I wonder if either of them knows anything."

"I think I'll ask," said Tina.

Tina left her drink on the bar and went around to where Sue was sitting.

"Sue, I just got off the phone with Ann. She was attacked earlier tonight up at Chapin Beach. Dee said you had drinks with her up at Chapin's earlier. Do you have any idea of who might have done that?"

"Is she all right?"

"Yeah. She said she has some bruises and scratches, and stitches but otherwise ok."

35

"I'm glad to hear she is ok. I know she had dinner with Kat at Gina's earlier tonight and then they stopped at Chapin's for a few drinks. I remember Ann trying to get one of the guys to take a walk on the beach with her but I didn't think any of them were interested."

Sue turned to Bobby, "Bobby, Ann was attacked by someone tonight up at Chapin Beach."

"You gotta be kidding."

"No. Tina just got off the phone with her. She was at the hospital before she called."

"Is she alright?"

Tina spoke up. "She said she only had a few stitches and a bump on her head."

"Bobby, you were there with them at Chapin's. Did you see Ann leave?"

"I left just after Ann did, but I didn't see her again."

Tina looked at Bobby, "So you didn't see her after that?"

"No."

"Did you see anyone follow her?"

"No. I went up to Chapin Beach shortly after she left but I couldn't find her. Her car was there but she wasn't."

"Did you see anyone there?"

"No. The lot was empty."

Sue turned back to Tina, "Maybe we should talk to Kenny and see if he knows anything."

Bobby pointed at the door. Kenny Brown was just coming in. Kenny Brown was thought to be a shady character. He was in trouble with the law a number of times and had a history of having a bad temper. There had been a number of occasions where Harry had to have one of the bouncers throw Kenny out after getting into a fight with another patron, sometimes a man, sometimes a woman. Bobby motioned to him to join them.

"Hey Bobby. What's going on?"

"Kenny, you were up at Chapin's earlier. Did you see Ann leave the bar?"

"I left just after Kat and that was the last I saw of Ann or you till now."

"I thought I saw your car and Kat's car in the corner of the parking lot when I was having a cigarette outside the bar. You were gone by the time I left the bar. What were you doing with her? Making love in the back seat?"

Kenny said, "Sort of. We were both in my car talking."

"I'll bet," exclaimed Bobby.

Tina looked at Kenny, "Kenny, you seem to be sweating. What have you been doing?"

"I just got out of the shower after working out for an hour."

"Can I get you a drink?" Tina offered.

"Sure. Where you sitting?"

"Right over there."

Tina led Kenny to her seat and the empty one next to it.

Bobby looked at Sue and they both watched Tina lead Kenny away to the other side of the bar. Sue had a quizzical look on her face. Bobby said, "What's bothering you?"

"Isn't it coincidental Ann was attacked not too long ago and Kenny is sweating?"

"He said he just finished showering after working out. Do you think he was involved?

"I don't know, but he was at Chapin's."

"So was I."

"Yeah, but you didn't see her or him after you left. You know he has a temper."

"So that makes him guilty?"

"I didn't say that, but it does put him as one of the last people to see her just before she was attacked."

"I wouldn't go jumping to conclusions if I were you Sue."

"I'm not. I'm just sayin."

"Well, let's get out of here. I'm sure we'll know more tomorrow." The two finished their drinks and left for other destinations.

Tina and Kenny listened to the band over the next few hours. At around midnight, Tina left the bar on Kenny's arm. Kenny smiled to Margarita as they exited Sundancers. Margarita said to Ron, "I don't like that guy. He gives me the creeps."

"He might have a temper but he is really a good guy. You might want to get to know him a little better."

"I'll pass. I hear enough from the women who come in here about him. He gets a little too physical for my taste."

"Could be your loss, Margarita."

"Ha, ha. Don't think so."

A little after one, Linda and Tommy left together for the night. Dee said to Margarita, "Looks like another cougar got her prey."

"Looks like it," said Margarita as she worked to clean up the bar and get ready for closing.

Chapter 5

As 2 a.m. approached, the night at Sundancers was coming to an end. Margarita finished up her tasks. She said goodnight to Dee and Ron. As she walked to the door to leave, she said to Ron, "Have a good breakfast." Ron smiled. Then Dee looked at her and just smirked.

Dee had just finished cleaning up the bar while Ron closed out the registers. Ron went to the door and locked it for the night. They would shut everything down and leave via the kitchen door. Ron walked up behind Dee and put his arms around her. She turned to face him.

"So Ron, it looks like I'm the winner."

"Yeah. Your cougar was the first one to strike."

"I know that guy she left the bar with. I'm not sure it was a cougar attack. He's a cop here in town. Maybe it was business."

"Oh, it was business. Just not police business."

"You're so sure of yourself aren't you?"

"I can tell when a cougar is on the prowl and that one was definitely on the prowl. She has been in the bar three or four times a week for the past month and every time she left with another younger guy. She's a real active one."

"You have seen her working the guys a lot lately have you?"

"Yep, and she did it again tonight."

"Ok. Now what was the bet?"

"I'm making you breakfast."

"So you have to make breakfast?"

"Maybe, maybe not. We'll see about it in the morning."

"You think you're staying at my house tonight do you?"

"I'd sure like to."

"Then let's get things wrapped up here and get going."

"I'm on it."

Ron went around the outside of the bar and straightened up all of the stools. He neatened the tables and took out the garbage. He put the proceeds in the safe and locked it. When all was done, he turned the lights off in the bar. When he went into the kitchen, Dee was finishing up putting the glasses away. She said she was ready to go. All of the other help had already left for the night so they had to lock up as they left. Outside in the parking lot, Dee went to her car.

"I'll meet you at my place."

"See you there in a few minutes."

Ron got into his car and followed Dee. They exited the parking lot and headed east on Route 28. They turned left on Route 134. After crossing over Route 6, they turned into the Condo complex where Dee lived. The two parked their cars and went in.

"Ron, get us a couple of beers out of the fridge. Would you?"

"Sure thing."

"I'm going to get changed."

"What about me? I need to get out of these clothes. They smell like the bar."

"Go ahead and change then."

Ron didn't have any other clothes with him so he just took off his shirt and pants. He took a seat on the couch in his underwear, although they could probably double for shorts.

40

He placed Dee's beer on the coffee table in front of him and took a sip out of his can of beer.

When Dee came into the room, she had on a skimpy top and her underwear. Ron could pretty much see right through the top and couldn't stop staring at her.

"So who do you think attacked Ann?" Dee asked as she sat down.

"I don't know. Probably some guy she pissed off."

"Do you think it could have been one of the guys at the bar?"

"Maybe, but I'd put my money on someone she met at Chapin's Restaurant. Maybe she ticked someone off and he went after her."

"Well, Bobby, Kenny and Ed were all there. Could it have been one of them?"

"I'd say no to Bobby. He has probably already slept with her and every other cougar we know."

"She did have an argument about something with him from what some of the others said."

"But Bobby doesn't get mad. He just moves on to the next woman. I don't think he has any problems getting laid."

"What about Kenny?"

"Now Kenny on the other hand can have a temper. I remember one time when he threw a drink in a woman's face."

"Yeah, I remember that night. He was pretty shit-faced."

"He was totally out of control."

"Didn't he get it on with Katherine in the parking lot up at Chapin's?"

"I thought I overheard a few of the cougars talking about it at the bar tonight. I wasn't sure if it was Kenny they were talking about."

"I think it was."

"Then that would probably rule him out."

"Why rule him out? I don't think Ann was sexually assaulted."

"Then I guess it could have been him."

"What about Ed?"

"Ed. I don't think so. Ed is kind of a geek. You know, a computer guy."

"I know he does something with computers for a living, but that hardly disqualifies him."

"It doesn't but I don't think it would be like him to stalk someone and then sneak up behind them and hit the person on the head. He just isn't physically that kind of guy. Any one of these cougars from the bar could probably kick his ass."

"You're probably right. Maybe it was someone we don't even know."

"That's a possibility."

Ron took a long sip of his beer. Dee leaned over to pick up a bottle-cap off of the floor. When she did, her breasts nearly fell out of her top. Ron kept looking at them as she sat back up.

"Ron you're staring."

"I can't help it. This is the first time I've seen you like this."

"You mean we've worked together all of this time and you never got a look at me before?"

"Well, I have seen what could be seen given the outfits you wear bartending, but this is the real deal."

Dee took off her top and holding her breasts said, "These are the real deal."

Dee looked down at Ron's underwear and could see he was now protruding from them.

"I'd say that is the real deal also. Wouldn't you?"

Ron was a little shy but quickly got over it.

"Why don't you come here and sit next to me?"

"I have a better idea. Grab the beers and let's go to the bedroom."

"I'm right behind you."

Ron picked up the two beers and jumped right up. As he followed her into the bedroom Dee said, "Shed those underwear and come here."

She had taken her underwear off and was laying on her bed looking up at him. He did as ordered. Ron joined Dee on her bed.

"So you are eleven years older than me. Is that so?"

"What of it?"

"Then I'd say that makes you a male cougar."

"You think so?"

"I think so."

Ron made a cat-like noise and Dee said, "Is that your cougar imitation?"

"Like it?"

"I'd say you are more like a pussycat. Now come here."

Ron got on top of Dee and began to kiss her. As he did, he explored the intimate parts of her body. Ron was ready. They made love for about twenty minutes. Ron was still breathing heavily when Dee said, "Want to try again?"

"Again? I need to catch my breath."

"I told you I would tire you out, old man."

"I think I satisfied your desire a few times tonight if I'm not mistaken."

She thought about it, "Yeah, a few times."

"Not bad for an old man wouldn't you say?"

"You're right. It was pretty good."

"*Pretty* good?"

He reached over to her and pulled her on top of him. As he did so, he started to get hard again.

"What do we have here?" Dee exclaimed.

Then she lowered herself and began to slowly move up and down. Soon, she moved at a feverish pace and they both climaxed at the same time.

"See, what did I tell you?"

"I need to sleep Ron. Thanks for the sleep aid. I have to work again tomorrow night."

"So who is the old person now?"

"I wouldn't say old, just tired."

Dee put her head on Ron's shoulder, "So, who do you think would have attacked Ann Benard?"

"You're preoccupied with what happened to Ann. Are you sure it was an attack?"

"How would you explain her getting those stitches on her head if she wasn't attacked?"

"Maybe she fell or something?"

"On the beach? Do you really think a person walking on the sand could fall and cut her head? How about the cut being where it is on the top back of her head? She would have to perform a flip or something."

"I guess you have a point."

"Do you think it's someone she knows?"

"I don't know."

"Could it have been one of the guys at the bar who has been hitting on her?"

"Come on Dee. You know the guys at the bar. They know they can get it from one of the cougars anytime they want."

"Oh, I don't think it's that easy."

"Easy? What about Easy Sue? Buy her a drink and you have the key to her pants."

"I don't think she's that easy."

"You don't? Just watch. She's slept with every guy in the place at least once. Even Ed."

"How do you know that?"

"I was there when she hooked up with Ed. I overheard her talking with one of the other women about him a few days later."

44

"Well, what about Tommy or Paul?"

"I don't know them that well. They are young and might be able to do anything if they drank too much."

"Or maybe it was just someone else?"

"I'm sure we'll find out over the next few weeks. I'm tired Dee. Can we call it a night?"

"Sure."

Dee rolled off Ron. She got up and put on her pajamas. Then she got back into bed and fluffed up her pillow. She turned off the light, kissed Ron and turned over to go to sleep. Ron, still naked, snuggled up to her back.

"If you feel something poking you in the back, roll over and we can go at it again."

"Who are you kidding Ron. I don't know any guy who can keep at it all night unless he's on something."

"You're probably right. I was just trying to impress you."

"You already impressed me. Twice. Now let's get to sleep."

"Ok, but if I have a good dream going, is it ok if I wake you up?"

"It had better be a good dream."

With that, the two dozed off into their respective dream worlds.

Chapter 6

Before each shift, the patrol officers meet with the Sergeant on duty to go over any items of importance that had to be communicated for the shift. Sergeant Grimes began the meeting.

"Last evening a woman, Ms. Ann Benard, was assaulted. The call came in from a Good Samaritan at 21:45 last night at Chapin Beach. Officer Trudy was the responding officer. Ms. Benard was transported to the Cape Cod Hospital where she was examined, treated and released. The ER doctor checked Ms. Benard for injuries and possible sexual assault. The victim had been knocked unconscious and the only visible sign of the attack ended up being a few stitches, a lump on the head along with some scratches. Anyone patrolling up at Chapin Beach today should take the opportunity to speak with any citizens you might encounter and ask if anyone saw anything out of the ordinary last night. Unfortunately, today is Saturday and most tourists turnover today. Anyone at the beach yesterday probably will not be back. Officer Trudy, is there anything you want to add?"

"Only that I'll be following up with the people who called 911 last night, Mr. and Mrs. Fields."

"While you're up there, stop in at the two restaurants Ms. Benard was at prior to the attacked, Gina's and Chapin's. See what you can find out from the people who work there. Maybe one of them will remember something of significance. Then report back to Detective Jenkins with your findings."

"Will do." Trudy scratched notes into her notebook.

"Anyone else coming up with anything that might add to the case, speak with Trudy or me. That's all. So let's get out there."

The seven patrol officers who had been attending the meeting got up and went about their duties for the day. Officer Trudy made plans to visit the Fields, then Chapin's and then Gina's to investigate the attack further. Sergeant Grimes knocked on Captain Tomlinson's door after the meeting briefing.

"Captain, I reviewed Trudy's report regarding last nights assault on Ms. Benard with the day shift. Trudy will follow-up with the places Ms. Benard last visited. Detective Jenkins will follow-up with the paramedics, hospital and the people Ms. Benard saw yesterday before the attack."

"Ok Grimes. Is there anything else?"

"It's not my place to bring personal things up, but do you think it's appropriate for Detective Jenkins to discuss the matter with Ms. Sterns?"

"What are you getting at Grimes?"

"Ms. Sterns was one of the last people to have contact with Ms. Benard before the assault and with the Detective having a personal relationship with Ms. Sterns, I was just thinking..."

"Stop right there Grimes. Are you saying Jenkins has a conflict of interest?"

"I guess not Captain. It doesn't seem appropriate that the Detective should interview a suspect whom he is sleeping with."

"Are you sure of this Grimes?"

"I have seen them together out in public, if you know what I mean."

"I don't know what you mean. I'll speak to Jenkins about it. That will be all Grimes."

"Yes Captain."

Officer Trudy gathered her notebook and cell phone and left the station to begin her canvassing duties. Her first

47

stop was at Gina's by the Sea Restaurant. Entering the establishment, a woman came up to her, "Can I help you officer?"

"Yes, my name is Officer Pam Trudy. I'm with the Dennis Police Department. I'm investigating an incident that took place near here last night and would like to speak with some of the staff who were working last night."

"Well, my name is Mary Lombardo. I was the hostess last night. What would you like to know?"

"Two women were here for dinner last night, a Katherine Sterns and Ann Benard. Do you know either of them?"

"Yes, I know both of them. They come here often for dinner. As you can see, we're not a big place, so it's easy to know the regulars."

"Well, Ms. Benard was assaulted last night near here and I'd like to ask a few questions if I might about their visit to your restaurant."

"Ms. Benard assaulted? Who could have done such a thing?"

"That's what I'm trying to figure out."

"What questions do you have officer? I'd like to help."

"What can you tell me about the two women while they were here last night?"

"Let's see. They came in around five and had a few drinks at the bar. The two of them seemed to be having a good time, laughing and chatting."

"Did anything seem out of the ordinary?"

"Not that I can think of."

"Did anyone else join them or leave with them?"

"No, and as I recall, they left at the same time after their dinner. Oh, here comes Jenny Andretti. I seated the women in her section last night. Maybe she can answer some of your questions."

"Jenny, this is Officer Trudy. Officer Trudy is investigating an assault that happened near here last night.

The victim was one of the women I seated in your section, Ann Benard."

"Ann? Oh my God, what happened to her?"

Officer Trudy said, "So you know Ms. Benard also?"

"Who doesn't?" said Jenny. "They come in here all the time."

Officer Trudy went through the same questions with Jenny. She did not learn anything new other than Jenny had overheard the women talking about going to Chapin's for a few drinks after dinner and Katherine having mentioned she thought there were going to be a few guys they both knew there. Officer Trudy gave each of them one of her business cards and asked them to call the station if either thought of anything else that might be relevant to the case.

Next, Officer Trudy went to Chapin's Restaurant. It was just down the road from Gina's. The hostess at the desk smiled warmly, "Hello."

"My name is Officer Pam Trudy and I'm investigating an incident that happened not far from here last night and would like to speak with some of the staff who were on duty last night."

The hostess identified herself as Amy Martin.

"Let me see if Mr. Newman can speak with you for a few minutes."

Amy Martin went through a door marked "Employees Only". Walking back to the hostess station together, Amy was telling Tony that Officer Trudy was following up on a crime.

"Officer Trudy, I'm Tony Newman. I'm the manager. How can I help you?"

"Mr. Newman, last night a woman was assaulted not far from here. The victim said she and a friend were here having a few drinks just before the assault."

"Can you tell me who it was?"

"Ann Benard was the victim. She said she had been here with Katherine Sterns sometime after seven thirty."

"I was here last night, but I don't remember the ladies. Generally I'm in back, in the kitchen or the office. If I come out at all, it's to deal with a particular situation. Possibly one of the bartenders might remember them. Please follow me and let's see what we can find out."

Mr. Newman lead Officer Trudy the full length of the building to the opposite end where the bar area is located. There were three bartenders waiting on customers around the spacious bar. Mr. Newman spoke to the nearest bartender, John White.

"John, Officer Trudy is investigating an incident that took place near here last night. The victim in her investigation said she was here sometime around seven thirty having a few drinks. Officer Trudy would like to find out if any of you were on duty last night and if you remember the women being here."

"Let me see, last night seven thirty. Yeah, I was on duty. Do you know the women's names?"

Officer Trudy spoke up. "Yes, the victim was Ann Benard and she was here with a Katherine Sterns."

"Yes, I remember them being here. Ms. Sterns comes in here often. I've seen Ms. Benard here before as well."

"What can you tell me about last night?"

"Well, they were down here at the end of the bar. The two had a couple of drinks. They talked to a few of the other patrons across the bar from them and eventually were joined by a few guys who had been sitting across the bar. Let's see, Bobby, Kenny and Ed, but only Bobby and Kenny joined the women. Ed stayed on the other side of the bar talking to some guy with a beard. After about a half hour Ms. Sterns left. It must have been a little after eight. Then Kenny left, and Ed and the guy he had been talking with left after him. The other lady, Ms. Benard was still here talking with the other guy, Bobby. Then she left and he left right after her. I'd guess it was eight forty five."

"Did anything seem out of the ordinary?"

50

"Well, it did seem like Bobby was a little perturbed about something. After the others left, their conversation turned from happy and smiling to frowns and little talk."

"Do you think they were having an argument?"

"I couldn't tell, but she did get up and leave pretty briskly."

"Anything else?"

"Not that I can think of."

Officer Trudy produced business cards and gave one each to the manager and to the bartender. She thanked them for their help and asked them to call the station if either thought of anything that might help with the investigation.

As Officer Trudy was getting into her cruiser outside, John White ran out, "One thing I just remembered."

"What's that Mr. White?"

"Well, right after Ms. Benard and the gentlemen left, I was cleaning up at the end of the bar and when I looked out the window, I saw Ms. Benard going up the street towards Chapin Beach. Bobby pulled out heading in the same direction at a pretty good speed not long after her."

"About how long would you say Ms. Benard left ahead of Mr. Jones?"

"I'd say it was about ten minutes. I had to ring the guy out and it took a few minutes since he paid by credit card."

"Are you sure it was Mr. Jones?"

"Yeah, Robert Jones was the name on the card." I don't know if that helps or not."

"It might. Thank you Mr. White. If you remember anything else, please call me."

"Will do."

Officer Trudy's next stop was at the Fields house. Knocking at the door, Mr. Fields answered. "Officer Trudy, what can we do for you?"

"I'm sorry for bothering you Mr. Fields, but I have a few questions I'd like to ask you and Mrs. Fields."

"Sure. Come in."

Mrs. Fields came into the living room from the kitchen and greeted Officer Trudy. "Hello Officer Trudy. How is the woman, what was her name?"

"Ann Benard and she's doing fine."

"I'm glad to hear it. Can I get you a cup of coffee or something to drink?"

"A coffee, black would be fine."

"I'll be right back."

Officer Trudy turned to Mr. Fields, "When you and Mrs. Fields were on your walk last night, was there anything you can remember that might be important to our investigation besides what we talked about last night?"

"Not much. I lay in bed last night replaying the events in my head to make sure that I hadn't forgotten anything. Walking along the beach one can't see the road. The houses and dunes between the road and beach kind of block everything out."

"Are you sure there isn't something you might have overlooked?"

"We went for a walk a little after eight. When Barbara and I were first walking along Dr. Bottero Road, before we got to the dunes by Chapin Beach, two vehicles passed us. The second vehicle was a few minutes behind the first one. That second vehicle, a Jeep, nearly hit us. The person driving was going too fast on that street. Maybe he was trying to catch up with the first vehicle? I didn't mention it last night because I didn't really see the connection between something that happened before we got to the beach."

"Did you see either vehicle leave the beach lot?"

"No, when we got to the dunes after the last house, we cut down to the beach and continued our walk on the beach. Then we cut up by the access road by the parking lot. That was when we discovered Ms. Benard. You know the rest from that point."

"Do you remember seeing the Jeep in the parking lot when the paramedics were there?"

"No, it wasn't there. The only vehicles in the lot were your cruiser, ambulance and a Toyota Rav4, which I assume belonged to Ms. Benard."

"The Toyota was Ms. Benard's."

"So that would mean sometime between our cutting down to the beach and finding Ms. Benard, the Jeep went the other way."

"Or it could have gone out on the off-road access to the beach."

"I would think we would have seen the tail lights or heard the vehicle if it was on the beach."

"Anything else?"

Mrs. Fields had been listening from the kitchen. When she came into the living room, she said, "I thought I heard a car running loudly when we were on the beach. You know, screeching the tires, that sort of thing. It made a loud squealing noise, like the fan belt or something. I thought at the time it was probably some kids getting a little out of control or something. It was definitely not coming from the access road direction; it was definitely from the parking lot."

"Anything else?" Trudy asked.

"I can't think of anything else other than what we have already told you," added Mr. Fields.

"Please call me at the station if you think of anything else," said Officer Trudy. She thanked them for the coffee and left.

While Officer Trudy was gathering information at the places the women had stopped, Detective Jenkins followed up with the hospital and paramedics. The Emergency Room doctor, Dr. Warren, confirmed what Jenkins already knew about the assault. Bump on the head, possible concussion, some cuts and scrapes, a few stitches but nothing more serious than that. When Detective Jenkins was about to leave Dr.

Warren's office, the doctor said, "Did you follow-up with the ZooQuarium people yet?"

"The ZooQuarium? What do they have to do with this?"

"I take my kids there from time to time. Out behind the Aquarium, they have a little zoo. I think they have a cougar back there along with a few other animals. We were talking about the possibility of it having escaped and perhaps being the attacker."

"I didn't see that in Officer Trudy's report."

"Maybe she didn't think it was worth noting."

"Well, thanks Doc. I'll look into it."

After talking to Dr. Warren, Detective Jenkins was walking by the nurse's station in the ER when he saw two paramedics talking with the nurses. He approached them.

"Are you Donovan and Jones?" Jenkins asked the paramedics.

"I'm Donovan, he's Jones."

"I'm following up on an attack which took place last night at Chapin Beach. The report Officer Trudy wrote up indicated you two were the paramedics who helped Ms. Benard."

"That's right Detective. How can we help you?"

Jenkins briefly read the report for them.

Paramedic Tom Donovan didn't have anything to add to what had already been put in the report, but paramedic Mike Jones did have some additional information.

"Mike is there anything else you can tell me that isn't in the report?" Jenkins asked.

"Yeah. Earlier today, I was talking with my brother Bobby, Bobby Jones. He was telling me about some trouble he was having with his social life."

"Why would that be of interest to this investigation?"

"One of the names he mentioned was Ann Benard."

Detective Jenkins expression changed to surprised. "What did he say?"

"He was telling me about having met her at Chapin's last night. Then he said he and Ann were having a discussion after the others left and Ann had told him she wanted to stop seeing him."

"And he wasn't happy about that?"

"He said she left the bar rather quickly before he could really talk to her about it."

"Did he say if he went after her?"

"He said he tried to follow her car up to Chapin Beach but she had already gotten out of her car and he couldn't find her so he left."

"So he says he didn't see her up at Chapin Beach?"

"That's what he told me."

"Anything else?"

"That's all."

"If you think of anything else, call me."

"Will do."

Next, Detective Jenkins called Katherine Sterns.

"Katherine, its Frank."

"Frank, I was just thinking about you."

"Was it good?"

"It's always good. I was just thinking about last night."

"That's kind of what I'm calling about."

"Is there a problem?"

"Not about us, but before I met you at Sundancers, you had dinner with Ann Benard at Gina's and then drinks at Chapin's, right?"

"Yeah. So?"

"So, she was assaulted last night up at Chapin Beach."

"She was?"

"Yes, and it happened right after you were together at Chapin's."

"Who did it?"

"That's what I'm trying to figure out."

"I'll bet it was Bobby Jones."

"Why do you say that?"

"Well, she wanted to break it off with him. He was one of the guys she talked with at Chapin's. I left before either of them so I don't know what happened."

"Was anyone else there?"

"Yeah, Kenny Brown."

"What do you know about him?"

"He left around the same time I did."

"What do you mean around the same time?"

"Oh, I mean when I walked out, he walked out with me."

"Was that it?"

"Yes. I don't know anything more about Ann and Bobby after that."

"No, I mean with you and Kenny?"

"Now Frank, you know I see other men. I'm not about to tell you what I do with them."

"Yeah, but you went to bed with me last night and I'm just trying to find out if you did the same with someone else between leaving Chapin's and meeting me at Sundancers?"

"If it makes you feel any better, I didn't sleep with Kenny last night."

"Did you do anything else?"

"I'm not going to answer that question. You're just going to have to leave it at that."

"Why are you so secretive about the men you have been with?"

"I'm not secretive. It's just not anyone's business."

"If anyone includes me, then I think I'd like to know more about the woman that I'm spending time with."

"Frank, you are being so old-fashioned."

"You think this is old-fashioned?"

"Can't we change the subject to something else?"

"Katherine, do you have any idea where I might find Bobby Jones or Kenny Brown?"

"Sure, they're probably at Sundancers."

"Then I think I need to go there and talk with them."

56

When Detective Jenkins finished his call to Katherine, he called Officer Trudy and asked her to meet him in a half hour up at Chapin Beach. He wanted to go over a few things with her at the scene.

When Katherine hung up the phone, she smiled. She checked her freezer. There was a box containing a few zip-lock bags off to one side. She held up the first bag and read out loud, "F. Jenkins". She picked up the second bag and read out loud again. "Kenny Brown". She closed the freezer and went about her business.

Chapter 7

Detective Jenkins and Officer Trudy met back to the scene of the attack at Chapin Beach.

"Over there is where the Fields found Ms. Benard." She was pointing towards the dunes near the off-road access path to the beach. "As you can see, there are quite a few tracks in this area."

"What do you make of these tracks?" asked Jenkins, pointing at a set of animal tracks just after where the pavement and sand met. The transition area was not as sandy as the actual off-road path. The tracks were pretty well defined.

Officer Trudy looking at the tracks said, "These look like some kind of big animal. Not your average dog tracks. See the four rounded toes above the heel?"

"They might even be large cat tracks like a bobcat or something."

"You mean like a mountain lion?"

"Yeah, or a cougar."

"You know, the ER doctor said he thought the ZooQuarium had a cougar in their zoo behind the Aquarium. He mentioned it to me when I followed up with him."

"I think he said something to me about it when I was there with Ms. Benard last night. I didn't think it was worth mentioning.

"Could they be from a large dog, such as a St. Bernard?"

"I guess. The claw area is not as clear as the pad area."

"The tracks are definitely from a big animal."

"Better follow-up with the ZooQuarium people and see if any of their animals are missing."

"I'll do it today."

There were only two tracks that were fairly defined. Then, the sand took over and the tracks became undistinguishable. There were vehicle tracks and human footprints as well, but there were none with enough clarity that could be used for identification.

"Trudy, when you were here with the victim, did you see any off-road vehicles anywhere on the beach?"

"No. I looked down the off-road access as far as I could see, but being nighttime, I didn't see anything from here. Why? Do you think the attacker was already here when Ms. Benard arrived?"

"I don't know. Didn't the Fields say they heard a vehicle leaving before they found Ms. Benard?"

"Ms. Fields said she heard someone peeling out of the parking lot just before they found her."

"Well then, I would guess we should be trying to find out who else was here last night?"

As the two were talking, two off-road vehicles came up the path from the beach. Detective Jenkins stopped them. The first vehicle was a four-wheel drive Ford pickup truck. Approaching the driver side, he said, "Excuse me sir, my name is Detective Jenkins. I'm with the Dennis Police department. Officer Trudy and I are investigating an attack that took place here last night. May I ask how long you were out on the beach?"

"Detective, my name is Bill Danvers. I came down to the beach around four this morning to fish the incoming tide. I didn't see anything when I came down here but Tim Zale might have. He's in the Jeep right behind me. I think he was here all night."

"Thank you Mr. Danvers. You can go."

Bill Danvers put his truck in gear and continued on to the pavement and left the area. Jenkins jotted down the plate number of the pickup into his notebook. Looking up, Officer Trudy had already approached the Jeep following the pickup. She had introduced herself and told Tim Zale what she and Detective Jenkins were doing. As Detective Jenkins approached the Jeep, Officer Trudy was asking Mr. Zale what time he had come down to the beach the night before.

"I got here about six o'clock," said Tim Zale. "I had my lantern and things I needed for the night. My plan was to fish the outgoing tide, then get a few hours sleep and catch the incoming tide in the early morning. My plan worked just fine. I got two nice stripers, one on each tide. They're in the cooler if you want to take a look at them."

"That won't be necessary," said Officer Trudy. "As I said, we are investigating an attack that took place here last night just after dark."

"I don't know anything about an attack. I was in the surf until about two hours after sunset. The fish were hitting pretty good, but mostly shorts."

"Did you see or hear anything unusual?"

"I wouldn't say unusual. It must have been around nine when I saw a set of headlights at the beginning of the off-road point back there by the parking lot. I thought another fisherman was coming down to fish but the vehicle only came a little way down the path and stopped right by the first high dune. I couldn't make out what was going on but I figured it was either someone going to the bathroom or some of the local kids because the vehicle was only there for a short period of time."

"Did you see anyone?"

"Nah, I only made out the lights because they stood out so clearly in the darkness. We're probably about a half-mile from where I was fishing down the beach. If you look down there, you can see where I was parked." Tim was pointing down the beach a ways to where the beach jutted out into Cape Cod Bay.

"Is there anything else you can tell us?"

"Not that I can remember."

Detective Jenkins produced a card and handed it to Tim Zale. "If you think of anything else Mr. Zale, please call Officer Trudy or myself at the station number on the card."

"Sure thing Detective."

Detective Jenkins turned to Officer Trudy as Mr. Zale was leaving, once again taking note of the plate. "Well, someone else might have been here last night when the attack took place. We have some more work to do."

"Or maybe Mr. Zale saw the headlights of Ann Benard or the attacker," said Trudy.

When the two got back to the station, Officer Trudy said she would write up a report detailing the findings from the visit to the scene. Detective Jenkins said he would update Captain Tomlinson. He asked that she have the report on Sergeant Grimes's desk so it could be reviewed during the shift briefings, and reminded her about the trip to the ZooQuarium. Jenkins was hoping someone would turn up a clue identifying the vehicle Mr. Zale had seen at the beach.

Later that afternoon, Detective Jenkins had a list of people he needed to interview. He called Katherine.

"Katherine, I have to interview a few of the people you had contact with yesterday. I thought you might have an idea of where I could find these people."

"Why would you think I know?"

"You know them so I just thought I could save myself some time trying to locate them."

"Ok, who do you want to interview?"

Jenkins read off his list. "Well, you said Kenny Brown and Bobby Jones could probably be found at Sundancers. What about Sue Kent, Tina Fletcher, Linda Sage, Darlene Crowe, Margarita Ortiz and Ron Jessup."

"Let's see. Darlene, or Dee, Margarita and Ron are the bartenders at Sundancers. For Sue, Tina, Linda, I'd start at Sundancers. You might get lucky and find all of them there."

"Thanks. I'll start there."

"I plan on going over to Sundancers in about an hour. If you are still there, we can have a drink."

"I'll be on duty."

"You can have a diet coke."

"Ok, but if I'm not there, I'll call you."

"Please do. I'd like to see you tonight."

"Goodbye."

Chapter 8

Detective Jenkins pulled into Sundancers parking lot. The place was full. As he entered the building, he could hear a Reggae band playing inside and realized conducting interviews there would be impossible. He decided to go in anyway.

Standing at the corner of the bar, he spoke to one of the female bartenders. "I'm Detective Jenkins of the Dennis Police Department. I'd like to ask you a few questions if I can."

Dee said, "You can see Detective we're pretty busy. If you can wait a few minutes, I'm taking my break and we can talk out on the deck."

"Thanks. I appreciate it."

"Can I get you something while you are waiting?"

"Just a diet coke."

Dee got the Detective a diet coke. Detective Jenkins took the drink and went outside and sat at a table on the far side of the deck. The noise level from the band wasn't so loud outside so Jenkins thought he could talk to people out there. After about ten minutes, Dee came out. She lit up a cigarette and took a seat.

"What can I do for you Detective?"

"I'm investigating an assault that took place last night up at Chapin Beach."

"Ann Benard?"

"You know of it? Do you know her?"

"Yes, some of the patrons were talking about it last night. What does this have to do with me?"

"Nothing, I don't think, but I'm looking for a few people who might have seen or heard something about the attack."

"Who are you looking for?"

Jenkins rattled off the names of the people he wanted to talk to. "I'm Darlene Crowe, but I go by Dee. Margarita and Ron are the other bartenders you saw inside. We were all working last night. The best tips are on the weekend nights, so we put up with it."

"I don't think I have anything that implicates either of them or you, but you might have overheard something that could be important to my case."

"What do you mean?"

"Well, you know how people talk at bars. I was hoping one of you might have seen something out of the ordinary or overheard something."

"We do hear a lot of things. Most of the time it's the drink talking or someone trying to put the moves on someone else. You know, impressing them."

"Even still, you never know when something said or done might be a clue to my investigation."

"Ok, I'll answer your questions. You'll have to limit our talk to fifteen minutes. I have to be back at the bar in fifteen."

Jenkins took out a pad and pen and prepared to re-read the names of the other people on the list.

"Do you know these people?"

"Sure. Most of them are inside at the bar right now."

"Can you point them out to me?"

The two stood at the door and Dee pointed out each person. "Is there anyone else here you think I should be speaking with?"

"No one else here, but I know Katherine Sterns had dinner with Ann last night."

"I've already talked to her."

Dee then looked right at Jenkins, "Oh, now I know where I've seen you. You were in here yesterday and left with Kat."

"So you have a memory for people and faces?"

"Not so much, but Ron and I had a bet going yesterday about the cougars."

"I'm sorry, the cougars?"

"Yeah, you know what I mean. The middle aged woman who are looking to score with younger men."

"So Ms. Sterns is a cougar?"

"I didn't mean," and she caught herself in mid-sentence.

"Ron, one of the other bartenders and me, from time to time, have a little wager as to which woman will leave the bar first with someone. It helps us pass the time and makes the job a little more interesting."

"That sounds interesting."

"Yesterday, when you came in, we had a bet already going and I remember you because you came in, stayed a few minutes and left right away. I ended up winning the bet."

"So you and Ron did have Ms. Sterns marked as a cougar?"

"I guess so."

"What about the others?"

"Let me see. Bobby left with Sue, but then again, they hook up quite a bit. Sue kind of has a reputation as being easy. Linda left with Tommy."

Jenkins stopped her, "Tommy?"

"Yeah, Tommy Anderson."

Jenkins made a note in his pad.

"Is Tommy here now?"

"No, I didn't see him today. He was here yesterday with his friend Paul Bremmer after their baseball game. When Paul left, Linda moved in and they eventually left together."

"So she is one of the so called cougars?"

65

"Yes, and she lived up to the title again yesterday."

"Please continue."

"And then Tina ended up leaving with Kenny."

"Anything else?"

"Not that this means anything, but I do remember when Kenny came in last night, he was rather sweaty. He said he had just taken a shower after having worked out but I thought it rather strange that he would workout so late on a weekend night."

"Thanks Dee. You've been very helpful."

"You're welcome. I'm going to have to get back to work."

Jenkins produced a card.

"If you think of anything else, or if something else gets said, please call."

"Will do."

Then Dee went back in and resumed her bartending duties.

Ron had seen her sitting out on the deck talking to Jenkins. When she came back in he said, "Isn't that the guy who came in here last night and left with Kat?"

"Sure is. He's a detective."

"What did he want with you?"

"Nothing really. He is investigating the attack on Ann Benard last night up at Chapin Beach."

"But why was he talking to you?"

"He's hoping one of us bartenders overheard something at the bar last night that might help him in his investigation."

"So he didn't pick up Kat last night?"

"Maybe not. He said he had already talked to her and I assumed..." Her voice trailed off.

"Hey, you might not have won that bet last night after all."

"You could be right. He was only here for a few minutes when they left. It could have been police business related."

"Then you owe me one."

"Oh, when can I pay off?"

"I'll think of something."

The two went back to bartending. Dee would come up with something appropriate to get even with Ron.

Detective Jenkins next asked Margarita Ortiz if she could come outside for a few minutes.

"Detective, I took my break a half hour ago. I don't get another one until closing. You can ask me what you want from here, but I have to keep tending."

"That's ok Ms. Ortiz. I'll come back if I need to talk with you further."

"Have it your way."

Detective Jenkins approached Sue Kent. As he did, Ed Phillips was trying to talk with Sue.

"Ms. Kent. I am Detective Jenkins with the Dennis Police Department. I wonder if I might have a few minutes of your time."

"Sure Detective."

"Can we talk outside on the deck? It might be easier." Jenkins pointed towards the band."

"I'll follow you."

Sue Kent had on a pink silk tee shirt, tight white shorts and sandals. Her hair was pulled back into a ponytail. She looked ten years younger than her actual age.

When they got outside, Detective Jenkins motioned for her to join him at the same table where he had talked to Dee.

"Thanks Detective. I needed to be rescued. Ed is always trying to get into my pants and he's kind of a nerd if you know what I mean."

"I'd like to talk to you about Ann Benard's attack last night up at Chapin Beach."

"I don't know much about it other than what I have overheard."

"And what did you overhear?"

"I was at Sundancers when Bobby came in. He said he had seen Ann and Katherine up at Chapin's bar a little earlier; Tina told us about Ann being in the hospital because she had spoken with her. I know Ed was there, as was Kenny. I think some of the others who are here now were there at some time as well."

"Did Bobby or anyone say anything about Ann?"

"Do you mean like they knew something about what happened to her?"

"Yes."

"No. I didn't hear anyone say anything like that."

"I know Bobby had some kind of argument with Ann because he said he went to look for her when they left Chapin's but he couldn't find her up at the beach. He wanted me to go to the beach and take a moonlit walk with him. He got the idea from Ann."

"Do you think he might have attacked Ann?"

"I don't think so. Bobby's not that kind of person. He might be aggressive trying to get into your pants, but I don't think he would resort to violence."

"What about any of the others?"

"Well, Kenny on the other hand can have a temper."

"Did he say or do something that might have implicated him with Ann's attack?"

"No, but when we saw him later that night, he looked disheveled."

"Did it look like he had been involved in an altercation?"

"I wouldn't go that far. He's in the bar, why don't you talk to him."

"I'll get around to him in a while."

"Are there any other guys who might have been after Ann?"

Sue, looking around the bar said, "Oh, I'm sure there are a few others in there that might have hooked up with Ann at one time or another. There are always those guys that don't seem to hookup at all, like Ed or Paul."

68

"Do you think any of them might have done this to Ms. Benard?"

"I don't know all of them personally. Of the ones I do know, I can't imagine any of them attacking Ann."

"Well, if you think of anything, please give me a call."

Jenkins handed her his business card and thanked her for her time.

Next, Detective Jenkins approached Kenny Brown and asked him for a few minutes of his time. The two went outside to the table Jenkins had been using as his desk and asked Kenny to sit down.

Kenny was dressed in a pair of Levi's jeans and a Red Sox tee shirt. He also wore a Red Sox baseball cap backwards. Kenny was just over 6'2" around 220lbs. He had brown hair, brown eyes. His physique was well toned as a result of working construction.

"Mr. Brown, I'm investigating Ann Bernard's attack up at Chapin Beach yesterday. I'd like to ask you a few questions."

"Sure thing, Detective. How can I help you?"

"Ms. Benard and Ms. Sterns said they saw you at Chapin's last night around seven thirty. Is that correct?"

"Yeah. I was there having drinks with Bobby and Ed. The ladies came in and sat across from us at the bar. After a while, they signaled us to join them. Well, not all of us, just Bobby and me."

"What about Ed?"

"Ed is kind of shy. He stayed on the opposite side of the bar. He was having a conversation with some guy that I don't know. I think his name was Tom something or other."

"So you and Bobby joined Ms. Benard and Ms. Sterns?"

"Yes. We had a few drinks and then Ms. Sterns and I left."

"You left with Ms. Sterns?"

"Well, not together, just at the same time. She had her own car there and I had mine."

"So you two just left at the same time?"

"Well, yes and no. We left at the same time and then went out into the parking lot and got into the back seat of my vehicle. I have an Explorer and I have one of those memory foam mattresses in the back."

"What is that for?"

"I put the back seats down and the foam mattress makes the back of my vehicle like a bed."

"So you and Ms. Sterns got into the back of your vehicle?"

"Sure did."

"Did you and she get it on right there in the parking lot?"

"I was parked way back in the rear corner of the lot. The last spot is blocked on one side by a big fence. Behind the lot are very thick bushes and Kat's car was parked next to mine. So the only view into my vehicle was through the windshield. I have a drop down cloth between the front and back seats and when dropped down, parked in the corner like that, we had pretty much complete privacy."

"So what happened?"

"She attacked me. She kissed me and took my clothes off. Then she tore her clothes off and got on top of me."

"Didn't you resist?"

"Have you ever taken a look at her? She's a 10."

"So you had sex with her right there in the parking lot."

"Sure did. When we were done, she did the strangest thing. She put the condom into a plastic bag and told me she would get rid of it. Then, I had to put my clothes on which had become all wrinkled. After I left the parking lot at the bar, I stopped to get gas, went to the liquor store to buy beer, dropped the beer off at my place and then went to Sundancers. When I walked in, everyone said I looked like I had slept in my clothes. I tried to fake an excuse of having worked out but I don't think anyone went for it."

"Some have said you came in sweating and looking like you were involved in an altercation. Someone said you even had blood on your shirt."

"Well, I probably did look sweaty, but I wouldn't call having sex with Kat an altercation. About the blood, I cut myself doing work around my place. The cut must have re-opened when things got rough with Kat."

"Did you go up to Chapin Beach at all that night?"

"No, like I said, I left the lot, ran errands, came here."

"I'd like to take a look at the shirt you had on if you could bring it to me at the police station if you haven't already washed it."

"I haven't washed my clothes yet for the week so I can bring it by."

"Please put it in a bag and drop it off at the station when you get a chance. Anything else you want to tell me?"

"Nah, but if you would, please don't tell anyone about my having sex with Katherine. She said she has a new guy she has been working on and doesn't want him to find out about it."

"I'm not here for anything other than information that might help me with my investigation. If you do think of anything else, though, Kenny, please give me a call."

He handed Kenny his card.

"Sure will."

Detective Jenkins went inside the bar to look for Bobby Jones. He wasn't sitting in the same place as he was when Dee had pointed him out. As Jenkins scanned the room, he saw Bobby over by the DJ booth talking with Linda. Jenkins approached the two.

"Are you Bobby Jones, and Linda Sage?"

Both answered yes.

"I'm Detective Jenkins of the Dennis Police. I'm investigating the attack on Ann Benard last night and I'd like to speak with both of you for a few minutes if I might."

"I was just telling Linda I was leaving for the night. Can we make it another time?"

71

"I only have a few questions. This won't take long. If you'll follow me outside to the deck, we can talk there where it isn't so loud, and I'll have you on your way in just a few minutes."

Linda started to follow the Detective as well when Detective Jenkins turned, "I'll come back and get you in a few minutes if that's all right with you Ms. Sage."

"I'll be right here at the bar Detective."

Bobby Jones was dressed in a pair of khaki shorts and a blue polo shirt. He wore a pair of leather sandals and sport sunglasses on his forehead. Bobby Jones was 5'11" and weighed 185lbs. He had a head of thick black hair cut about mid-ear length. Bobby's skin was well tanned and kept himself fit as he fancied himself as a ladies man and had a self-proclaimed image to uphold.

Jenkins led Bobby Jones to the interview table on the deck. Jenkins sat down and asked Bobby to take a seat.

"Since this isn't going to take much time, I'd prefer to stand."

"Have it your way. Let me start by asking you if you were at Chapin's Restaurant last night around seven thirty?"

"Yes, I was there with Ed, Kenny and other people I know."

"Were these other people Ms. Katherine Sterns and Ms. Ann Benard?"

"Yes."

"Did you have a disagreement with Ms. Benard while you were there?"

"I wouldn't call it a disagreement. I was trying to hook up with her for the night but all she wanted to do was take a walk on the beach."

"By hook up with her, you mean you wanted to sleep with her?"

"That kind of fits the picture. We had a few words at Chapin's but then she left. I kind of felt bad about how our conversation ended and I tried to follow her shortly after she left Chapin's."

"Did you find her?"

"No, I went up to Chapin Beach. Her car was in the parking lot but I couldn't see her. She must have already gone on her walk down to the beach."

"Why didn't you go after her?"

"I had no idea which way she went. I waited for her for a few minutes in the parking lot but when she didn't return, I left."

"Did you spin your tires when you left the lot?"

"Why would that be important?"

"Because there were people on the beach who heard someone peel out of the parking lot around that time and if it was you, then the story starts to come together."

"I might have. I had been at the bar for a while and had a buzz."

"So you were impaired?"

"I didn't say that."

"Do you think it's possible you had too much to drink where you don't remember everything that took place?"

"If you are asking me if I attacked Ann, I didn't."

"That's what I'm getting at."

"Well, I didn't do it."

Bobby started to turn away.

"I still have other questions."

"I don't think I am going to answer any more questions Detective. You can either charge me with a crime or I'm leaving."

Bobby turned and went back into the bar. He didn't stop to talk to anyone. He headed right out the front door, got into his car and went home.

Detective Jenkins went back inside and found Linda Sage. When the two went out to the deck, she said, "What was up with Bobby? He left in a hurry."

"He didn't like the way the questioning was going."

"Did he say what he was talking about with me? I'll bet he told you he was talking with me about leaving but that was just not true. He was talking to me about the clothes I have on."

She turned for him to be able to take a look at her clothing. She wore a sheer tan blouse with a tan tank top underneath. She had on a pair of white jeans and tennis sneakers. Linda had her shoulder length hair combed straight. She pulled out a chair and sat. As she sat, she leaned forward making sure the Detective could see down her blouse. Jenkins did look. He just stared at her as she took her seat.

"You can look if you want Detective. They're real."

"Excuse me Ms. Sage. I have a few questions I'd like to ask you regarding the assault on Ms. Benard."

"I don't know anything about that other than what I overheard."

"That's what I want to talk to you about."

"Ok. What do you want to know?"

"Is there anything you can recall from last night that someone might have done or said that would involve Ms. Benard?"

"Some of the people were talking about Ann being attacked up at Chapin Beach. Some of the people who were here had drinks with her up at Chapin's Restaurant before the attack. Some people were talking about who might have done this to Ann."

"Who might some of these people be?"

"Oh, you know. People at the bar."

"Can you be more specific?"

"I don't remember who said what. I know Kenny and Bobby had drinks with Katherine Sterns and Ann Benard at Chapin's Restaurant last night."

"How do you know that?"

"Because I overheard Bobby telling some of the other people about it."

"Anything else?"

"Yea. Kenny had come into Sundancers later on last night and when he was asked why he was sweaty, he said he had just gotten out of the shower. I know it wasn't true because I was outside having a cigarette when he pulled into the parking lot and I talked to him before he went into the bar. He had told me he had just had sex with someone in the parking lot up at Chapin's Restaurant and that was why he was sweaty."

"Did he say who it was?"

"He didn't have to. It had to be Katherine."

"Why do you say that?"

"Put two and two together. Ann went for a walk on the beach. Bobby tried to find her. That left Kenny and Katherine."

"I see what you mean."

"Anything else?"

"No. That's about it."

"If you think of anything else, please call me."

He handed her a card.

The next person Detective sought out was Tina Fletcher. When he asked Tina to join him for a few minutes on the deck, she took her drink with her and followed Jenkins out. Jenkins took his seat. Tina took the chair Jenkins designated for her and moved it close to Jenkins.

Tina was dressed in a tight yellow v-neck shirt and jean skirt. Being about 6' tall and slender, Tina liked to show off her long attractive legs. As she adjusted her skirt when she sat, Jenkins could see the top of her thong above the waistband of the skirt.

"Ms. Fletcher, what can you tell me about last night?"

"I'd rather talk about tonight."

"I'm investigating the attack on Ms. Benard and I'd like to know what you know about last night. Some of the people I have interviewed indicated you left Sundancers last night with Kenny Brown. Is that correct?"

"Yes. Kenny and I left here late last night."

"Do you remember what time that was?"

"No, just late."

"And where did you go?"

"To my place, but things just didn't work out. Kenny was spent."

"What do you mean spent?"

"He couldn't get it up."

"Why do you think that?"

"Look Detective. I'm good at certain things. If I couldn't get a rise out of him, no one could. You should let me show you some time."

"Maybe some other time. Did he say anything about Ms. Benard last night?"

"Not much. Just that they had a few drinks when they were up at Chapin's Restaurant."

"Do you think he was involved in her attack?"

"Kenny? No, I don't think so. If you asked me about his involvement with Katherine, I might have something to say, but not Ann."

"So Kenny and Katherine have a thing?"

"Not really a thing. Just sex. Kat likes a certain kind of man."

"What kind is that?"

"You know, well endowed."

"Detective, I need to get another drink. Can we hold up on the questions for a few minutes? Or, I have a better idea. Why don't we continue this discussion at my place?"

"I don't have anything else at the moment. If you think of anything else, please get in touch with me." He handed her his card.

"You sure you don't want to continue this at my place?"

"I'm on duty. Maybe another time."

"I look forward to it."

76

Detective Jenkins got up and went inside, following Tina's very entertaining display of legs. The bar was very busy so he decided to put off talking to Ron Jessup until another time. He had been there for an hour and a half by this point and the bar was very crowded and noisy. He decided to end his interviews for the day and pick it up tomorrow. He wanted to have a conversation with Katherine anyway.

Chapter 9

Detective Jenkins had been reading his incoming e-mails when he opened one from Officer Trudy. She indicated she had put a copy of her report in his in-basket and would be available at the end of her shift to discuss it if he wanted to speak directly to her. Jenkins looked though his in-basket and found her report. He took a few minutes to read it through. She had summarized her interview with the personnel at Gina's by the Sea, with the bartender at Chapin's and identified the tasks still open. The one task Jenkins was hoping to see resolved was of the bloodstains on Kenny Brown clothing which had been sent to the lab for analysis. Jenkins called dispatch and asked the officer on duty to call Trudy and have her stop into his office at the end of her shift.

Later in the day, at the end of Officer Trudy's shift, she stopped into Detective Jenkins office.

"What's up Detective?"

"Oh, Trudy, thanks for stopping in. Any news from the lab yet on the Browns clothing?"

"Not yet. I put in a call before I came here and the technician said they are almost done."

"Well, let me know as soon as you hear from them?"

"Will do. Anything else?"

"Did you learn anything from the people at the ZooQuarium?"

"Not yet. They are closed two days a week and don't re-open again until tomorrow. I'll let you know if I find anything out."

"Do you know any of these people who we have been investigating?"

"Not really, but I do know Bobby Jones's brother Mike. He was one of the paramedics who were on scene after Ms. Benard was attacked."

"When I talked with Mike, he said his brother knew Ms. Benard and had told him about some things that have happened between him and her," said Jenkins.

"Mike's a pretty straight guy. I know his parents as well. They're good people. So if Bobby is involved, I don't think it's something from his childhood upbringing."

"Sometimes guys change when they get involved in social situations especially where the hormones get involved."

"You think he has some male identity issues?"

"I don't know. From what everyone says about him, he fancies himself as a ladies man. His conduct is definitely suspect. He was a little too standoffish when I tried to talk to him at Sundancers."

"Do you want me to bring him in for more questioning?"

"No, but stop into Sundancers from time to time and see if he's there. Ask some questions of some of the other people we've talked to and see if he gets nervous. Sometimes when the heat's turned up, a perp shows his colors."

"Ok Detective. I can do that. Do you think they will talk to me?"

"Sure they will Trudy. You're pretty good looking, so do some of the work out of uniform."

"Like undercover?"

"He knows who you are, but if you show interest as a woman, then he might slip up."

"Ok. I'll report back to you if I find out anything."

"Report back to me even if you don't uncover anything new."

79

"Will do."

Detective Jenkins was bothered by Bobby's story. He was at Chapin's. He went to the Chapin Beach lot around the same time as the attack being committed. He had some sort of disagreement with Ms. Benard at Chapin's Restaurant. He left the restaurant abruptly and in haste. His Jeep was observed by the Fields on Dr. Bottero road traveling towards the parking lot at a speed beyond the posted speed limit. He was not present when the Fields found Ms. Benard by the beach. He seems to be hiding something during questioning. Jenkins knew he needed to talk to Ms. Benard.

Looking at Officer Trudy's report from the attack, Detective Jenkins found Ms. Benard's home phone number. He called it.

"Ms. Benard. It's Detective Jenkins."

"Hello Detective."

"How are you doing?"

"Better. My head doesn't hurt as much and the medication the doctor prescribed is helping."

"Ms. Benard. I'd like to meet with you to ask you a few questions."

"Would you like me to come to the station?"

"I can come to your residence if it would be convenient?"

"That would be fine with me. When would you like to meet?"

"Do you have anytime free today?"

"Sure. I'm just sitting here resting. Anytime would be fine."

"Then I'll be there in about a half hour."

"See you then."

Detective Jenkins gathered his notes from the interviews and the various reports he and Officer Trudy had prepared. He put them into a manila folder and headed over to Ms. Benard's residence.

80

Ms. Benard lived in a big house on Cove Road in West Dennis. Her back yard had about two hundred feet of frontage on the Bass River. As Jenkins drove down Cove Road, he thought it was a very nice upscale neighborhood. He pulled into the loop driveway and parked his unmarked cruiser.

The front door opened and Ms. Benard greeted him.
"Detective Jenkins, come in please."
Jenkins looked at her with raised eyebrows. She had on a bikini and a sheer wrap around her waist.
She said, "I've been resting on a lounge chair in the back yard. It's such a nice day. Let's sit out back and talk."
"What ever makes you most comfortable is fine with me."
"Well, most comfortable is probably in the bedroom but out back will do for now. Can I get you something to drink?"
"Do you have any diet cola or iced tea?"
"I have iced tea. I'll bring you a glass."
She got two glasses of iced tea from the kitchen and a small glass flask containing a clear liquid. Placing the tray on the table in the back yard, she said, "High test or regular?"
"Regular please."
She put some of the liquid from the flask in her drink and left his as it was.
"How can I help you Detective?"
"I have interviewed most of the people you had contact with on the day of your attack and I have a few questions you might be able to answer."
"Sure Detective. I'll answer what I can."

"Let's start with your dinner. The staff at Gina's by the Sea indicated you and Ms. Sterns had a few drinks and then had dinner. Your waitress, Jenny Andretti, said she knows both you and Ms. Sterns and she recalled waiting on you. She said the two of you were in a jovial mood, laughing and having a good time."

"Katherine and I did have a good time at Gina's. We were talking about some of the men we have in common."

"What do you mean, in common?"

"You know. Dated."

"Later on, I talked with John White at Chapin's Restaurant."

"John, he was our bartender. Nice guy."

"He said you come there often and the two of you had a few drinks there by yourselves and then were joined by a few guys who had been sitting across the bar from you."

"That's right, Bobby and Kenny joined us."

"Mr. White indicated you had a few more drinks with the guys who joined you and then Ms. Sterns and Mr. Brown left together."

"Oh, I don't think they left together, just at the same time."

Jenkins looked through his notepad and scribbled something down. When he looked up, Ann said, "Does this have anything to do with Katherine?"

"What do you mean?"

"Well, I know you and Katherine have a thing going."

"What do you mean a thing?"

"You know, sleeping together."

"Did she tell you that?"

"She told me about the two of you when we were at Gina's. Is there something you want to ask me about Katherine?"

"No, I'm investigating the attack on you."

"Then why all the questions about what Kat and I did or who she was with?"

"Because any one of the people you had contact with might have been your attacker."

"After Katherine and Kenny left, I had another drink with Bobby. Bobby had been at Chapin's for some time drinking with Kenny and Ed before Katherine and I got there. After Kenny and Bobby joined us, Ed just sat on the other side of the bar looking at us. After Kat left, Bobby said he was going to ask Ed to join us. I told him not to. Ed kind of gives me the creeps. I had to go to the bathroom and when I returned, Bobby was over on the other side of the bar talking to Ed. Ed shot me a nasty look and I knew Bobby had told him I didn't want to be near him. Then Bobby rejoined me at my side of the bar."

"Did Ed join you, too?"

"No, he was talking with another man who took up one of the stools Bobby and Kenny vacated. I didn't know the guy but just before Katherine left, she said the guy looked like a friend of her former husband, except this guy had a beard. When Bobby came back to talk with me, I asked him what he had said to Ed. He said he told him that he gave me the creeps and I didn't want to be near him. That was when I had words with Bobby."

"What did you say to him?"

"I told him he was very insensitive and I had only said what I said in confidence."

"Didn't you mean it?"

"Well, yeah, Ed does give me the creeps. He's always trying to pick one of us up, but saying something like that to someone's face is mean."

"Who is one of us?"

"Linda, Sue, Tina, Kat, me, you know, one of the girls."

"Do you have some kind of club or something?"

"No, we just all know each other."

"Did Katherine go over and talk with the guy with the beard?"

"No. She said the guy she thought he looked like moved to Virginia with his family shortly after her husband died."

"Did Ed seem to know the guy?"

"I don't know. I think they were talking about fishing or something. I really didn't pay much attention to them."

"If you do think of anything else, let me know. Will you?"

"Sure."

Jenkins made more notes in his book. He scanned a few other pages, "When Officer Trudy and I visited the site of the attack the next day, we talked with a fisherman who had been on the beach all night. He indicated that at a little after dark, another vehicle started down the off-road access path but stopped by the dunes. The vehicle was not there for very long and then left abruptly. Did you see any other vehicles when you first went to the beach that night?"

"No, the parking lot was empty and I had only walked to the point where I was attacked. Then the next thing I knew the paramedics and Officer Trudy were helping me."

"Did you see the Fields walking along Dr. Bottero Road when you drove to the beach?"

"Let me think. There were a few people walking along the road back by the houses. I remember because the street isn't very wide back there and I had to slow down to pass them."

"That matches the story the Fields reported. They also said another vehicle went in the Chapin Beach direction shortly after you went by but that vehicle was driving faster. Do you have any idea who that might have been?"

"No. I didn't see anyone else."

"Could Bobby have been coming after you?"

"Why? Because of our disagreement at Chapin?"

"That or for some other reason."

"Look Detective. Bobby and I see each other from time to time. We know each other pretty well. I don't think he would attack me for any reason."

"You never know what will trigger someone's aggression."

"Not Bobby. He knows I was only being me."

"But you embarrassed him in public. Some men can't take that."

"Bobby can. He knows if he ever hurt me, he'd never be with me again."

"He told me he tried to find you at the beach but couldn't. If you didn't go much past the access-road entrance, I don't see how he could have missed you?"

"Unless the attack had already taken place."

"What do you mean?"

"I was unconscious for some time. Maybe he tried to find me and I was lying on the ground knocked out all the time he was looking?"

"I guess that's a possibility."

"Bobby couldn't have done it."

"What about Kenny? Didn't he leave before you?"

"Yes, as I said he left when Kat left."

"Could he have gone to Chapin Beach and waited for you?"

"How would he have known I was going to Chapin Beach?"

"Didn't you tell Bobby you wanted to take a walk on Chapin Beach in the moonlight?"

"Yes, but Kenny was deep in conversation with Kat when I was talking to Bobby about a moonlight walk."

"But you did say it out loud, didn't you?"

"Why are you asking it that way?"

"John White remembered you talking to Bobby about walking on the beach so I'm pretty sure others at the bar overheard you. Plus, you already said you had a number of drinks by this point in the evening so the conversation might have been rather loud."

"I'm not a boisterous person Detective."

"Maybe not, but other people at the bar heard you talking about it. My guess is someone who was at the bar went to the beach and waited for you."

"But Bobby left after I did and I didn't hear or see his vehicle so it couldn't have been him."

"That's why I'm asking about Kenny."

"I thought you were asking about Kenny because he left with Kat."

"I thought you said he didn't leave with her?"

85

"You know what I mean. He left at the same time she did."

Ann's back yard had a high fence on one side blocking any view into her yard from the neighbor's house. On the other side of the yard was a wooded area covered with vegetation at least ten feet high. The only view of her back yard to the outside world existed from across the river and that was probably a half-mile away, or from a passing boat. As the questioning went on, Ann began to feel the heat. She sat up in her lounger and took off her top.

"It's getting a little hot out here don't you think Detective?"

Jenkins looked at her breasts, "You really can't do that."

"Why not? This is a secluded area. I'm not bothering anyone."

"Because it's a town ordinance. No nude bathing."

"I'm not nude bathing. I'm just getting a little hot. If it really bothers you, we can continue inside."

"I only have a few more questions."

"So stop looking at me and ask."

"What about the other guy at the bar, Ed. Did you see him leave?"

"I didn't notice him again from the time Bobby spoke to him. I think he went to the other end of the bar and talked to other people but I'm not really sure."

"Do you think he could have attacked you?"

"I don't know."

Jenkins made another note in his pad.

"What about Katherine?"

"What about her?"

"You said she left before you. Remember? She left at the same time as Kenny."

"Kat would never hurt me. We do everything together."

"Maybe you hurt her in some way, say with a guy and she wanted to get back at you."

"I can't think of a single thing that would cause her to want to hurt me, even where men are concerned. We talk, compare notes and have a few laughs but we would never let a man come between us. Well, at least not like that. It's gals before pals where we're concerned."

"Still, she was there. She knew your plans. She left before you."

"So did Kenny and I'm sure there were other people who overheard my plans."

"But none that might have had a reason to attack you."

"Or maybe it wasn't even someone I know."

"That's a possibility as well."

"Detective, I'm getting too hot to continue out here. Can we go inside and continue."

Jenkins thought about it for a minute and then responded, "I think I'm done with the questioning for today."

"Then how about we go inside and you allow me to investigate you?"

"That will not be necessary. I'm still on duty."

"Then why don't you come back when you get off duty?"

"I have other plans."

"Well, if your plans change, I'll be here. If you don't come back later, maybe we can make it another time."

She got up and walked to her back door. She turned to look back at Detective Jenkins. Her upper exposed body was clearly visible to him. As she turned, she smiled, "Detective, can you bring the glasses and my top into the house?"

Jenkins thought about it for a minute. "Where was this headed?"

He picked up the half full glasses and the pitcher of iced tea. Then he picked up her bikini top and walked towards the door. He stopped at the door and remained outside the house.

"Here are your things."

"Can you put the glasses in the sink and the pitcher in the refrigerator," he could hear her say from another room. He did as she asked and then went back to the open door. He turned to see her come back into the room. She had nothing on.

"I've got to be going."

"Can't you stay for a little longer?"

"Not really." He was starting to blush and get interested.

"Come on in and make yourself comfortable for a while. Who would miss you for an hour?"

"I really can't."

He turned and closed the door behind him.

Jenkins thought to himself. So that's what a cougar attack is like.

Chapter 10

After wrapping up his visit with Ann Benard, Detective Jenkins returned to the station. He logged into his computer and selected e-mail. There was an entry from Officer Trudy. He selected the entry and began to read. "The lab report of the clothes obtained from Kenny Brown did not have any of Ms. Benard's DNA on them. All blood traces matched the DNA of Mr. Brown. The written report from the lab will be on your desk in the morning. Trudy."

Jenkins took out his notepad and filled out e-reports for everyone he had spoken to. When done, he filed each one in the electronic file for the Benard case. Something was bothering him about the information that had been gathered. Someone who knew she would be going to the beach may have attacked Ms. Benard. The circle of people who knew was very small. If it wasn't someone who was at Chapin's Restaurant the attack was a completely random event and Jenkins didn't believe there were very many truly random attacks.

Near the end of her shift, Officer Trudy went to the ZooQuarium on Route 28 in West Yarmouth. The ZooQuarium sits back off the road behind Captain Parker's Restaurant. She parked her cruiser in the parking lot and entered the main entrance. She approached the ZooQuarium ticket window and asked to see the manager. The cashier pointed to an office door and Officer Trudy went in that direction.

Trudy knocked on the door and opened it.

"I'm Officer Trudy of the Dennis Police Department. I'm investigating an attack that occurred recently and would like to speak with the manager."

"I'm Mary Harper, I'm Mr. Carson's secretary. He's the manager here."

"Is he in? I'd like to speak with him for a few minutes."

"Yes, he's here. I think he's out on the grounds talking with the caretakers. I can call him in if you like?"

"If it wouldn't be too much trouble."

Ms. Harper picked up her phone and pressed a button. Trudy could hear her say over the intercom, "Mr. Carson, can you come to the office. Mr. Carson to the office please". She hung up the phone and asked Officer Trudy to take a seat. A few minutes later, the door opened and a man walked in. He approached Officer Trudy, "I'm Mr. Carson. I'm the manager here. Can I help you?"

"Yes Mr. Carson. I'm Officer Trudy of the Dennis Police. I'm investigating an attack that took place recently up at Chapin Beach. I'd like to ask you a few questions if you have a minute."

"Please, come into my office Officer." He led her through the door into his office. The back wall of the office was all glass overlooking the Zoo grounds. "How can I help you officer?"

"As I said, an attack took place up at Chapin Beach and I'm investigating a few leads."

"How is the ZooQuarium involved?"

"During our investigation, it came to our attention that you might have a cougar here on the premises."

"That is, or was true."

"What do you mean was true?"

"Well, sometime the day before yesterday, our cougar got out of his compound and left the zoo property."

"Did you report it to the Police?"

"Yes, we called the Yarmouth Police and reported that Charlie, that's the cougar's name, had gotten out of his cage."

"Has he been recaptured?"

"Not yet, but we're sure he'll turn up when he gets hungry."

"Cougar's are predatory animals aren't they?"

"Yes they are."

"Then he will probably hunt for food once he gets hungry won't he?"

"Charlie isn't a wild cougar. He's been raised in captivity since he was a cub. We've had him here at the ZooQuarium for three years and he's rather tame. He's part of the regular show we put on in the amphitheatre on weekends. In fact, we let some of the kids even pet him. Trust me, his idea of a meal doesn't include the local cat or dog."

"Do you think he is capable of attacking someone?"

"No, Charlie might try to play with someone like wrestling but I don't think he'd attack anyone."

"How big is your cougar?"

"I'd say he's about one hundred seventy pounds."

"And about how tall is he?"

"Probably the size of a Doberman, just a little stockier."

"And if he stood on his hind legs, how tall would he be?"

"About six foot."

Mr. Carson stood and walked over to a wall, which was covered with pictures. He pointed to one 11" x 14", "This is Charlie."

Officer Trudy came over and looked. Charlie the cougar was standing with his paws on Mr. Carson's shoulders. He was as tall as Mr. Carson. In the background, the stands were full of people watching the show that had been going on when the picture was taken.

91

Mr. Carson said, "As you can see, Charlie is part of the show."

"What were you doing with him in the picture?"

"In part of our act, Charlie stands on his hind legs and tries to wrestle the trainer to the ground. I was the trainer during the show where the picture was taken."

"And just how does he do it?"

"He uses his weight and lunges at you putting his paws on your shoulders. If the trainer isn't paying attention, Charlie could knock him down."

"Interesting," said Trudy.

"As I was saying, Charlie jumps up like he's going to attack the trainer but just then music is pumped into the amphitheater and Charlie starts to do a dance with the trainer. Everyone always laughs and can't believe they are seeing a cougar dance."

Mr. Carson went back to his desk and pulled out a brochure. Inside, it showed a picture of Charlie and had a caption under it that read, "Would you dance with a cougar?" He handed it to Officer Trudy.

"Where do you think Charlie is right now?"

"I don't know, but he's been gone long enough now where he will be hungry and unless he finds some cat's dish outside someone's house, he'll be back here to eat very soon."

"Do you think he could have gone to Chapin Beach?"

"I wouldn't think so. That's quite a way from here. Then again, cougars can travel a pretty good distance on any given day."

"Thank you Mr. Carson for the information. Will you call us as soon as you find your cougar?"

She handed him her business card.

"I'll call as soon as he shows up."

Officer Trudy took the brochure and left the ZooQuarium.

Returning to the station, Officer Trudy had about twenty minutes left on her shift. It would be just enough time to enter her report into the computer before checking out for

92

the day. She completed the e-report and sent it to Detective Jenkins. In it, she indicated the people at the ZooQuarium said their cougar was at large but he's a trained animal and has never shown any aggression at anyone. She indicated the cougar might get playful with humans as he does during his act at the ZooQuarium.

When Detective Jenkins later read the report, he wanted to speak with Trudy about some of the details. He thought about what had been written and about the details of the attack. The claw marks on Ms. Benard didn't sound like they came from a playful animal, but rather a savage attack. Jenkins called Trudy's desk phone first, but there was no answer, so he dialed her cell phone.

"Pam, its Frank Jenkins. I was just reading your report from the ZooQuarium and have a few questions. Can you come to my office for a few minutes?"

"I'm on my way home for the night. I left the station about fifteen minutes ago and have an appointment. Can it wait until tomorrow?"

"Can you talk with me for a few minutes while you drive?"

"Sure, what do you want to know?"

"In reading this report, it indicated the ZooQuarium has a cougar and it has escaped. Do they have any idea where it might be?"

"Mr. Carson, the manager there, indicated Charlie, he's the cougar, would probably return when he gets hungry. Mr. Carson said their cougar works in the shows they put on and it is a very tame animal."

"If it were their cougar that attacked Ms. Benard, how would you explain the scratch marks?"

"Mr. Carson said Charlie can stand on his hind legs and does so in their show. He might have been imitating the act and stood up to Ms. Benard. If he did, he might have knocked her over and accidentally scratched her in the process."

"I guess that might have happened, but what about the rock with the blood on it?"

"We assumed she was hit on the head with the rock. Maybe it never left the ground and Ms. Benard struck her head on it when she fell to the ground."

"It all sounds possible."

"So you think this whole thing might be a situation of unfortunate circumstances?"

"I don't know, but it's certainly a possibility."

"Do you want me to continue investigating the people Ms. Benard had contact with?"

"No, you return to your normal duties tomorrow and I'll take the case from here."

"Will do. I'll make sure all my information is on your desk or online tomorrow."

"Thank you Pam. Have a good night."

"You too Frank."

Chapter 11

Detective Jenkins wrapped up the day at the station and called Katherine. "Katherine, I'm just finishing up for the day and was going to stop for a drink on the way home. Care to join me?"

"What did you have in mind?"

"I thought I would stop in at Sundancers."

"I'll meet you there in twenty minutes."

"See you there."

Twenty minutes later, Detective Jenkins walked into Sundancers. Katherine was sitting on the opposite side of the bar where she could see everyone who came in. Tina was sitting right by the door and turned to see Jenkins come in. She said, "Detective, nice to see you here again. More questions?"

"I'm off duty. I just stopped in to have a drink."

"Well come and join me."

"Thank you for asking, but I'm meeting someone."

"Anyone I know?"

Just then, Katherine approached him. She greeted him and gave him a kiss on the cheek. Tina remembered what Jenkins had told her when he had interviewed her. She said, "I guess I wasn't quick enough about getting back together."

Jenkins just ignored her and took Katherine's arm and went around to where she had been sitting. He took up the chair next to hers and ordered a draft.

Margarita Ortiz was bartending and took his order. When Margarita went to pour the beer, Tina said to her, "looks like Katherine is hooking up tonight."

Margarita looked at her, "Yeah, and so early."

"It could have been me," Tina said.

Margarita took the beer and walked back over to where Jenkins and Katherine were sitting and put it on the bar in front of him.

Katherine, looking at Frank Jenkins said, "What did Tina mean about getting back together?"

"I have no idea. I interviewed her in regards to the case I'm working on and I had said I might have more questions. That must be what she was referring to."

"She is always looking for new meat if you know what I mean."

"I think I do."

"Well, she's not getting you, at least not tonight."

Sue Kent was sitting two chairs away from Katherine on the other side. Bobby Jones had been talking to her and trying to get close to her. Sue kept turning to guys who walked by attempting to get the attention of one of them. She made it obvious she didn't want Bobby. Finally Sue got up and went around to the end of the bar where Linda Sage was sitting.

Sue said to Linda, "That Bobby, he keeps trying to get into my pants."

"Well, you have been known to take him home from time to time."

"Yeah, when things get slow, Bobby is there, but he gets so touchy."

"I know what you mean. I had him once and he couldn't keep his hands off me."

"That's because you're so big." Sue looked down at Linda's chest.

"Could be, but he didn't stop there."

"Kind of creepy."

96

"With Bobby, all I want is to get off and move on."

"Yeah, me too."

Linda looked around, "And what's Ed's problem?"

"Oh, Ed doesn't have a problem. He's just inexperienced," said Sue with her eyebrows raised.

"What do you mean?"

"I used to think he was creepy too but my curiosity got the best of me one night and I had him over."

"And what happened?"

"I mean he has to have one of the biggest I have ever had."

"You slept with Ed?"

"Sure did and I'd do it again if I had the chance."

"Why don't you just go after him right now?"

"He is preoccupied with someone. I don't know who, but he has no interest in anyone but her."

"So you say he's blessed?"

Sue is holding her hands about twelve inches apart gesturing. The two laughed and both turn and look at Ed at the same time.

Linda said, "You're kidding me, right?"

"Well, maybe a little, but I'll tell you he's going to make some woman very happy."

Tina saw the two laughing and pointing. She walked over, "What's so funny girls?"

Linda pointed at Ed and repeated what Sue had told her. She made the gesture with her hands. Tina said, "Wow, I'd sure like to see that."

"I'd like to do more than look at it," said Linda.

During all of this, Ed, who had been sitting along at the other end of the bar trying to make contact with the older woman next him, saw the women pointing at him and laughing. He wasn't sure what they were talking about but when Tina joined Sue and Linda and the three looked in his direction laughing, he made a mental note. He finished his drink. When he was about to order another, Linda walked over to him, "Ed, can I buy you a drink?"

"I saw you women laughing. What was so funny?"

"Oh, just girl talk."

"Well, you were pointing at me and laughing. What was Sue saying?"

"It wasn't anything bad, well not in the bad sense. In fact, I'd say she was complimenting you."

"What did she say?"

"Oh, I can't tell you that Ed. It was just girl talk."

"I think it's rude when you point at someone and laugh."

"Ed, you're taking this all the wrong way. Let me buy you a drink and we can start from there."

"What do you mean start?"

"The night is still young."

"No thanks. I'm still a little put off by your laughing at me."

"Then why don't we just get out of here and go to my place?"

"Your place? What do you have in mind?"

"I'd like to get to know you better."

"No, I don't think so. Maybe another time."

Ed asked for his tab. He paid it and left Linda just sitting there at the bar. He didn't even say goodbye. Ten minutes after Ed left the bar, Ann Benard walked in as Tina was walking out, by herself.

Katherine Sterns and Frank Jenkins had been sitting at the bar having a drink when Ann walked in. Katherine motioned to her to come over. Ann took up the open seat next to Detective Jenkins.

"Ms. Benard, how are you feeling?" Detective Jenkins asked.

"Detective, its Ann."

"And it's Frank when I'm not on duty."

Katherine leaned in, "So, Ann, are you OK?"

"I'm doing ok. I just have a headache that doesn't seem to want to go away. I thought I'd come down and have a drink and see if that helps. I tried calling you Friday night after I got home from the hospital, but you weren't home."

Katherine thought about it, and then remembered the phone rang, as she and Frank were getting ready to enjoy dessert.

"Gee, I was there. Perhaps I was in the shower."

"Are you sure having a drink is the right thing to do? Didn't you say you were taking medication?" Frank asked.

"My doctor said I just need to take it easy. He said I have a mild concussion."

"Just take it easy Ann. You don't want to make it any worse than it has to be," said Katherine.

"I plan on taking it easy for a few days," responded Ann. "Frank, or should I say Detective, have you found anything out?"

"As I said, call me Frank. I'm not on duty and even if we talk about your case, I'm still not on duty. Yes and no in answer to your question. We are pursuing a number of leads, one of which is rather interesting."

"What do you mean, interesting?"

"Well, it seems that a large cat, or rather a cougar got out of his enclosure at the ZooQuarium and is at large."

"What does that have to do with my attack?"

"I don't know yet. It may not have anything to do with your attack. When Officer Trudy looked around after your attack, she identified some large tracks that were created by an animal. The tracks looked like large cat tracks."

"Do you think I could have been attacked by a cougar?"

"Let's just say the facts are interesting. When Officer Trudy talked with the people at the ZooQuarium, they indicated the cougar is part of the show they put on and the cougar is accustomed to having contact with humans."

"Could it have attacked me?"

"I don't know if attack is the right term. Apparently, the cougar is known to stand on its hind legs and put its paws

99

on the shoulders of the adult trainer during the ZooQuarium show."

"I was knocked to the ground and hit on the head. I don't remember what hit me from behind and don't remember hearing anything."

"So it could have been an animal or a person?" Questioned Katherine.

"I guess it could have been either," responded Ann.

"We are continuing our investigation and that is one of the leads we are pursuing."

"Could I have been mauled by that animal?"

"From what the people at the ZooQuarium said, the cougar was probably only playing with you. It has never demonstrated any aggression towards any human being in the past and may have been playing with you."

"If it was a cougar, I'm glad I was knocked out. Had I seen it, I probably would have had a heart attack right there on the spot."

Katherine added, "It would have scared me to death as well."

Frank ordered them each another drink and they continued talking. After a little while, Sue waived to Ann and motioned for her to come over. Ann picked up her drink and excused herself. She took up a stool next to Sue.

"How you feeling Annie?" Sue asked.

"Better now that I have had a drink. This headache I have has been really bothering me."

"If you are up to it, I think I can persuade Tommy to show you a good time?"

"Tommy Anderson? He's young for my taste."

"Ann, you know my theory about men. Check out their shoes. Big feet mean big you know what. Age means nothing."

"Yeah, I know. You've said that before."

"Well, Tommy has size twelve or fourteen, and I can tell you, he fits the bill."

"Oh really? But is he good?"

"If he hasn't had too much to drink, he knows his way around. He might be a little young, but trust me it will be worth it. Want me to call him over?"

"Sure. I could use something positive about now."

Sue motioned to Tommy to come over and join her and Ann.

"Hey Sue. How you feeling Ann?"

"I'm ok. Thanks for asking."

"Tommy, I was just telling Ann about how good you are with your hands. You know, giving a massage."

"I thought you might be talking about something else."

"Well, now that you mention it, that did come up."

"It always comes up."

"Anyway, I was telling Ann you give a great massage and given what happened to her, I thought you might be able to help her out."

"Are you sore Ann?"

"Somewhat, and I have had this terrible headache."

"You know, a good massage can help relieve a headache in addition to sore muscles."

"I didn't know that," said Ann.

"Yeah, a massage can help you relax and in turn, your mind will relax. You think about other things and the headache seems to just go away."

"I guess that could happen."

Sue said, "Tommy, why don't you take Ann home and see if you can help her out."

"Sure. If you'd like," he said looking at Ann.

"Let me finish my drink and we can go."

"I'll pay my tab and meet you by the door," said Tommy as he got up and went back to where he had been sitting before joining the girls. As he left, Sue said to Ann, "Remember what I said Ann. He might be young but he's pretty good."

"I remember. I'll let you know tomorrow what I think of him."

"I'm sure you will. Now go relax."

Ann said goodbye and waived to Katherine and Frank as she left the bar with Tommy.

"Looks like Ann is getting back to her old self," exclaimed Katherine to Frank.

"Maybe he's taking her home or something," said Frank.

"More of the *or something*," said Katherine as she set down her drink and waived to Ann. "Well, it doesn't look like she's any worse from the attack."

"So are you saying she's back in action?"

"You saw it, what do you think?"

"I don't know what to think. Remember I'm a Detective. I need facts."

"Well Detective, that one is a real cougar. Real cougars are always on the prowl."

"Ha, ha. Now you're an expert?"

"In those matters I am."

"So you consider yourself a cougar?"

"No, I'm just a horny feline. You know, a real pussy cat."

"Oh please. I've been with you. You're no pussy cat."

"Ok, Ok. So I have an appetite for certain things."

"Appetite. I'd call it an obsession."

"Because I like sex?"

"No, because you like sex all the time."

"Is that a bad thing?"

"Guys like a girl who likes sex. They just don't want to be following each other if you know what I mean."

"I guess I don't know what you mean."

"Well, a guy wouldn't want to be having sex with a woman shortly after she just had sex with another guy."

"Do you mean the same day, same hour or what?"

"If you're having sex with multiple partners on the same day, I'd say that you are either a nymphomaniac or a prostitute."

"Well, I don't charge. So I'm not a prostitute."

"So you are a nympho?"

102

"I didn't even say I have had multiple partners on the same day."

"But you didn't say you didn't either."

"Isn't that a double negative?"

"I think if you did those kinds of things, you would call it a double positive."

"I'm not going to elaborate on my sexual preferences."

"So now its preferences?"

"You know what I mean."

"I'm not sure I do. I think we should change the subject before it creates a problem between us. Remember, I'm a cop."

"I didn't know sex between consenting adults was a law enforcement issue."

"I'm not saying it is, but I wouldn't want to put our relationship in a position where I had to become a cop."

"Ok. Let's just leave it at that."

"Sure."

The two went back to their drinks and didn't say much for a few minutes. Dee came over and asked them if they wanted another drink. Frank said he thought it was time to go and asked for the check. Katherine shot him a look showing her frown. She realized the conversation was heading down a road that might be a problem for him so she didn't say a word. When Frank had paid the tab, the two got up and left together.

Outside the bar, Katherine said, "Will you follow me to my place? I'd like to ease your concerns about me."

"I've got a busy day tomorrow. If you don't mind, I'd like to pass."

"Can't you spend the night?"

"No. I really need to get some rest and going home with you would mean I wouldn't get much rest."

"You could just lie back and I'd do all the work."

"I'm sure you would. I really have to get a good night's rest Katherine. I'll talk to you tomorrow."

He kissed her on the lips and turned towards his vehicle.

"Ok. Tomorrow then."

Dee had been looking out into the parking lot as the two left. She said to Margarita, "Looks like Kat struck out tonight."

"Looks like it," said Ron as he looked out into the lot.

"Sure does," added Margarita.

"And Tina left by herself as well. Must be something about today that all of the cougars are going hungry," said Ron.

"Yeah, and the prey isn't doing much better," added Dee. "I saw Kenny leave by himself. Ed, although I don't think I would call him prey, left by himself as well."

"Well, Sue's still here. We'll have to see if she gets her prize for the night or not."

"Only Ann connected today. Maybe the cougars are off their game."

"Or maybe the prey just isn't appetizing."

"Or maybe the recent attack has put them on guard?" Margarita added.

"That could be. Give them a few days and I'm sure things will be looking up," said Dee as she cleaned up the bar area where Frank and Katherine had been sitting.

"We'll see," said Ron and he went back to waiting on the other patrons who were still seated at the bar.

Margarita walked over to Dee, "Do you think one of the guys who come in here is targeting the cougars?"

"Don't know," replied Dee.

"Well, Detective Jenkins is working close to one of the cougars. Do you think his interest is part of the job, or is he interested in her?"

"They've been in here a few times together even before the attack, so I think it might be a little of both. It does appear Katherine is limiting her prey to just a few targets lately. I'm sure she will return to her ways once he figures her out."

"We'll see."

The two went back to waiting on the other patrons at the bar.

Chapter 12

Tina turned left out of the parking lot heading east. When she got to Old Main Street, she turned left again. After a few minutes, she passed town hall and continued for another fifteen minutes until she reached 6A. She turned left and then right. The blue sign read, Mayflower Beach. After another few minutes and a few turns, she turned into her little bungalow overlooking Cape Cod Bay.

She locked her car and walked up to the door. She reached over and took her key out from under the flowerpot sitting on the stoop. Tina was happy she had a motion sensor installed on her outside door light, as the night was rather dark. While the moon was just rising in the eastern sky, Tina's house stood behind a large oak tree that would block the moonlight for another hour or two. She flipped on the light switch as she entered the foyer illuminating that portion of the house.

She put her things away and went to the refrigerator. She selected the open bottle of Pinot Grigio and poured a glass. She opened the sliding doors at the back of the house and walked out on to the deck overlooking the bay. She could see the tide was out and the beach seemed to extend out a half mile, maybe more. Taking her glass of wine, she kicked off her shoes and walked down the stairs to the beach. The sand was still warm from the sunny day that had departed only hours before. Tina liked the feeling of the sand under her feet as she walked along. She continued out as far as she could walk without touching the ripple waves. Turning and looking back towards her house, she could see a number of other homes lit up along the ridgeline above the beach. She decided to walk east along the water edge until she was abreast of Mayflower Beach parking lot. Then she walked up to the now closed concession stand. She could see the parking lot had some gravel on top of the pavement so she decided to walk back along the dunes to her house. Tina had walked about a half mile up the beach when she turned in to Mayflower Beach.

She passed a cottage that had lights turned on inside. She didn't see anyone outside and guessed the residents were watching TV based on the flickering blue glow behind the blinds. Just after walking past the house, she had to walk out fifty feet or so from the dunes to navigate around a couple of large boulders, which extended from the beach up onto the dunes. As she walked around the landscaping boulders, which seemed to be over ten feet high, she could feel the cool water running out from around the boulders into the bay.

"Miss, are you all right," said the young man.

"Who are you? What happened?"

"My name is Martin and this is Tammy. We found you here on the beach."

Martin had a flashlight and was shinning it in Tina's eyes.

"Can you turn the light away a little? I can't see anything with it in my eyes."

"Sorry," said Martin.

"We found you lying on the beach and thought you might be ..." Tammy didn't finish her sentence. She had picked up and was holding the empty wine glass that Tina had been carrying.

Tina felt the back of her head, "Ouch. Someone must have hit me from behind. I don't even remember it. What time is it?"

107

Martin shined the flashlight on his watch, "eleven thirty."

"I came out for a walk on the beach a little before ten. Could I have been knocked out for over an hour?"

"We really don't know," said Martin. "We were just taking a walk along the beach and came across you."

"I would have walked on the road to my house down there if I had my shoes with me. The gravel on the road would hurt my feet so I decided to walk along the beach."

"So you live right down the beach?"

Tina pointed to the west and indicated she lived a little ways further past the last house they could see from their vantage point on the beach.

"Can we help you get home?" Martin asked.

"If you don't mind. I feel a little uneasy and would really appreciate it."

"No problem," said Tammy.

"Give me one hand and Tammy the other. We'll be your crutches in case you feel like you are about to fall. Our car is in the Mayflower Beach parking lot. Let's go there and we can give you a ride to your house."

"Thank you Martin. I really appreciate it."

Martin and Tammy took Tina's arms and helped her back along the beach towards Mayflower Beach parking lot. When they got near the concession building, the high power lights on the building provided enough light where Martin and Tammy could see Tina better.

"You're bleeding," exclaimed Tammy.

Tina put her hand to her head and when she brought it back around, it was covered in blood. Martin pointed to a picnic table next to the building under the light and asked Tina to take a seat. He ran back to his car and got a first aid kit he had in the trunk and a roll of paper towels. When he got back, he put a paper towel on the back of Tina's head. After absorbing the wet blood, he was able to see a cut. It looked to be about two inches long and a half-inch wide. He took another piece of paper towel and asked Tammy to hold it over the cut and apply pressure. After a minute, Tammy pulled the paper towel back and the blood began to flow again.

"I think you are going to need a few stitches," said Tammy. "Do you want us to take you to the hospital?"

Martin said, "I don't think we should. It would probably be better to call the police and have them send paramedics over to transport her."

"Do you think the cut is bleeding too much to take me there?" Asked Tina sounding scared.

"The cut is bleeding pretty bad every time we take the pressure off. The paramedics would have the right bandages that would keep pressure on the cut sufficient to be able to transport you to the hospital. Tammy, keep the pressure on and I'll call for help."

Martin took his cell phone out of his pocket and flipped it open. He pressed 9-1-1.

"911 operator, please state your emergency."

"My name is Martin Wagner. My girlfriend and I were walking on Mayflower Beach when we came across a woman who was unconscious on the beach. She has a cut on her head and she is bleeding quite a bit. She's conscious now, but I think we need an ambulance to come to Mayflower Beach parking lot by the concession stand."

"Do you know the name of the person who was hurt?"

Martin took the phone away from his head, "The 911 operator wants to know your name."

"It's Tina Fletcher."

Martin got back on the phone and gave the information to the operator.

"Paramedics are being dispatched to Mayflower Beach right now. Can you have someone meet them in the parking lot and show them where Ms. Fletcher is at?"

"Sure. My girlfriend Tammy will be waiting in the lot for them, but you'll probably see us. The lot lights are on and we're the only people here."

"Do you need to stay on the line with me while you are waiting for the paramedics?" asked the operator.

"No, as long as one of us has pressure on her cut, we can control the bleeding."

"The paramedics will be there in about eight minutes. If you need my help again, just call 911."

"Thank you," said Martin. He pressed the end key and closed his phone.

"The operator said the paramedics would be here in a few minutes. Tammy, keep pressure on the cut and Tina should be OK."

"I can't thank you enough for all you're doing," said Tina.

"We're happy we could help," said Tammy.

Off in the distance, the three could hear sirens. As the sound got louder Martin took over for Tammy and asked her to go meet the paramedics at the parking lot entrance and to then bring them down to where they were. Pulling in first was a Dennis police cruiser, followed by an ambulance. Paramedic Mike Jones pulled up to the woman waiving her arms at him. As he exited the ambulance, he said, "I'm paramedic Mike Jones. Where's the person who's hurt?"

"She's over there by the concession building. She's with my boyfriend sitting at a picnic table on the other side."

"Let us get our first aid kit out of the back and we'll follow you."

Tammy led the paramedics and officer over to where Tina and Martin were sitting. Paramedic Jones put on a pair of plastic gloves and asked Martin to let him see the wound. "I'm Mike Jones and this is my partner, Tom Donovan. We're EMTs and we're here to help you. This is Officer Henderson of the Dennis Police Department. Can you tell us your name?"

"Thank you. I'm Tina Fletcher."

"What happened to you Ms. Fletcher?"

110

"It's Tina. I was taking a walk on the beach and the next thing I know, Martin and Tammy here are helping me. When I asked Martin what time it was, he said it was eleven thirty. I went out on my walk on the beach a little before ten so I must have been knocked out on the beach for over an hour."

"You're fortunate the tide was going out or you might have found yourself in the water."

"I hadn't thought about that."

"She might've drowned," said Tammy to Martin.

"It sure is a good thing we found her before the tide came back in," remarked Martin.

Jones looked at Donovan, "This sounds like it might be very similar to the call we had Friday night. Maybe you should ask the Officer Henderson to contact Detective Jenkins."

"Detective Jenkins? I know him," said Tina.

"I recently talked to him about an attack that happened over on Chapin Beach to a friend of mine."

"You know about the attack on Chapin Beach?" asked Jones.

"Yes. A friend of mine, Ann Benard, was attacked there."

"We know. We were called to transport her to the hospital that night."

"Do you think the same thing happened to me?" Tina asked quizzically.

"Don't know, but Detective Jenkins will probably want to talk to you."

"I'd like that," said Tina. The response caught Jones off guard. He didn't know what to make of her response.

Tom Donovan asked Officer Henderson if she would contact Detective Jenkins, and explained why. She pulled a cell phone from her shirt pocket and dialed the station. She then handed the phone to Tom.

111

The desk phone rang and Jenkins picked it up, "Jenkins here."

"Detective, this is paramedic Tom Donovan. I'm up at Mayflower Beach with Mike Jones and Officer Henderson. We're working on an assault victim, Tina Fletcher. She has a cut on the back of her head and needs to be transported to the hospital for stitches. She says she knows you."

"Yes, she's one of the people I interviewed in the Benard case."

"That's what she said. Anyway, the circumstances look and sound very much like those in the Benard case and Mike thought you might want to know about it."

"Thank you Tom. I am interested. How long do you think it will be before you transport her?"

"Probably twenty minutes or so."

"Can you wait there until I can get there? I should be there in fifteen."

"Sure Detective. The woman seemed eager to see you anyway."

Jenkins thought to himself about his encounter with Tina at Sundancers. He had to keep it professional. "I'll be there soon."

Paramedic Donovan walked back to the others and told them Detective Jenkins would be there soon. Tina smiled.

Jenkins buzzed the front desk and asked if Officer Trudy was still on duty. She had been working a double shift and was, but was on the road. So he had the dispatcher contact her and connect her to his desk phone.

"Detective Jenkins, this is Officer Trudy. What can I do for you?"

"Trudy, I just got off the phone with paramedic Donovan. He's up at Mayflower Beach attending to a woman who was attacked. He said it looked like Ms. Benard all over again. I'm going there now. Can you meet me there?"

"Sure Detective. I'll meet you there in a few minutes."

Officer Trudy pulled her cruiser into the next parking lot, and reversed direction. She didn't turn on the flashing

112

lights, as the situation did not warrant. When she arrived at the Mayflower Beach parking lot, she saw that Jenkins's car was already there parked next to the ambulance. Getting out of her cruiser, a woman in her bathrobe walked over to her.

"Officer, I'm Doris Hamilton. I live just down the street. Do you know what's going on?"

Officer Trudy looked at her and then down the street. She could see a house a few hundred feet away had all the lights on illuminating the front yard and into the street. "We're investigating a possible attack on someone here at the beach. Is there something you want to tell me?"

"Yes. About two hours ago, I was sitting out on my front porch when a vehicle came out of the beach parking lot and didn't have its lights on. Who ever was driving waited until the car turned down the next street before turning them on."

"Do you know what kind of vehicle it was?"

"It was one of those SUV things."

"Did you get the make or license plate number?"

"No I only saw the outline of the vehicle as it went past my house and I couldn't see it after it turned the corner."

"Can I have your name and address?"

"Sure. It's Doris Hamilton. My house is 37 Dunes Road, right over there."

"Is there anything else you can recall?"

"Yes. When that car started up in the parking lot, it made a screeching noise like something was wrong with the motor, and then it did it again when it turned the corner down there and started to speed up."

Trudy made a note in her pad and then looked up to Ms. Hamilton.

"Thanks Ms. Hamilton. Someone from the department will be getting back to you. It's pretty dark out here. Do you want an escort back?"

"No, I'm fine. Call or come by anytime. I don't mind."

"Thank you again."

Officer Trudy turned and walked to the concession building where she could hear people talking. Turning the corner, she saw the group, "Detective, I just talked with one of the residents who live just down the street. She said she saw a suspicious vehicle leaving this area a few hours ago with its lights turned off."

"Did she get the make and plate number?"

"No, she said it was too dark but the vehicle was an SUV."

"Ok. We can follow-up on it later. Right now, let's have a look around and see what we can uncover."

"Sure. Where was the victim found?"

Paramedic Mike Jones said, "Mr. Wagner said they found her down on the beach to the left of the path. You'll know the spot by the big rocks that come out from the dunes."

Officer Trudy took out her flashlight. She and Officer Henderson went down to the beach. While they were doing that, Jenkins talked with the paramedics and Tina.

"Ms. Fletcher, how are you doing?"

"I'm better now, you're here," she smiled at Jenkins. Jenkins looked at Donovan who just rolled his eyes. "Do you have any idea who would have done this to me Detective?"

"Not yet, we'll see what we can find out." Turning to Jones, Jenkins said, "What do you think about the cut on her head?"

"It looks like she struck her head on the rocks either before going down, or as a result of going down. Fortunately for her, her head landed on a clump of wet seaweed that acted like a bandage and stopped the flow of blood. When the people who stumbled on her helped her up, the bleeding started again. It looks like she will need stitches. We should have her ready to transport in a few minutes."

Donovan had applied a small clip to the cut and a gauze bandage. He wrapped Tina's head with a soft gauze roll to secure the bandage and told her not to touch it. He used tape to secure the end of the roll. When he was done, Tina looked like she had a toothache and a large wrap was applying pressure on it.

"She's ready for transport," announced Donovan.

"Can you walk to the ambulance?" Jones asked.

Tina looking at Jenkins said, "Can you help me Detective. I think I can walk but I want to make sure I have someone holding on in case."

Jenkins took her arm and Mike Jones took the other. Donovan packed up their equipment and they headed back to the ambulance. Martin Wagner and Tammy Gardner were waiting by the ambulance.

"Are you the folks that found Ms. Fletcher?" Detective Jenkins asked.

Martin spoke, "Yes sir. Tammy and I were walking on the beach when we came across Ms. Fletcher. She was out cold just lying there on the beach."

"And your names?"

"Tammy Gardner."

"Martin Wagner."

"Did either of you notice anyone else when you found her?"

"No," said Tammy. "There were no other cars in the parking lot when we came here and we didn't see anyone else on the beach other than Ms. Fletcher."

"Ok. Give me your phone numbers and addresses. Someone from the department will be following up in a day or two. If there is anything you can recall, please give me a call."

Jenkins handed Martin and Tammy his business card.

"We will officer." Martin was looking at the card and continued, "I mean Detective."

Jenkins turned to the paramedics, "I think you're good to go. I'll meet you there in a little while."

"See you at the hospital Detective," said Donovan.

Tina was put into the back of the ambulance. Jones stayed with her in the back while Donovan drove. The ambulance left the parking lot quietly without any flashing lights. Jenkins walked back to the beach and went down to where Officer Trudy and Officer Henderson had been looking around. Officer Henderson was a little past the rocks and Trudy was standing near where Tina had been found.

"Find anything Trudy?"

"Yes." She held up a pair of woman's underwear. Then she shined her flashlight near the rocks. There was a set of human prints in the sand.

"What do you make of those tracks?"

"I'd guess someone was down here with a big animal sometime tonight."

"Why do you say that Detective?"

"Because the tide line is up past the end of the line of boulders and those tracks could only have been made since the tide went out. You see those tracks there? They're from a large animal just like the tracks we saw at Chapin Beach."

"I see what you mean."

"What other kind of big animal do you think might have been up here?"

"I was just thinking about the cougar from the ZooQuarium."

"Well, look here. The human and the animal prints both lead back towards the parking lot. To me, that would indicate a person was walking with the animal."

"Or the animal was stalking the person."

Jenkins thought about it for a few seconds, "Could be."

"Where did you find the panties?"

"Right there, where the blood is on the seaweed."

"You think they belong to Ms. Fletcher?"

"I'll find out when I talk to her at the hospital. Bag and tag them for identification, will you Trudy?"

"Will do Detective. Anything else we can do here?"

"No, I think that will be it for tonight. Write up your report and leave it for me at the station."

Detective Jenkins called out to Officer Henderson.

116

"Henderson, we are going to wrap it up for the night. I think we have all we need. Thanks for your assistance. I'll take it from here."

Officer Henderson said, "Ok Detective. I'll write up my report and leave it for you at the station."

"Thanks Henderson."

"I'll write up my notes as well Detective. I'll check in with you tomorrow," added Officer Trudy.

"Thanks Trudy." They walked back to their respective vehicles and left Mayflower Beach.

Detective Jenkins was heading to the hospital to talk with Tina Fletcher. Officer Trudy went to the station to do her report and wrap up what had already been a long day.

Arriving at the hospital ER, Detective Jenkins went into the room Tina had been placed. Dr. Peter Stone had just finished putting a couple staples and stitches into Tina's head when Jenkins arrived. Tina looked up, "Detective Jenkins, I'm glad you came to the hospital."

"I have some follow-up questions I need to ask you."

"I can answer your questions but I need a ride home as well. Can you take me home when the good doctor is done with me?"

Jenkins didn't want to sound cold in front of the medical personnel so he said, "Sure. How long before she can leave doc?"

"I just need to finish the paper work and then she is free to go," said Dr. Stone.

"Anything other than the cut on the head Doctor?"

"Not that I've found. I didn't get a chance to do much of an examination as Ms. Fletcher said she wanted her head fixed and then to get out of here."

"I don't like hospitals," Tina said sarcastically.

"The good doctor is just trying to help you," Jenkins said in a father to daughter tone.

Doctor Stone made a few notes and then handed the file to the attending nurse. "Ms. Fletcher, you'll need to come back in ten days to have the staples and stitches removed. Until then, have this prescription filled and be careful of your head."

"Thank you doctor. I'll be careful."

Tina took the prescription and got up. She took Jenkins arm, "We can continue your questioning while you take me home."

Detective Jenkins thanked the doctor and left with Tina. They got into his car and Tina moved over closer to him.

"That isn't necessary," said Jenkins.

"I feel a little light headed and just wanted to be next to you in case I fall over," exclaimed Tina.

"Oh. OK."

Tina put her head on his shoulder. As they were driving down Route 28, she let her hand slide down to his right leg. She slowly moved it until it was in the intended position.

"Ms. Fletcher, we're here."

Tina looked up and saw they were at her house. The lights she had turned on when she went for her walk were still on. They got out of the car and went into the house. She asked Detective Jenkins to have a seat on the couch while she put her things away. She went into the kitchen and poured two glasses of white wine and came back into the room. She sat next to Jenkins on the couch and handed him a glass of wine.

"I'm on duty and I don't drink on duty."

"Oh, just one glass."

"Can't do it."

"OK. Leave it there. I'll drink for both of us."

"Are you sure you should be drinking anything given what you have been through?"

"I have a slight headache and the wine will help it go away."

"Suit yourself."

Jenkins took out a pad and read through his notes. He turned to Tina, "I have a few questions."

"So do I."

"What time did you go out for your walk?"

"I think it was around ten."

"Did you see or hear anything unusual?"

"No. Not that I can remember."

"Do you have your panties on?"

"Isn't that a little forward of you, Detective?"

"Do you have them on?"

"Why do you want to know about my panties?"

Tina put her hand down on her mid section and slowly moved it to her waist. Then she picked up her skirt and was surprised that she did not have her panties on. "I don't know what happened to them!" she exclaimed.

"Officer Trudy found a pair near where you were found."

"That's funny. I don't remember taking them off. Do you think whoever attacked me might have removed them?"

"Do you feel like someone had sex with you?"

"I usually know when someone has had sex with me."

"But this time you might have been unconscious. Did the doctor check to see if you were sexually assaulted?"

"No. I wouldn't let him."

"Why not?"

"Because that would have just caused problems for others."

"What do you mean others?"

"Come on Detective. You know what I mean. I had sex with someone else earlier tonight and the doctor would have found evidence of my lover and that would have led to a bad situation."

"Why would it have been a bad situation?"

"The man I was with earlier tonight has his own privacy that needs to be protected."

"Oh, I think I get it. He's married."

119

"Kind of."

"There is no *kind of*. He either is or is not."

"He is."

"Even if you had sex with someone earlier, if you were raped, the lab might be able to isolate the attacker's DNA."

"Well what if I had sex with more than one man earlier today?"

"That might be a problem."

"Plus, wouldn't the lab have to get DNA samples from anyone I had sex with in the past day or two?"

"Probably, and from the sound of it, you wouldn't want that."

"That's why I didn't let the doctor do his thing."

Jenkins made a few notes in his pad. "Can you tell me the names of the men you slept with?"

"I'd rather not."

"Then you're making it difficult for me to find your attacker."

"I don't know if the attacker had sex with me or not. Finding DNA on my underwear will not mean much unless you test all of the men I've had sex with in the past few days and I'm not prepared to get them involved."

"How many exactly have there been?"

"In the last day or two?"

"Yeah. Let's start with the last twenty-four hours."

"Two men, but one I had sex with twice. Two on Sunday and one very late on Saturday."

"You've had sex three times in the last twenty-four hours?"

"Well, it could be four," she put her hand on his leg moving it up slowly. "But it seems it's been more than twenty-four hours."

"Your attacker might have been number four."

"No, you would be number four," she leaned in to kiss him.

"I can't get involved," said Jenkins.

120

"You're involved with Katherine."

"That's different."

"Why is that? She's a cougar also."

Jenkins had to think about the comment for a few minutes. He closed his pad and stood. "I'll follow-up with you at another time Ms. Fletcher. We're done for tonight." Then he started walking to the door.

"Are you sure you can't stay for awhile?"

"I'm sure." Then Jenkins let himself out.

Chapter 13

Detective Jenkins called the station on his way home. He would file his report in the morning when he got in. He said he was tired and was going home to get a few hours sleep. He thought he had just fallen asleep when his phone rang.

"Jenkins here," he said in a sleepy voice.

"Frank, it's Kat. Aren't you going to work today?"

"What time is it?"

"It's ten. I called the station and was told you hadn't come in for the day yet. Are you OK?"

"I had to go out on a call around mid-night last night and didn't get back to bed until after two. I must have been really tired because I never heard my alarm."

"I was calling to see if you're available tonight."

"I don't know. There was another attack last night. You know Tina Fletcher?"

"Yeah, what about Tina?"

"She was attacked while walking on the beach by her home last night."

"Is she alright?"

"Yeah. She had to get stitches on her head. Otherwise, she is fine." Jenkins was making a pot of strong coffee, and threw an English muffin into the toaster.

"Was it a sexual attack?"

"Don't know. She wouldn't submit to an examination so the doctor couldn't tell."

"What did she say?"

"She told me she was with a few men yesterday and the night before and didn't want to get them involved in her problems."

"That is so like Tina."

"She had told me one of the men she slept with is married and she didn't want him involved. So doing DNA testing is out."

"Isn't there any other way you can find out who attacked her?"

"Sure, but we need some facts to go on. Right now, the only lead we have is a resident in the area where the attack took place saw a suspicious SUV leaving the area with its lights off a few hours before the victim was found."

"That could be anyone. Even I have an SUV."

Jenkins thought for a minute. "You remember who else was at Sundancers last night and has an SUV?"

"I don't know for sure, but I'm sure Dee, Margarita or Ron would know."

"I guess I could drop by there today and see what they can remember."

"That would probably be a good idea. I'll meet you there."

"OK. Meet me there about four. That will give me some time to ask them questions before you arrive."

"See you at four."

"Bye."

Jenkins took a shower, brushed his teeth and got himself ready for the day. He had a cup of coffee along with a peanut butter English muffin and then went to the station. There was a message on his desk from Officer Trudy indicating the resident who had seen the suspicious SUV in the area the night before had called. She also saw a large animal in the parking lot just before dusk. Jenkins made a note in his pad of the woman's name and address from Trudy's report and would visit her first.

Next, he stopped in to talk with the Captain.

"So you have another case?"

"Yeah. I got the call around midnight and went to the scene. This one took place by Mayflower Beach. Similar MO. Woman walking alone, struck from behind. Cut on the head."

"Any sexual attack?"

"Can't tell. The vic isn't cooperating."

"Why not?"

"She had sex with a few other men recently and one of them is married. She doesn't want to get the other men involved and realized DNA testing would involve them."

"Doesn't she know DNA is the surest way to ID a perp?"

"She knows. She isn't going there."

"Sounds like a loose woman. What's her name?"

"Tina Fletcher."

Captain Tomlinson looked up at Jenkins, "Tina Fletcher?"

"Yeah, you know her?"

"Didn't I see her name in the Benard report from Officer Trudy?"

"Probably. Or it might have been in my report on Ms. Benard. Ms. Fletcher was one of the friends of Ms. Benard we interviewed."

"Isn't it suspicious that a woman Ms. Benard knows was attacked?"

"I'd say."

"Is she alright?"

"As I said, she has a few bumps, bruises and stitches. Otherwise she's fine. I don't know why she's being so secretive about the men she slept with recently. We don't need to talk to any wives, and each of the men don't need to know about each other either."

"Don't pressure her if you don't have to. It doesn't look good for the department if we come down hard on a victim."

"Ok Captain. I'll go easy on Ms. Fletcher."

"Well let me know how this one turns out."

"Just another cougar, but I'll keep you informed."

"Speaking of cougars, did the ZooQuarium catch theirs?"

"Not that I know of."

"Well, follow-up with them and see if anything has changed."

"Will do Captain."

"And Frank, try to not get caught in the cougar trap."

"What's a cougar trap?"

"You'll know when you're there."

"Thanks Captain, I think."

"You're welcome. Let me know how things progress."

"Will do."

Jenkins picked up his keys from his desk along with the notes he had on the two cases. He got into his car and headed towards Mayflower Beach. He stopped his vehicle in front of 37 Dunes Road. He got out and went up to the front door and knocked. The door opened and a short older lady appeared, "Can I help you?"

"Ms. Hamilton, I'm Detective Jenkins. May I speak with you for a few minutes about last night's incident at the beach?"

Jenkins had out one of his business cards and he passed it to her through the crack in the door. She read the card and then opened the door. As he walked past Ms. Hamilton, he could smell a strong odor of alcohol.

"Come in Detective."

"I'd like to follow-up on the information you gave Officer Trudy."

"She is such a nice woman. Don't you think so?"

"She is a good officer. Now, you told her you saw a suspicious vehicle in the parking lot last night. Is that correct?"

"Yes. I saw a vehicle with no lights on coming out of the parking lot last night. It went all the way down to the corner before the lights were turned on."

"And you didn't know the make or see the plate?"

"As I told Officer Trudy, it was too dark for me to see much detail with my eyesight being what it is and all."

"Officer Trudy also said you called and left her a voice message about a large animal in the parking lot around sunset. What did you see?"

"I was putting things away on my front porch after sunset when I saw what I thought was a big cat over there in the parking lot. It was sniffing around the garbage cans. Most of the time I see raccoons going through the garbage just after sunset but this animal looked like a big cat."

"How big would you say it was?"

She held her hand up around two feet off the ground and then spread her arms as wide as she could. "I'd say it was at least that big. I'm saying that because its head was almost as tall as the trash can."

"Do you think you saw a mountain lion or cougar?"

"Now that you mention it, it looked like one of those animals you see on the television. Yes, a mountain lion. We don't have any of those in this area. Do we?"

"Not normally, but a cougar is missing from the ZooQuarium in South Yarmouth."

"Then that must have been it."

"Where did it go?"

"As I said before, I don't see so well in my old age. The animal went to the left down the dunes. Then I lost sight of it. There are no lights over there, as you know."

"And what time was it?"

"I'd guess around nine. Yes, it was right before nine. My favorite show hadn't started yet. Murder She Wrote. Do you watch it?"

"No, I don't. I have one more question if you don't mind Ms. Hamilton. Did you see anyone else here last night?"

"I thought I heard car doors in the parking lot around the time the eleven o'clock news came on. I didn't pay much attention to it. People come and go here all hours of the night when it's nice. I figured it was some young couple doing what young couples do, if you know what I mean."

"The couple that found the victim on the beach last night indicated they had parked their car in the lot around that time."

"I didn't pay any more attention until I saw the flashing lights a little later. That's when I spoke with Officer Trudy."

"Well, thank you Ms. Hamilton. You've been a big help."

"Any time Detective, and say hello to that lovely Officer Trudy for me will you?"

"I'll do that. Good Bye."

"Goodbye."

Jenkins looked at his notes and thought to himself that this was the same woman who told Trudy about the vehicle with no light on and with the screeching engine. He wondered about her credibility. Her details were pretty specific, so he'd give her the benefit of the doubt.

Leaving Ms. Hamilton's, Detective Jenkins headed towards Sundancers, stopping first to get a bite to eat at the American Pub. They had the best fish sandwich, and that along with sweet potato fries was just what he wanted today.

As he finished lunch, Jenkins reviewed his next assignment. He wanted to have a talk with the bartenders and anyone else there who might be able to shed some light on last night. The parking lot at Sundancers was pretty full. Jenkins had to park in near the water at the end of the lot. As he walked up to the door, Ron was looking out the windows, "Here comes that Detective who's been investigating Ann's attack."

"He has been in here a few times recently, not only to talk with us but with Kat," said Dee.

"You think he has something going with her?"

"It wouldn't surprise me."

Detective Jenkins took up a stool at the end of the bar. "Ms. Crowe, I'd like to talk with you for a few minutes."

"Ron, can you handle the bar for a few minutes?"

"Sure."

"I'll be in the back room talking to the Detective."

Dee walked to the back room with Detective Jenkins. They sat at a table in the far corner. The back room, or dining room was about half full so there wasn't so much volume the two couldn't talk to each other.

"Ms. Crowe, there was another attack. This time it was Tina Fletcher."

"Tina? I just saw her in here last night."

"That's when it happened, after she left here last night someone attacked her."

"How can I help you?"

"I think it's someone who was here at the bar and left right after she did. Whoever is doing these attacks, knows the women, knows where they live and knows what they're doing. That both victims know each other is not just a coincidence."

"So you think it's someone who comes to Sundancers?"

"I think so. Now, tell me what you can about those who were here last night?"

Dee thought about it for a few minutes. "Well, you and Katherine were here, so you probably know everyone I know."

"I was talking to Katherine, not really paying attention, and others I don't know may have been here, others may have come back. I'm sure your perspective is far more detailed than mine."

"You know, Ron and I were talking last night about how the women kind of struck out last night. I don't think Tina left with anyone."

"I don't think the victims are leaving with the person who is attacking them. I think the attacker is either leaving right before them or right after."

"Do you think the attacker is stalking the victims?"

"Not in the traditional sense. I think the attacker somehow finds out information about the victims that creates an opportunity and then he acts on it."

"Let me think. Kat left with you. Then I saw you two split in the parking lot."

"I needed to get my sleep so we went in different directions."

"Kenny left early, by himself. Sue and Bobby had a spat. Tommy hooked up with Ann after Ann and Sue had a talk. Ed left shortly after Sue, Linda and Tina were laughing and pointing at him. Tina left by herself shortly after Ed. Sue left by herself. There might have been a few other people who left here around the time Tina left, but I don't remember."

"Thank you. It's certainly helpful. If you think of anything else, please call me."

"I will Detective. I've to get back to work."

Dee went back to the bar. Ron came over, "So what was that all about?"

"Tina was attacked last night."

"Why haven't we heard about it?"

"I don't know. Word usually spreads pretty quickly around here when it involves one of the big cats."

"It's still early and the regulars haven't come in yet. Just give it some time."

"The Detective thinks the attacker has been here."

"Why would he say that?"

"He thinks the attacker knows the victims; someone who just waits for the right opportunity, then attacks."

"Knowing how these cougars act around the guys, I can't imagine who would attack them. I think every guy in here has had at least one of the cougars at one time or another. It's almost not predator and prey anymore, its friends with benefits."

"Maybe it's someone who isn't so lucky, like Ed."

"Oh, Ed gets lucky from time to time. Only last night I overheard Sue telling Linda and Tina about doing Ed. The

129

three of them were sitting across the bar from him giggling as she described her conquest."

"I thought they were making fun of him. It wasn't much later when Ed left the bar," Dee said, as she poured a new draft for one patron who was seated in front of the two of them. "He probably should have hung in there. What Sue was saying wasn't insulting or anything, but rather very complimentary. Both Linda and Tina were very attentive. I think one of them would have targeted Ed had he stayed a little longer."

"What about Kenny? He left by himself."

"Yeah. I talked to Kenny for a little bit. He said he had a date."

"So that rules him out," Ron said with a frown.

"Tommy left with Ann, so I don't think he was involved."

"Bobby left by himself although he leaves with all of them at one point or another. I think he's the most laid guy in here."

"Now that you mention it, you're probably right."

"How about you Dee, you ever get it on with Bobby?"

"A girl never tells. We're not like you guys who have to blab your conquests to everyone you meet."

"I don't think the cougars are very discrete. You women seem to talk quite a bit about to each other about your conquests."

"Are you calling me a cougar?"

"No, I didn't mean that. I was referring to our patrons."

Dee smirked at Ron and went to the end of the bar where a patron was waving at her for another beer. Detective Jenkins came up to Ron and asked him if he could speak with him for a few minutes.

"Dee, you have the bar. I'm up."

"Go get'em cowboy."

Ron and Detective Jenkins went back to the same table Jenkins and Dee had used. The two sat down and Jenkins said, "You probably already know that Tina Fletcher was attacked last night. I'd like to ask you a few questions about who was in here last night."

"I talked to Dee for a few minutes after you questioned her. There isn't much I can add to what she already told you."

"Mr. Jessup, isn't there something you could add?"

"You know about Kenny, Ed, and Bobby. What about Tommy Anderson?"

"Ms. Crowe didn't say anything about him?" Jenkins flipped through his note pad. That name had come up before.

"Tommy is kind of young. He can be immature at times. I think he and Tina had something going at one point in time. Maybe it didn't work out or something."

"Why do you think there might be something there?"

"Well, last night, I saw Tommy talking to Tina in the parking lot before Tina came into the bar. It looked like they were having some kind of argument or something. Tommy never did come in. He just left after their encounter."

"So you think they had a fight or something?"

"You might want to ask Tina. I only saw them talking in the parking lot."

Jenkins made a note in his pad. While he was doing that, Ron stood and started to go back to the bar. He turned back, "You can ask her right now if you want. She just came through the door."

Detective Jenkins walked over to where Tina had taken up a stool at the bar. "Ms. Fletcher, how are you doing?"

"Better, but I still have a headache."

"I was just talking to Mr. Jessup and he said you and Mr. Anderson had some kind of disagreement in the parking lot last night and then Mr. Anderson left without coming in."

"That was earlier in the night. I'd say it was even late afternoon."

"What was the disagreement about?"

131

"Oh, nothing really. Tommy wanted me to meet him after his date last night and I said nothing doing."

"Why would he want to meet with you then?"

"I think he's working on someone new and didn't think he would get anywhere. He wanted me to be available, if you know what I mean."

"So he wanted to have sex with you after his date?"

"I don't think he thought he would score so he wanted to bet on a sure thing."

"Do you think he might have attacked you because of that?"

"No, Tommy and I are friends."

Jenkins made another note in his pad and thanked her for her time. He glanced at his watch. It was only just three thirty, so he decided to pick Katherine up instead of hanging around for the extra half hour waiting for her to arrive. Detective Jenkins left Sundancers and went over to Katherine's house. The lights were already on inside, but he didn't see any movement. He knocked loudly three times. Quickly he could see Katherine pull back the blinds and peek out.

"Frank, come in."

"I was in the area and thought I'd pick you up instead of waiting at Sundancers."

"I'm glad you did. I totally forgot the time. Is it almost four already?"

"Yea. I finished up talking with some of the people there and they provided me with some leads about the cases and I wanted to run something by you."

"Go ahead."

As Jenkins began to speak, the door of the bathroom opened and Tommy Anderson walked out.

"Mr. Jessup was telling me about an argument Tina Fletcher had with a Tommy Anderson last night before the attack."

Tommy walked into the living room and Jenkins was startled.

"Why don't you ask him yourself?" said Katherine pointing at Tommy.

"Why Mr. Anderson, I was just asking Ms. Sterns about you."

"What did you want to know?"

"Did you have an argument with Tina Fletcher in Sundancers parking lot yesterday?"

"I did speak with her there about five thirty."

"What did you talk about?"

"I wanted to get together with her later on last night."

"Well, did you?"

"No, she had other plans."

"And what about yours?"

"I had a date."

"Why did you want to get together with her?"

"We see each other from time to time."

"So your story is you wanted to hook up with her after your date. Is that right?"

"Something like that."

Katherine wasn't sure where the conversation was going. She wondered if Frank was jealous because Tommy was at her place or was he really asking questions about his cases. "Detective, can I speak with you privately?"

Katherine led Jenkins to the kitchen, and whispered. "I'm not really feeling up to going out right now. Can you just call me later and maybe we can meet somewhere then?"

Detective Jenkins looked at Anderson in the next room, and then at Katherine, "Sure Katherine. I'll call you."

He got up and went to the door. Before he left, he said, "Mr. Anderson, I'd like for you to come to the station tomorrow so we can continue our discussion."

"What time would you like me there, Detective?"

"How about three tomorrow afternoon?"

"I'll be there."

When Detective Jenkins had left, Tommy said, "What's his problem?"

"He might be a tad jealous."

"Why would he be jealous?" Tommy paused. "Oh, I get it; you and the Detective have a thing going, don't you?"

"We see each other from time to time."

"Do you see him like you see me?"

Katherine stood and walked over to Tommy, who was now sitting on the couch. She turned off the light and took off her top. She reached back and undid her bra. She leaned in on him and kissed him. "Tommy, I don't see anyone unless I want to." She worked her tongue into his mouth and reached down. Tommy was ready to go.

"Do you have protection Tommy?"

"Always."

He picked her up and carried her down the hallway to the bedroom.

Chapter 14

Late in the afternoon, a call came into the Dennis Police Station that got the attention of the desk sergeant.

"Dennis Police Station, Sergeant Grimes speaking. How may I help you?"

"Sergeant, my name is Donald Ward. I live at 72 Old Bass River Road. I was going out to my car when I was confronted by a mountain lion in my driveway. It scared the crap out of me."

"Mr. Ward, you say a mountain lion was in your driveway?"

"That's correct officer. When I went out of my house to get into my car, a mountain lion was right there in my driveway. I think it had been eating my cat's food that was on the side porch."

"Is the animal still there?"

"No, it just looked at me and then wandered off through the neighborhood."

"About how big was the animal?"

"I'd say it was about two maybe three feet high, maybe three feet long."

"So you think it was eating your cat's food?"

"I think so. I had just put out a full dish of cat food before I was going out and when I came out, the bowl was empty and the lion was there."

"Is your cat around?"

"I haven't seen it and if the cat sees the mountain lion, I might not see my cat for days."

"If you see your cat Mr. Ward, take it inside. It isn't a mountain lion. It's a cougar."

"Are you sure?"

"I think so. One escaped from the ZooQuarium recently and it's still at large."

"Shouldn't someone tell the public that this thing is on the loose?"

"Yes. There's an article in tomorrow's Times as well as radio news stories telling about the cougar escape."

"I think you should send someone up here to see if it can be captured."

"I'll report it to the appropriate people and someone will be there soon."

"Thank you Sergeant. I'll stay home for another hour or so in case the mountain lion, or rather cougar, comes back."

"Don't put any more food out. Let the authorities take care of the situation."

"Ok. Will that thing attack me if I see it again?"

"It's supposed to be a tame animal, but you never know what will happen when one of these animals gets back into the wild."

"I'll stay clear of it if I see it."

"Thank you Mr. Ward. If you do see it again, please call back."

"I will." Mr. Ward hung up and went back outside to look around to see where the cougar went.

Sergeant Grimes called the ZooQuarium and asked to speak with the manager.

"Officer, this is Mr. Carson. I'm the manager at the ZooQuarium. What can I do for you?"

"Mr. Carson. This is Sergeant Grimes of the Dennis Police department. I just took a call from a Mr. Ward who lives at 72 Old Bass River Road. He said he saw your cougar a few minutes ago in his driveway. He said it looked to him like the cougar had been eating his cat's food which was on a side porch."

"That could be. By now, Charlie would be pretty hungry. He doesn't know how to hunt and would probably take any meal he could find."

"Do you think that could include attacking someone or someone's pet?"

"Charlie has never been known to attack another animal or person, but one can never be too sure when hunger is involved."

"Look Mr. Carson. Can you have someone go up to Mr. Ward's neighborhood and see if they can capture your cougar? It should probably be someone whose voice Charlie would recognize and respond to."

"I'll have one of our handlers go right up there and see if he can find Charlie."

"I'll also call Environmental Protection and let them know your people will be on Old Bass River road trying to trap your animal."

"Just make sure you tell the DEP guys not to shoot Charlie."

"I'll tell them, but if your cat makes an aggressive move, I can't guarantee the cougar's safety."

"I'll get someone right up there." Then Mr. Carson hung up.

Mr. Carson went out of his office and into the zoo area. He called over to Joe Mains, one of the animal handlers. "Joe, go up to Old Bass River road and see if you can find Charlie. A Mr. Ward who lives at 72 Old Bass River Road reported seeing Charlie in his driveway a little while ago."

"What do you want me to do if I find Charlie, boss?"

"Bring some food. Mr. Ward thought Charlie was eating his cat's food."

"Then he must be hungry because he hates cat food."

"See if you can lure him into your custody. Bring Charlie's collar, a tranquilizer gun and at least one other handler. I'm not sure who's working today, but make sure whoever it is can handle the cat. Don't use the gun unless you

137

have to, and Joe, be careful. The DEP guys will probably be in the area as well. They'll have real guns."

"I got it boss. I'm on it. I'll call you and let you know what I find."

"Thanks Joe. I'll be here at the zoo for another hour. Then you can reach me on my cell."

Joe Mains gathered his things, Charlie's collar, a leash and the tranquilizer gun along with a few rounds of drugs that would put Charlie into a deep sleep if he had to use them. He called out to the handler's maintenance area, and Bob Hermot poked his head out.

"Bob, you and me gotta go out to Old Bass River Road. Charlie's been seen roaming around up that way. Shake a leg."

The two got into the animal transport pickup truck and headed out.

Driving down Old Bass River road, Joe stopped in front of number 72. There was a drab dark green jeep in the driveway along with a red Toyota Camry. The writing on the door of the jeep told Joe the DEP guys were already there.

"Bob, you stay in the truck and get the gun ready. We might have to use it. Be ready if I call you."

"Ok Joe."

Joe got out of the truck. He walked up to the door and rang the bell.

"I'm Joe Mains, from the ZooQuarium," said Joe to the two gentlemen who greeted him at the door."

"I'm Mr. Ward and this is Officer Becker from the DEP."

"Hi Ben," said Joe Mains to Officer Becker. You here to help me catch our cougar?"

"I got a call from Sergeant Grimes of Dennis PD stating a cougar was loose in a residential area. I'm here to do what ever I can to help catch the animal."

"Listen Ben, Charlie, that's our cougar's name, is a pretty tame animal. I don't think he'll hurt anyone."

"The Sergeant told me two women were attacked recently up at the beach and there were big animal prints nearby. He said it might have been your cougar. Grimes didn't say it was your cat that attacked the woman, but he didn't say it wasn't either."

"Charlie has never attacked anyone. I wouldn't believe he would start now."

"Well, maybe the animal is hungry or frightened."

"Nah. Charlie might lick someone's face or try to wrestle with them, but he wouldn't attack anyone."

"In any event, I'm here to see what I can do to help."

"Thanks Ben."

"Now Mr. Ward, can you tell me what happened?"

Mr. Ward went through the same story again for the umpteenth time. When he got done, he showed the men where he had seen the cougar and where the cat's dish had been. He pointed to a wooded area behind his house in the neighborhood. That was the last place he had seen the cougar. Joe and Ben walked back to the wood line to take a look. They could see cougar prints in the dirt at the edge of the woods right where Mr. Ward said the cat disappeared.

"Those are Charlie's prints," said Joe Mains.

"How do you know that?" asked Ben.

"Look here. Do you see the spacing between the outside toe and second toe on the right track?"

"Yeah?"

"Well, Charlie had gotten his paw caught in a cage when he was little and broke his outside toe. It never healed properly and as a result he has a toe that kind of points to the right."

"I see. I'll have to report that back to the police in case they get any more calls about the cougar."

"Its kind of Charlie's calling card."

"Couldn't another big cat have a similar print?"

139

"Unlikely. How many big cats are you aware of here on Cape Cod?"

"Good point. We have our fair share of cougars or pumas as they're typically called now, but they're all of the two legged variety."

"My guess is if you find more of these tracks, its Charlie."

The two walked a ways into the woods but the tracks disappeared as the ground became covered with leaves and grasses. "It looks like we lost track of him," said Ben Becker.

"I guess so," replied Mains. "I'm going back to my truck and ride around the area a little to see if I can spot Charlie again. Here is my cell number, Ben. If you see him, call me."

"Will do. You call me if you find him, too."

"Sure."

The two men walked back to their vehicles and began a patrol of the residential area to see if they could locate Charlie. While driving around, Ben called the police station and asked for Sergeant Grimes.

"Sergeant, I just met with Joe Mains of the ZooQuarium up here at the Ward house on Old Bass River Road."

"Did you confirm it was their cougar?"

"Yes. Joe told me how to identify their cougar's tracks and we were able to find tracks matching their cougar's prints."

"Were you able to tell where the animal went?"

"We followed the tracks until they disappeared. It was in a wooded area behind the Ward house when we lost the tracks. Right now, Mains is driving around trying to spot the animal. I'm doing the same."

"Let me know if either of you find it."

"I will. For your information, you can identify their cougar by its front right paw print. The outer most toe was broken when the animal was smaller and it now has a very distinct print. The outside toe points to the right and has a gap between it and the next toe."

"I'll make a note and inform our personnel at our next shift meeting."

"I'll get back to you if I find out anything else."

"Thanks Ben."

Ben Becker, Joe Mains and Bob Hermot drove around for about an hour and neither party had a sighting of Charlie. Joe Mains picked up his cell phone and called Ben.

"Ben, its Joe. We're going back to the ZooQuarium to drop Bob off. I didn't see any sign of Charlie anywhere other than what you and I saw at the Ward house. I'll report back to my boss and I'm sure he will send someone else out here tomorrow to look around again."

"Ok Joe. I'm going to call it a day as well."

As Joe Mains was driving back to the ZooQuarium, he called his boss.

"Mr. Carson, the animal that was spotted was Charlie. I was able to see his tracks and it's definitely him."

"What do you think?"

"We lost his tracks in the woods. He could be anywhere within a mile circle by now. We're on our way back to the ZooQuarium. I'll try again tomorrow."

"Ok Joe. I'll see you when you get back."

The three men left the area without having found Charlie. About a half hour after the search was abandoned, a Ms. Claire Watson, who lives on Driftwood Lane by Follins Pond was looking out her kitchen window when she gasped. "Oh my God! Look at the size of that cat."

Her husband Marshall who had been reading the paper came to the window, "That's not a cat, that's a mountain lion. I'm getting my gun."

Mr. Watson went into the garage and got out his shotgun. He loaded a number four turkey round into the chamber and went into the back yard. When got there, the mountain lion was about a hundred and fifty feet behind his house just on the edge of the woods. He took aim and pulled the trigger. The mountain lion turned and raced away into the woods. Marshall didn't know if he hit the animal or not. He just knew it was gone. He went back into his house and put his gun away.

"Marshall, did you kill it?" Claire asked.

"I don't know. It took off into the woods."

"Do you think you hit it?"

"I don't think so. It was moving pretty good the last I saw of it."

"Do you think we should call the police?"

"Nah. If I wounded it, it will probably die over night in the woods. If I missed it, I'm sure it won't come back."

"But what if you wounded it. Might the animal become more dangerous? I hate to think of it suffering all night."

"Don't know, but there isn't anything I can do about it now Claire. It's getting dark."

"Don't you think someone heard the shot and will report it?"

"Nah, people are duck hunting in this area all the time. Forget about it for tonight. I'll look again in the morning."

"Ok, but I'm not going outside unless it's light outside."

"Don't be afraid. I'm sure I scared that thing off."

"If you say so."

Joe Mains pulled into the ZooQuarium driveway and drove around the back of the main building. He parked the truck by the back entrance and he and Bob went inside to speak with Mr. Carson.

"So it was Charlie, eh?" came a voice from outside the office as Mains came in the back door.

"Sure was. I saw his tracks, with the abnormal right paw. It's Charlie."

"Did you get a look at him?"

142

"Nah. He was gone by the time we got there. The resident, Mr. Ward, saw him go into the woods behind the neighborhood. That was where I saw the tracks."

"Do you think he'll return?"

"I don't know. Charlie was eating the cat food the homeowner had put out for his cat. He might come back and might not. If they don't frighten him off, he'll probably stay in the general area as long as he can find things to eat."

"Then we'll go back there tomorrow and scout around to see if we can find him, maybe around the same time as when Mr. Ward saw him."

Mary Harper was concerned about the welfare of Charlie. Mr. Carson came out of his office, "Joe will find Charlie. Don't worry."

Joe Mains turned to Mr. Carson, "I'm going home for the night. I'll see you in the morning."

"Oh, Joe, what did you do with the tranquilizers?"

"They're still in the truck in the dart box."

"Good. Leave them there as we may need them tomorrow."

"Ok. Good night."

"Find Charlie," said Mary as Joe was walking away.

On Ben Becker's way home, he stopped into the Dennis Police station and spoke with Sergeant Grimes.

"Joe Mains from the ZooQuarium and I looked all around the area where the cougar was sighted. We did see some tracks but didn't see the cat. When we met with the resident, Mr. Ward, he indicated he confronted the cougar in his driveway and it ran away."

"Was anyone or any of the domestic animals in the area hurt?"

"Not that we know about. The cougar had apparently been eating Wards' cats' food on a side porch and then Mr. Ward surprised it."

"Did Mains have anything to add?"

"He said the cougar was starting to improvise in finding food. He did say the animal is very tame and he didn't think it would attack anyone."

"That's good to hear, but the cougar may have already attacked one or more individuals already. We don't have concrete answers to the two attacks that have taken place up in that area and the fact that a cougar is loose in close proximity might implicate the animal."

"Mains said the ZooQuarium will probably have people back up there at first light trying to find the cougar. My office will have personnel out trying to find it as well."

"I'm sure the department will make an extra effort to patrol the general area until the cougar is captured. I just hope these attacks that have been taking place at the beaches come to an end."

"I hear you Sarge. I'll report in if we find anything."

"Thanks Ben. I'll mention what you have told me at tomorrow mornings briefing."

"Thanks. I guess that's all so I'm going home for the night."

"Have a good night."

"You too."

Chapter 15

While the search for the cougar was going on, Detective Jenkins met with Officer Trudy. They talked about what had been discovered at the latest attack at Mayflower Beach. Trudy took out the evidence bags she had assembled from the crime scene and began to look through the contents. She held up the bag with the panties in it, "Where do you want to go with this one?"

"Get it to the lab and have DNA analysis performed."

"What do you think they'll find?"

"My guess is there will be evidence there if Ms. Fletcher was sexually attacked. If there is, then we just have to match it up with our suspects."

"But we already know she had sex with multiple men earlier. Plus, she didn't know if she was sexually assaulted at the beach or not."

"True, but if there is DNA on those panties, we can narrow the playing field."

Officer Trudy took the bag and left the office. She went to the lab and filled out the paperwork to have the panties analyzed.

Detective Jenkins picked up the phone. "Katherine, I just finished going over evidence obtained from Mayflower Beach where Tina Fletcher was attacked. One of the things we found was a pair of panties."

"Were they Tina's?"

"I think they could have been. They were found in the same area where she was found unconscious."

"If I remember correctly, Tina has her initials on her panties. She does that so her conquests can show off their souvenirs to the other guys and everyone knows they came from her."

"Tell me you're kidding."

"No kidding. All her panties have a TF embroidered on the upper right side."

"Hold on a minute," Jenkins said as he put her on hold. He called Trudy's cell phone. She had just arrived at the lab but hadn't checked the evidence in yet.

"Trudy."

"Yes Detective?"

"Look at the panties in the bag and see if they have a TF embroidered on the upper right side?"

Pam picked up the plastic bag and looked at both sides. She examined them and then came back on the phone. "I see the TF. Does that tell you something?"

"I'm on the phone right now talking with someone who knows Ms. Fletcher and that person told me about the monogram."

"So you think this is a lock?"

"I'll show them to Ms. Fletcher the next time I see her and get her to confirm they belong to her. You go ahead and have the DNA testing done. Have the lab send the panties back once they are done."

"Will do detective."

Jenkins punched the blinking line button. "Sorry Katherine, but I wanted to have the panties checked."

"And?"

"They had the TF monogram on them."

"I'm sure they're Tina's then."

"So somehow she became separated from her panties up at the beach. Either someone took them off her or she did."

"Why would she have done that?"

"Maybe she had to pee or something, but more likely, someone else took them off."

"But you said she didn't remember being sexually assaulted."

"Maybe she wasn't sexually assaulted."

"Oh, you mean she had consensual sex with someone at the beach?"

"That's a possibility."

"Knowing Tina, it sure is."

"Or, her attacker took them off her after he knocked her out."

"Is there anything I can help you with?"

"Not really. I just wanted to ask you about her. While I'm thinking about it, she tried to come on to me when I took her home from the hospital."

"That would be just like Tina. How did you fight her off?"

"I didn't have to fight her off. I simply stood my ground and told her I was on duty."

"I'm sure that made her want you even more."

"Why do you say that?"

"She likes men of authority and she really likes a challenge."

"Well, she didn't succeed with me."

"Oh, she'll try again. You're prey now and she has reasons to talk with you. You wait and see."

"I'll be on guard. So what are you doing tonight?"

"I'm hungry."

"Do you want me to pick you up when I get off work?"

"I want you to pick me up and take me right up stairs."

"I meant, out to dinner."

"We can eat here."

"Ok. I'll try and get things wrapped up in an hour or two. If I can't I'll let you know."

"I'll be waiting."

After hanging up the phone, Jenkins got a call from Officer Trudy.

147

"Frank, the lab technician says there's definitely DNA evidence on the panties plus he found some hairs as well."

"How long will it take for him to classify it?"

"He says it will be ready tomorrow. The new machine they have there can analyze and report on the samples in a few hours. He'll look for a match in the data bank, too. He thinks there might be more than one report coming back."

"Why does he think that?"

"He said there are some stains that will come back to life once the testing solution has been added to the panties. He said the hairs will take a little longer to analyze, maybe a day or two more."

"Tell him I'd like the information as soon as possible."

"Will do. If I get anything else tonight, I'll leave a voice message for you at the station."

"Thanks Pam. See you tomorrow."

When Officer Trudy got in the next morning, her phone was already blinking. She called in for messages. The first one was from the lab. She hit the number one to play the message. "Officer Trudy. This is Ken from the lab. I have the information you wanted from the materials we tested last night. I'll forward you an e-mail with the results."

She was amazed at how fast the lab technicians were able to process DNA materials. She turned on her computer and logged into her e-mail account. Sure enough, one e-mail was from Ken at the lab. She opened the e-mail, "Two different DNA models identified on the materials. Profiles are available in the lab under the code DPOT08021. Please reference the code number if requesting any future sample comparisons. I hope to have the hair analysis done later today. I'll leave another message when I'm done."

Trudy now had a base for sample comparisons. She selected the forward button and selected Detective Jenkins as the target destination. In the response area she wrote, "Detective, here are the DNA results from the lab. As you'll

148

see, there were no hits with our data bank. If we get samples from the suspects, the lab can compare them to the results taken from the panties. I have attached the lab report to the case file for Ms. Fletcher for future reference. Trudy."

At the morning shift briefing, Officer Trudy was asked to give a summary of the situation involving Ms. Fletcher. She described the scene and relevant information including the lab report. Sergeant Grimes asked about the possibility of the attack being caused by the cougar that was loose. He mentioned about the DEP and ZooQuarium personnel search for the animal and personnel from those operations would be in the area again looking for the animal. He asked the officers to be on the lookout for the cougar during patrols and anyone finding anything suspicious should report it to him or Detective Jenkins.

When the shift meeting was over, Officer Trudy went to see Detective Jenkins.
"Good morning Frank."
"Hi Pam. Did you brief the shift on the case?"
"Yes. Sergeant Grimes talked about a cougar from the ZooQuarium that's loose and asked about the animal's possible role in our case."
"I have thought about it and there could be a tie."
"Do you want me to tag along with DEP and the ZooQuarium personnel today and see what turns up?"
"That might not be a bad idea. I'll follow-up with the suspects and try to get DNA samples from them."
"If DEP or the ZooQuarium people turn up anything, I'll call you."

Officer Trudy left Jenkins office. She contacted the DEP office to find out what time the search for the cougar would resume and indicated to the DEP officer she would be tagging along.

149

Detective Jenkins went through his notepad to find the phone numbers of the suspects he had identified in the case. He called Bobby Jones and Ken Brown and both agreed to come in for three o'clock for DNA collections. While Tommy Anderson wasn't really a suspect at that time, Jenkins wanted to talk with him more for other reasons. Jones and Brown were done quickly, but Jenkins spent a few more minutes with Tommy Anderson, asking some questions about his whereabouts at the time of the two attacks. His alibi for both seemed plausible; he was either working, at Sundancers or sleeping. Of course, Jenkins also knew he could have been with Katherine, too. He would cross that bridge when he got to it, but the thought of having to ask Katherine to provide information on her partners on the days of the attacks didn't appeal to him.

That afternoon, Jenkins took the samples to the lab and had them compared to the results from the panties Trudy had analyzed the night before. When he got the results back a few hours later, he had a hit on one of the suspects. Kenny Brown was a match. The other sample from the panties did not match anything the lab had on file.

While he was at the lab, the lab technician told Jenkins that the analysis of the hairs lifted from Tina Fletchers panties had been completed. The results did not match any of the samples the technician was asked to compare against. Jenkins told the technician he would update the files at the police station with the hair analysis report.

Jenkins picked up his phone and made a call.

"Ms. Fletcher, its Detective Jenkins."

"Detective, I was just thinking about you."

"I have some information in the case I would like to discuss with you."

"I'd like that. Can you come over?"

"I think we can do this over the phone."

"But Detective, we could cover even more if you come here."

Jenkins ignored her advances.

150

"Ms. Fletcher, the DNA tests from your undergarment revealed samples from two contributors. Can you comment on that?"

"Sure Detective. I had sex with someone who will remain unidentified within the past twenty-four hours and with Kenny."

"So the presence of Kenny's DNA isn't a surprise?"

"As I previously told you, I also had sex with Kenny that day."

"The lab says they retrieved two different DNA samples, not including your own, of course."

"I had told you I had sex a couple of times in the past twenty-four hours. I'm not hiding anything."

"You said three."

"You would have been number four, but you wouldn't cooperate. One was the same man twice."

Jenkins thought to himself he was glad he didn't fall for her advances. How would he explain his DNA showing up on the lab report had he given into her?

"Listen Ms. Fletcher. I need to know the names of any of the men you had relations with so that tests can be done."

"I'm only talking about sex with Kenny. I won't talk about the other."

"I know. You said one's married."

"He is. Bringing him in would only complicate things for me."

"Why would they complicate things for you?"

"Because he's in a position of authority. If his name were revealed, it would not be good for him or me."

"Is this person someone you met at a bar?"

"Oh, no. That would be a problem in itself. He is pretty well known around town."

"Well, it is important to the investigation that I identify this mystery person."

"I can't help you there Detective, but if you come over, maybe you can get it out of me."

151

"That's ok. I'll go on what I already have."

"Anything else, Detective?"

"I'll call you if I have any more questions."

"Better yet, come by."

"Goodbye Ms. Fletcher."

Detective Jenkins decided to call Katherine back.

"Katherine, it's Frank."

"Hi Frank. What can I do for you?"

"Keep me away from your friend Tina Fletcher."

"What has she done now?"

"Every time I talk with her, she keeps trying to get me alone with her at her place."

"Don't say I didn't warn you. You apparently are presenting a challenge to her and she wants you."

"I'm investigating a case where she was attacked."

"That isn't how she sees it. She sees you as prey and she wants you."

"I'm not prey."

"To a cougar you are."

"Let me change the subject. Did you sleep with Tommy Anderson?"

"Why do you ask?"

"Because he was at your place when I came over."

"Tommy and I are friends. That's all."

"Did you sleep with him?"

"No I didn't sleep with him. Are you getting jealous or something?"

"Maybe a little."

"Frank, that is so sweet."

"Look Katherine. I'm not used to the women I'm seeing with other guys while I'm seeing her."

"I didn't know we were an item."

"I just thought..." his voice trailed off.

"Frank. I told you I see other men from time to time."

"Yeah, but I didn't expect to see you see them as well."

"Your timing just wasn't right."

"My timing?"

"Yes. Coming to my house without calling first. I could have saved you from the surprise."

"I'll have to think about this arrangement Katherine."

For a moment, no one spoke. Jenkins continued.

"Tell you what. I'm still pretty backed up with paperwork here. I'll call you later if I'm able to get out."

"Ok, but don't let my indiscretions become an issue for us."

"Like I said, I'll think about it."

Chapter 16

The next morning, Joe Mains rendezvoused with Ben Becker. Officer Trudy had followed Becker to the area where the cougar had been sighted the day before.

"Joe, this is Officer Trudy of the Dennis Police. She will be helping us today to see if we can find your cougar."

"Nice to meet you Officer Trudy."

"Same here Mr. Mains."

"Please, call me Joe."

"Ok Joe. So what's the plan?"

Mains went to the back of his truck and opened one of the storage compartments on the driver's side rear panel. He took out a container. "I have some of the food Charlie loves in here. My plan is for us to set a trap for him in the area behind the neighborhood and see if he shows."

"Do you think he would come out for it?"

"Since Charlie has been foraging for domestic animal food, I think if he gets a whiff of his favorite meal, he'll respond."

"Do you have enough for a few traps?"

"What are you thinking Pam?"

"If the three of us each take some of the food, we can increase our chances three fold."

"True, but I only have one capture loop. I'm the only one here who knows how to handle Charlie."

"How about we use our cell phones and if any of us see the cougar, we contact you Joe?" Ben asked.

"I guess that could work."

"It would increase our odds of sighting the animal."

"Ok. Just in case, Ben, you take my tranquilizer gun. If you get a clear shot, hit him in the hindquarter. The drug will immobilize Charlie in a few minutes."

"And Pam, if you see Charlie, call me right away."

"Will do. I'll set up down by Follins Pond."

"Good. Ben, you go down by Old Bass River Road."

"Ok."

"I'll set up in back of the Ward house. Charlie already knows he can get food there."

"Didn't someone take a shot at him yesterday?" Pam asked.

"Yes, we had a report of a gun shot in the vicinity, but I think he missed. Plus, Charlie doesn't know what a gun is. We use some props at the ZooQuarium show that make popping noises so Charlie wouldn't be scared off by a shotgun blast. He's kind of used to it."

"Officer Trudy, here is my cell number as well," said Ben. "Call me if you can't get Joe."

"Will do."

The three went to their respective locations and set out the meal bait Mains had brought along. Then the three got into their respective vehicles and began the stakeout. After about an hour, Mains decided to take a walk around the wooded area to see if there was any new sign. As he walked in the woods, he heard a shot. He thought to himself that Ben had gotten lucky and shot the tranquilizer into Charlie. He called Ben's cell phone but didn't get an answer. He tried Officer Trudy next.

"Pam, did you shoot?"

"No. I heard a shot and thought it was pretty close by. It wasn't me. Maybe it was Ben?"

"He isn't answering his cell."

155

"I'm going to go over to his location and see if I can find him," said Joe.

"Let me know what you find out."

Joe Mains went to Old Bass River Road where Ben Becker had said he set up. When he located Ben's vehicle, Ben was not in it. Joe yelled out his name and listened for a response.

"Over here."

The DEP officer came walking out of the woods. He had the tranquilizer gun in his hands.

"Did you get off a shot?" Asked Mains.

"No. I was just looking around when I heard a shot off in the distance."

"I heard it also," said Mains.

"Where do you think it came from?"

"I spoke with Officer Trudy and she said it wasn't her. Let me get her on the cell."

Joe called Pam again and put his phone on speaker, "Anything?"

"No. Ben didn't shoot. It must be someone else."

"I'm going to take a ride around and see if I can figure out where the shot came from."

"Ok. I'm going back to my stakeout and Ben, can you continue here?"

"Sure"

Officer Trudy drove around Follins Pond. When she came to Driftwood Lane, she saw a person coming out of the woods from behind a house holding a shotgun. She pulled her cruiser into the driveway. Approaching the person with the gun, she said, "Sir, did you discharge your shotgun a few minutes ago?"

"Yes Officer. My name is Marshall Watson. I live here. I saw a big cat in my back yard. I took a shot at it last night and again this morning but I missed."

"Can you describe the animal for me?"

"It was about this tall." He held his hand palm down about half way between his knee and waist. "And I'd guess three feet long."

"What was it doing?"

"I think it was trying to get to my pet's food on my back deck."

"Did it look like a bobcat or mountain lion?"

"I'd say more like a mountain lion."

"So you took a shot at it and it ran away?"

"Yes. It took off into the woods heading north."

Officer Trudy took out her cell phone and called Joe Mains.

"Joe, I'm up on Driftwood Lane with a Mr. Watson. He's the person who took a shot. He says he saw a mountain lion in his back yard last night and again this morning and he took a shot at it both times."

"Did he hit it?"

"He said he missed."

"Thank God for that," was Joe's response.

"Which way was Charlie headed?"

"He said north."

"So that will put him up by Cape Cod Bay."

"Looks like it."

"Why don't we set up our stakeouts up in that area and see if we can lure Charlie in."

"Sounds good to me. Let's meet in the Players Plaza parking lot at the intersection of 6A and 134."

"I'll meet you there in a few minutes."

Officer Trudy produced a card and asked Mr. Watson to call if he saw the big cat again and not to shoot. She explained to Mr. Watson that the cat was actually a cougar that had escaped from the ZooQuarium and the authorities would be in the area trying to capture it.

"If that thing comes back, I can't guarantee I won't shoot it," came the response from Mr. Watson.

157

"Please try to call us first Mr. Watson. The animal isn't wild and shouldn't harm you."

"I'm not taking any chances. If I see that thing and think it's getting aggressive, I'm shooting. I've got two dogs that spend a great deal of time outside, and a young grandson that spends time with them."

"Please call us first," said Officer Trudy as she got into her cruiser and headed to route 134.

Driving to the agreed meeting place, Trudy thought about the exchange with Mr. Watson. If she encountered the cougar and it was acting in an aggressive manner, she might have to shoot it. As she got out of the cruiser in the parking lot, Joe and Ben were standing at the back of the ZooQuarium truck.

"I think we should set up the food traps along Corporation Road and William Crowell Road."

"What are you thinking Joe?" Asked Ben.

"Well, if Charlie was trying to get food at the Watson place, then he's hungry. That could be a good thing if we can get him to take our bait."

"Ok. Why don't I set up at this end of Corporation and Ben at the other end up by Nobscusset Point? Then Joe, you set up by the William Crowell Road intersection. That way we have a pretty good area covered."

"If anyone sees Charlie, get on the cell phone," instructed Mains.

The three agreed. They got into their respective vehicles and went to their designated spots. All three deployed the bait meal they had taken from the earlier sites and waited.

Chapter 17

After getting off the phone with Frank, Katherine decided to get out of the house for a while. Katherine went to Sundancers dressed in a light blue summer dress with sandals. From the front, the dress was quite demure, for Katherine. But from the back, it was open from her neck to her waist with a small bow holding the neckline together. She had her hair pulled back with a brown hair clip. She wore a gold necklace around her neck with a locket on it. She took up a stool at the far end of the bar next to Ed Phillips. Margarita Ortiz was bartending. She came over to Katherine, "What will it be Katherine?"

"I'll have a martini, dirty."

"Can't be any other way now, can it?" Margarita said with a smile.

"Where have you been lately Margarita? I haven't seen you here?"

"I had to put my dog Pete down last week. He had medical problems."

"Wasn't Pete just a puppy?" asked Katherine.

"Sure was. He was only eleven months old."

"That's too bad."

"I've been bummed out for a while."

Chef Antonio who had been standing near the bar overheard the conversation and approached Katherine.

"Can I make you something special Ms. Sterns?"

"Thanks Antonio, but I'm only here for a few drinks."

159

"I heard what you said to Margarita. It was nice of you to ask about her dog. She's been really bummed out over it. Are you sure there isn't something special I might be able to make you for an appetizer at least?"

"That's so thoughtful of you Antonio. Thanks again, but maybe some other time."

"Let me know if you change your mind."

"Oh, I will. I remember the last sauté you made me and it was just fabulous."

"I don't have a big enough kitchen to make dinners like that all the time, but for you, I'd make an exception."

"You're so sweet Antonio. Thanks again."

Antonio went back into the kitchen to work.

Dee heard Antonio talking to Kat, "Is Antonio trying to pick up one of the cougars now?"

"Who knows," Ron replied.

Margarita, after having made the martini, came back over and put it in front of Katherine. Katherine took a sip and turned to Ed.

"Hi Ed. How are you doing?"

"I'm fine. How about you Mrs. Sterns."

"Ed, don't be so formal. Call me Katherine."

"Ok, Katherine it is. You know I used to know your husband. I mean your former husband, er, your dead husband, ah, well, you know who I mean."

"You knew Sam?"

"Yes. I'm a fisherman also. I met him once when I was casting for bass at Chapin Beach."

"Sam was an avid fisherman."

"That was too bad about his death and all."

"Yes it was, but that was some time ago and I'm past all of that."

"Maybe you would like to go for a ride with me up to Chapin's to see the sunset sometime?"

"Do you do that often?"

"I take a few beers and go up there whenever I get a chance. I have a beach permit for my vehicle so I can drive out at low tide. The sight is really breath taking when the sun sets."

"I think I'd like that. When are you going again?"

"I was thinking about going out there tonight. There aren't many clouds so the sunset should be great. Would you like to join me?"

"Let me think about it. I was going to meet someone tonight. I'll have to see if the date is still on or not."

"Well, let me know. I'll be leaving here in about an hour."

Ed was dressed in a pair of khaki shorts with a white and yellow striped polo shirt. He had on a pair of brown loafers, no socks. Ed had a watch on his left wrist that looked like a computer. It had a number of buttons and had a multi-display face. Katherine took an interest in Ed's watch.

"What kind of watch is that Ed?"

"It's a multi-function watch. It not only tells time, but gives the date, tides, sunrise, sunset and GPS location."

"Why would you need all of those things?"

"It comes in handy when I go fishing."

"Oh, I see." She really had no idea why he had all of those things on his watch. "Why not just get a Blackberry?"

"Too big to carry around. Plus, I couldn't take it into the water with me. My watch is also waterproof so if I'm out in the surf fishing, I can still wear it."

"How convenient."

"Want to see what time sunset is tonight?"

"Sure."

Ed pressed two of the buttons and a time appeared on the digital screen.

"See," he remarked. Katherine leaned closer to Ed's arm, letting him smell her perfume while she brushed his forearm with her breast.

"How handy."

161

Ed smiled as he proudly showed off his watch.

"Say, Ed, you said you knew Sam from fishing."

"Well yes and I did some work for his company a few times."

"What kind of work do you do?"

"I'm a computer technician. I did some work for Sterns and Dunn setting up a new network for them a few months before Sam died."

"So you know things about computers?"

"Yeah, it's what I do."

"I've been having some trouble with my home computer. It keeps freezing and I have to re-boot it to be able to do anything. It happens at least a couple of times a day."

"Sounds like some kind of virus got into it."

"Is that something you could resolve?"

"Sure. You probably just need some anti-virus software installed and then run the scan program to check the computer out. The software would remove any infections and you would be good to go."

"I can remember having the same problem right after my husband died. Someone I used to know fixed it and it has worked fine for a while. Now it's broke again and fixing it sounds complicated."

"Not really. If you want I could come by and take a look at it."

"I would really appreciate it."

"When would you like me to stop by?"

"Let me see if my evening plans are firm or not. If not, how about tonight, after we go see the sunset?"

Ed looked up and down Katherine's body as she said those words. Katherine didn't notice him looking as she was digging her cell phone out of her purse. She made a call.

"Hi, it's me. Do you still think you're going to be tied up tonight? Ok. Then I'll talk with you tomorrow."

"Well Ed, it looks like my evening is free."

"Then let's get a few beers and head up to Chapin's. You'll love the sunset. Then I'll take you to your place and see what's up with your computer."

162

"Sounds good to me. Dee, can I get my tab and add Ed's to my bill."

"Sure Katherine. I'll be right there."

Katherine and Ed left Sundancers together. Ed followed her out of the parking lot in his truck. The two drove to Katherine's place and left her car there. She stopped into the house and picked up a sweater, a beach blanket and a six-pack of beer. When she got into the truck, she said to Ed, "We're all set. I had beer here. And a beach blanket can't hurt either. Take me to a romantic sunset."

"Coming up," Ed replied and headed to Chapin Beach.

Ed took the access road on to the beach at the Chapin Beach parking lot. As he drove on to the sand, he put his truck into four-wheel drive and put the transmission into low gear.

Katherine said, "Why do you do that?"

"Because the sand can have soft spots and if I were to hit one going too fast, it might mess up the truck front end or get stuck."

"How far down the beach do you usually go?"

"Sometimes I go all the way down by Barnstable Harbor if the tide is way out. Sometimes I stay back here by the beach access point."

"How far do you think we can go tonight?"

"Most of the way as the tide is out pretty far."

"I'd like to go all the way. I always want to go all the way."

Ed wasn't sure what she was saying but he thought he knew. He had heard that Katherine was a pretty busy woman especially since her husband passed away. He could think of a half dozen times in recent weeks where she left the bar with a different guy although she seemed to be with only one guy recently, but tonight was different. She was there with him and the setting couldn't be any better.

Ed stopped the truck about a mile from the access path. From their vantage point, the two could see for miles across Barnstable Harbor to the left and across the bay.

"This is absolutely beautiful Ed," remarked Katherine.

"Yes it is. Let's get out and grab a beer."

"Sounds good to me."

The two got out of Ed's truck. Katherine spread her blanket on the bay side of the truck so only someone on the water would be able to see the two. She took the six-pack out of the truck and opened a beer. She sat down on the blanket facing the sunset, "Come and join me Ed. This is really spectacular."

Ed grabbed a beer and opened it. He sat on the blanket a few feet away from Katherine and looked towards the sun. "Sure is colorful isn't it?"

The sun had changed the wispy clouds in the western sky into shades of red and orange making the sky look like there was a raging fire on the horizon. "I can't get over the color," said Katherine. She took a pull on her beer and then moved closer to Ed. Ed looked at his watch. He pressed a few buttons.

"Only a few more minutes."

"Wouldn't it be wonderful to make love right here at this most romantic moment?" Katherine softly said in Ed's ear.

"I'm sure it would, but right here out in the open?"

Katherine looked around. There were no other vehicles or any people. "We have to be miles away from everyone else plus we could see and hear anyone who might be approaching," she said in a suggestive voice.

"I guess."

Then Katherine untied the bow at the back of her neck and let the dress slip away. She wore no bra, and Ed looked at her healthy well-formed breasts. As he did, she unbuttoned his shirt and removed it for him. Then she undid his belt, unbuttoned his jeans and pulled his zipper down. She took control. Ed lay back on the blanket allowing Katherine to work her magic. Soon he was at attention and Katherine kept up her maneuvers. She grabbed on to both sides of his shorts and pulled them down.

"Do you have protection Ed?" She asked him as she reached his ankles.

"No, is that a problem?"

"Hand me my bag."

She pointed to her purse. Ed retrieved it and handed it to her. She opened it and took out a condom. She opened it and handed it to Ed. He opened the package and put it on.

She looked at him and remarked, "How nice." Then he bent his knees and allowed her to take the shorts completely off him. Next, she fully removed her dress and panties. She moved up and kissed him and coaxed him to take the top position. Soon, the two were moving in unison in the soft sand. Katherine reached climax first. She said she hadn't had a man like Ed in quite some time. Then she rolled him over and got on top. She worked the pace into a frenzy until Ed held his breath and achieved climax. She did again at the same time.

As the two lay there spent, Katherine looked at Ed, "I'd like to see more of you."

Ed looked at her. "I thought you were seeing that police officer who's investigating the attacks on Ann and Tina?"

"You mean Frank?"

"If that's what his name is. I wouldn't know."

"I have been seeing him a little, but after this..." She squeezed him. "I'd settle for this every day." She removed the condom and put into a zip-lock bag she had taken out of her purse when she got the condom. She put the zip-lock back into her purse.

"What are you doing?" asked Ed.

"I don't want to litter such a beautiful place. Plus, the zip-lock will minimize any mess."

"I try to be environmentally conscious as well."

"No sense ruining a pristine place like this."

"I agree. So do you like the sunset?"

"Call it what you want. I like the sex."

"You know I can make myself available whenever you want."

"I'll keep that in mind Ed. Now let's enjoy the rest of the sunset and these beers."

Ed rested his head on her bare mid-section and watched the sun set. The two were completely naked as the sun went down. Ed noticed Katherine's features were reacting to the change in temperature as the sun set, "Looks like you're starting to get cold?"

"That or I'm ready again."

Ed kissed her breast and looked down. He wasn't ready. The two began to get dressed. When they had completely dressed, Katherine said, "Maybe after you look at my computer you might want to look at my equipment again."

"Anything you say. Let's get out of here."

The two packed up the blanket and picked up the empty beer bottles. They got into the truck and drove back to Katherine's house. Just as Ed had thought, Katherine's computer had picked up a virus. He went to the Internet and downloaded a copy of Avast anti-virus software and installed it on her computer. Then he ran the scan. It picked up three different virus infections and quarantined them. When it was done, he said, "Your computer should be all set. Avast has fixed the problem."

"Do I need a license for the software?"

"No. It's free for home use. I downloaded it from the Internet and you'll get periodic updates from Avast so your machine stays current. New viruses come out all the time. If you don't keep your virus software current, they won't get picked up."

166

"Thank you Ed. Let me repay you."

Katherine took Ed's hand and led him to her bedroom. She shed her clothes and suggested he do the same. At first, he just stood there watching her take off her things. Then he quickly got out of his clothing. She got on the bed and motioned for him to join her. As he did, she reached out. Ed was already aroused. She used her skills until he was at his maximum potential. She reached out to her nightstand and took a condom out of the drawer. She took it out of the wrapper and put it on Ed. The two began to move in one motion.

Katherine let out a loud sexy noise that was followed by a "Yes, yes", then she reached climax. Ed followed shortly after her. It seemed like the two were locked into that position for a half hour before Ed began to lose interest. As Ed lay on his back, she removed the condom and squeezed him. She said, "I want more."

"You'll have to give me a few minutes."
"Let me know when you are ready?"
"Oh, you'll know."
She took another zip-lock out of her nightstand and put the condom in it.
"You really are cautious about making a mess with these things," Ed said as he watched her seal the bag.
"I don't have to be outside to want to keep things clean and neat."
"I guess not."
She continued to work on him.

In a few minutes, Ed came to life again. When he was fully extended, she got on top. This time, she didn't require him to wear a condom. She worked feverishly sitting perpendicular on his mid-section. From time to time, Ed would reach up and hold her. Finally, she reached climax again. Ed did not but he faked it. She never knew. As the two fell back into the pillows, Katherine was thinking about how good a lover Ed was. He was really impressive. She had found the thing she had been seeking for some time. How would she deal with Frank?

When they finished, Katherine said, "Ed, remember when I saw you up at Chapin's Restaurant the night Ann was attacked?"

"Yeah."

"After Bobby and Kenny came over to talk with me and Ann, you were talking with a man with a beard. Who was he?"

"That was Tom Bowman. Tom was one of the people I knew from fishing just like Sam. I remember a couple of times when the two of them came down to the beach to surf cast. When they were done fishing, they would ask me if I wanted to join them for a beer. I did join them on a few occasions. That's how I got to know Sam and eventually got to do some work for his firm."

"I thought that was Tom, but he looked different with the beard. Plus he looks like he has lost some weight."

"Yeah, he said he has lost about sixty pounds. The beard does make him look different."

"Did he move back here with his family?"

"No, he said he ended up getting divorced. Something about some infidelity that he and his ex couldn't work out."

"I'll bet."

"Did he say what brought him back to Cape Cod?"

"He told me he was interested in someone back here."

"Did he say who it is?"

"No, but he said he was going to do everything he could to win her over. Pretty obsessed I'd say."

"Really?"

"I don't know what he meant but it sounded like he's definitely hooked on someone."

"Yeah, sounds like it. Ed, why don't you spend the night? I might need more help with my equipment in the morning."

"Oh, I'm sure your computer is all set."
"I wasn't thinking about my computer."

He put his head on the pillow and closed his eyes. When Katherine looked at his face, he was fast asleep with a smile.

Katherine thought, "That worked out just fine."

Chapter 18

The next day, after reviewing the information the Police Department had collected regarding the attacks, Jenkins met with Tomlinson, Grimes and Trudy. Jenkins started the meeting.

"Captain, it looks like the attacks we've been pursuing could have been relatively harmless attacks by the cougar that escaped from the ZooQuarium. Joe Mains, who is a handler there, indicated the cougar might have confused the victims with handlers from the act they do at the ZooQuarium."

"How so?"

"Well, it seems this cougar does dancing and wrestling as part of the act they put on for their customers."

"That wouldn't explain the victims getting knocked out."

"If they had hit their head when the cougar knocked them over, then it might have happened that way."

"And what about the panties?"

"I don't have an answer for that yet. Maybe Ms. Fletcher took them off to take a swim or go the bathroom?"

"I'd continue with looking for a sexual attacker. I'm not convinced an animal from the ZooQuarium did these attacks."

"Then how do you explain the cat like scratch marks?"

"I don't know Detective. That is one of the things *you* need to pursue."

"OK Captain. I get the message."

Captain Tomlinson got up and left Jenkins' office. After he was gone, Jenkins turned to Grimes, "Did any of yesterday's patrols report anything about the cougar?"

"No Detective. The only thing that remotely happened with regards to the cougar took place up by Follins Pond."

"What happened there?"

Officer Trudy said, "A resident shot at an animal the night before and again when I was on stakeout with DEP and Joe Mains from the ZooQuarium."

"Did you see the animal?"

"I didn't, it was gone before we got there."

"What about the resident?"

"He took a shot at the animal with a shotgun he uses for duck hunting."

"Did he hit it?"

"He said he didn't think so."

"So now we have an animal out there that may or may not be injured. What will happen next?"

"Look Detective, we can't really blame the public for taking action against a cougar. That animal would scare me pretty good if I came across it."

"You have a good point. We had better find it before something else goes wrong."

Grimes added, "We did review the case at the morning briefing. Nothing was reported back as of last night."

Officer Trudy said, "Frank, do you want me to follow up with the DEP and ZooQuarium people and see how their search is going again today?"

"Yes Trudy. Let me know what they think."

"Will do." Officer Trudy then got up and left the office.

Sergeant Grimes turned to Detective Jenkins, "So we have someone out there acting like an animal with claws and attacking middle aged women. If that isn't the ultimate."

"What do you mean?"

"Here you have these cougars being attacked by what appears to be a cougar. Then at the same time, the cougars are seeking their prey. Are we sure there is a crime here?"

"Look Sergeant, we might not like it, but an attack is an attack."

"Yeah, but what if we find out the supposed attacker is one of the men the cougars regularly sleep with?"

"I know. That would make our case pretty difficult."

"What if the DNA tests come back and identify someone who is important in the community? Should we bring that person or persons into the investigation?"

"Grimes, we bring in any and all suspects that produce solid leads."

"Ok Detective. I'll review the attacks again at the shift meetings."

"Get back to me if anything develops."

"You know I will."

Sergeant Grimes got up and left for the morning shift meeting. Detective Jenkins continued to review his notes and the various reports that had been generated.

Around noon, the bar at Sundancers was starting to fill up with the lunch crowd. Ann and Tina were sitting near the door. Bobby and Kenny were talking with Linda on the far side of the bar. Katherine was down in the corner talking to Ed. He had his back turned to the door. As Katherine was leaning in to Ed saying something, Tom Bowman walked in.

"Oh no," said Katherine.
"What's the matter?" asked Ed.
"It's Tom Bowman."

Ed turned and waived to Tom to join them. Tom walked to the corner and held out his hand to Ed.

"Hey Ed. How are you doing?"

"Fine Tom. You know Katherine, don't you?"

"Sure. Hi, Kat. How you doing?" He leaned in to kiss her on the cheek. She pulled back so he couldn't touch her.

"I'm fine Tom. What are you doing back in these parts?"

"Things didn't work out for me in Virginia so I have moved back."

"I thought I saw you at Chapin's a few days ago and again here at Sundancers. When did you move back?"

"I got back two weeks ago."

"So what have you been up to?"

"A little of this, a little of that."

"Come on Tom. I saw you fishing up at Chapin Beach a few nights ago," said Ed.

"Yeah, I have been doing a little fishing."

Tom ordered a draft and took up the stool next to Katherine with Ed sitting on the other side of her. Katherine turned more towards Ed so as to block Tom.

"Wasn't that fun going up to the beach to see the sunset Ed?" Katherine said.

"It was nice. I had a good time."

"And afterwards, did you enjoy yourself then also?"

Ed kind of blushed because he knew Tom could hear everything she was saying, "That was good also."

"Good. That was the best sex I ever had," Katherine said and turned a little to Tom to make sure he heard her. Tom didn't react.

"Excuse me for a minute if you would Katherine, I have to visit the men's room." Ed got up and went to the bathroom. When he did, Tom said, "So how have you been Katherine?"

She turned to Tom, "Things have been pretty good. I have a comfortable income coming from my investments Sam had set up for me and I have found a good set of friends here who take me for who I am."

"And who is that?"

"Look Tom. I never got over what you did when Sam died; trying to give me that card and gift after he died. How could you think I would sleep with you after that?"

"You might not believe me Katherine, but Sam got you those things and he had asked me, when he knew he was dying, to give them to you."

She thought about it for a few seconds, "Well, I have no way of knowing if it's true or not. I do know you tried to get into my pants after Sam died. To me it looked like you were trying to take advantage of my situation."

"I never intended to offend you Katherine. You are a beautiful woman and I haven't forgotten the time we had at the Route 28 motel."

"Tom. We had sex. That was it. What happened? Did you fall in love with me?"

"You know I have feelings for you Katherine. Why don't you just give me a chance?"

"Look Tom, I'm seeing someone now."

"That never stopped you from being with more than one man in the past."

"And it still hasn't."

"Are you seeing Ed or just sleeping with him?"

"That's none of your business."

At that moment Ed returned from the men's room.

"I heard my name. What did I do?"

"Nothing," said Katherine.

Katherine took a sip of her drink and looked toward the door. Frank Jenkins and Lou Tomlinson were just coming in. "Oh shit," she said. Ed turned to see the two. "Looks like more questions."

Tom asked Ed, "What do you mean?"

"Those are a couple of the cops who are investigating the recent attacks on a few of our friends."

"So why are they here?"

174

"Because they think someone who knows the victims or who is stalking the victims is frequenting the local bars."

"No kidding?" said Tom.

"That's what they think," said Katherine. She picked up her drink and got up. Walking over to Detective Jenkins she said, "Hello Detective, Captain. Out for lunch are you?"

Captain Tomlinson spoke first. "Hello Mrs. Sterns. How are you today?"

"Just fine Captain. How about you Detective?"

Detective Jenkins looking around at the bar said, "I'm just fine Ms. Sterns."

"Looking for anyone in particular Detective?"

"No one in particular."

"Well, Ms. Fletcher will be right back from the ladies room if she's the one you are looking for."

"Thank you for the information Ms. Sterns, but we are only here for lunch."

"Then have a good lunch." She turned and went back to the bar taking up the stool Ed had been sitting at. Ed had moved next to Tom when Katherine had walked over to the cops. As she sat, she heard Tom and Ed talking about going surf fishing up at Chapin Beach. Tom was telling Ed about his four-wheel drive vehicle.

"I can't go today though. My Jeep is in for service. One of the belts is loose and has been making a screeching sound."

"We can take my truck," said Ed. "How about I pick you up around four this afternoon."

"Ok."

"Where are you staying?"

"At the Travelodge."

"You're kidding me? Right across the street?"

"That's right. I haven't gotten a place yet so I'm renting a room there."

"Ok. I'll be there at four."

"OK, then I'll check out of here now and get my gear ready." Tom paid his tab and left. As he was walking out the

175

door, Katherine said to Ed, "So you and Tom are going fishing?"

"Yeah. Like old times."

Then Ed realized he might have hit a sore spot with Katherine because Tom and Sam had been fishing buddies.

"I'm sorry. That was insensitive of me."

"That's alright Ed. I know you didn't mean anything by it."

"Even so, I should be more considerate of your past."

"Thank you for thinking of me that way Ed. It means a lot. Why don't you come by my place after you're done fishing with Tom?"

"That might be kind of late. The tide is around eight tonight. By the time it turns could be close to midnight, especially if the fishing's good."

"I'll be home. Come anytime."

"If you don't mind my being too late."

"I don't mind Ed. You're worth waiting for, and Ed?"

"Yea?"

"Plan on staying the night."

Ed turned a little red. He kissed Katherine on the cheek, paid his tab and left to get ready to go fishing.

Jenkins and Tomlinson took up a table just off the bar. Dee came over to the two, "What'll it be?"

"We're here for lunch today. Can we have menus?"

"And two diet cokes," added Tomlinson."

"Two diet cokes it is," responded Dee as she went back to the bar.

When she came back with the menus and sodas, Jenkins said, "Ms. Crowe, do you know what vehicles some of the people in here drive?"

"Sure. What are you looking for?"

"Anyone with four-wheel drive and an off-road permit."

"That could be anyone of the guys here. I think they all have four-wheel drive and most of them have off-road permits. This is a fishing hot spot you know."

"We know," added Tomlinson. "We're looking for someone who was on the beach the night the attacks against some of your patrons took place. More specifically, we're looking for a vehicle that makes a screeching noise."

Dee thought about it for a few seconds.

"You know, I heard a screeching vehicle a few times in the past few days when I was bartending. Normally, it wouldn't have bothered me but the windows have been open in the evening and the screeching sound was rather obvious on a few occasions."

"So you know someone here who has a four-wheel drive vehicle that makes a screeching sound?"

"I can't say who has the vehicle that is making the sounds like that, but I can say I have heard screeching sounds as you described recently."

Jenkins then added, "Can you try to pay particular attention to a sound like that if it happens again in the next few days?"

"Sure. If I hear it again, I'll try and see who's driving the vehicle."

"Thanks," said Captain Tomlinson.

"You know Detective. I know Ed has a four-wheel drive, and I overheard him talking to another patron about going surf-fishing tonight on the bay side. Something about the tide, moon and abundance of big fish. He already left but if you're lucky, you might find the vehicle you are looking for if you go up there tonight.

"Thank you Ms. Crowe. That's good information."

The two men ordered lunch. Dee went back to the bar and put in their order.

"What do you think Captain?"

"I think you might want to take a ride up to Chapin Beach tonight and check out the vehicles and people who are there."

"Maybe this will be the break we need."

"Maybe. Let me know if you find anything. Otherwise, we can pick it up again in the morning."

Dee brought their lunches over. The two ate and then left when they were done. As Dee got back to the bar, she looked to Ron, "I don't think the good detective knows what Kat is up to."

"What do you mean?"

"I overheard her talking with Ed a little while ago and inviting him over to her place later on tonight."

"So?"

"So? She's been in here a few times with the detective and I thought she had a thing going with him. Like an exclusive thing."

"She has things going with a lot of men."

"You still on the cougar thing?"

"I don't think women like that ever shake the cougar thing."

"Am I a cougar?"

"You're different."

"How so?"

"You know what I mean. Those women are always on the prowl."

"And I'm not?"

"No you are not."

"How do you know that?"

"Ok. Let's see. How many of these guys here at the bar have you slept with?"

"Other than you? None."

"See. Had you been a real cougar you would've slept with a number of them, both workers and customers. You'd be curious. But you're not."

"I see what you mean."

178

Chapter 19

Later that afternoon, Detective Jenkins changed into casual clothing so he would look the part as he went surf fishing up at Chapin Beach. He parked in the lot right near the off-road access. Taking a surfcasting rod and small tackle box from the back seat, he walked down to the beach about fifty yards past the access point.   He took out a surface plug, attached it to his rod and set it down. Next, he picked up his PVC rod holder and worked it into the sand. When done, he placed his rod into the holder so anyone arriving at the beach would just see another fisherman waiting for the bite to start. He unfolded the bag chair he had brought with him and set it up facing west.   From his vantage point, he could see completely down the beach off-road access path. He sat in his chair with notepad ready to write down the description information of any vehicles coming onto the beach. He thought about what a brilliant sunset he would see in a few hours.

About a half hour later, the off-road vehicles started to arrive. The first few vehicles were pick-up trucks with one or two men in them. They stopped as the vehicles reached the access road. Jenkins figured the drivers were shifting their vehicles into four-wheel drive and low gear. As each vehicle began to move again, they would move forward at a crawl pace so as to not sink in the soft sand.   The next vehicle coming on to the path was a Jeep Wrangler. The driver got out of the vehicle when it reached the path and let air out of all four tires. Jenkins made a mental note that the Jeep had regular tires and guessed the thinner tires needed to be made softer or they would dig into the sand easier.

As each vehicle drove in, Jenkins wrote the description of the vehicle in his notepad. When he could, he made note of the plate number as well. While he was writing down the information for an Explorer that had come on to the beach access road, a screeching sound got his attention. He snapped his head around to see a Jeep Laredo coming to a stop at the access point. The driver had turned the wheels as far as they could go causing the power steering to make the screeching sound. For a minute, Jenkins thought he might be on to something and then realized the occupants of the vehicle probably didn't meet the criteria of his perpetrator. The driver was an elderly man about sixty-five years old. He had two young boys with him who looked like they were ten or twelve years old. He guessed it was a grandfather taking his visiting grandsons fishing. He just jotted down the plate.

The next vehicle coming on the beach was a Chevy Silverado. The truck had a cap on the back. Jenkins recognized the driver. It was Ed Phillips from Sundancers. Ed's truck didn't make any sound out of the ordinary. It moved easily over the sand. Jenkins continued to watch as the truck went on down the beach access road until it stopped about a half mile away. When it stopped, he could see two men get out of the truck and set up for fishing. Jenkins looked through his binoculars attempting to see who was with Ed, but he couldn't identify the other man. He looked familiar but no name came to mind. Had he been at Sundancers? Maybe.

The tide had changed and most of the fishermen along the beach were standing knee deep in the surf, casting. Jenkins decided to take a few casts himself. To his amazement, he caught a fish on the second cast. The fish pumped hard and darted across the top of the incoming waves. Jenkins held his rod tip straight up keeping constant pressure on the fish. After what seemed like a half hour, the fish gave up. Jenkins brought the fish in on its side on an incoming wave. He had landed a thirty-five inch stripped bass. Jenkins thought, "Maybe I'll take this over to Katherine's later and we can grill it."

He cleaned the fish and put it in a black plastic bag he kept in his tackle box. He went back to fishing and caught another fish right away. This one was a blue fish about two feet long. He cleaned it and put it in the plastic bag with the striper after he bled it out in the surf. After finishing up with the fish, he sat back down in his chair. He picked up his notepad and looked down the beach. The Silverado was gone. In all the excitement of catching fish, he didn't see the truck leave.

The sun was beginning to set and Jenkins thought he wouldn't gather any more information at the beach. He gathered up his things including the bag of fish and headed back to the parking lot. When he got to his vehicle, he stowed the gear and catch. Standing in the lot, he took out his cell phone.

"Katherine, it's Frank. I am up at Chapin Beach doing a little fishing. I caught a blue fish and a pretty big bass and wondered if you have dinner plans?"

"Frank, you caught fish?"

"What? You think detectives can't do anything other than detect?" Based on how things had ended Monday, he decided to maintain an upbeat, positive tone.

"I know you can do other things."

"I meant other than that."

"What did you have in mind?"

"Why don't you come over to my place and we can have grilled fresh fish. I'll even open a good bottle of wine. I make a wonderful bluefish wasabi dip for an appetizer. Put the dip on Ritz crackers and you'll love it."

Katherine thought about it for a few seconds.

181

"I don't think I can make it tonight. I have already made plans." She was thinking of Ed.

"Anyone I know?"

"That's unfair Frank. You know I see other people."

"Well then why don't you get back to me?"

"Frank, you don't have to be that way."

"Just how am I being?"

"Kind of jealous."

"I'll put this fish on ice. You give me a call when it is convenient for you."

"I'll see you tomorrow."

"If you say so."

As Jenkins was closing his phone, he heard a loud screech again. A vehicle that had just come off the beach entering the paved road had made the noise. He turned to see it, but the vehicle had already moved past the dunes that separated the parking lot from the road. He ran over to the corner of the lot so he could see down the road. When he got there, he just caught site of the right taillight of the vehicle as it rounded the turn. All he knew is the vehicle had a square tail light. With darkness now nearly complete, he returned to his vehicle and put his catch on the floor in back of the driver's seat. It was a good thing he had the plastic bag.

Jenkins got into his car and left the lot. He traveled a little faster than the posted speed limit hoping to overtake the vehicle that had made the noise. As he went down Dr. Bottero Road, he could just make out the vehicle about a half-mile ahead of him making the turn by Gina's by the Sea. When he got to that point, he picked up speed but was unable to find the vehicle. He slowed as he passed Gina's and then again by Chapin's. The parking lots were full at both places. He decided to keep going. When he reached 6A, he thought he probably should have stopped at Chapin's and asked if someone just came in, and who. Maybe he would get lucky. He turned his vehicle around.

Jenkins stopped at Chapin's Restaurant. He went inside. As he approached the hostess station, Amy Martin, the hostess said, "How many in your party?"

"I'm not here for dinner. I'm Detective Jenkins of the Dennis Police. Did someone just came in here in the last few minutes?"

"Are you looking for a man or a woman?"

"A man, probably late twenties or early thirties. His vehicle just left Chapin Beach a few minutes ago and I lost it coming down the street."

"Only a couple came in during the last fifteen minutes. Our busy hours have already gone by."

"The person I'm pursuing might not have come in here. I lost sight of the vehicle up on Dr. Bottero drive and should have caught up with it. So it must have turned somewhere."

"There is a back entrance to the bar. You might want to check with the bartenders."

"Thanks." Jenkins went back to the bar area.

John White was bartending as Detective Jenkins approached him.

"I'm Detective Jenkins of the Dennis Police Department. I'd like to ask you a few questions if you can give me a minute?"

"Sure Detective. I can give you a minute or two but as you can see the bar is pretty full."

"Can I have your name for my file?"

"It's John White."

"John, have you been on duty for the past hour or so?"

"Sure. What's this all about?"

"I'm looking for a man who would have come in here in the last fifteen minutes or so."

"A few have come in during the last half hour or so. I've been pretty busy. I did set up a few guys but I don't know their names."

"Can you point them out for me?"

"Sure. You see that guy at the end of the bar with the beard. He came in recently. He's drinking a beer and shot."

Jenkins looked at the man. He looked to be around fifty years old. Jenkins thought the man might be too old for the person he was looking for. "Anyone else?"

John looked around and said the two guys across the bar who were talking to each other had come in recently. Jenkins surveyed the two. They looked like they were in their late twenties or early thirties. One was a bit overweight and the other seemed to be in the thin side. He guessed the overweight one probably wasn't the person he was seeking as he looked to be about five foot ten and two hundred eighty pounds. That person was probably not nimble enough to have been pulling off the attacks. The other one looked like he might be a candidate. "Any others?"

John looked around again.

"I don't think so, but there might be one or two I didn't notice come in."

Jenkins approached the two. He spoke to the slim man. "I'm Detective Jenkins of the Dennis Police Department. I'd like to ask you a question or two if you don't mind?"

"How can I help you?" said Zack Aaron.

"Do you have some identification?"

Zack took out his drivers' license and handed it to Jenkins.

"Mr. Aaron, can you tell me what kind of vehicle you're driving?"

"That red '69 Camero out there in the parking lot." Zack pointed through the windows in the back of the bar to a beautiful, antique 1969 Camero Z-28 that was parked on an angle in the lot.

"Nice car," said Jenkins.

"Sure is. I restored it myself. What's this all about Detective?"

"Nothing you need to worry about Mr. Aaron. I'm looking for someone driving a four-wheel drive vehicle that can be used off-road."

"Well, that wouldn't be me. I'd never try to take the Z off-road."

Jenkins handed Zack his license back. "Thanks for the time Mr. Aaron. Sorry to bother you."

"No problem."

Detective Jenkins walked back to the hostess station and spoke with Amy Martin again.

"Did anyone come to mind while I was talking to the bartender?"

"Sorry Detective. I didn't come up with anything new."

"Thanks anyway," said Jenkins and he exited the restaurant.

Getting into his vehicle, he remembered he had put his catch in the cooler in the back and decided it was time to get it home and into the refrigerator. He headed for home. After stowing his gear, he put the striper in the refrigerator. Then he took the blue fish and cut off the fillets.

Next he took out a frying pan and put about a quarter inch of water in it. He put the skinned fillets into the frying pan, covered it and turned the range on to medium high heat. In a few minutes, the fish was being poached. When the fish looked tender, he took a teaspoon and carefully removed the dark stripes from the fillets. He discarded the dark meat. Then he took the fish and put it into a food processor. He added two tablespoons of tartar sauce and one tablespoon of sweet pickle relish. He turned on the food processor just long enough to blend the mixture. He poured the mixture into a plastic container and covered it. He put the mixture into the refrigerator to chill. The dip would be ready for Katherine tomorrow. The flavors would be better blended if it sat overnight.

After cleaning up, Jenkins decided he would take a ride by Katherine's to see who was there. He parked a few houses away so he had a clear view of her place. In her driveway, he saw a Silverado truck. He thought it might be the same one he saw when he was up at Chapin Beach the one Ed Phillips was driving.

After a half hour or so, Jenkins could see the downstairs lights go off and the upstairs lights in the house come on. They were only on for a few minutes and then the whole house was dark. The Silverado remained parked in the driveway. He knew what it meant so he decided to leave.

Since he was already out, he decided to stop in to Sundancers and see if he could learn anything new. He took up a stool by the door. Dee Crowe asked him what he would like to have.

"I'll have a beer."

"So Detective, anything new?"

"I have a few leads I'm working on. Have you overheard anything here at the bar?"

"Now that you mention it, Ron and I were just talking about the attacks on Ann and Tina. The two of them are sitting over there in the corner and we overheard them talking about it."

"Anything interesting?"

"Could be. One of them said something about wanting to keep things private because she was having an affair with one of the higher ups in town."

"Did you hear who they were talking about?"

"Someone named Lou. I didn't get the last name."

Jenkins thought about it. His boss had the first name of Lou. Could Tomlinson be having an affair with one of the cougars? As he was sipping his beer, Linda Sage who had been sitting a few stools away was having a conversation with Bobby Jones that Jenkins could hear.

"Bobby, why don't we get out of here and go over to my place."

"I'd like to go somewhere private with you Linda. You know I have been after you for some time."

Linda put her hands on the outside of each breast and pressed in. "You have been after these for some time. Now it's time you met them. Plus, I talked with Sue and she said you'll make it worth my while."

"Sue said that, did she?"

"She did."

"Well, she would know."

"Yes, she would. Now let's go to my place."

"I'm all yours."

The two got up and left the bar. As they did, Ron took out a dollar and handed it to Dee. "You win," he said.

Jenkins had just observed one of the cougar attacks first hand. When Linda and Bobby had left, Jenkins turned his attention to the other side of the bar. Kenny Brown who had been there just watching Linda and Bobby started to get up and knocked his stool over. He seemed to be a little inebriated. Kenny headed for the door right after Linda and Bobby. Jenkins wondered if Kenny was going after them.

When Kenny was gone, Jenkins took his beer and walked to the back corner where Ann Benard and Tina Fletcher were sitting talking. The two were talking about Tina's situation as he approached. He only caught a little of what they were saying but he did hear Tina say, "How did you know about Lou?" They stopped talking when they saw him a few feet away from them.

"Hello Detective," said Ann.

"Yes, hello Frank," added Tina.

"How are you doing Ms. Benard, Ms. Fletcher?"

"Just fine detective," said Tina. "What brings you in here tonight?"

"I was just finishing up my shift and wanted to stop in for a cold one on the way home."

"Do you have any plans for the night, Detective?" asked Tina.

"Just to get some rest and wind down."

"I know a great way to unwind. Care for company?"

Ann Benard sensing Tina was about to pounce said, "I'll talk with you tomorrow Tina. I'm going to see if I can get that new guy to buy me a drink."

"Ok Ann. Later."

Ann Benard got up and left the two sitting in the darkened corner at the back of the bar.

Tina moved closer to Detective Jenkins and put her hand on his knee. She moved it up a little. "I could help you relax."

"I think I know what you mean. I'm not sure I'm up to it."

"Why don't you let me be the judge? Why don't we get out of here?"

"Where would you like to go?"

"I have a king size bed at my place, why don't we go there?"

"Do you want to come with me or have me follow you to your place?"

"I want you to come with me."

"What about my vehicle?"

"You can get it later."

The two left the bar together. They got into Tina's Pontiac G-6. She had Jenkins drive. As they pulled out of the parking lot, she dropped out of sight. She said, "You drive, I'll warm you up."

Jenkins pulled out onto Route 28 heading east with a big smile.

Chapter 20

At around mid-day, a call came into the Dennis Police department.

"Dennis Police Department, this is Officer Trudy speaking, how may I help you?"

"Officer, my name is George Fishman. I live at 283 Whig Street in Dennis. I was just outside working in my yard when I was confronted by a mountain lion."

"Mr. Fishman, you say you were attacked by a mountain lion?"

"Not attacked, but confronted."

"Are you sure you saw a mountain lion?"

"It was certainly a big cat. Not a tiger or lion in size, but smaller. It was the size of a Great Dane."

"About how long ago did you see the animal?"

"Hold on a minute."

Officer Trudy could hear the phone being put down on a counter. He could hear footsteps going away and then coming back.

"Officer, the animal is still in my back yard. The thing is playing with my kid's basketball."

"What do you mean playing?"

"It keeps hitting the ball around the yard with its paws and then chasing it."

"Mr. Fishman, the animal you see is a cougar we think escaped from the ZooQuarium in Yarmouth. While it's a trained animal and not known to attack people, we would like you and your family to remain inside until the ZooQuarium people can get there."

"Ok officer."

"Mr. Fishman, if the animal looks like it is going to leave your yard, please call back right away."

"Got it officer."

Officer Trudy hung up and immediately summoned Sergeant Grimes.

"Sergeant, I just got a call from a resident on Whig Street. He says the cougar we're looking for is in his back yard right now."

"Trudy, have Officer Brickman take over the desk and you go up to Whig Street to assist in the capture of the animal. I'll call Detective Jenkins and have him meet you there."

"Will do Sergeant."

Officer Trudy went back into the squad room and got Officer Brickman to man the phones. Then she left to go to the Fishman home. After talking with Officer Trudy, Sergeant Grimes called the ZooQuarium. He asked to speak with the zoo manager.

"Mr. Carson speaking."

"Mr. Carson, it's Sergeant Grimes of the Dennis Police Department. We just got a call from a resident at 283 Whig Street who said your cougar is in his back yard. Can you send someone up there to try to capture the animal right away?"

"Sure Sergeant. I'll have Joe Mains go there right away."

"I've dispatched Officer Trudy to meet your guy at the location and I'll be calling Detective Jenkins as soon as I hang up."

"I'm on it Sergeant."

Mr. Carson punched the intercom for the zoo and asked Joe Mains to come to the office right away. A few minutes later, Joe Mains came through the door.

"What's up?"

190

"Charlie has been seen up on Whig Street. A Mr. Fishman who lives at 283 Whig Street called the police station and said Charlie was in his back yard."

"Is he still there?"

"Sergeant Grimes of the Dennis PD said he's still there. Get up there right away and see if you can capture him."

"Will do."

Sergeant Grimes called the Department of Environmental Services offices in Town hall. Ben Becker was on duty.

"Becker here, whom am I speaking with?"

"This is Sergeant Grimes from Dennis PD. Listen Becker, do you have anyone who can assist with the capture of that cougar that escaped from the ZooQuarium?"

"Where is the animal?"

"Up at 283 Whig Street in a back yard. The homeowner called in and said a mountain lion is in his back yard right now."

"I'll handle it myself Sergeant."

"Officer Trudy is responding as we speak and someone from the ZooQuarium is en route."

"I'll look for them when I get there."

"You might be the first one on site as you're probably the closest right now."

"Got it. I'll look for Officer Trudy and the ZooQuarium people once I'm on site."

"Thanks Becker."

Ben Becker closed up the office right away and hung a sign on the door indicating the office was closed for the afternoon. He got into the drab green Jeep and headed up to Whig Street as fast as he could go. As he raced up Corporation Road nearing Whig Street, he thought he saw the cougar going in the opposite direction. He kept going around the bend and didn't turn on to Whig Street.

Joe Mains left the office and got into the pickup truck with the cage in the back. He had left the tranquilizer gun in the truck from the previous attempts at finding Charlie so he was already prepared to try to catch him. It took him about twenty minutes to make his way from the ZooQuarium on Route 28 all the way up to Whig Street on the north side of town.

As he pulled up to number 283, a Dennis PD cruiser was parked at the end of the driveway. Some of the neighbors where starting to mill around in the street. The police officer, Pam Trudy as he recalled, was asking them to please go inside. She was explaining that an animal had escaped from the Zoo and they were trying to capture it. Joe Mains knocked on the front door. Mr. Fishman answered it.

"I'm Joe Mains from the ZooQuarium. Are you the person who reported seeing a cougar in your yard?"

"The officer I talked to at the police station said the animal was a trained animal. That's probably why it was playing with the basketball in the back yard. It wandered off a few minutes ago."

"Mr. Fishman, can you show me where you last saw Charlie?"

"How did you know my name?"

"The Sergeant who called us gave us your name and address. That's how I knew where to show up."

"Come this way Mr. Mains."

Mr. Fishman escorted Joe Mains through his house to the kitchen at the back of the house.

"Please wait here Mr. Fishman. I'd like to see if I can catch Charlie without spooking him."

They both looked out the windows but Charlie was nowhere to be seen.

"I don't see him," said Mains.

"But he probably didn't go far. He seems to be comfortable in this neighborhood. We've had a number of sightings over the last couple days."

Joe Mains opened the back door and stepped out onto the back deck. He looked to the shed and then all around the yard. Charlie wasn't in view. There were woods in back of the shed. Joe couldn't see any other houses as he looked around. He walked back to the door and opened it.

"Mr. Fishman, how far do those woods go?"

Mr. Fishman said, "Down to Beach Street in that direction and then to Corporation Road the other way. There is another street with homes on it about a quarter of a mile back through the woods."

Joe Mains thought about it for a minute and then went to the front door. He motioned for Officer Trudy to come and talk with him.

"Officer Trudy, Charlie left the back yard before I could get a chance to see him. Since you've been out here, have any of the neighbors reported seeing Charlie?"

"No they haven't. I've been trying to keep them inside while you checked on the cat."

"He's only been gone for a few minutes so I don't think he's gone very far."

"What do you want to do?"

"You go that way towards Corporation Road and I'll go the other way. Go slowly and keep an eye out for him. He will probably show himself very soon."

"Ok Joe. I'll call your cell if I see him."

"Thanks. I'll do the same."

The two got into their respective vehicles and started off in opposite directions. After about five minutes, Joe Mains heard a gun shot. He turned his vehicle around and headed back in the direction he had come on Whig Street. Just around the turn from the Fishman residence near the intersection with Corporation Road, he could see the police cruiser stopped in the middle of the street with the door open. He approached and stopped his vehicle. Getting out, he didn't know what direction to pursue until he looked further down the street and saw Officer Trudy coming out of the woods with her weapon drawn. He ran up to her.

"Did you see Charlie?"

"No. Someone else took a shot from over there." She was pointing around the bend on Corporation Road. "I was afraid it might be one of the residents taking matters into their own hands."

The two started to walk back in the direction Officer Trudy thought the shot had come from when a man in a dark green uniform appeared coming out of the woods. The two immediately recognized him.

"Ben, did you just take a shot?"

"Sure did. He's laying over there about a three hundred feet into the woods."

Joe Mains heart was racing. Ben didn't have a gun with him.

"What did you shoot him with?"

"My shotgun. I used one of those tranquilizer rounds you left with me yesterday. I left my shotgun next to a big oak tree so I could easily find the animal when we go back in. Charlie will probably be out for a while as the tranquilizer takes hold so I thought I would just walk away and let the tranquilizer do its thing."

"Good thinking Ben. Let's get back to my truck and get the stretcher. He'll probably be ready to transport by the time we get back to him."

Officer Trudy said, "I'll stay here and keep everyone away from the scene while you two round Charlie up."

"Thanks Officer Trudy," said Joe.

Ben Becker led Joe Mains to the spot where he had left his shotgun. A few feet further and there he was, sound asleep from the tranquilizer.

"I'm glad we were able to recapture Charlie. He's a good cougar. My boss is sure going to be happy."

194

"How long will the tranquilizer last?"

"It should be good for about two hours."

Joe put the stretcher along side Charlie and got Ben to grab the hind legs while Joe took hold of the front legs. They pulled Charlie onto the stretcher. Joe tucked Charlie's head between his front legs. Then he used the tie down straps to secure the animal to the stretcher. Ben took the back and Joe the front. The two lifted Charlie and walked out of the woods. As they reached the truck, Officer Trudy already had the cage door open in the back. Joe put the front of the stretcher on the truck floor and assisted Ben in pushing Charlie into the back of the truck. While they were loading Charlie into the truck, some of the neighbors had come out and were talking about it.

"Did you see the size of that lion they just loaded into the truck?" said one woman.

"I can't believe that thing was in our neighborhood," said another.

Officer Trudy asked them to please keep back. She also said the animal was actually a cougar and it could be seen at the ZooQuarium in Yarmouth. With Charlie secure in the truck, Joe Mains thanked Officer Trudy and DEP officer Becker. He drove Charlie back to the ZooQuarium.

As the pickup left the scene, Detective Jenkins pulled up and got out of his vehicle.

"Officer Trudy, what's going on?"

"We just captured the cougar that had escaped from the ZooQuarium."

"Alive or dead?" asked Jenkins.

"Alive. DEP Officer Ben Becker was able to tranquilize the animal. Joe Mains from the ZooQuarium just left with him."

"I passed a ZooQuarium truck on my way here."

"He has the cat in the back."

"Well, thank God that ended well."

195

"Yes it did."

"Now if only the other cougar investigations will go as well."

"Is there anything more you want me to do here Frank?"

"No. Write up your report when you get back. I think we're all set here."

"Got it."

Officer Trudy started to walk back to her vehicle.

"Pam?"

"Yes Frank."

"Can you go by the ZooQuarium and make sure they get the cougar back into its compound? I just want to make sure this has ended."

"Will do Frank. I'll see you back at the station in about an hour."

"Thanks Pam."

Jenkins got back into his vehicle and went back to the station. Officer Trudy stopped in at the ZooQuarium. Charlie was already back in his compound, still resting comfortably. Joe Mains saw her looking at Charlie. "He's back home. He'll eat and then sleep for a while. Tomorrow, I'll check him out just make sure he's all right. He looks like he missed a few meals. You might want to come by and see the show sometime Officer Trudy. Here are a few passes. Thanks for helping me capture him."

Officer Trudy took the passes, "You're welcome. Maybe I'll do that."

Chapter 21

Arriving back at the Police Station, Officer Trudy reported in to the desk Sergeant.

"Sergeant Grimes, we caught the cougar that had escaped from the ZooQuarium."

"That's good news Trudy. I'm sure Detective Jenkins will be happy to hear the news."

"He already knows. I saw him up on Whig Street where we caught the cat. Is he in his office?"

"Yes. He came in a few minutes before you."

"I'm going to go and talk to him for a few minutes. Then I'll write up my report."

"Sure. Anything I need to know?"

"No. I'll cover the whole capture in my report."

"Ok. Let me have a copy of it before you leave for the night."

"Will do."

Officer Trudy went down the hall and knocked on Detective Jenkins office door.

"Come in."

"Frank, I went to the ZooQuarium like you asked and the cougar is safe and secure. The folks over there gave us a few passes for any show as a token of their appreciation. Mr. Carson said to say thank you for your help."

She handed him the passes for the ZooQuarium show and he put them in the file he had for the case.

"Good. Now I can put that aspect of the attacks to rest. Tell me again what happened."

Officer Trudy took the next ten minutes to summarize what had taken place. When she was done, Detective Jenkins asked her to put everything into her report and to send him a copy. She said he would have it in about a half hour. Officer Trudy left his office to begin writing her report.

A little after five in the afternoon, Linda was sitting at the corner of the bar at Sundancers talking with Ron Jessup. Tommy Anderson and his baseball teammate Paul Bremer came in and took up the stools next to Linda. Paul kept looking past Tommy at Linda. She was dressed in a pretty skimpy outfit for her figure. She had on a pair of shorts, sandals and a rather snug low cut blue turquoise top.

Ron, seeing Paul starring at Linda said, "What will it be gentlemen?"

"Two cold buds Ron," came back the reply from Tommy. "And get Linda here another of whatever she's drinking."

"Why thank you Tommy," Linda replied. She turned and looked at the two. "Another baseball game?"

"Yeah," said Tommy. "We beat up on A-1 Auto."

"Tommy hit two home runs," added Paul.

"How about you Paul, hit any home runs lately," said Linda looking past Tommy aware of Paul starring at her.

"Nah, but I did score a few times."

"I'll bet. What about tonight? Either of you want to score again?" Linda asked as she took a sip of her vodka and tonic.

"What do you have in mind?" Tommy asked.

"Well let's see. Paul scored. Tommy, you hit a home run. I think I might be up for a double."

Paul looked at Tommy and smiled. Then he thought about what Linda was saying. "Too bad I have a prior

198

commitment for tonight. I would have loved to be in that game." He kept starring at her rose tattoo.

Linda saw him looking down at her. She looked down and then looked back at him and smiled. "Too bad."

Tommy, taking the lead said, "How about a single?"

"I might be up for single, but I was hoping for extra bases."

"I swing a big bat and I'm always looking for the long one."

"Me too," Linda came back.

The door to the bar opened and Tom Bowman came in. He took up a stool on the opposite of the bar from Linda, Tommy and Paul. He ordered a rum and coke, and for the next half hour, he sat and watched as Tommy tried to work his magic on Linda. After another two drinks, Paul Bremer got up to leave and Tommy went outside with him for a few minutes. When they had gone outside, Linda found herself sitting there alone. As she scanned the bar, Tom Bowman was the only target she could see who was by himself. She picked up her drink and walked over to where he was seated.

"Hi, I'm Linda Sage."

"Tom Bowman."

"Mind if I join you?"

"Please do."

Linda took up the stool next to Tom. They started up some small talk. Tommy Anderson came back in taking up the stool he had left. He saw Linda on the opposite side of the bar talking to another man. He had lost his chance for that night.

"I've seen you in here a few times before," said Linda.

"I used to live in this area and had moved out of state for awhile."

"Where did you move to?"

"Virginia."

"Didn't like it down there?"

"Things didn't work out for me down there."

Linda looked carefully at Tom's hands to see if he had a ring or not. He did not. "So, are you here with anyone?"

"No. I just stopped in for a drink."

"Have any plans for the night?"

"Not yet. Do you have anything in mind?"

"Could be." She ran her hand along her shirt making sure she exposed more than she should have. "It looks like it might be a hot night."

"Yeah, it's kinda humid."

"I like to go skinny dipping up in the bay on humid nights."

"That sounds like it could be fun. I would love to get to see you skinny dipping."

"Maybe we could try it sometime."

"I'd like that."

The two chatted like old friends for well over an hour. The time passing as quickly as the many drinks they had.

"Please excuse me for a minute Tom; I have to go to the ladies room."

"I could use a pit stop myself."

The two got up and went to the respective rest rooms. Tom came out of the restroom first and went back to where the two had been sitting. He took up his stool. He took something out of his pocket and dropped it into her drink. He looked towards the ladies room waiting for Linda to return.

When she came back, she picked up the drink and took a sip. The contents of the capsule he put into her drink while she was away was colorless and tasteless making it undetectable to the drinker.

About a half hour later, Kenny Brown came into Sundancers. He walked over to where Tommy Anderson was seated and talked to Tommy for a few minutes. Then he

200

walked around to where Linda was seated talking with Tom Bowman and took up the other stool on Linda's other side.

"Hey Linda. What's going on?"
"I'm just having a drink with Tom here."
Kenny leaned back and extended his hand.
"Kenny Brown."
"Tom Bowman."
"Tom just moved back from Virginia. I was just telling him about how I like skinny dipping in the bay on humid nights like tonight."
"I'm going up there in an hour or so. Maybe I could join you?"
"A double after all, what a game," Linda responded.
Tom said to her, "Maybe another time."
"You might enjoy it Tom. Why not give it a try?"
"I'll pass," he replied.

Linda said she was going to go home and get the things she needed to go to the bay. She told Kenny she would meet him at Corporation Beach in about an hour and he should meet her there. Linda got up and left Sundancers. After a few minutes, Tom Bowman paid his tab and left. Around forty-five minutes later, Kenny paid his tab and left.

Driving home, Linda started to feel a little groggy. When she got to her place at 26 William Crowell Road, she parked her car in the driveway and went inside to gather her things. She packed a bag with a beach towel, pint of vodka and bottle of tonic. She put two plastic glasses in the bag along with a zip-lock bag with a few ice cubes in it. She went to her bedroom to put on a throw dress to wear while driving to the beach. She took off all of her clothes and that was the last thing she remembered doing.

When he got to her house, Linda's car was in the driveway. He knew she was home. There were only a few lights on. He parked down the street and walked up to the edge of the yard. The houses on the street were spaced out fairly well. Linda's house was on a lot that was about four acres in size. On the east side of the house stood a stand of trees and shrubs that blocked the view from everyone except someone in the house who might be looking out of a window. He crept up to the back window that was illuminated with light. Peering in, he could see Linda lying naked on her bed. She didn't stir. He watched her for ten minutes. She lay in the same position the whole time. The only movement he could detect was in the rise and fall of her large breasts that moved up and down with each breath. She had one leg bent into a triangle position presenting a partial view as he looked up past her thighs. She looked stunning. He knew the drug had taken effect. Walking to the side door by the driveway, he found it open, and stepped inside.

He worked his way down a hallway to the room at the end that had the light on. He checked to see if anything had changed. Linda lay in the same position on the bed, naked. For a minute, he looked at her naked body and smiled. He walked over to her and bent down so as to speak softly into her ear. He said to her, "I'm here for you." She did not respond.

Throughout the whole episode, Linda maintained a normal breathing pattern. She had no idea of what was taking place. He couldn't help but notice she had no expression at all. He reached into his pants and took a zip-lock out of his pocket. He opened it and then squeezed the contents on to her. He sealed the zip-lock back up. Then he put the zip-lock back into his pants pocket. He left the same way he had come in.

After waiting at the beach for nearly an hour, Kenny decided he would have to see what happened to Linda. He drove over to her house. Linda's car was in the driveway so he pulled in. He parked behind her car and went to the side door. It was unlocked so he let himself in.

202

"Linda, you home?"

No answer. He could see the light was on at the end of the hall so he thought she might be in the adjoining bathroom. He walked down the hall. When he looked in, he saw her out cold lying naked on the bed.

"Drank too much," he said disappointedly.

He went over to her and kissed her on the lips. She stirred.

"I thought you and I were going skinny dipping at the beach?"

Linda was groggy, "What time is it?"

"Around eleven thirty."

"I must have passed out."

"Looks like it."

"I had a dream I was having sex."

"Why dream? I'm here."

"Then join me."

Kenny took his clothes off and joined her. He took a condom out of his pocket and put it on.

"You know I don't like those things."

"Just being careful."

"You don't have to be with me."

"I have to be with everyone."

"You guys. Well then bring it here."

The two embraced in the traditional position. Kenny moved in and they spent the next half hour sweating and moaning in ecstasy. As Linda got up, she could feel liquid going down her leg.

"Looks like it broke," she said as she wiped herself with a towel.

"I don't think so," said Kenny as he retrieved the condom from the trash and held it up. It contained a fair amount of semen. There was nothing leaking out.

"Then where did this come from?" asked Linda quizzically.

"Not me," Kenny replied. "Maybe someone else was here before I got here," he added.

"Not funny."

Linda was concerned because she always knew her partners. She had been raped once before and didn't want to find herself in a situation that might jeopardize her health. That certainly could happen if she wasn't careful.

Kenny got dressed, "That was pretty good although I was looking forward to skinny dipping."

"Kenny, you just wanted to have sex and you did. Now go home."

"Ok Linda, but next time, we go skinny dipping."

"Sure. Next time."

Kenny left and Linda kept thinking, "How did that semen get there? Maybe it wasn't semen. Maybe it really was Kenny's and the condom only looked intact. I don't remember having so much to drink that I would lose hours. What happened that I don't remember?"

In the morning, she would find out. She took the used condom out of the trash and put it in a small zip-lock bag and then went to bed for the rest of the night.

When she got up the next morning she dressed and took the zip-lock bag with her. She drove to the Dennis Police Station. Approaching the desk, she explained her concern to the desk officer who called for a detective.

"Detective Jenkins."

"Ms. Sage, what brings you here?"

"Detective, last night, after having sex with a man at my house, I noticed semen."

"Isn't that what usually happens?"

"Yes, but he used a condom."

"Maybe it didn't work."

"It did, but I can't explain how semen is inside the condom and outside."

"What do you mean outside?"

"When I was cleaning up, liquid was going down my leg."

"Did you have sex when your partner didn't have the condom on?"

"No, and that's what's bothering me. I have the condom with me. Can you have it tested?"

"We don't usually do that unless a crime has been committed."

"One might have been. I may have been drugged or something last night, because there are hours that I don't remember before my date found me."

"Don't you know if you had sex with someone else recently?"

"Look detective, I'm very careful with whom I have sex. And I always use protection."

"Ok Ms. Sage. Give me the condom. I'll see what I can do."

"Thank you Detective."

Linda Sage handed him the zip-lock bag. Detective Jenkins took it and placed it in an evidence folder. He wrote her name on it and sealed it.

"This will take a little while. Once I have the results, I'll get back to you."

"Thank you."

Linda left the station. Detective Jenkins took the folder to the lab and asked that DNA tests be performed on the condom inside and outside. Later that afternoon, he got the results back. The lab indicated there was DNA on both the inside and outside of the condom and that the DNA was from three people. The strange thing the lab technician reported was that the condom was intact, yet the semen both inside and outside were from the same person. There was vaginal DNA on the outside of the condom. The lab technician also said they found a few hairs on the condom but the hairs were from another person.

Jenkins read the report, "Bad memory Ms. Sage. Looks like you had sex with the same man multiple times in the last day, both with and without a condom." He read further down and noticed the DNA for the semen matched the DNA the lab had on file from a recent test performed in another case. That DNA matched Kenny Brown. Now, who did the hairs belong to?

Chapter 22

Jenkins turned back to his computer and opened up the file for the Linda Sage. He spoke out loud to himself, "There were two male DNA samples on the condom plus the DNA from Ms. Sage and hairs from an unidentified person. The male DNA samples were from the same person, one on the inside, one on the outside." He thought about it for a few minutes. Turning away from the computer, Jenkins said, "So you had sex with the same guy with and without the condom, Ms. Sage. Now I'm going to have to find out if you were attacked or if your memory is just lacking."

He closed the file in his computer and finished up his paperwork. As he left his office, he stopped at the duty desk. "I'll be over at Sundancers trying to get more information about the attacks I'm investigating. If anyone needs me, call me on my cell."

"Got it Detective," said the duty officer.

Walking into Sundancers, Detective Jenkins observed most of the people he had been interviewing were seated around the bar. He saw Linda Sage on the far side and went over to her. Linda was dressed in her usual, tight top; low cut showing more than it should over a pair of shorts.

"Ms. Sage, may we talk for a few minutes?"

"Sure Detective. Let's go out on the deck. It will be a little quieter there."

The two walked out onto the deck overlooking the Bass River. There was only one other couple on the deck making it easier to find a quiet corner to talk.

"What's up Detective?"

"I got the lab report back on the evidence you gave me. It showed semen DNA from only one male, Kenny Brown. The strange thing is the DNA was on the inside and outside of the condom and the condom didn't have any leaks. The report also said they found hairs from another person."

"How could that be?" Linda said loudly.

"You must have had sex with the Mr. Brown with and without the condom."

"Impossible. I only had sex with Mr. Brown after he came over to my house and found me. He used a condom and who could those hairs be from?"

"Are you sure he didn't do something to you that you just don't remember?"

"Think about it Detective. Why would he? We had sex once he woke me up. Wouldn't he have had to have sex with me back to back within a short period of time? I don't think so."

"So how do you explain the DNA?"

"Look Detective. I know I'm pretty active sexually. One thing I know is when I'm doing it and with whom."

"That may be, but if you passed out, maybe someone went home with you and you just don't remember."

"I'd remember. Plus, I didn't have enough to drink to pass out. I drove myself home. Someone must have drugged me."

"If you think that, then I'd like you to have your blood tested. Since it has been less than twenty four hours, there is a good chance that if you were drugged, traces of the substance might still be in your body."

"Tell me where to go and I'll have it done."

"I'd suggest you go down to the Cape Cod Hospital Emergency Room and ask the admissions manager to have a blood sample taken. I'll call ahead and let them know you're coming in at my request. Before you go, tell me again about last night."

"I spent the afternoon shopping at the Cape Cod Mall. Then I stopped in here around four. Tommy Anderson and that friend of Tommy's, Paul came in after their baseball game. There were others, but I didn't talk to them."

"Did any of them buy you a drink?"

"Sure. Tommy bought me a drink. Oh yeah, Tom Bowman bought me a few drinks too."

"So you know Mr. Bowman?"

"I didn't until recently. Why do you ask about him? Do you think he drugged me?"

"I didn't say that."

"Do you know him?"

"He was involved in another case I worked on a while back."

"I think I know the name. Isn't he the guy who was with Katherine Sterns husband when he died in the ice fishing accident last year?"

"He's the same person."

"I'll have to talk with Kat about him."

"I'd prefer it if you didn't. For now, leave the investigating up to me. If he has anything to do with this, you might spook him."

"Oh I wasn't talking about the case. I want to know more about him."

"What do you mean?"

"I think he likes me and if Katherine knows him, I want to know more."

"Like what else?" Jenkins thought to himself.

Linda continued, "A little while later, Kenny Brown came in. We had a drink and then decided to go up to the bay for a swim."

"All three of you?"

"No. Tom didn't want to be a threesome so it was just going to be Kenny and me."

"So you left with Kenny?"

"No, I left by myself. I was stopping at my place to get a few things and then Kenny was supposed to meet me at the beach."

"Do you know if Kenny went there?"

"He said he did, and waited over an hour for me. When I didn't show up, he came to my house."

"Do you know what time that was?"

"After eleven. I remember because he woke me up and then joined me in bed."

"Is that when you had sex with Mr. Brown?"

"Yes. I owed it to him after making him wait all that time for me at the beach. Plus he was thoughtful enough to check on me when I didn't show."

"Does Kenny have a key to your house?"

"No. My side door wasn't locked because I was just stopping in for a few minutes to pick up things to take to the beach."

"About how long would you estimate elapsed between your getting home and Kenny waking you?"

"I'd guess about two hours."

"And when you woke up, did anything seem out of the ordinary?"

"Everything was out of the ordinary. I was naked, lying on my bed. I had a headache and was rather groggy. The lights were on in my bedroom."

"Do you have window treatments on your windows?"

"Yes."

"Do you know if they were drawn or not?"

"They were not."

"So someone could have looked in from the outside and observed you in your bedroom?"

Linda stopped for a moment and thought about it. "If someone were outside my house, that person could have easily looked into my bedroom. If I didn't have any clothes on..." She stopped and didn't finish the sentence.

"Someone could have followed you home and waited until you passed out. If someone were looking through your windows and saw you lying naked on the bed passed out, that person could have come in the same unlocked door and assaulted you."

"Who would have the nerve to do something like that?"

"Let me tell you Ms. Sage, there are some real perverted people in this world. You laying on your bed naked like that and out cold would have been an easy invitation for a predator."

"Then I need to get to the hospital and have that test done right away."

"Ok. You go to the hospital and I'll phone in the request to the ER."

"Thank you Detective."

Linda Sage got up and left. She was on her way to the hospital ER to have the blood test performed.

After Linda had left, Jenkins called the hospital emergency room and told the receptionist he was sending down a Linda Sage to have a blood test. He told her the tests were part of an ongoing investigation and a copy of the report would need to be sent to the police department. The receptionist said they would have Linda sign the appropriate paperwork releasing the information to the police and the department would be billed for the test. Before hanging up, Jenkins said he would like to have an internal test performed as well. He told the receptionist the case might be a drug rape case. The receptionist said she understood and she would talk with the doctor. Jenkins thanked the receptionist and hung up.

When Linda arrived at the hospital ER, she approached the receptionist.

"My name is Linda Sage. I'm here for a test at the request of Detective Jenkins of the Dennis Police Department."

"Yes Ms. Sage. Detective Jenkins called and said you would be coming in for a test. If you will fill out these papers, the doctor will be with you in a few minutes."

"What are the papers for?"

"Name, address and such. Plus you have to give the hospital permission to release the test results to the police department."

"Ok."

She filled out the form and took a seat.

A few minutes later a nurse came out.

"Ms. Sage."

Linda followed the nurse into an examination room.

"Ms. Sage, please remove your blouse, shorts and underwear and put on this smock. Then come up on the table."

"My shorts and underwear. Why do I need to remove them for a blood test?"

"We need to do an internal as well."

"Why an internal?"

"The Detective requested an internal be performed to determine if there was evidence of rape."

"I gave the Detective the condom that was in my house and supposedly it had DNA on it."

"That may be Ms. Sage. If foreign DNA is found during an internal, the lab test can confirm the DNA. The Detective thought it might prove helpful in his investigation and possible prosecution. Evidence collected at a hospital may be viewed more favorably in court than what you provided."

Linda did as instructed. She got up on the table and sat on the edge. After a knock on the door, a doctor came in.

"I'm Dr. Warren Ms. Sage. I'll be taking the samples. Could you please lie back and put your legs in the stirrups."

"Sure," she said as she lay back and spread her legs placing a foot in each

"This shouldn't hurt."

212

Doctor Warren took a long thin swab and took a sample from Linda. He removed it and placed it in a container and sealed it. Then he repeated the procedure a second time. When he was done, he took a syringe and took a blood sample from her arm. He labeled the test tube and put a bandage over the needle mark.

"That's it. I'll send these to the lab and the results will be sent to the Detective in a little while."

Linda got up. She dressed and then left the hospital. Driving down Route 28, she thought, "I need a drink." So she made the left turn after crossing the Bass River Bridge back into Sundancers parking lot.

Walking into Sundancers, she observed Detective Jenkins still sitting at the bar talking with Dee, Margarita and Ron. She approached.

"The doctor said you should have the results in a little while."

"Thank you for going down there promptly Ms. Sage. If your suspicion is correct, the test results might help us identify who has been committing these attacks on you and your friends."

"I hope so Detective. Having that test is very humiliating."

"How so?"

"I'm used to having men down there in moments of lust, but having a doctor and nurse looking at my open legs and inserting something up there isn't my idea of a good time."

"It was necessary in order to get a good DNA sample. What we're hoping for is a sample that does not match Mr. Brown."

"Why?"

"Well, if Mr. Brown's DNA is found, then the condom theory is out, but if his isn't the only one present, then someone else was there."

"I hope you can use the results to find out who did this to me."

"I'll let you know what the lab says when I get the results."

"Thanks Detective."

Linda got up and went around to the other side of the bar. She saw Katherine Sterns sitting talking to Ed Phillips. She took up the stool next to Katherine on the other side from Ed.

"How are you doing Linda?" asked Katherine.

"I've had better days. I need a drink."

"What happened?"

"I just came back from the ER."

"Why? Are you OK?"

"No, not really. I think someone raped me last night."

"What do you mean, you think?"

"When I left here last night to meet Kenny at the beach, I went home to pick up a few things. On the way, I started to feel funny, like fuzzy. While I was changing, I must have passed out. A few hours later, Kenny woke me up when I didn't show at the beach."

"Did Kenny see someone at your house?"

"No, he said he found me lying naked on my bed."

"What makes you think someone raped you?"

"Kenny and I had sex, with a condom. But when I was cleaning up afterwards, there was semen on my leg that couldn't have come from the condom. Kenny took it off in the bathroom. Plus, in the morning I had it sent to the lab for testing. Detective Jenkins had me go to the ER and be tested. The results came back with semen DNA from only person, Kenny. But there was hair DNA that wasn't Kenny's and hasn't been matched to anyone yet. I have this weird lost feeling not knowing."

"Wow. So now you've been attacked. That makes Ann, Tina and now you. This has to be someone we all know."

"That's what the Detective thinks."

214

"I'm going to talk with him."

"Katherine, you don't have to pretend with me. I know you've been seeing him."

"I'm not pretending. This will be an official talk."

Ed had already picked up his drink and moved away to the other end of the bar. He started up a conversation with Ron about surf fishing. Neither Katherine nor Linda gave any thought to Ed moving as they were in a deep discussion about Linda's incident. After a few minutes, Linda looked past Katherine. "Good."

"What's good?" asked Katherine.

"That Ed moved down the bar. He blew me off the last time I talked to him here. Why do you talk to him?"

"What do you mean? Ed is good in bed and he's not a bad guy. He's well endowed, too."

"You've slept with him?" Linda asked in a surprised voice.

"Yes I have. I can tell you he knows his way around."

"Ed? Are we talking about the same geeky guy?"

"Don't let those looks and his act fool you. He's good."

"I never would have guessed."

"It's true. You should give him another try."

"Maybe I will, if he's nicer to me."

The two changed the subject. Linda indicated she just wanted to have a few drinks and forget about the events of the past twenty-four hours. After a few minutes, Kenny came over.

"How you doing Linda?"

"Better, now that I have had a few drinks."

"What did the doc say?"

"Not much but he sent samples to the lab for DNA testing."

"You know they'll find my DNA."

"It should only be in the condom."

"Where else could it be?"

"Inside me."

"That couldn't be. I used the condom and it didn't break."

"I know, but the lab found seminal DNA from one person, but other DNA from two different men. There were hairs that had a different DNA than the semen. It wasn't you. And on top of the DNA, a lubricant was identified."

"I didn't use any lubricant. Maybe it came from the condom."

"The lab report said the lubricant didn't come from the condom I sent them so I have no idea where it came from."

"So you slept with someone else before me yesterday?"

"If I did, it wasn't consensual. Someone might have gotten to me while I was out cold and that would be rape."

"You let me know if the lab can identify whose DNA it is. I'll take care of it."

"That's so like you Kenny. What are you going to do that the police can't do?"

"I would take care of it, properly. You don't worry."

"Kenny, Detective Jenkins over there is already investigating the incident. I don't think he would welcome your involvement."

"Just the same, let me know if you find out."

Kenny picked up his empty glass and went down the bar to the area where Ed was sitting. He took up a stool two away from Ed and told Ron he wanted another drink. When Ron brought him the drink, they talked about what Linda had told him. He reiterated his thoughts to Ron, "I'll get the bastard who did that."

Linda eventually came down and took up the empty stool between Ed and Kenny. She talked to Kenny for a few minutes and then turned to Ed.

"Ed, Katherine had some good things to say about you."

"Oh yeah, what did she say?"

"She just said that you are someone I should get to know better."

"She did, did she?"

"Yes, would you like to buy me a drink?"

"I don't think so. I don't think I'm interested," he mumbled under his breath something about seconds.

Linda didn't hear him.

"What did you say, Ed?"

"Nothing. Why don't you go back to talking to Kenny? He's more your type."

Linda was now more than a little put off. She turned her back on Ed and started to talk with Kenny again. When she did, Ed picked up his drink and moved away.

Ed had walked over by the DJ booth where a group had taken up seats around a few of the high top tables. Tina, Ann, Bobby, Tommy, Paul and Katherine were all talking about the attacks that had taken place. Ed stood behind Katherine and just listened.

"I'm telling you Bobby, someone is out to get all of the women who frequent this place," said Tina. "First it was Ann, then me, then Linda. I'll bet Katherine is coming up on the list."

Everyone turned and looked at Katherine.

"I don't have any enemies," Katherine responded.

"I don't think this is an enemy thing Katherine," said Ann. "I think it's a sex thing."

"What do you mean sex thing?" asked Katherine quizzically.

"Well, someone seems to be making a game out of stalking us one at a time and then attacking us. Sex and Sundancers seem to be the only things in common," added Ann.

"But you weren't sexually assaulted Ann," said Katherine.

"I was knocked out so I don't know what was done," said Ann.

"Didn't the doctor at the ER check you out for sexual assault?" asked Katherine.

"He did. He said there was no sign of forced penetration, but that doesn't mean the attack wasn't sexual in nature. It only means I didn't have any evidence of violence present when I was examined."

"You think who ever attacked you cleaned you up before leaving you?" asked Tommy.

"Anything could have happened Tommy. I was out cold."

Paul had a smile on his face. Ann looked at him. "What are you smiling about Paul?"

"I was just thinking about what it would be like to have my way with a woman to do anything I wanted," said Paul.

"You're sick Paul," said Katherine.

"Not sick Kat, just fantasizing."

"That isn't even fantasy Paul. Maybe we need to have the detective have a talk with you," added Ann.

"Don't bother with him Ann," commented Tommy. "Paul has had limited success with women."

"That's no excuse to be insensitive," said Tina.

"You're right, but you could cut him some slack," said Tommy.

"Cut him slack? Some sicko is out there attacking us. He could be doing who knows what to us when he renders us unconscious. I think the women here are the ones that should be given the consideration," fired back an angry Tina.

"Calm down Tina. I'm not saying anything about your predicament. I'm just saying Paul has some issues," replied Tommy.

Paul sat straight up. "What issues Tommy?"

"You know you're shy when it comes to women Paul. That's all I'm saying."

"I do ok," was Paul's response as he picked up his drink and got up from the table. He went back to the bar and left the others talking.

"See what I mean," said Tommy.

"Look Tommy, the ladies are concerned about what's been going on. I don't think anyone here has anything against Paul," said Bobby.

"Unless he's the one doing all the attacking," remarked Tina. "If he likes the sound of taking advantage of a woman, why wouldn't he act on it?"

"Paul is harmless," said Tommy.

"Maybe so, but I'm not going to be comfortable until the person who is doing all this is caught," said Ann.

"Me either," added Tina. "And you be careful Katherine. You may be next on the list if there is one."

"Why would anyone want to attack me?" Katherine laughed as she got up and started to walk away."

"Just be careful Kat," said Ann as she walked away with Katherine.

The group disbanded. They got up from the tables and took their drinks to different places at the bar.

Chapter 23

Detective Jenkins knocked on Captain Tomlinson's office door.

"Come in."

"Captain, I'd like to run a theory I have regarding the recent attacks against the middle aged women by you."

"Give me a minute Jenkins. I just need to finish this e-mail and then I'm all ears."

Captain Tomlinson completed the e-mail he had been working on. He logged out of the e-mail system and then got up and took a seat at the conference table in his office. "Ok, what do you have?"

"It looks to me like we have a stalker who wants to rape his victims. The stalker knows the victims, or at least knows of them. The stalker identifies his target at a public place and using information obtained by observation, he is able to position himself in front of his target and wait. When the situation is to his liking, he strikes."

"How do you know it's a man?"

"When you look at each situation, you will see how I arrived at that conclusion."

"Proceed."

"The first victim, Ms. Benard, was attacked at Chapin Beach. I think the attacker has a four wheel drive vehicle and had been there before, possibly a fisherman."

"Why do you say that?"

"The couple who found Ms. Benard said they heard a vehicle leaving the scene just before they found the victim. Ms. Benard said her vehicle was the only one in the lot and she didn't see another one arrive before being knocked out. So that means the person could have been waiting having driven his vehicle onto the off-road access. That would have hidden the vehicle from Ms. Benard."

"So you think this person attacked the victim, then re-entered the road from the access-road and took off?"

"Pretty much. Plus, a fisherman I spoke with remembered seeing a vehicle leaving the off-road access point shortly before the ambulance arrived. Since ninety-nine percent of the off-road vehicle usage is by male fisherman, I'd say any vehicle being driven off the beach at night was probably being driven by a man."

"What do you make of the scratch marks on the victim?"

"That kind of threw me off at first. The cougar escaping from the ZooQuarium made me think possibly the animal had been involved. Upon closer inspection, the scratches were too clean. Had an animal scratched her, the paramedics should have seen some dirt or sand in the scratch area. They were too clean. I think the attacker wore a pair of gloves. Take a look at these."

Jenkins handed a pair of gloves to the captain. They were durable cloth with plastic grips on the inside of the palm and fingers. The grips were pointed. They were not pointed enough to immediately cut the Captain's hand when he ran his fingers over them. They left scratch marks.

"Put one of the gloves on and grip your other hand with it," instructed Detective Jenkins.

Captain Tomlinson did as instructed. When he pulled the glove hand away from the exposed hand, visible scratches were on the non-glove hand.

"If the attacker were to squeeze hard enough and pull away, then scratches like those found on Ms. Benard could have happened."

"I see what you mean."

"So, given the strength required to make the marks, the off-road access probability and having knocked Ms. Benard out, I am pretty sure the attacker was a man."

"So if I buy the attacker being a man, how did the attacker know where to attack?"

"There were a number of suspects that knew Ms. Benard would be alone at Chapin Beach that night. Ms. Benard and Ms. Sterns had talked about Ms. Benard going to Chapin Beach while they were at the bar in Chapin's Restaurant. Anyone sitting at the bar could have overheard them."

"But why would the attacker be at Chapin's Restaurant at that time?"

"That might have been coincidental. I'm inclined to think the stalker knows the victims and where they frequent. The opportunity just happened and he took advantage of it."

"Seems like a coincidence to me," Tomlinson said.

"Not really. The bartenders at Chapin's Restaurant said a number of the single men at the bar knew the women. Some even talked with them. The bartender remembered a few of these men leaving around the same time as Ms. Benard."

"Why didn't the attacker sexually attack Ms. Benard?"

"When I talked with one of the men who had talked to Ms. Benard at the bar, he indicated he went up to Chapin Beach shortly after Ms. Benard did."

"Why didn't he see the attacker or the attacker's vehicle?"

"I think the attacker either heard or saw the other man's vehicle and hid. By then, Ms. Benard had already been knocked out and when she didn't answer the other man's calls, he left the scene. Then the attacker decided the risk level was too high and he decided to leave."

"When the two people who came upon Ms. Benard and found her, the woman had said Ms. Benard's pants were undone and slightly pulled down. I think the attacker was about to sexually assault her when the other vehicle arrived."

"Was there any DNA evidence on her?"

"No. So the attacker was probably just getting started."

"So you have a short list of suspects?"

"I do. If you'll bear with me, I think you'll see where all of this goes."

"Ok. What about the other attacks?"

"In the Tina Fletcher case, the facts get stretched a little. Ms. Fletcher had gone home and then on the spur of the moment took a walk on the beach. The only way the attacker could have known she was talking a walk on the beach would be if the attacker were watching her house or followed her home from the bar. Ms. Fletcher has motion sensors on the outside of her home that probably would have picked up the movements of any intruder approaching her home."

"About how long was it from the time she arrived home until she went outside to take the walk on the beach?" asked Tomlinson.

"She said she got herself a glass of wine and then went out to her deck. That was when she had decided to take the walk on the beach."

"If I recall, most of those motion sensor devices stay on for a little while after being activated. What if she activated the sensor in the front of her house when she got home and then activated the back sensor when she went out onto her deck? That might have provided a window for the attacker to approach without being noticed."

"That could be an answer. If that were the case and the attacker saw her heading towards the beach, he could have out flanked her and sought the right spot from which to spring an attack."

"So the facts aren't really far fetched are they Detective?"

"Plus, having found the woman's underwear that did have DNA on them along with Ms. Fletcher being tested for rape have provided us with the DNA we need to accurately identify the attacker."

Tomlinson looked at the things Jenkins had written on his board and asked, "Why is this guy knocking these women out and then having sex with them. Wouldn't that be like having sex with a dead fish?"

"He probably doesn't want to take any chance of being identified by the women. If they already know him or see him around, he could be easily identified."

"If we get a DNA match that will be just as good."

"I think the attacker isn't thinking about the DNA. If he knows these women, then he knows they are cougars and are having sex regularly with different men. He probably figures DNA evidence might be a real challenge in these cases."

"Detective, I think you have a pretty smart attacker here. He's probably right. We might have a real problem with DNA especially if your assumptions are right about the activity levels of the women. I wouldn't try to make too much out of the DNA of the Fletcher woman."

"Good point Captain. Once the DNA match is found, I'll work on ensuring there are other facts that corroborate the case."

"And the third attack?"

"That would be Ms. Sage. Her case was a little different. She was drugged from what the lab could tell although the others weren't tested because it wasn't suspected. One problem with her case is she is a casual recreational drug user and had a few drinks before her attack."

"What kinds of drugs were detected?"

"The lab report indicated marijuana and a few prescription drugs along with alcohol were present."

"Are you sure she was drugged and had not just taken in a mix of things that rendered her unconscious?"

"No I'm not sure. The things we do know are she did take prescription drugs, smoked some pot with a guy before going to Sundancers and then had a few drinks at the bar. She had gone home to pick up a few things in anticipation of meeting another man at the beach but never made it. When she didn't show up, the man she was supposed to meet went to her home and found her passed out naked on her bed. He was able to wake her and the two had sex. He used a condom. The next morning, she had the condom tested and it had semen on the inside and outside. The semen inside the condom and outside the condom was from the same man. The lab found a hair from a third person and a lubricant on the outside of the condom, which couldn't be explained. She said she only had sex with the man she was supposed to meet at the beach. I'm not sure how credible her story is. She might have had sex with someone else earlier in the day but right now she is saying she only recalls having sex with one man and he used a condom."

"So where do you go with that one?"

"We have the DNA from the condom. Plus, Ms. Sage was tested as a possible rape victim and we have the DNA from the internal. It matched the DNA on the outside of the condom."

"Now all you have to do is identify who the hairs belong to?"

"We already know who owns the DNA from the inside of the condom. That was from the man she was meeting for the swim who eventually found her passed out. That person was Kenny Brown. For a while I was suspicious of Mr. Brown, but his alibi is credible."

"What about the hair?"

"Nothing yet, but I'm sure we will identify a suspect soon."

"Ok Detective. Keep me informed."

"Thanks Captain. You've given me a few thoughts that might help. It's a real benefit to have a former Detective as Captain. You still have the detecting instincts."

"Come in anytime. I don't mind being a sounding board."

Chapter 24

Katherine Sterns parked her car and got out. She pressed the lock button on the remote to lock the door. She opened the door to Sundancers and walked in. Looking around, she decided to take a stool on the side of the bar nearest to the parking lot. As she sat, Ron said, "What will it be Katherine?"

"I'll have a margarita, no salt."

"No salt. Isn't that illegal?"

"I'm trying to cut down."

"Why, are you getting high blood pressure or something?"

"No. I'm just trying to cut back on some things."

"Ok. Margarita, no salt."

Ron went and made her the drink. He brought it back and put it in front of her. "Anything else?"

"How about a KENO ticket?"

"Here you go," and he placed the rack of blank KENO tickets in front of her. "What numbers do you like to play?"

"I like 69, 4, and 2."

"Interesting."

"Do you like 69?"

Ron smiled and responded blushingly, "When the time is right."

"Maybe we could get together sometime and compare timing?"

"Kat, are you coming on to me?"

226

"I just think we could get to know each other better."

"Let me think about it."

"You do that Ron."

Margarita Ortiz was bartending that night as well. She overheard Katherine talking to Ron. "Ron, are you getting in on the cougar action?"

"Just a little word play."

"Oh, I'm sure she's serious. Just look at how she's dressed. If that isn't a cougar attack outfit, I don't know what one is."

Katherine was dressed in a red halter-top over a pair of white short shorts. She had a pair of white high heels on that elevated her to about six-one. Her hair was combed straight and covered a portion of her face. She looked sexy.

Ron walked around to the other side of the bar to wait on other patrons. Dee came up behind him. "What was that all about?"

"She wanted to play KENO."

"She wanted to play, but it was definitely not KENO."

"Are you jealous Dee? You and Margarita are getting this all wrong."

"Come on Ron, you know these cougars. They are all aggressive."

"Still Dee, it sounds like you're a little jealous."

"Ron, if you want to sleep with any of them, I'm not in your way."

Ron turned. "Well actually you are. Can I get by?"

"You know what I mean."

"Ok. You're right. I think she was propositioning me."

"Did you take the bait?"

"Well, I'm still here, but just look at her. I don't know many guys who wouldn't jump at the opportunity."

"Just be careful Ron. She is seeing a guy with a gun."

"I'm always careful."

They went back to tending bar.

As Katherine surveyed the bar, she saw Ed talking with another man at the far corner of the bar. At first, she couldn't make out whom Ed was talking with until he turned to say something to Dee. Then she saw his face and immediately knew it was Tom Bowman. She picked up her margarita and walked around to where Ed and Tom were sitting.

"Hi Ed."
"Hello Katherine," Ed responded.
"How are you Tom?"
"I'm fine Katherine. You?"
"I was just sitting here having a margarita when I noticed you and Ed talking. So I understand you both used to fish with my husband?"
"I don't think we ever went as a group, but yes, we were all fishing together a few times," Tom said.
"Sam, Tom and I went surfcasting a couple of times up on the Bay," Ed added.
For a moment, no one spoke.

"If you'll excuse me, there's someone I see I'd like to speak to before they leave," Ed said as he picked up his beer and rose.
Katherine took up the stool when Ed left and continued her conversation with Tom.
"So Katherine, are you seeing anyone right now?"
"What's your interest Tom?"
"I was just thinking about that night you called me to the Route 28 motel."
"Well, I only date single men."
"Well at the time, that wasn't the case. But regardless, I don't know if you know it or not, Lisa and I got a divorce a few months ago."
"So you're a single man again?"
"Yep."

228

"What happened?"

"We moved to Virginia and tried to put things back together after Sam's death. It didn't work out. She just couldn't get past my having an affair with you."

"What affair? We had sex once, that was all."

"I know you said that but Lisa didn't look at it that way."

"I got to know Lisa a little when you and Sam went missing. I think she has her head on pretty straight. You must have done something else that drove her to the point of seeking a divorce."

"She said I would talk in my sleep and say your name. Then one night, she said I came on to her and called her Katherine."

"That's sick Tom. What are you obsessed with me or something?"

"When you made love to me at the Route 28 motel, you changed me. I think about you all the time and want to sleep with you again."

"Tom, you're having an infatuation with sex and my body. That's all it is, lust. We don't have any mental or emotional connection."

"Maybe you don't, but I do."

"Look at the facts. I called you out of the blue one night. We met at a motel and had sex. That was it. We didn't have dinner, see a movie or anything else. We just had sex."

"I can't get you out of my mind."

"So what is it you want from me?" She spoke loud enough that Margarita and Dee could hear them.

"To be with you."

"What do you mean *with me*?"

"You know, to spend a few nights together and see where it takes us."

"So you want to have sex with me again and see what happens."

"That's about it."

"I'm seeing someone else these days and I'm not sure how he would take it if I took you home."

"Is he living with you?"

"No, but I entertain from time to time."

"Are you concerned that seeing me might mess up that opportunity?"

"I don't depend on anyone or anything else for what I want. I have things under control at all times."

"I remember you like that."

"When do you propose trying to see where it takes us?"

"How about tonight?"

"I had other plans."

"That's what Ed said."

"Ed? What did he say?"

"He said you probably had other plans."

"My plans didn't include Ed although I could be convinced to change my plans."

"Give me a chance Katherine. You won't regret it."

"Ok Tom. Pay the tab and let's get out of here."

Tom paid their tabs and the two left. As they were leaving the bar she said, "You remember where I live?"

"I remember."

"Then I'll meet you there in a few minutes."

Arriving at Katherine's home, she took out her keys and let them in the front door. Walking into the living room, Tom couldn't help but feel Sam's presence. Some of the mementos Sam had collected were still in the home. Katherine went to the kitchen and poured two glasses of white wine. She walked back into the living room and sat next to Tom on the couch. They sipped their wine.

"Tom, you have been around when my friends were attacked. Are you involved?"

"It looked to me like you wanted something to happen to those women to take them out of competition."

"Where did you get that impression?"

"I overheard you talking at Chapin Restaurant with your friend and those two guys. Didn't you tell your friend

Ann she needed to be careful walking on the beach at night and if something happened to her, she would be out of commission?"

"I might have said something like that but I don't think I wanted anything to happen to her."

"What do you have against those other women?"

"Nothing really. I see them as competition."

"From what?"

Katherine took a sip of her drink. She sat back. "Enough shop talk. Tom, why don't you make yourself more comfortable."

"What would you suggest?"

"Take your shoes off and sit back."

He did as instructed. Katherine had on the halter-top and short shorts. She reached back and undid the catch to the top in the back. As it fell off, she rose. "I'll be right back."

She walked down the hall and into her bedroom. When she came back into the room she wore an oversized men's shirt he could practically see though. Her body was very visible under the sheer material. She had also unbuttoned the shirt mid-way. As she sat and reached for her glass of wine, Tom could easily see inside her open top and it aroused him.

Katherine noticed a bulge in his pants, "What do we have here?" She put her hand on the outside of his pants and lightly pressed down.

Tom took this as the cue to kiss her. Their tongues touched and he sighed. As they continued to kiss, he unbuttoned her shirt the rest of the way and reached in to touch her. She in return undid the buckle of his belt and unzipped his pants. She could feel his strength when she touched him. Tom had all he could do to contain himself. When he could take it no more, he stood up. As Katherine rose, he pushed her shirt off, and gripped her hands behind her back with just one of his hands. The two stood in embrace naked in the middle of her living room.

"Follow me," she said.

Katherine took his hand and led him to the bedroom. She pulled back the blankets and lay down in the middle of the bed. As she enticed him, he joined her on the bed. Katherine reached over to the nightstand and opened the drawer. She took out a condom and opened it.

"What is that for?" he asked.

"Protection."

"From what. I've been fixed."

"From anything and everything."

"I don't like using those things."

"Try it, you'll like it."

"If you insist."

"I do."

The two made love for the next half hour. When they were finished, Tom said, "That was all I remember it being."

"Tom, you need to get a life. It was just sex."

"Maybe to you, but it was heaven to me."

"You must have had good sex with Lisa. You had kids."

"With Lisa it was all mechanical. You do this, I do that and five minutes later it's all over."

"I'm sure it was more than that."

"Not sex like this. You really know how to please a man."

"Tom, this is my life. I live for sex."

"I thought you wanted to have a family."

"That was when Sam was alive. When he died, it all changed."

"But you were pregnant once. What happened between then and now that so convinced you that kids weren't for you?"

"When I lost the baby, the doctors told me I would never have children of my own."

"So you gave up?"

"No. I just accepted me for who I am."

"And who is that?"

232

"I'm a cougar. I like men. I like sex. I like everything that goes with it."

"Isn't there more than that?"

"You tell me. You're here because you have some sexual fantasy for me."

"It isn't a fantasy. It's a quest. I never had sex like we had at the Route 28 motel again until today. That's the feeling of satisfaction."

"Haven't you had other women since Lisa?"

"I have been with a couple, but the circumstances were never like this."

"Have you ever been with another cougar?"

"Recently, I…" he stopped in mid-sentence and didn't say any more.

As Tom looked up, he saw Sam's picture on the dresser. He got out of bed and walked over to it. Picking it up, he said, "I don't know how it has all come down to this Sam. Things were so better when you were alive?"

"I'd agree with that," added Katherine.

"But Sam is gone. You're divorced and here we are."

"Do you think we could have a future together?"

Just then, the doorbell rang.

"Who could that be coming over without calling?" asked Tom.

"I'll get it. You stay here," instructed Katherine.

She put on a silk robe and went to the door. She had the condom in her hand.

"I went to Sundancers to meet with you. The bartender said you left about an hour ago."

"Yes, I met an old friend."

"So I understand. Is that friend here?"

"Yes."

Tom Bowman came out of the bedroom just then with just his pants on.

"I see you were in the middle of something. I'll call you sometime," said Jenkins.

"Frank. It's not what you think."

"It's exactly what I think."

Tom Bowman walked into the kitchen while Katherine talked to Detective Jenkins. While in the kitchen, he opened her refrigerator to get a drink. He poured himself a glass of iced tea. Then he opened her freezer to get an ice cube. He noticed the box with the zip-lock bags. He picked up the first one. It had E. Phillips written on it. He looked at the contents and saw the condom. Then he looked at the second bag. It had K. Brown written on it. He could hear Detective Jenkins telling Katherine he was leaving and heard the door close. He grabbed the two zip-lock bags he had read and put them in his pocket. He picked up the glass of iced-tea and walked back into the living room.

"What was that all about?"

"I think Frank isn't happy about you being here."

"I'd be unhappy if I found the woman I care about with another man."

"I'm not married to him. I'm not even engaged to him. He knows I see other men."

"Maybe so but as a man he can't be happy."

"I'll make it up to him."

"I'm sure you will. Anyhow, I have to get going. Can I call on you again?"

"Let's see how things go."

"I'll call you."

Tom walked over to Katherine and gave her a kiss. She put her arms around him to hug him but didn't open her left hand. Tom didn't notice. She walked Tom to the door seeing him out. After Tom left, Katherine went back into the kitchen. She got out a zip-lock bag and put the used condom in it. She took a black magic marker out of a utility drawer and marked T. Bowman on the zip-lock. Then she put it in her

234

freezer in the back of the box with the other zip-locks. She didn't notice two were missing.

Chapter 25

Detective Jenkins walked into Sundancers and looked around. Dee saw him. "Looking for someone Detective?"

"Yes, Ms. Sterns."

"Oh, she left an hour ago or so."

He already knew.

"Did she say if she was coming back?"

"I don't know. She left with someone she knew, Tom something or other."

"Thanks."

Jenkins asked for a drink. As he took a sip, Linda Sage approached him.

"Out by yourself tonight Detective?"

"Oh, hello Ms. Sage. I'm just stopping in for a drink."

"Care for company?"

"What'll you have?" Jenkins said as he pulled the stool next to him out for her to have a seat.

"I'll have sex on the beach."

"I'm not sure sex on the beach is a healthy thing to request these days."

"It's only a drink. I'll take it any way I can get it these days."

"What would you say if I told you I don't like the beach?"

"And how about just sex?"

"Now that's an interesting approach."

"Why don't we go some place a little more private?"

"Where do you have in mind?"

"Oh, I'm sure I'll think of something." She ran her fingers down her blouse separating it a little so he could see she didn't have a bra on.

"Let's finish these drinks and I'll take you up on your offer."

The two finished their drinks and then left together. Linda took him to the Route 28 motel where she already had a key to a room. They got out of their vehicles and she told him to follow her. She went to the last room on the bottom floor and produced a room key from her bag.

"Here we are," she declared.

Linda opened the door and Jenkins followed her in. He closed the door behind him. Linda had a small cooler with her that she had in her car. She opened it and produced two beers.

"Can you open these for us?" she asked as she handed the bottles of Coors Light to him.

"Sure."

"Why don't you make yourself comfortable? I'll be right back."

Linda Sage went into the bathroom. She changed into a skimpy teddy that didn't leave anything to the imagination. When she came into the room, Frank had taken his shoes off and was sitting on the edge of the bed.

"Let me help you," she unbuttoned his shirt and pushed it back off of his shoulders. He helped by undoing the buttons on the sleeves and pulled his arms out. She threw the shirt on a chair next to the bed. Next, she undid his belt buckle, unclipped his pants and pulled his zipper down.

"Can you stand for a minute and I'll take care of these?"

Jenkins stood and she took his pants off for him, carefully folding them and putting them on the dresser. She came back to him and put her hands around his neck and began to kiss him, slowly at first. After a few minutes, she reached down, and sighed.

237

"Very nice, Detective."

Then she opened her mouth and let the tip of her tongue touch his. He reached up and put his left hand on her right breast. As he did, she reached around and undid the string holding the teddy on. It easily fell off. Frank then lightly touched her. Linda had begun to move her hands in a stroking motion getting Jenkins more aroused.

"Lie back on the bed Frank and enjoy the moment."

Jenkins went back. As he did, she got on top of him. She straddled him in such a way that he found himself inside her. She sat up and moved her body in an up and down motion. Jenkins was amazed at the size of her breasts that moved up and down with the rest of her body. He occasionally reached up and held both of them. Linda smiled. She reached around and touched him. At that moment, he exploded inside her. As he did, she did the same. They continued for another few minutes until both were spent. Finally, she leaned forward and allowed him to take her in his arms. They kissed.

"Well Detective, did that take your mind off of things?"

"You certainly did. I don't remember the last time I had such good sex."

"Oh come now Frank. I know you've slept with Katherine."

"Maybe so, but she doesn't have the skills you do."

"You mean tits, don't you?"

"There is that. You do tend to take over as well. The other women I have been with tend to be less aggressive."

"When it comes to sex, I believe in being aggressive. If a person doesn't take control, then that person might not be satisfied. If a person is going to all the trouble to have sex, then there is no reason to not be satisfied."

"You have an interesting perspective Linda."

"I've been told that."

"Well, I'm glad we were able to get together."

"Me too. Maybe we could get together again sometime."

"I'd like that."

"You like these." She put her right hand under her breasts palm up. He reached down and tickled her with his fingers between her legs. "They are nice, but this is where the action is at."

"I like a man who can see through the distractions and focus on what's important."

"That's probably the detective in me."

"That and this," she squeezed him in the right place.

The two hugged and kissed for another half hour. Finally, Frank said, "Thanks Linda. You've been a big help. I have to get going as I have a few things I need to follow up."

"Those attacks huh?"

"Yeah, that and paperwork."

"Anything you can talk about yet?"

"Not yet, but I think I'm getting close."

"I'd like to get together with you again and hear what you have come up with."

"Is that an excuse for us to have sex again?"

"Could be."

Jenkins got dressed and left.

As Frank Jenkins closed the motel room door, he saw another man he knew coming out of one of the other rooms. The man had his back facing Frank and was kissing a woman who was standing in the door dressed in just a bath towel. When the man turned around to walk away, Frank Jenkins said, "Hey Captain."

Captain Tomlinson looked at Jenkins and his face turned very red.

"Jenkins, what're you doing here?"

"It looks like the same thing you're doing here."

Jenkins waved. "Nice to see you Ms. Fletcher."

"You too Detective." Tina smiled and waved at Jenkins, not the least bit embarrassed.

Captain Tomlinson walked over to Jenkins.

"Look Frank, this isn't what it looks like."

"It never is Captain."

"You know Tina, don't you?"

"Yes, from the case I'm investigating, but I don't know her nearly as well as you obviously do."

"Come on Detective. She told me she has a thing for cops and you two have had some time alone together."

"That's true, but we only discussed business. How did you end up here with her anyway?"

"She came into the station one day to see you. You were out in the field so she talked with me. One thing led to another and the next thing I knew we were at a bar having a drink. Then she suggested we come here. I've been here a few times with her over the last few weeks."

"What about your wife?"

"What about her? Like Tina says, its just sex."

"It might be to her but if Helen finds out, you're toast."

"That may be true but I'm discrete."

"You may think you are, but I bumped into you here."

"It seems a number of the cougars like this place."

"Yeah. There seems to be a small group of women that share some of the same likes and desires."

"If you mean sex, you're right. I'll bet the group is bigger than you think. I've come to know a few of them as a result of the cases I'm pursuing. They're all cougars."

"A fitting label."

"It sure is. Well your secret is safe with me Captain."

"Thanks Jenkins. I appreciate it."

Detective Jenkins turned and walked to his car. He got in, started it and drove away. Captain Tomlinson did the same.

Chapter 26

The next afternoon, Tom Bowman went to Sundancers and was sitting at the bar. He had already had a few beers when Ed walked in. Ed took up the stool next to Tom.

"Doing any surf fishing Ed?"

"Later tonight. It's low tide now and the fish should be biting once the incoming tide starts to move. I figure the fishing should be good in about two hours."

"Going with anyone?"

"Nah. I'm solo tonight."

"If I had my gear with me, I'd go."

"I'll be here for another hour or so if you want to go and get it."

"I'd like to, but I'm waiting for someone."

"Too bad. There's supposed to be a good bite on tonight."

"I'm hoping for my own luck."

As they were talking, Tina Fletcher walked in. She looked like she just got out of the shower. Her hair was still wet. She approached the two.

"Hey guys. How are you two doing?"

"Just fine Tina. You just get out of the shower?" asked Tom.

"I did. I had a busy afternoon and needed to clean up."

Tom looked at Ed.

Ed's eyebrows rose up and he tilted his head in Tina's direction.

"I'm waiting for someone," said Tom.

"And I'm going fishing," added Ed.

"Well, you two will be no fun."

"You could always come fishing with me," said Ed.

"No thanks. While I do like a good rod from time to time, I don't get into things with strings."

Tom laughed. He turned to Ed. "Looks like you're still going solo."

"Looks that way," said Ed.

"Well, enjoy yourselves guys. I'm looking for other fish."

Tina turned and walked away. When she took up a stool on the other side of the bar, Ed picked up his drink and got up.

"Going to give it another try?" asked Tom.

"Can't hurt."

"Oh yes it could. If you do get her to go to the beach with you, don't let her touch anything you don't want her to touch."

"Why is that?"

"Because she has a one track mind. You let her get to your tackle and she'll have you hooked."

"I see what you mean."

Ed left Tom and went over to talk with Tina again. The door to the bar opened and Katherine walked in. Tom looked over to her and gave her a wave. She came over to where he was sitting. She was dressed in black slacks and a tight halter-top that accentuated her features. Tom took note that neither her pants nor top had any accompanying lines that usually show from undergarments. Plus, her top had two rather pronounced protrusions.

Tom looked at her top. "Are you cold?"

"No. Why do you ask?"

He looked down at her breasts. "Don't be silly Tom."

242

"Sure looks like you are cold to me."

"Oh, don't worry. I can be as hot as I want when I want."

"I'm sure you can."

"If you are cold, I could probably do something to warm you up."

"I'll bet you could," she said.

Then Katherine saw Tina on the other side of the bar and waved to her. She told Tom she would be back in a few minutes. She walked over to where Tina and Ed were talking.

"Hey Tina. How are things?"

"Just fine."

"You look like you just got out of the shower."

"I did."

"Oh. I went over to your house but you weren't home."

"I wasn't. I took a shower at the Route 28 motel."

"Busy afternoon?"

"Sure was, and fun."

"Anyone I know? Check that. Was it who I think it was?"

"Who do you think I was there with?"

"A certain Captain?"

"How did you know that? Did Linda tell you?"

"No. Was she there also?"

"Yes. She was there with a certain detective?"

"Oh, she was, was she?"

"You don't mind, do you?"

"Why would I mind if you were there with a certain Captain?"

"Not me. Linda."

"No, Linda can be with whomever she wants."

"But with your detective?"

"He isn't *my* detective. He's free to be with whomever he wants."

"I'll have to talk with Linda and see what she's up to?" Tina said.

"I'd say she's up to the usual."

"Probably."

While they were talking, Tom paid his tab and got up to leave. Tina saw him walking to the door. "He told me he was waiting for someone."

"Did you try to hook up with him?"

"Not especially, but I might have. Are you interested in Tom?"

"Tom and me go back a long way. He used to be friends with Sam. I slept with him a long time ago."

"He sounded like he was interested in someone."

"Oh, we got together again yesterday. He's probably fallen for me again."

"Did that happen before?"

"I think so. When Sam died, he tried to get me to sleep with him again. He used the excuse he was trying to console me, but I know what he wanted."

"Why did that bother you?"

"I kind of got to know his former wife when the two had gone missing for a few days and I didn't feel right hooking up with him again."

"What happened?"

"They moved to Virginia."

"And he came back for you?"

"I don't know. He says they got divorced. He said he came back here because this is where he knows the area and has friends. I think he came back here for me."

"What happened yesterday?"

"We had sex."

"Was it worth it?"

"Linda, sex is always worth it."

"But does he want more?"

"Probably."

"What do you plan to do?"

"Nothing at the present time. I'll let things take their course and see what happens."

244

Katherine got up and went to the door. Tom was just getting into his car when she went out.

"Where you going Tom?"

"I was going to get my fishing gear and join Ed fishing up at the beach tonight."

"Tina said you were waiting for someone?"

"I changed my mind."

"I have a better idea."

"Why don't you join me?"

"Ed asked me to go fishing with him tonight and didn't we just do that yesterday?"

"So? You want to go fishing or be with me some more?"

"But Ed..."

"You come with me. You don't need any bait, line or hooks. I have everything you will need right here with me. Just bring your rod."

"What do you have in mind?"

"Let me gather my stuff and I'll be right back."

Katherine went back inside. She gathered up her purse.

"That was quick," Tina said.

"We're going fishing."

Ed looked at Katherine, "I asked him if he wanted to go fishing with me. He said he was waiting for someone."

"I just threw the bait at him and he was hooked. Now he gets to go fishing."

Katherine smiled at Ed and turned and left. She walked over to Tom's car. He pressed the down arrow on his window button of his Jeep and looked at Katherine.

"Follow me to my place, Tom."

"I'm right behind you."

"Keep that thought in mind. Here we go again."

The two left Sundancers. Tom was following Katherine in his car. When they got to Katherine's house, she saw that she had left a flat of flowers on the front walk, waiting to be planted. "They can wait a little longer," she thought to herself. So she went into her garage and put on her gardening gloves, walked back to her front porch and picked up the tray and moved them into the garage.

"What gives with the gloves?"

"I had to move some plants that were on the walk."

She took the gloves off.

Then she reached down and put her hand on the front of his pants. She looked over to the neighbor's house just in time to see her neighbor looking out the window. She rubbed him. "Time to go fishing."

Then she led him into the house.

When they were done, Tom fell asleep. Katherine got up. She went to his side of the bed and took the condom out of the trashcan. She went to the kitchen and retrieved another zip-lock bag, labeled it T. Bowman and put it into the freezer along with the other bags. She returned to the bedroom and slid under the covers. Tom stirred.

"Can't sleep?"

"I just had to use the bathroom."

He struggled to raise his head enough to give her a kiss and then fell back on to his pillow. In another few minutes, he was snoring.

"Thank you Tom. I got what I was after."

Tom didn't respond. He remained fast asleep.

Katherine smiled and closed her eyes.

Chapter 27

When Detective Jenkins arrived at the station the next morning, he reviewed the overnight reports. There was a report of a woman being attacked overnight in Barnstable Harbor. He read the report indicating a woman walking on the beach was attacked before midnight. The report was sketchy with details so Jenkins decided he would call Barnstable PD to see if he could obtain more details. He had a friend, Ben Lang, who worked at Barnstable PD. Jenkins gave him a call.

"Detective Lang, how may I help you?"

"Ben, its Frank Jenkins from Dennis."

"Hey Frank, how are you doing?"

"Ok. I saw something on the morning briefing where a woman was attacked at Barnstable Harbor last night. Can you give me some details?"

"Sure. What's your interest?"

"I'm working on a few cases here that sound similar."

"Here's what we have."

Lang described the attack information to Jenkins. The details sounded similar to those of the other cases Jenkins had been pursuing. The woman was hit from behind and when she awoke, she had a bump on her head and a few scratches on her legs. Otherwise, she was ok. She had not been raped. Lang told Jenkins a worker from the Matakeese Restaurant found the woman lying on the beach when he went to get into his car to go home. The report indicated the woman was found around ten o'clock. The woman had said she went for a walk on the beach a little after nine. The report indicated the officer figured the worker must have surprised the attacker and left the scene. The worker did not see or hear anyone leaving.

"It sure sounds familiar. The cases I'm pursuing in Dennis are similar. The lady was lucky someone scared the attacker off."

"What happened to the victims in your cases?"

"Some were raped, some were not."

"Anything I can do to help you with your cases just let me know."

"I'll do that. Thanks Ben for the info."

"No problem. Most of the info has not been released to the press yet so you might be able to get a jump on it."

"I'll talk with my boss and I'll get back to you."

"Thanks again."

Jenkins hung up the phone. He went into Captain Tomlinson's office.

"Captain, there was an attack in Barnstable last night. Same MO."

"Get anything we can use?"

"Not really. The details are similar to the cases we are pursuing."

"So the perp is branching out?"

"Looks that way."

"I'll see what I can find out about the victim. Maybe she has something in common with the victims in our cases."

"Do that. Let me know if you need any help with the higher-ups in Barnstable."

"Will do."

The information Jenkins had obtained from Lang was not public yet. Lang had told Jenkins the name of the victim, Carrie Morgan, along with her address. Carrie Morgan's address was listed as 97 Pond Street, West Dennis. Jenkins decided to stop in and see if Ms. Morgan could provide some additional details.

He arrived at Ms. Morgan's home and knocked on her door.

"Ms. Morgan. I am Detective Jenkins of Dennis PD. I understand that you were attacked last night up in Barnstable Harbor."

"Yes Detective."

"I'd like to ask you a few questions if you don't mind?"

"Come in."

Carrie Morgan looked to be about thirty years old although Jenkins knew she was forty-three. She was dressed in a hot pink terry cloth jogging suit along with a pair of flip-flops. Detective Jenkins said Detective Lang of Barnstable PD had provided some information but he had some questions he would like to ask her.

Ms. Morgan's home was a typical Cape Cod house; three bedrooms, cedar shingle home surrounded by pine trees, shrubs and hydrangea bushes. The interior was nicely laid out with bright colors on the walls and nautical teak furniture. Ms. Morgan had pictures on the mantle over the fireplace. Most of the pictures showed her with a man at various settings around Cape Cod and other vacation locations.

When he was talking to her, Jenkins said, "Is Mr. Morgan around?"

"My husband died two years ago in an automobile accident. I'm a widow."

"I'm sorry to hear that."

"Thank you. I'm dealing with it as best I can."

"Ms. Morgan, what can you tell me about last night?"

"I had gone to Chapin's Restaurant for dinner last night around seven. I had dinner at the bar and then decided to take a ride down to Barnstable Harbor. I parked in the lot next to Matakeese Restaurant and started to take a walk along the beach. I remember hearing some noise in the brush near me and when I turned to look, something was coming at my head. That's the last thing I remember until the nice man who worked at the restaurant helped me."

"Did you talk to anyone when you were at Chapin's?"

"Yes. A nice quiet man, Ed Phillips, sat next to me and we talked for a while. He left the bar just before I did."

"Did you get a look at your attacker?"

"Not really. What I did see was someone in a hooded sweatshirt lunge at me and strike me. I think the person had long hair."

"Why do you think that?"

"Because the person's hair was showing at the base of the hood."

"So you saw the person's face?"

"No, I only saw the hair as I was turning. Then I saw something coming at my head. Then lights out."

"Do you know if it was a man or woman?"

"No. The person wasn't large in stature."

"About how tall would you say the person was?"

"Under six foot. I'd guess five-eight or five-ten."

"Anything else?"

"No, that is about it."

Jenkins made a few notes in his pad. Carrie tried to see what he had written and she brushed up against his arm. Carrie Morgan had long jet-black hair and piercing blue-gray eyes. She was about five-seven with a slender body reflecting her vigorous workout schedule, which occupied much of her time since her husband had died. Jenkins could feel the softness of her breast against his arm as she looked over his shoulder.

"Just a few notes about your attack," he said as he looked at her.

"Why are you interested in the attack on me, Detective? I was attacked in Barnstable."

"There have been a number of attacks in our town recently and the circumstances of your attack seemed similar."

"Where did you get the information about my attack?"

"It was on the morning briefing at the station today. The Dennis PD and Barnstable PD work together on these kinds of things. I talked to Detective Ben Lang earlier and he filled me in with the details."

"Oh, Detective Lang. He's a nice man."

"Sure is. Tops."

"Is he married?"

"No. A confirmed bachelor."

"I'll have to follow-up with him then."

"Ms. Morgan."

"Call me Carrie."

"Ok, Carrie. Do you ever go to Sundancers in West Dennis?"

"Sure. It's right near my house."

"Do you know any of the other patrons who go there regularly?"

"Let me see. Sue Kent, Tina Fletcher, Ann Benard, Linda Sage, Tommy Anderson, Paul Bremmer, Bobby Jones, Kenny Brown and a few others."

"So you know Sue Kent?"

"Who doesn't know Sue? She gets around. You don't think Sue was involved in my attack do you?"

"Not really. How about Ed Phillips?"

"As I said, I had talked to Ed when I was having dinner at Chapin's."

"So you know Ed as well?"

"Sure. I've known Ed for a few years now. Nice guy. Shy, but a nice guy."

"Have you ever dated Ed?"

"That's getting a little personal don't you think?" She thought for a minute and then added, "You don't suspect Ed do you?"

"Right now, everyone is a suspect."

251

"Well, I have dated Ed a few times. What would he have to gain by attacking me?"

"Are you still in good terms?"

"Sure."

"How about the other men?"

"Tommy and Paul are too young for me. They are always trying to show how macho they are. I don't go for those kinds of guys."

"What about Bobby or Kenny?"

"I've dated Bobby a few times and Kenny once. That Kenny is a sex crazed guy."

"Did something happen between you two?"

"We fooled around in his car in the parking lot up at Chapin's once. That was it."

"He seems to do a lot of his shenanigans up in Chapin's parking lot."

"Kenny's at Chapin's every night, always looking to pick someone up."

"So he doesn't go to Sundancers very much?"

"I didn't say that. When he can't score at Chapin's, he usually ends up at Sundancers trying to hookup with one of the regulars."

"Interesting."

Jenkins made a few more notes in his pad. Carrie Morgan asked if he would like something to drink. Jenkins said no and he had all he needed for the time being.

"Maybe you can come back sometime and stay longer."

"I may have a few more questions."

"I didn't mean to discuss the attack on me. I'd like to get to know you better."

"Maybe. You never know," was Jenkins reply as he closed his pad and stood to leave. "Thank you for talking with me Ms. Morgan."

"Anytime Detective."

Detective Jenkins left. Driving back to the station, he thought she was another cougar, more selective, but still another cougar. He decided to stop at Sundancers. He walked into the bar and saw Linda Sage seated near the door having lunch. She wore a sundress, flip-flops and little else.

"Ms. Sage, can I ask you a few questions?"

"Detective Jenkins. Sure. Have a seat."

"Do you know a Ms. Carrie Morgan?"

"Yes. Carrie comes in here from time to time."

"Did you know she was attacked last night up at Barnstable Harbor?"

"No I didn't. Is she ok?"

"A few bumps and scratches but otherwise she's fine."

"Did they catch the attacker?"

"Not yet."

"I hope someone catches this guy soon. It seems like every woman who I know, including myself, is being attacked."

"Do you have any ideas as to who might be doing the attacks?"

"I have my own ideas. Plus, I'm trying to get DNA samples from the guys I think might be doing the attacks."

"How are you doing that?"

"I have my ways.'

"What do you think about Kenny Brown?"

"It's not Kenny. He might be a little oversexed, but he doesn't need to attack women to get laid."

"What about Tommy Anderson or Paul Bremmer?"

"Tommy definitely not, but I'm not so sure about Paul. I don't know him intimately so I can't say."

"What about Ed Phillips?"

"Ed is quiet and shy. He's kind of a nerd. I don't think he could do those things."

"Anyone else?"

"There are a few others I have questions about, but nothing I care to talk about right now."

"Listen Ms. Sage. You probably ought to leave the detective work to us. You might get hurt."

"Detective, anything I uncover will be without the guy even knowing. I make them use protection. That protection can be very telling."

"If you want to get your evidence tested, call me and I'll have it sent to the lab."

"I don't need you to do that. My brother runs the lab in Hyannis."

"How will you match the attacker up with your suspects?"

"As I said, my brother runs the lab. Everything goes through his computers."

"He isn't supposed to tell you those things."

"Come on Detective. If one of your relatives were asking about something like this, do you think you would keep quiet?"

"Good point."

"I'll let you know if I come up with anything."

"Thanks Ms. Sage."

Detective Jenkins got up and left the bar. Now he had a hobby investigator helping him with the cases, and a pretty nice one at that.

Chapter 28

Early in the morning the next day, Officer Trudy walked into Detective Jenkins office.

"Frank, I did as you asked and went to the Route 28 Motel this morning. The manager there was happy to cooperate and let me into the room you had indicated. In going through the waste can, I found a condom, which I bagged and sent to the lab. I just got the report back and the lab confirmed the DNA found on the condom matched one of the DNA samples taken from Ms. Fletcher after her attack. We now have identified two of the DNA samples taken from Ms. Fletcher."

"Thank you Pam. If you can send me a copy of the report, I'll include it in my files."

"Do you know who's the owner of the sample I sent to the lab?"

"Yes."

"Care to tell?"

"Nope."

"Frank, I'd like to know who the owner is of the sample?"

"I'm not at liberty to tell you Pam. Just leave it at that."

"Why can't you tell me?"

"The person is someone who holds a position of importance and I would prefer to keep the name secret at this time."

"Ok Frank. If you say so."

"If a time arrives where the name can be revealed, I'll let you know."

"I guess I'll have to leave it at that."

"You will. Anything else?"

"No."

"You do good work Pam. Thanks."

"You're welcome Frank."

Officer Trudy turned and left Detective Jenkins's office. She wondered who the sample belonged to and why Frank wouldn't reveal the name to her.

Detective Jenkins picked up the phone and called Captain Tomlinson.

"Captain. This is Jenkins. I just got the results of a DNA test I had performed on an item. The lab indicated the sample matched one of the DNA samples found on Ms. Fletcher right after her attack."

"Good Jenkins. Whom did the DNA belong to?"

"You."

There was a silence on the phone. Then Tomlinson said, "Well, as I told you when I saw you at the Route 28 Motel, I have been seeing Ms. Fletcher."

"You did tell me, but you should have told me you had sex with her within twenty-four hours of the day she was attacked."

"You're right, but I didn't want to get involved."

"Captain. You're now a suspect."

"Jenkins. I'm no suspect. If you interview Ms. Fletcher, she will tell you about our consensual relationship."

"I'll have to do just that Captain."

"Just keep it discrete if you would."

"I'll keep it under wraps as long as I can, but something may come up if we charge someone and this evidence gets questioned."

"I understand Detective."

"I'll do all I can Captain."

256

"Thank you Detective."

Tomlinson hung up the phone.

Detective Jenkins called Tina Fletcher.

"Ms. Fletcher. This is Detective Jenkins."

"Detective, please call me Tina. What can I do for you?"

"I have some questions that I need to speak to you about."

"Go ahead."

"I'd rather do it in person if you don't mind?"

"How about noon?"

"That will be fine with me. Can you come to the station?"

"How about we meet at Sundancers. I'll buy you lunch?"

"I'll be on duty and I can't accept anything from someone I am investigating."

"Ok. Then you can buy me lunch."

Can't do that either, but we can both have lunch. I'll see you at noon."

When noon arrived, Jenkins went to Sundancers. Tina was already there. She was seated at the bar near the door. When Jenkins entered, she said, "Detective, right on time."

"I like to be punctual."

"Would you like to talk here or at a table?"

"I'd prefer we go somewhere with a little privacy."

"Ok. How about we talk over there at the table off the corner of the bar. It's pretty private back there."

"That'll do."

The two went to the table and sat down. A waitress came over and asked if they wanted a menu. Tina said yes. The two looked at the menu and then told the waitress what they wanted. Jenkins ordered a burger, medium, with fries and a diet coke. Tina ordered a sausage, peppers and onions grinder, with fries and a draft.

257

When the waitress had left, Jenkins said, "Tina, some of the questions I have are rather sensitive."

"Go ahead."

"After I saw Captain Tomlinson with you at the Route 28 Motel, I had an officer investigate the motel room you and the Captain used after you left. The officer found a condom in the trash. We had it tested for DNA and there was a match with the DNA found after your attack as a result of the internal examination from the hospital."

"So? I slept with Lou the night before I was attacked."

"So you don't deny it?"

"Certainly not. I've had a few rendezvous' with Lou recently, and I did tell you there was someone else involved that I couldn't reveal."

"Well, he did confirm it to me as well."

"So why are you asking me?"

"It's my job to follow up on all leads for corroboration."

"My having sex with your Captain is a lead?"

"Since you didn't tell me about it, it was."

"Well, now you know. Lou wasn't the attacker."

"I know that now. I just had to confirm it."

"Consider it confirmed. What about the other DNA?"

"We have positively identified the other sample as coming from Kenny Brown. The only remaining unknown in your case is to identify the person the hairs belong to that the lab technician lifted off your panties. The hairs didn't belong to you or either of the men you had sex with.

"How could that be?"

"I'm working on it. I'll let you know when I have something to report."

"Thanks Detective. Anything else?"

"No, that's about it for now."

"Why are you being so secretive about this?"

"The Captain asked me to be discrete."

"Oh, the wife. I get it. So where are you going from here Detective?"

"More leads."

"Want to join me at my place?"

"No thank you Tina. I have work to do."

"Your loss Detective."

"Thank you again Tina."

The waitress came and cleared the table, and brought two checks. Tina got up and left the table, carrying her check with her. She walked over to the bar and started up a conversation with a man who was sitting alone at the far end of the bar.

Detective Jenkins was about to leave when Katherine walked in. She approached him, "Leaving Frank?"

"I was."

"Care to join me for a little while?"

"Here or somewhere else?"

"Your option."

"Can we talk outside for a few minutes and then decide?"

"Sure."

The two walked outside and down by the waterfront. There were a few Adirondack chairs at the waters edge. They each selected a chair.

"What's going on Frank?"

"I just finished an interview with Tina Fletcher. She's been having an affair with Captain Tomlinson."

"I knew that."

"Why didn't you say something about it when we talked about the attack on her?"

"I don't think he attacked her. I didn't think it was relevant."

"I know he didn't, but his DNA has now been linked to her. When we apprehend the attacker, that information will certainly come out at trial."

"What if it does?"

"Tomlinson is married. He's also the Captain of the police force."

"Look Frank. Many of the men the girls sleep with are married. It happens all the time."

"Tomlinson doesn't want to create any problems for himself at home."

"Then he shouldn't be sleeping with Tina."

"Maybe so, but the damage is already done."

"I'd say the damage was done a long time ago."

"I'm still looking for the attacker. When the lab tested the material from Tina's attack, they found semen DNA from different individuals. Two have now been identified. I still don't have any answers about the hair found on the outside of the condom."

"The lab found hairs belonging to someone else?"

"Yes. It's like someone planted the hair or it belongs to the person planting the evidence."

"Do you think that could be possible?"

"Stranger things have happened, so anything is possible."

"Do you have ideas about how it happened?"

"Not yet, but I'm getting closer."

"What do you want from me?"

"Think back to the attacks. Of the people I have interviewed, they have all had alibis or their DNA didn't match in the instances where we recovered DNA. Is there anyone you can think of that might have committed these attacks?"

Katherine looked around at the scenery. The Bass River Marina was straight ahead and to the right. She could see across the river to a golf course and to the left, she could see the bridge leading to Yarmouth. Jenkins could see she was going through her mind trying to identify a possible suspect for him. She turned to him, "No, I can't think of anyone."

Just then, a Jeep drove down the driveway and parked a few spots away from where they were seated. The door opened and Tom Bowman got out. Tom didn't notice Katherine and the Detective seated down by the water.

"Did your DNA testing include him Frank?"

Detective Jenkins looked back into the parking lot and saw Tom heading to the door.

"No it didn't."

"Well, as I recall, Tom was at Chapin's Restaurant when Ann and I were there. He has been hanging around Sundancers for a few weeks now although I didn't recognize him at first. I know he's been hitting on some of the girls."

"I'll have to see if I can get a DNA sample on him without him knowing it."

"I might be able to help you out."

"How could you do that?"

"Tom came over to my place recently. One thing led to another and we had sex. He used a condom and I still have it. If you come over, I'll give it to you."

"Can we go there right now?"

"Sure."

The two got into Detective Jenkins car and left. When they got to her house, Katherine went into the kitchen and got a zip-lock bag. She walked to the bedroom asking Frank to follow her. He said he wanted to use the bathroom first. She proceeded to the bedroom. After using the bathroom, Frank went to the kitchen and poured himself a glass of iced tea. He opened the freezer to get ice cubes and saw a box with zip-lock bags in it. He picked one up and read the magic marker writing, "E. Phillips". He picked up another and it read "K. Brown". He looked at a third and it read "B. Jones". There were a few more but he had seen enough. He put the zip-lock bags back and closed the refrigerator. He joined her in the bedroom. Katherine held up the zip lock bag. It was labeled "T. Bowman". She handed it to Detective Jenkins.

He said, "Thanks. I'll have this tested and see if this is our suspect."

"Now that your business is done Detective, why don't you stay for a while?"

261

Katherine took off her shoes. She reached around and undid her bra and let it drop to the floor. She reached out to Jenkins and ran her hands down his chest over his shirt until they reached his zipper. With one hand she unzipped it and reached in with the other.

"I'm still on duty."

"You certainly are," was the response as he was becoming aroused.

She knelt down and continued to bring him around. While there, she unbuckled his belt and unhooked his pants. They fell to the floor. She pulled his underwear down. While she was doing this, he shed his shirt. The two fell into bed. Along the way, he removed her pants and panties. They assumed the traditional position and had sex for the next half hour. When done, she said, "I only hope I have provided you with the proper assistance in your investigation Detective."

"You're a beautiful woman Katherine. I'll have to remember that in the future."

"So you're saying we have a future?"

"I'm just saying I'll have to be aware of your skills in the future. You certainly know how to get your way."

"Oh come on Frank, you wanted me."

"You're right."

"And now you've had me, again."

"Katherine, I'm sure this doesn't mean anything. I didn't use a condom."

"That's ok. I'm not concerned."

"What if you get pregnant?"

"Then you'll have to marry me."

"That isn't what I was thinking."

"What were you thinking?"

"I guess I wasn't"

"Look Frank. If you have sex and don't use a condom, don't be surprised if the woman gets pregnant or if you contract a disease."

"A disease, do you have something?"

"Not that I'm aware."

"That's good to know."

"I'm just saying. Having unprotected sex is playing Russian roulette. You have to accept the consequences."

"You're right. Now I have to get back to business."

"Well, if I can be of assistance again, please don't hesitate to call on me."

"I'll keep that in mind."

He couldn't stop thinking about the zip-lock bags she had in her freezer. What could she possibly be saving them for? Had he used a condom, the next bag would most certainly be labeled "F. Jenkins".

Frank got dressed and left. He went directly to the lab to have the condom tested. When he got to the lab, he gave the technician his cell phone number and asked that the DNA test sample be compared to the DNA of the cases he had been pursuing. The lab technician took the number and said he would call once the comparisons had been completed.

Chapter 29

After dropping the specimen off at the lab, Jenkins thought it would be a good time to talk to Captain Tomlinson about the new evidence. He called the station and asked to speak with him. The dispatcher told Detective Jenkins the Captain was out having lunch. Detective Jenkins then called the Captain's cell phone. When Tomlinson's phone rang, he looked at the caller id and saw who it was.

"Yeah Jenkins, what is it?"

"Captain, I have some new evidence in the attacks I'd like to review with you."

"Ok. I'm on my way to Sundancers to have lunch."

"Are you meeting anyone?" When the Captain said Sundancers, Jenkins immediately thought the Captain was looking to run into Tina.

"No. I'm not meeting with anyone in particular."

"I just thought since Sundancers is where Ms. Fletcher hangs out you might be meeting her there."

"I don't know if she'll be there or not Jenkins. I'm just going there to have lunch."

"Then do you mind if I join you?"

"Come on down. I'd like to hear what you have."

Jenkins got off Route 6 at exit 8 and headed south on Station Avenue. In a few minutes, he was driving down the driveway to Sundancers. The parking lot was about half full. He parked next to Tomlinson's Crown Victoria. Walking in, Jenkins could see Captain Tomlinson seated at a table in the dining area. He bypassed the hostess and walked over to the table.

"Hello Captain."

"Jenkins."

"As you know, I've been following up on leads in the attacker cases. I've narrowed my suspect list down to a few people and have been able to secure DNA samples from all of my current suspects."

"And you even have DNA from some people who are not suspects, right?"

"Captain, I had to check everyone to eliminate some."

"Just don't get me in trouble."

"I don't plan on getting you involved other than in an official capacity."

"Make sure of it."

"I will."

"So, you've got new evidence?"

"I think so."

"What do you mean, think so?"

"I was able to get hold of DNA from the last person I suspected."

"How'd you do it?"

"You know Ms. Sterns?"

"Yes."

"She assisted me in obtaining the DNA and I'm having it tested at the lab right now."

"How did she assist you?"

"She was able to capture his DNA and gave it to me."

"And how did she do that? Why are you being so vague?"

"She had him use a condom during sex, saved it, and gave it to me."

"So you procured the evidence using one of the cougars in a sex sting?"

"No, nothing like that."

"Then how did you get her to provide the sample?"

"I had been talking with her about the suspects, one of which I had no DNA on, and she said she might be able to help."

"And?"

"She told me she had the last suspect over to her house the day before and he had left a used condom at her house. She provided it to me."

"So you're saying she gave you the condom from her conquest of the night before?"

"That's right."

"Look Jenkins, I know you haven't been a detective for long but you have to know this was not collected legally. She's telling you it's his, but you don't know that for a fact. And he wasn't told it was being collected for testing purposes. I'm not sure this will be admissible evidence."

As Captain Tomlinson was talking, Jenkins cell phone rang. "Detective Jenkins."

He listened and then said, "Thank you for being so prompt in performing the test." Then he closed his cell phone."

"The lab says the DNA matches the unidentified hair samples. The same person was at the scene of both attacks."

"Ok, who owns the DNA?"

"Captain, you remember the accident where Ms. Sterns' husband died during an ice fishing trip?"

"Yes."

"Well, the unidentified DNA belongs to the guy who survived, Tom Bowman."

"You gotta be kidding?"

"That's what the lab technician said. The DNA on the condom I brought in matched the previously unidentified hair samples from the Fletcher and Sage cases."

"So where do you go from here?"

"I was going to pick him up and bring him in for questioning if the DNA matched, and based on his story, arrest him."

266

"I don't think that'll be such a good idea. There are going to be a few problems with the evidence. Unless you can flat out ask him for a random contribution, you'll need more."

"What would you suggest?"

"Follow the guy for a few days and see if he gives you hard evidence you know you can make stick. Then you can bring in this other evidence and it will confirm your charges."

"Ok. I'll take that approach."

"Now, let's order lunch."

"I'll pass if you don't mind Captain. I want to get to work planning my strategy, plus, I think there is someone else who wants to have lunch with you."

The two turned and looked towards the bar. Tina Fletcher was standing there in a pair of navy shorts and a red and white striped halter. Her hair hung down in its usual unkept look. She had on a pair of designer sunglasses on her head, holding her hair back, and looked like she was on the prowl.

As she approached, Jenkins said, "I'm just leaving." He held out a chair for her to sit.

"Why thank you Detective."

"My pleasure."

"Another time," she responded.

"How are you today Ms. Fletcher?" asked Captain Tomlinson.

"Just fine Captain. May I join you?"

"Sure."

Jenkins shot Captain Tomlinson a look. The Captain's eyebrows raised a little but he didn't say a thing.

Jenkins turned and left. As he was walking to his car, he opened his cell phone and called Katherine.

"Katherine, its Frank."

"Hello Frank. How are you?"

"Not so good. I just met with Captain Tomlinson and he says there might be a problem with the evidence I got from you."

"What kind of problem?"

"How it was obtained, third party and like that."

"Did you have it tested?"

"Yes. I just got the results and the DNA matched the unidentified hair DNA from Linda's and Tina's attacks."

"So you know who was involved, but you can't use the information? So why did I bother to help?"

"Well, that's part of the problem. I didn't get the DNA myself and it didn't come through any other approved channels. You provided it."

"Look Frank, I got you the sample. You had it tested and it was a match. What more do you want?"

"In court, it would be your word against his as to how you got the DNA sample. The evidence and situation might have flaws. We don't want him to be able to walk."

"There were no flaws. I had sex with the guy and he used a condom. Then I gave the condom to you."

"The Captain and I agree more is needed."

"Do you want me to sleep with him again and let you watch?"

"No nothing like that. I just wanted to know if you know how I can get in touch with Mr. Bowman."

"I usually see him at Sundancers or around town. He moved last week and said he was staying at one of the hotels in Yarmouth until he gets a new place."

"So he hasn't been in town for very long?"

"Only a couple of weeks."

"Interesting. The attacks didn't start until he got back. Look, if you see him again, give me a call on my cell. I'd like to talk to him. Katherine, be careful with this guy. He's hurt a couple of your friends already. The guy could be capable of anything."

"Frank, I slept with the guy. Why would he attack me?"

"Who knows what goes through the mind of guys like him."

"Why don't you just go down to Sundancers for the next couple of nights? I'm pretty sure he'll show; he's been there pretty much every night for the past week. I've watched enough detective shows to know if he drinks from a glass, and leaves it in a public place, you can pick it up. Then you'll have your DNA sample, again."

"Thanks Katherine."

He closed his cell phone and went back to the station. He asked the dispatcher to have Officer Trudy come in to his office.

"Frank, what can I do for you?"

"Pam, I got a lab report back that has positively identified the unknown in the Fletcher and Sage cases, and it's the same person."

"Who is it?"

"Tom Bowman. He has a history with Ms. Sterns and has recently come back to the area."

"Do you plan on arresting him?"

"Not yet. I talked with Captain Tomlinson and he thinks we need more. The DNA had a few strings attached that might present problems in court."

"What can I do?"

"I'm going undercover for a few nights to see if I can get solid evidence on this guy. I need someone to accompany me so that I don't look suspicious."

"I think I can do that."

"I also think the attacker is making his way through the group of cougars that frequent the local bars. The only two that haven't been attacked are Sue Kent and Katherine Sterns. We might have to follow the two of them for a few days and see if either of them gets targeted."

"When do you want to start?"

"Tonight. Can you be here at say eight o'clock? Dress casual. We might be going to a couple of bars."

"That sounds like a date Detective."

"Kind of, or that's how it needs to appear."

"I'll be here at eight."

Officer Trudy left Detective Jenkins office and went home. She would have to be back on duty in a few hours. She went home and selected her clothing for the evening. She picked a jean skirt and a sleeveless tank that snugly fit her body. It had graphic artwork that resembled an Andy Warhol portrait. For shoes, she picked out a pair of espadrille wedges. The outfit would allow her to fit in with the regulars at the establishments that Jenkins planned on visiting, and still be comfortable. This was a uniform she could get used to. She went into her bathroom and turned on the shower. Stepping into the hot shower, she sighed and took her time. When done, she prepared herself for the night. She put on perfume, dressed and left her home to meet up with Detective Jenkins.

At eight o'clock, she walked into Jenkins office.

"Well you sure look the part," said Frank with a big smile on his face.

Pam Trudy was pretty good looking. Without the police uniform, she was actually attractive.

"I'm ready."

Frank had dressed in a pair of slacks, knit shirt and loafers. He looked like an off-duty policeman, which was OK, because everyone at the bars knew him as one. The two left the station in her personal car with Frank driving.

"Why did you want me to drive Detective?"

"Call me Frank tonight. I want it to look like we're on a date."

"Ok."

"And Pam, we might have to make it convincing at some point in the night if we run into your suspect."

"What do you have in mind?"

"Nothing specific really, but I just don't want you to freak out if I have to get close to you all of a sudden."

"Ok Frank. I promise not to give you away. Where do you want to start?"

"Let's start at Sundancers. And Pam, sit close to me when we pull into the parking lot. That will give the impression to anyone who's looking that we're seeing each other."

"I can do that."

As they drove down the driveway, Pam slid over on the seat and was toughing Frank's right side. Jenkins pulled into the first parking space right next to the door and turned on his interior light. If anyone was looking, it sure looked like they were on a date.

The two got out of Pam's car and walked into the bar. Pam held his hand as they entered.

Chapter 30

The sun had set and the cool of the evening could be felt in the air. A fog came in off Nantucket Sound making the air heavy. Katherine parked her car and walked into Sundancers. She was dressed in her prowl clothing; a tight low cut red wrap dress and heels. The height of the heels was perfect to define her calves. When she walked in, she turned heads.

Katherine took up a seat on the far side of the bar. Ron just stood behind the bar looking at her as she came in. Dee hit Ron with a towel. "Stop drooling Ron. See if she wants a drink."

"I'm not drooling."

"Oh, sure," said Margarita.

"He can't help himself," said Dee.

Ron went over to her. "What will it be Katherine?"

"I'll have a dirty martini, please."

"Sure thing."

"So Ron, you like the getup? It's new."

"Katherine, you always look good."

Another hit of the towel from behind.

"What was that for Dee?"

"You're on duty."

"I can still be polite."

"That's what you call it."

"It's Ok Dee. I don't mind the admiration."

"Katherine, I think Ron is lusting for you."

"That wouldn't be a bad thing, now would it?"

"I guess not, but he needs to be focused on his job. We're expecting a big crowd tonight and if Ron isn't on his best game, then the rest of us end up picking up the slack." Dee pointed to Margarita.

"You'll work your ass off anyway," responded Ron.

"Well thanks for the looks Ron. A girl always likes to be desired."

"If you say so."

Then Ron went around to the other side of the bar to make the martini and wait on other patrons.

Katherine took a sip of her martini and sighed.

"Tough day?" Dee asked.

"I'm just trying to sort things out."

"It looks like someone else is sorting things out as well," added Margarita. She shook her head in the direction of the back corner of the bar to Dee.

Dee looked to the back corner of the bar where there's only one table and it's rather dark. Two people were sitting back there. She said, "I know what you mean."

Katherine followed Dee's gaze and she saw Frank sitting there facing her. He was sitting with a woman whose back was to the bar so Katherine couldn't make out who he was with.

Katherine asked Dee, "Who's that with Detective Jenkins?"

"I think it's one of the female officers on the force."

"Isn't that interesting?"

"Aren't you still seeing him?"

"I thought I was, but I guess he's getting back at me."

"It looks like he's putting the moves on her tonight."

"We'll see about that."

273

Katherine picked up her martini to have another sip. When she did, Dee noticed her fingernails. "I love the color of your nails. That shape, I don't think I have ever seen that one before."

"These are false nails. They're acrylic. I used to use the snap on nails that are actually caps that snap into place over your real nails. They kept coming off so I went back to acrylic."

Katherine held her hand out for Dee to see.

"If you look closely, you can see what my real nails looked like when I used the snap on nails."

Dee could see that Katherine's real nails had been cut into a funny design, kind of like those of a cat.

"Didn't it hurt when you had your nails shaped like that?"

"No. The beautician who does this has a special formula you apply a day before the procedure. Then when she shapes your nails, you don't feel anything. I think the solution you apply has numbing qualities to it allow the procedure to take place without pain. You have to leave some real nail for the fake one to attach to."

"That's interesting. I've never heard of it before."

"It's new. I thought I would give it a try. But like I said, the snap on nails kept coming off. So I went back to using acrylic nails."

"And what about the color of the fake nails?"

"You can get the nails in any color you want. They have a full array of choices you can select from."

"So the false nail is kind of wedged in place?"

"Kind of. Plus, the base of the false nail snaps around the real nail base. It all works together and what you get is a pretty sturdy false nail that snaps in place and can be easily removed if necessary."

"When would you take the false nails off if your own nails look like claws?"

"You never know when you need a claw."

"Maybe I'll give the snap on nails a try some time."

"They look great. They just didn't work for me."

Katherine smiled and picked up her martini for another sip.

Dee went about her business waiting on other patrons. After a little while, Tom Bowman came into the bar. He waved to Katherine and walked over to her. He took up the stool next to Katherine and ordered a beer. He and Katherine started a conversation and Dee could see Katherine pointing to the back corner of the bar where Jenkins and Trudy were seated.

Detective Jenkins saw Tom Bowman coming in through the door. He moved his seat around a little so he was on the side of his companion. He could still see Tom Bowman when he took up his seat and had started talking with Katherine. When he noticed the two looking in his direction, Jenkins tried to put the move on Trudy. He put his arm around her shoulder and tried to kiss her. At first, Trudy leaned away.

"What are you doing?"

"We have to make it look good and one of my suspects just came into the bar. If he's our guy, I want to make it look good and see if he notices."

She came back to him and allowed him to kiss her lightly.

"I'm not sure that will do. It looks like we are brother and sister with a kiss like that."

Trudy leaned over to him and opened her mouth. Her tongue tip split Jenkins lips and found his. The two kissed passionately.

"Is that better?"

"Much better."

"Did he notice?"

"He keeps looking this way."

She leaned in again and kissed him again. As they kissed, his hand came up to her breast.

"Is that necessary?"

"It makes this all look real. In a few minutes, you get up and leave. I'll stay behind and observe the suspect. If he is our guy, he might follow."

"Ok."

They French kissed a few more times. She allowed his hands to drop below the table out of site. After a few minutes, Trudy got up and gave Frank a kiss and left the bar. As she left, Jenkins ordered another drink and sat back with a smile on his face.

Katherine noticed Trudy leaving and told Tom she would be right back. She left right after Trudy. Detective Jenkins just sat and looked around gazing from time to time at Tom Bowman.

Katherine got into her car and followed Trudy home. When Trudy got out of her car and went into her house, Katherine made note of the address and watched Trudy go in. Trudy had gone into her garage and retrieved a key. She used it to open the side door and then put the key back into the garage then returned to the house. The key seemed to be hanging on a nail or something to the left of the side door. Katherine had all she needed. She started up her car and went back to Sundancers.

When she got back into Sundancers, she took up the same seat she had before. Tom had ordered her another martini when he saw her pull into the parking lot. She took a sip. "Thanks Tom."

"Did you get what you needed?"

"Sure did."

"So what are your plans for the rest of the night?"

"I have something in mind. Let's finish our drinks and get out of here."

"Sounds good to me."

The two finished their drinks. Tom paid the tab and they left.

After Trudy had left, Jenkins called the station and asked that someone pick him up at the bar as soon as possible. He asked the person picking him up not to use a police car. Detective Jenkins paid his tab and waited outside the bar. After a few minutes, Sergeant Grimes pulled into the parking lot in his Toyota Camry. He instructed Grimes to drive to the station where he picked up his car. Then he drove to Katherine's house. He knew Katherine and Tom Bowman had more than a few minutes lead, but he already knew where Katherine lived so he went right to her house. When he arrived, there were no lights on and no car in the driveway. Katherine and Tom Bowman had gone somewhere else. Jenkins didn't know where Tom Bowman lived and he wasn't sure they had gone to his place anyway. He decided to call it a night but he wanted to make sure Trudy got home safely so he went by her place.

As Detective Jenkins turned onto Trudy's street, he didn't notice a Jeep parked a few houses down the street with two occupants in it. The house had a foreclosure sign on the front lawn and was obviously empty. There were no curtains and no visible personal effects at all. Jenkins parked in Trudy's driveway and walked up to her door. He rang the bell and Trudy came to the door.

"Anything happen Frank?"

"No. Our suspect left and didn't go where I thought he was going."

"So what do you do now?"

"That's it for tonight. We don't know where he went so we can pick it up again tomorrow. I came by to make sure you made it home safely. If my theory is right, you might become a target."

"I didn't see anyone following me and no one has come by but you."

"I think we might have to follow Katherine and Sue Kent. I just have a feeling this guy is going to strike again soon and if we're lucky, we can catch him red handed. Maybe we'll start at Chapin's Restaurant."

"Ok. Then I'll see you there tomorrow."

Pam had already changed into her pajamas. She wore a pink camisole over pink boy shorts. It wasn't obviously sexy, but it was cute. As Frank turned to leave, she said, "Why don't you come in for a while?"

"I'm kind of tired."

"I know just the thing to relax you."

"Ok. Just for a little while."

The two went inside. Frank looked around and thought the house looked just as he imagined it would, she was very organized. The furniture was all very neat, clean and modern. There was a bookcase containing law enforcement books along with the various awards she had achieved. The wall coverings were all pastel colors, with pictures and paintings of flowers and ocean settings. Frank was impressed.

Katherine took note of everything from her vantage point. She watched as the outside lights went off, then the living room lights went off and finally a light at the back of the house turned on.

Inside, Pam had put her arms around Frank as they closed the door and she took up where she left off at the bar. They kissed passionately. In a few minutes, she shed her pajamas and opened Frank's shirt. She ran her hands over his chest and then down to his pants. She undid the belt, unhooked his pants and unzipped them. They fell to the floor. Frank picked her up and carried her down the hall. As they went, she reached over and hit the wall switches turning the lights off.

"Last room on the left," she whispered in his ear.

As they entered, she turned the light switch on. The shades were not pulled down and Katherine could see into the bedroom from her vantage point. She could see the upper half of both of their naked bodies as Frank took her to the bed. He laid her on the bed and the two disappeared from the window view. The kissed and explored each other's bodies. The bedroom was just as organized as the rest of the house. Nothing seemed out of place. The walls were done in soft-green stripped wallpaper. The bed had big feather pillows accompanied by a half-dozen throw pillows. A thick light pink comforter was on top of the bed. A large bureau with what looked like a six-foot mirror stood against one wall. Another small table surrounded with lights was against the other wall. One door led to a large walk-in closet. The other led to an oversized bathroom that had a whirlpool bathtub.

"Do you want me to turn the light off?" he asked.

"No. I like to see what I'm doing," and she rolled him over and got on top. She moved down his body kissing him from time to time. He lay back and relaxed.

"Most of you can relax, just not here."

She squeezed him. Then, she straddled him. She began to move up and down taking command.

"You like to be in charge."

"I do. That's why I joined the police force."

"Well you certainly know how to put someone at ease."

"All part of my training."

"So they teach this at the academy to female cadets?"

"This comes with being an aggressive woman."

"Kind of like the cougars?"

"Kind of."

She leaned forward and allowed him to hold her. She continued down and they kissed. He rolled her over and took command. They both began to breath heavily and reached climax at the same time. When done, Frank lay next to her. "You certainly relaxed me."

Trudy reached down and responded, "Certainly did."

"Well, I have to be going. I need to be at the station early tomorrow and I have a few things I need to pick up at my place before I go in."

279

"Detective, work can wait until morning."

She reached over and flipped the light switch to off. She cuddled up next to him. "We can do this again in the morning."

"If you insist, but I have to be in by eight. I'll have to set my cell phone for seven so I can swing by my house for clean clothes."

"My shift starts at noon, but I'll get you out of here by seven."

"Ok."

He reached over her and kissed her passionately. In another few minutes, she had hold of him as he began to grow again.

"Why wait until morning?"

Jenkins got on top and they were at it again. In another few minutes, the two were breathing heavily again.

When the back bedroom light went out, Katherine said, "That bitch. Let's go."

"You don't like her very much do you Kat?"

"No I don't. Something bad should happen to her."

Tom started up the Jeep and pulled out of the driveway, "Where to now?"

"My place."

Chapter 31

While having English Muffins and coffee the next morning at Pam house, the two discussed how to go about following the two cougars they thought might be attacked next.

"Pam, instead of both of us going to Chapin's, why don't you go to Sundancers tonight and start looking for Sue Kent. If you aren't sure which one she is I'm pretty sure I have a picture of her in the file at the station. I'll watch for Katherine Sterns. We'll just both follow our targets and see how it goes."

"Ok. I think I can make a good impression."

"Just be careful not to exaggerate too much. These cougars are cagey."

"I'll be careful."

"If Bowman makes a move, follow him. Call me right away. I want to catch him in the act. That way, we won't have to rely on any of the questionable evidence that has already been collected."

"Do you want me to wait until he's leaving the scene or step in right away?"

"Wait until he's leaving, but don't let him actually leave. Then we will have him red handed. If he stays true to the pattern, the victim will be unconscious."

"Isn't that rather dangerous for the victim?"

"Somewhat, but we need solid evidence."

"Ok, but if I think the person is in jeopardy, I'll have to react."

"I understand."

"I'll follow Ms. Sterns. If it looks like she's the next target, I'll call you to assist."

"Don't you think she'll see you?"

"I know my way around her place so I think I can remain unseen."

"Sounds like a plan. I'll start tonight after dinner."

"Ok. So will I. Call me on my cell when you're starting."

"Will do."

Later that night, Detective Jenkins parked down the street from Katherine's home. He sat in his car, behind a large bush but with enough of a view to see comings and goings. The motor was running for about half hour when his cell phone rang.

"Frank, its Pam. I'm watching Ms. Kent."

"Anything yet?"

"Nothing out of the ordinary. Just wanted you to know I found my target."

"Ok Pam. I'm watching Ms. Sterns house. Call if anything happens."

"Will do."

He turned the vehicle off and sat in the dark observing her home. The lights were on in a number of the rooms and from time to time he could see the shadow of a person moving around as the silhouette on the shades. After about an hour, a Jeep came down the street and pulled into the driveway parking next to Katherine's car. A man got out and went to the door. He knocked. Katherine answered and she let the man inside. Jenkins could see into the living room and the two people sat there talking. About forty-five minutes later, someone came out of the house and got into the Jeep and left.

Detective Jenkins decided to see if Katherine was all right. He went up to the door and knocked. The door opened, and Tom Bowman stood there in front of him holding what looked like a prescription bottle.

"Can I help you?" Bowman asked.

"Is Katherine home?"

"No. She stepped out for a while."

"Do you expect her back soon?"

"I'm not sure when she'll be back but it shouldn't be too long. Haven't I met you before, or seen you around?"

"Just tell her Frank Jenkins stopped by."

"I will."

Bowman closed the door and Jenkins walked back to his car. He got in but didn't start it. He just waited again in the dark.

Tom Bowman returned the bottle he had in his hand back to Katherine's nightstand but not before taking a few pills and putting them in his pocket. He might need these again in the future.

Meanwhile, Officer Trudy had gone to Sundancers. She found Sue Kent there talking with Kenny Brown. Trudy had a drink. She talked with Margarita about the weather and other small talk. When Sue got up to leave, Trudy followed her.

Officer Trudy parked a few houses away from Sue Kent's place. She watched as Sue went into her home. Lights came on and went out in a pattern that suggested that Sue was moving from one end of her house to the other. Eventually, the only lights turned on were at a room in the back of the house. Trudy could just make out the windows at the back of the house from where she parked.

Not too long after Sue had gone to the back of the house, a Jeep drove down the street with its lights off. The Jeep stopped in front of Sue's home. The door opened but the interior light did not come on. Someone got out and went up to the house. The person didn't go to the front door but rather went around to the garage. After a few minutes, the person came back around and using a key, gained entry into the house. Trudy thought this was it. She would catch the attacker in the act. Trudy got out of her car and went to the Jeep. She noted the license plate number. Then she went around to the back of the house. Looking into the only window that had a blind open, she could see two people. One was lying on the bed and the other person was standing over the person on the bed. The person on the bed did not move. Trudy could not make out the face of the person standing as that person had a hood on blocking Trudy's clear view of the face.

Officer Trudy's eyebrows went up when she noticed the person standing over Sue was holding a zip-lock bag. The attacker was squeezing something out of the bag onto Sue's stomach and pajamas. Trudy started to panic and decided to move in. As she turned, she tripped over a rainspout and it made a clanging noise. The attacker heard it. The attacker made a break for it and ran out the front door. Officer Trudy, now floundering on the patio under the window, was trying to run to the front yard. Just as she got there, she could see the Jeep, with lights off, turn the corner.

Officer Trudy took out her cell phone and called Detective Jenkins as she walked back to the house.
"Frank, the attacker was here."
"Where are you Trudy?"
"I'm at Sue Kent's home. I saw the attacker."
"Who was it?"
"I didn't see the attacker's face, but I got the license plate."
"It was a Jeep wasn't it?"
"Yes, how did you know?"
"I think I know who it is."
"What do you want me to do with Ms. Kent?" Trudy was looking back in the window, and Sue had rolled over and pulled up her covers. She seemed unharmed.

"See that she's all right. If she needs medical attention, get it for her. Otherwise, call it a night."

"Ok. No, she looks Ok. She's sleeping. But, there are some strange things I saw going on over here that I'll put into my report. I'll tell you about it in the morning."

"Ok Pam. I'll see you in the morning."

Officer Trudy knocked on the door. The door opened slightly.

"Ms. Kent?"

There was no answer. Officer Trudy entered the house and worked her way to the bedroom. Sue Kent was out cold on the bed. Trudy lightly shook her.

"What happened?" asked Sue.

"It looks like someone drugged you and then tried to attack you. We have been following you recently to see if an attempted attack would be made against you and it looks like it just took place."

"You say you were following me?"

"Yes. Detective Jenkins is following another person we suspect might be another target and I was assigned to follow you. I saw a person enter your house and when I was looking around I saw the person standing over you in your bedroom. Unfortunately, I tripped over your down spout and scared the person off."

"Did you see the attacker?"

"Not good enough to identify the person but I did get the vehicle make and marker number the attacker used to get away."

"Then you should be able to find out who it was."

"It will be a start. Are you all right Ms. Kent?"

"Yes. I'm a little groggy but otherwise I think I am fine."

"If you don't feel ok, you should go to the ER and get checked out."

"No, I'm fine."

Officer Trudy handed her a card and told her to call if she had any questions. Trudy looked around and saw what she was looking for. There on the floor next to the bed she found the zip-lock bag the attacker had been holding. When she held it up, she could see what was inside.

"What is that?" asked Sue.

"This is what I saw the attacker holding over you when I looked through your window."

Sue turned to her bedroom window. The shade was up.

"You could see in through my window?"

"Yes. I saw the attacker squeezing something on you out of this bag. It looks like there is a used condom in the zip-lock."

Sue looked at the bag.

"Sure is."

"I'll have this analyzed at the lab to see if we can determine whose DNA is in there."

"Why would someone have a condom in a zip-lock bag?"

"We think the attacker is trying to throw us off and accuse an innocent party of the attacks."

"If you find out whose DNA is in there, can you tell me?"

"I'm not sure. I'll have to ask Detective Jenkins."

"I understand."

"Get some rest Ms. Kent. Someone from the department will call on you in the morning to make sure you are all right. Lock your doors."

"Thanks Officer Trudy."

"You're welcome."

Pam Trudy closed the door behind her as she left with the zip-lock in hand.

Chapter 32

The next night at the Bridge Bar, just across the Bass River in Yarmouth, things were just getting going for the night. A few of the regulars from Sundancers were there. Ed, Tommy, Paul, Tina, and Ann were all seated around the bar. They had come to see a new comedy act appearing for the first time. The Bridge Bar had its own regulars, including cougars. Tim Hurst was the bartender on duty when Bobby Jones walked in. Bobby saw his friends seated at the bar and he joined them.

"Hey Tommy, Paul. What's going on?" said Bobby.

Tommy looked around the bar. "It looks like this place is going to be hopping tonight. I guess a lot of people want to see the comedy act."

Paul added, "I don't know about the comedy, but the cougar show should be interesting."

"Got your eye on anyone specific?" said Bobby to Paul.

"Yeah. Do you see that red head at the end of the bar? I'd like to hook up with her."

Ann had overheard the guys talking, "Paul, you don't have it in you to go after something like that."

"I do too."

"Paul, this is Ann you're talking to."

"I know."

"And besides, I know Ruby. She's way out of your league."

287

"You really know her Ann?" Paul asked.

"Yeah. Why? You want to meet her that bad?"

"Sure."

"Then come with me Paulie."

Ann walked over to Ruby Crane.

"Hi Ruby."

"Hi Ann."

"Ruby, my friend here Paul would like to meet you."

"He would?"

She turned to Paul and stuck out her hand."

"Ruby Crane."

Paul took her hand, "Paul Bremmer."

"Nice to meet you Paul."

Ann turned to walk away, "I've done my job Paulie. The rest is up to you."

"Thanks Ann," said Paul.

Ann walked back to the others. Paul looked at Ruby.

"Is anyone sitting here?"

"It's all yours Paul."

Paul seated himself next to her and continued the conversation. "So Ruby, how do you know Ann?"

"Ann and I have many of the same friends, and we definitely have the same hobby," she winked at him.

"Oh, I think I understand."

"I'm sure you do."

"I just came over here with my friends tonight to hear the comedy show."

"Look Paul, if someone like me wanted to hook up with you tonight, would you do it?"

"Well, that would certainly improve my night."

"Now, how about we get to know each other a little better?"

"What would you like to know?"

"I already know you're a friend of Ann's, and the rest I'll learn as I go." She put her hand on his thigh and slowly moved it up. As she reached the top of his leg, she looked at Paul's face. He was blushing.

Ruby Crane was wearing a denim skirt that had slid up her legs as she sat on the barstool. She was showing a little more than just her legs now, and Paul was enjoying the show. She wore a crisp white button down blouse. It had short sleeves and was pulled tight across a firm set of 36 Ds. Her complexion was creamy smooth and very tan. Her hand was now between his legs. Ruby was aggressive and Sue was probably right about Paul's ability to handle her. He hung in there anyway.

"Say Paul, why don't we get out of here for awhile? I have a place just down the street."

"I don't know. I was going to see the show with my friends."

"Look Paul, do you want some of this or not?"

Paul looked at her again. "I guess a little while won't hurt."

"Oh, it'll hurt. I promise you that. Finish your drink and follow me to my place."

"Ok. I'm just going to tell my friends I'm going with you."

"No need to Paul. Ann will see us leave and she'll know what's going on."

"If you say so."

"Come on. Let's go. We'll take my car and I'll bring you back."

Ruby got up and left the bar with Paul following her. The two got into her car. They headed west on Route 28. Just past McDonalds, Ruby took a right, then a left. She turned into the first driveway. She turned the car off and got out. Paul got out and followed her.

"Come on in."

Paul followed Ruby into her house.

The house was a small ranch with three bedrooms, two baths and a large family room off the kitchen. The house was neat and nicely appointed. Ruby turned on the lights as they entered.

"Paul, there's a bottle of wine and beer in the fridge. Open the wine and pour me a glass. Help yourself to some, or have a beer. Your choice."

"Sure."

"I'll slip into something more comfortable while you're doing that."

Ruby went down the hallway and into one of the bedrooms. She came back dressed in a red silk robe. Paul came out of the kitchen with two glasses of wine and stopped in his tracks when he saw her seated on the couch. Ruby had long flowing strawberry blonde hair that came around to the front of her robe, which was undone. Paul could see she had nothing on under the robe. Ruby motioned for Paul to sit next to her on the couch. He put the drinks down on the coffee table and started to sit. Before he could, she said, "Hold on a minute if you would Paul."

He stood in front of her for a minute. Ruby undid his belt and his pants. She unzipped his fly and pushed his pants and underwear to the floor in one smooth motion. Then she stood and helped him pull his shirt off over his head. Paul stood there in front of her naked. He was very aroused and Ruby took control of things at that point. At one point, Ruby leaned over and put a blue pill into Paul's drink. It quickly dissolved. Paul didn't see her do it.

The things she did drove him absolutely crazy. He wasn't sure if he could keep himself from going too far and was relieved when she stood. She looked down at an aroused Paul and said, "A toast to your stamina."

Paul didn't understand. He picked up his glass and finished it.

"Let's take this to the bedroom."

Paul followed her into the bedroom where they both got onto the king size bed in unison. Ruby held on to Paul. "Come here and let me have you."

Soon the two were moving as one. Paul began to breathe heavily and had all he could do to hold back. He tried but she was just too much. He felt his entire body tense up and then was relieved. Just as he was about done, Ruby's motions quickened and she climaxed.

"I wasn't sure I would be able to hold out long enough for you Ruby."

"You did just fine Paul. Give it a few minutes and we can go at it again."

"I don't think I could be ready in another few minutes."

"You leave it to me. I'm sure I can have you ready to go again in another few minutes."

"Ok, but I have never done it twice in the same night."

"Paul, I know my business. Twice is easy. Heck, three or four times is easy."

"You're kidding me?"

"I don't kid about sex. It's easy for us women. We just have to lie back and be in the mood. You guys have to get it up and I've taken care of helping you out."

"After doing it once, I'm not sure how long it will take to do it again."

"It's all mind over matter. When I get done with you, you'll see what I mean."

In another twenty minutes, Paul was ready to go again. This went on for another hour. In that time, Paul responded three times and Ruby did many times. When Paul looked at his watch, an hour and half had passed and he had done things he had never done before in his life. In fact, he actually hurt from going at it for so long.

When he winced, Ruby said, "See, I told you I would hurt you."

"Yes you did, and yes you did."

"Paul, now you know what it means to be with a real cougar."

"I don't know about the cougar part but you are certainly a skilled beautiful woman."

"I am at that."

"I feel a little stuffed up. That has never happened to me after sex."

"You probably never had Viagra before either."

"I haven't."

"Now you have."

"I don't understand."

"It was in the wine."

"Will it hurt me?"

"You'll have to be the judge of that Paul. But from what I can see, it only helped you."

"I guess."

"How about if we get back to catch some of the comedy show if it isn't over."

"Ok. I'd like to go back there as well."

The two got dressed and went back to the Bridge Bar. As they entered the bar, the comedy act was in full swing. The comedian, Johnny O'Reilly, was into a portion of his act where he interacts with the audience. When he saw Ruby and Paul come in, he said, "Now here's an interesting couple."

Paul put his head down in embarrassment, while Ruby stood up straighter flipping her long strawberry blond hair back. Ruby went over to talk to some of her friends. Paul went over to Tommy and stood behind him. Johnny, seeing the two go in different directions said, "Was it something I said?" The audience laughed.

Ann saw Paul hiding. "So, did she work you over?"

"I'll say."

Tommy turned around, "Paulie, got your pipes cleaned?"

"You don't know the half of it Tommy."

292

"Oh, I think I get the picture."

"I'll tell you about it another time."

Ann added, "With Ruby, I'm sure she gave you the whole enchilada."

"Aw Paulie, I'm sure you gave as good as you got."

Ed had been seated on the other side of Tommy and heard the whole conversation. He didn't say anything to Paul. After a while, he just kept looking down the bar at Ruby, watching her. When the comedy show was over, Ruby finished her drink, waved to the group, and left the bar. When she did, Ed paid his tab and left right after her. As she left the parking lot headed west, Ed followed her in his car.

Ruby pulled into her driveway. She turned her car off and got out. As she walked up to her front door, she thought she heard another car door close nearby so she hurried up to get her key out. At first, she cursed for not leaving the porch light on as she couldn't find the key in her purse but eventually she found it. As she reached to put the key into the lock, someone jumped her from behind. That was the last thing she remembered.

When Ruby woke up, she was lying on the floor in the middle of her living room. She was completely naked. She had some red marks on her upper legs and could feel warm sticky liquid on her thighs and on her breasts. She knew exactly what it was. As she got up, she reached for her phone and called 911.

Chapter 33

The 911 call came into Yarmouth PD around one. The dispatcher asked the caller to state the emergency.

"My name is Ruby Crane. I've been assaulted."

"Ms. Crane, this is Officer Mike Posner. Do you need immediate medical attention?"

"I have a cut on my head. I think I was raped."

"Do you have any idea who might have done this to you?"

"No. I was attacked from behind as I was opening my house door. I never saw or heard anyone coming at me."

"I have your address and I'm sending a patrol car and an ambulance to your location. You should hear and see them coming in a few minutes."

"Thank you Officer Posner. I need to put some clothes on."

"Ms. Crane. Please stay on the phone with me until help arrives. Do you know if your attacker is still at your home?"

"I don't think so. I got home around eleven so the attack happened around then. I don't think anyone hung around."

Ruby could hear the sirens approaching her house. Then in another minute there was a knock on the door. She hadn't gotten anything on yet and had to make a quick decision. She went to the door and turned on the outside light.

"Ms. Crane, this is Officer Glen Simon. I'm here with paramedics to help you. Can you open the door and let us in?"

The door opened and a woman stuck her head out from behind the door.

"Are you all right?" asked Officer Simon.

He could see blood dripping down the side of her head and neck. The paramedics saw it also, "She might be in shock."

Officer Simon carefully pushed the door back and held Ruby's arm. The two paramedics came in and set their first aid gear on the floor. When the paramedics turned around a frightened, naked Ruby Crane stood there in front of them covering her eyes, sobbing. Paramedic Justin Parker went down the hallway to a bedroom and got Ruby's robe that had been thrown on the floor. He came back and handed it to Officer Simon. He carefully put it around Ruby. Then, paramedic Richard Michaels got bandages and gauze from the first aid kit and applied them to the cut on Ruby's head.

"Ms. Crane, the dispatcher indicated you were attacked. Is there anything you can tell us?"

"I came home from the Bridge Bar sometime around eleven. I remember hearing a car door close somewhere nearby as I was going to open my house door and that's the last thing I remember until I called 911."

"Did you come home alone?"

"Yes and no."

"What do you mean yes and no?"

"I had come home earlier in the evening with someone. We went out a little while later and then I came home alone after that."

"What is the name of the person you came home with?"

"Paul Bremmer, but Paul didn't do this."

"Are you sure?"

"Look officer. Paul and I were intimate for about an hour and a half. I wanted him to stay longer but he wanted to see the comedy show at the Bridge Bar tonight. He wouldn't have had any reason to do this."

"I'd like you to go to the hospital with the paramedics and have a sexual assault kit completed. You may need stitches as well."

"Yes, but I had sex with Paul tonight so I'm sure his DNA will show up."

"If you were sexually attacked by someone else, that DNA will show up also."

Paramedic Parker and Officer Simon had a conversation and then Parker and Michaels prepared Ruby for transport. When they were ready, they put Ruby into the ambulance and left for the hospital.

Officer Simon called dispatch from his patrol car and spoke with Officer Posner.

"Posner, I'm just wrapping up here at the Crane residence. She's going with the paramedics to the hospital to have a cut on her head looked after and for a rape test. Is there anything else that the Captain wants me to do here?"

"We're all set Simon. Captain said for you to turn in your report as soon as you can. He thinks the attack might be linked to attacks that have been taking place in Dennis."

"Will do. I'm on my way back to the station now."

Captain Barnes of Yarmouth PD had known Captain Tomlinson of Dennis PD for years. They had both come up through the ranks in their respective departments. The two regularly met for lunch and discussed happenings in their respective departments. Over the years, the cooperation had helped both solve cases. Tomlinson had discussed the recent attacks in Dennis with Barnes so Barnes put in a call to Tomlinson after reading the morning briefs.

"Lou, its Phil Barnes. We had an attack on a woman in Yarmouth last night and the MO sounds like the cases you've had in your area."

"Where did it take place Phil?"

"Over near Stop and Shop. A woman who had been at the Bridge Bar was attacked as she was unlocking her door. She woke up a few hours later naked lying on her living room floor with a pretty bad cut on her head."

"Sounds similar. I'd like to have Detective Jenkins look at the info if I can."

"Sure. Have him ask for Officer Glen Simon, he's the investigating officer."

"Thanks Phil."

Captain Tomlinson hung up and then immediately called Detective Jenkins.

"Frank, its Lou. A woman was attacked in Yarmouth last night and it looks like it might be our guy. Can you get over to Yarmouth PD?"

"Sure. Who should I see?"

"Ask for Officer Glen Simon. He was the officer on the scene. If you run into any problems, speak with Captain Barnes."

"Will do."

Jenkins hung up the phone. He got into his car and headed to Yarmouth PD. When he got to the Yarmouth station, he asked for Simon. The dispatcher called Officer Simon on the intercom.

"Detective, I'm Officer Glen Simon."

"Frank Jenkins. My Captain called me and asked me to come right over. Your boss called him and said there was an attack last night that looked like it might be similar to a number of cases we are pursuing. Can you tell me what you have?"

Officer Simon handed him a copy of his report. Jenkins read it, "Sure sounds similar."

"How can we help you?"

"I'd like to talk to some of the people at the bar where the woman had been before being attacked."

"Sure, would you like our assistance?"

"That would be a help. When can you join me?"

"How about later today, say four?"

"Ok. I'll come by and pick you up. I'll catch up with Ms. Crane earlier and get some names."

"I'll be ready."

Jenkins took the copy of the report and left the station. He had some research to do and wanted to review the information with Captain Tomlinson.

Detective Jenkins went back to Dennis PD. After checking his computer, he knocked on Captain Tomlinson's door.

"Captain, I followed up with Yarmouth PD regarding the attack there last night. The attack looks a lot like the attacks that have taken place in our jurisdiction recently. I met with an Officer Simon, who was the investigating officer. I asked him specifically about the conditions of the victim such as cat-like scratches, DNA samples etc. He indicated the victim did have a rape kit taken but the results haven't yielded any matches to any of our samples. He's going to get names of people the victim was with last night at the Bridge Bar before the attack, and then we're meeting up there to conduct some interviews. That'll be at sixteen hundred hours. I'll let you know if the they yield any positive results."

"Thanks Jenkins. Captain Barnes is a good friend and has told me they would like to work with us in resolving these attacks."

"Maybe they will see something we missed."

"Maybe. Let me know if I need to get involved."

"Will do."

Detective Jenkins went back to his desk. He logged on to his computer and entered the information he had gathered into the electronic case files he had been gathering regarding the cases. He sent an e-mail to Officer Simon of Yarmouth PD and provided him with the access information to the case files he and Officer Trudy had assembled. This would allow Officer Simon to be able to see all of the information Dennis PD had gathered. Officer Simon had already provided Detective Jenkins with the appropriate access information to the Yarmouth PD files so Jenkins called up the Yarmouth information and reviewed it. The profile certainly matched those already on file in the Dennis PD files.

At 3:45 Detective Jenkins got into his cruiser and went to Yarmouth PD. He picked up Officer Simon and the two set out to conduct interviews.

"Frank, I wasn't able to speak with Ruby earlier. I guess she had some appointment or something. But she did agree to meet with us at 4:00. I figured we could go together before we head to the Bridge Bar."

"Works for me. The bar will be busier later anyway. Better chance of hooking up with some of the same people."

The first stop was a visit to Ruby Crane. They arrived at Ruby's house a little after four.

Knocking on the door, Ruby greeted them. "Officer Simon, right on time."

"Ms. Crane, this is Detective Jenkins of the Dennis PD. He's been investigating similar attacks in Dennis recently so our departments are working together to see if your attack might have been committed by the same attacker. It might help both departments solve the cases faster."

"Hello Detective Jenkins."

"Nice to meet you Ms. Crane. We would like to ask you a few more questions about the attack if you don't mind."

"Please come in."

The two went into the house. Ruby asked them if they would like coffee or something. Both officers said coffee would be fine. She led them to the kitchen where the two sat around a small table while Ruby made a pot of coffee.

"How do you men take it?" She smiled as she asked the question.

Jenkins said he would like it with cream, Simon had his black.

"What questions do you have?"

Jenkins opened his pad and took out a pen. "Did you notice any unusual scratches on your body after the attack?"

"Now that you mention it, I do have scratches I can't explain."

"Are they like bruises from scratches?" asked Jenkins.

"Yes. How did you know?"

"Can we see them?"

"They are in a rather private place. Since you are investigating the attack on me, I guess you can." She lifted up her blouse and showed them the scratches on the side of her left breast. The two officers looked at each other but didn't say anything.

"I thought the scratches must have happened in a fall or something. Do you suspect something else?"

"Some of the other victims have also had cat-like scratches. It seems to be some kind of signature. Do you have any scratches anywhere else?"

"A few inside my thigh." Ruby stood up and started to undo her pants when Officer Simon said, "That will not be necessary Ms. Crane. We get the picture."

"I don't mind Officer. I want you to catch the pervert."

Detective Jenkins added, "Did the hospital take any pictures of the scratches?"

"No. Would you like to take a picture?"

"If you don't mind," said Jenkins.

"I don't mind. Plus, these have been photographed many times already."

Jenkins took a digital camera out of his bag. He turned it on and asked her to stand sideways. He asked her to cover her other breast and only expose the scratches. Then he moved in to about two feet away and took a picture. He made a note in his file of the picture number, the date, time and who was present.

"Do you need a bigger picture showing my face Detective?"

"No. Officer Simon is a witness. If we need to use this, we have all we need."

Then Jenkins asked her to show him the other scratches. Ruby stood up and pulled her pants down. She

300

lifted her left leg so the scratches on her right leg could be easily seen. Jenkins took his camera and stood about two feet away from her leg and took another picture.

"Thanks Ms. Crane. These might be a big help. You can pull your pants back up."

Ruby pulled her pants up, with a little left to right action for good measure, and then slowly re-buttoned her blouse.

"What will you do with those pictures?" she asked.

"I'll log them into our computer under the electronic file for your case. If they have to be recalled for use at a later time, then they will probably be printed."

"Who has access to the pictures?" Ruby said in a soft voice.

"Only officials at the PD who have a reason to look at your case file. The pictures are put into a secure file that can only be accessed with the proper credentials. Only people who need to have access to the pictures will be aware of that information."

"Then I shouldn't have to worry about them becoming public knowledge or showing up on some sordid website?"

"No, you don't have to worry."

"Thanks Detective. While I might be a little outgoing, I don't want my body spread around."

"That can't happen Ms. Crane."

"Good."

Jenkins put the camera back into the bag. Then the two walked through Ruby's recollection again. She provided the officers with the names of the people she could remember at the bar: Ed Phillips, Tommy Anderson, Paul Bremmer, Tina Fletcher, Ann Benard, Bobby Jones, and the bartender, Tim Hurst.

"Is there anything else you can think of Ms. Crane that might help us with this case?"

"I don't think so Detective. I've told the same story to Officer Simon and you. I don't think I can think of another thing."

"Well, if you do, please give me a call."

He handed her his card.

As they got into Jenkins' cruiser to go to the next place, Officer Simon said, "Did you get a look at her body?"

"How could I miss it?"

"She's very well built."

"And likes to show it off."

"Do you think there's any possibility her story has holes in it?"

"The other victims in the cases my department has been pursuing have all been pretty good looking women mostly in their forties. I would characterize them as cougars, women who like younger men and are pretty aggressive about it. Ms. Crane seems to be cut from the same cloth. The only thing that differs in this case that I can see right now are the scratches on her thighs. In the other cases, the scratches are mostly on the upper body, looking like they occurred during a struggle. These lower scratches look like they took place during a sexual attack. Our attacker already has the victims unconscious by the time the attack takes place, but not every victim was sexually assaulted. It's almost like they got interrupted. I don't know what to make of it yet."

"Then you have some doubt about her claims?"

"No. I don't doubt she was attacked and probably raped, but a difficult issue in these cases is the role the victims played in the attacks."

"What do you mean?"

"Well, did the victims mislead the attacker?"

"How could the victim mislead the attacker?"

"Let's say the victim and the attacker were at a bar. Let's say the victim was flirting with the attacker, and let's say alcohol was involved."

"Yeah?"

"If we charge someone and a scenario like that is uncovered, then there might be circumstances indicating consent or would at least lessen the severity of the crimes.

Random acts of violence somehow don't play out the same as non-random acts in a jury case."

"So why would any of that affect the case?"

"An all male jury might have some sympathy for the attacker and hostility towards the victims."

"I see what you mean."

"Let's go to the Bridge Bar and talk with the staff there. Maybe we'll catch up with some of these people Ruby named, although I already know many from my cases. Either way, we'll get a better picture of what transpired."

"Good idea."

Detective Jenkins and Officer Simon pulled into the Bridge Bar parking lot. The two went inside. They introduced themselves to the bartender, Tim Hurst, and asked if he could answer a few questions.

Tim said, "Sure Detective. What do you want to know?"

Detective Jenkins started the questioning.

"Mr. Hurst, do you know a Ms. Ruby Crane?"

"Yes. She comes in here all the time."

"Were you bartending last night during the comedy show?"

"Yes."

"Do you remember Ms. Crane being here?"

"Yes. Has something happened to her?"

"She was attacked last night."

"I thought something was up with her."

Officer Simon spoke up. "What do you mean?"

"She was here having a few drinks. Some of the guys who come in usually after baseball games were sitting down the bar. One of the guys left with her before the show. They were gone for about an hour and a half and then came back. When they got back, they went their separate ways. The comedian made a joke about them when they came in and I'm not sure the guy appreciated it."

Detective Jenkins asked, "Do you know the name of the man?"

"Yes. It was Paul Bremmer."

Continuing, Jenkins asked, "Did something happen later on in the night?"

"Well, sort of."

"What happened?" Officer Simon asked.

"Well, Paul was talking with Tommy Anderson. He was telling him what he and Ruby had done. This other guy, Ed, was listening. He seemed to be interested in Ruby. Later on that night when Ruby left, after the show, Ed left right after her."

"Did the two have any conversation that you know about?"

"Not that I'm aware. Ed kept looking at her after he overheard the Paul and Tommy conversation."

Detective Jenkins asked, "Anything else?"

"No. That's all I can remember involving Ruby."

Officer Simon asked, "Did anything else happen with anyone else at the bar?"

"Look Officer, these women are on the prowl all the time. This is pretty much the same way most nights go. Its difficult keeping track of who is with who if you know what I mean. We had a group of them in here last night because of the comedy show."

"Do you know the names of any of them?"

"Sure, there was Sue Kent, Ann Benard, Tina Fletcher, Linda Sage and of course Ruby Crane. Linda was here much earlier than the rest and left way before the show."

"Do you know who any of them talked with?"

"Let's see. Bobby Jones, Tommy Anderson, Paul Bremmer, Ed Phillips. I don't remember who talked with whom, but I know Paul left with Ruby for a little while. Katherine Sterns was also here, she sat away from the group a little with Tom Bowman."

"Tom Bowman?"

"Yeah. He used to come in here a lot until Katherine's husband who was Tom's fishing partner, died in a fishing accident."

304

"So you knew her husband?"

"Sure. A lot of sportsmen come into the Bridge Bar. Sam and Tom used to come in here all the time."

"How would you characterize the relationship between Mr. Bowman and Ms. Sterns?"

"I don't know. They know each other. They didn't seem to be romantic if that's what you are asking."

Officer Simon asked, "Is Ms. Sterns one of those cougars you described?"

"Since her husband died, she has been known to be with a number of different men. I don't know to what extent she seeks out younger men, but I'm sure she's lonely."

Detective Jenkins said, "Why do you say that?"

"After being in this business, I can tell you women that look like her and drink a lot are searching for something."

"I think we get the picture Mr. Hurst."

"Anything else?" asked Jenkins.

"No, that's about it."

"Thank you for you help," said Officer Simon.

Detective Jenkins produced a card and handed it to Mr. Hurst. "If you think of anything else, please call."

"Will do."

Frank looked around the bar, which was still pretty quiet, looking for any of the regulars. Just a couple of mailmen sitting having a drink after work, so the two left the bar. When they got into the cruiser, Simon said, "So you think this guy Ed had something to do with the attack?"

"I don't know, let's see if he's at Sundancers. If he's there, we can ask him to step outside for a few minutes. If he's involved, our questioning will probably shake him up."

"We can do a good guy bad guy routine on him."

"Good idea."

"Ok Frank, you be the bad guy."

Chapter 34

When Detective Jenkins and Officer Simon arrive at Sundancers, they were happy to see Ed Phillips was standing outside, having a cigarette. Detective Jenkins approached him. "Mr. Phillips, may Officer Simon and I have a word with you?"

"What's this about?"

Ed was a little nervous and kept looking around.

Officer Simon asked, "Mr. Phillips, were you at the Bridge Bar last night?"

"Yea. I was there to hear the comedy show."

"Do you know a Ms. Ruby Crane?"

"Not personally, but I know who she is."

"Did you have any contact with her last night?"

"No."

"Mr. Phillips, Officer Simon and I are investigating an attack on Ms. Crane last night."

"And you think I did it?"

"Well, did you?" said Jenkins.

"Mr. Phillips, can I call you Ed?" Simon said pleasantly, playing the good cop to perfection.

"Sure. Whatever." Ed threw his cigarette into the bucket nearby.

"Ed, you were observed leaving the bar right after Ms. Crane but before she was attacked."

"I didn't attack her. I might have followed her home, but I didn't attack her."

Jenkins jumped on the statement, "So you admit to following her home?"

"I was trying to get up the nerve to talk with her here, but chickened out. When she left, I thought I'd have more guts one on one at her house. But I just drove past her driveway when she got home. I didn't stop."

Even more aggressively, Jenkins said, "So you followed her home. Maybe she wasn't interested in you, and so you got angry?"

"No. I didn't. That's not what happened. I didn't even get out of my car. I swear."

As Jenkins was about to ask another question, Simon stopped him.

"Ed, would you be willing to provide a DNA sample?"

"I wouldn't mind. I didn't do anything."

"A simple DNA test will probably do."

"You tell me when and where and I'll be there."

"You got it tough guy. I can take the sample right now and right here," Jenkins forcefully countered. He went to the cruiser and got a collection kit. He walked back and asked Ed to swab inside his cheeks, and to place the swab in the sterile beaker. Jenkins put the cap on and labeled it, E. Phillips. "That's all I need. We'll get back to you."

"I telling you I didn't do anything. I've been trying to get up the nerve to ask her out. I'm not the most outgoing person. That is all I'm guilty of."

"Do you have a problem with women Ed?" Simon gently asked.

"Not a problem. I'm just a quiet person. I'm not aggressive like those other guys at the bars. It takes me longer to get to know someone."

"You don't seem to have any problems with the women at Sundancers," Jenkins probed.

"It took me a long time to get to know some of them."

"So if you can't get to know them here, you get to know them at home?" said Jenkins.

"You make it sound like I'm stalking these women. That's not how it is. These women are always looking for men, and they find them."

"We know all about the cougars Ed," said Simon.

Jenkins wrapped things up, "Mr. Phillips, don't leave town. Once we get the results of the sample, we'll be looking for you."

"Didn't you want to check inside, see if there was anyone else we should talk to?" asked Simon.

"Nah. I've been talking to most of the others, and the place will be there tomorrow. I got a hunch about this Phillips."

Jenkins and Simon got into the cruiser and left, with Ed looking on helplessly. "I know you think he's guilty Frank, but I'm not totally convinced yet."

"The DNA test will tell us more."

"Anywhere else you want to try tonight?"

"No. I think we have enough for today. If you don't mind, I'm gonna take this swab to the lab Glen and have it tested against the DNA that was collected from Ms. Crane. I'll let you know what they find."

"No, I don't mind. Just keep me in the loop."

Jenkins drove Officer Simon back to the Yarmouth police station. Then he went to the lab and dropped off the sample. He remembered his conversation with Linda Sage and decided to have a talk with the lab manager, Vince Maurcaux.

"Vince."

"Hey Detective."

"Vince, I had a talk with Linda Sage recently and she said she's your sister. How come you have different last names?"

"She used to be married and still goes by her married name. What's she done now?"

"Well, she's playing private eye and trying to get DNA samples from people she thinks might have attacked her, or anyone else in Dennis."

"Yeah, she's always been the nosey type."

"She said she's obtaining DNA samples from men she suspects might be involved and having you test them against the DNA samples the police have turned in."

"She said that, did she?"

"You know you're not supposed to be doing that, right?"

"What harm can it do?"

"She isn't an official. She could get hurt. Plus it compromises our cases."

"I'm sure she's very discrete in how she gets her evidence."

"I wouldn't call it discrete. She's sleeping with men to get evidence."

"I don't think she's sleeping with them to get evidence. I think she's collecting evidence after the fact just to see if any of the guys she knows might be. She's just protecting herself."

"I hope you're right. Do me a favor and call me if any of the samples she turns in match up."

"I intended to do that anyway. After all, she's my sister and a victim."

"And don't tell her about our conversation."

"I won't."

"Vince, did you do any testing on samples submitted by Yarmouth PD involving a Ruby Crane?"

"Yeah, why do you ask?"

"I'm working with Officer Simon trying to see if there are similarities between the attacks happening in my town."

"I ran the samples and only identified Paul Bremmer's DNA. There was DNA from someone else that I couldn't identify."

"Did you check it out against Tom Bowman's DNA?"

"No. But I can."

"Can you call me once you have checked it?"

"If you can wait five minutes, I can tell you right now. My computers are very fast and I have both samples in the computer."

Vince sat at his keyboard and typed a few strokes. The computer started to process and in about twenty seconds the screen came back with two profiles. The one on the left was from Ruby Crane's sample. The one on the right was from the condom sample Detective Jenkins had previously turned in identified as Tom Bowman. Large letters were displayed on the lower part of the screen. **"Exact Match."**

Jenkins left the lab. Driving back to the station, he thought about the details of the attack against Ms. Crane. Something wasn't right. This was the first time the attacker moved outside of the circle of cougars from Sundancers. While the Sundancers cougars knew Ms. Crane, the stalker would have expanded his range to another town and other bars. Could the attacker be branching out?

Getting back into the station, Jenkins got on to the Internet and looked up the recent police briefing reports for the surrounding towns. He specifically searched for rape attacks. He didn't get any hits within a fifty-mile radius of Dennis for the thirty-day period he requested. He thought if the same attacker had attacked Ruby Crane, then it must be one of the men who went to the comedy show that night at the Bridge Bar.

Jenkins opened his pad. He had the names Tommy Anderson, Paul Bremmer, Ed Phillips, Bobby Jones and Tom Bowman written. He checked them off one by one as having DNA samples already at the lab. Then it hit him. These were the same names of the samples he had seen in Katherine's freezer. Why would she have these samples? Was she doing

310

the same detective work Linda Sage was trying to do? He would have to confront her and find out.

Chapter 35

When Detective Jenkins got back to the station, he summoned Officer Trudy to come to his office.

"Did you find out anything new with the Yarmouth case?" Pam Trudy asked as she sat down.

"Yes and no. The victim there had scratches on her upper legs. Those differ from the victims in the cases we have investigated so far. Up to now, all of the scratches have been on the upper body as if occurring during a struggle. The scratches on Ms. Crane in Yarmouth looked like they took place during a sexual attack."

"Frank, when I was following up on Ms. Kent, I could see the attacker through the window as I approached the house. The person standing over Ms. Kent was doing something with a zip-lock bag over Ms. Kent's body. That was when I tripped over the rainspout and fell. The attacker was tipped off by the noise and got away. But I found this dropped on the floor next to the bed. Trudy held up a zip-lock bag.

Inside, the two looked at a used condom. On the outside of the zip-lock was an inscription. Pam Trudy read it out loud.

"T. Bowman. What does it mean?" asked Pam quizzically.

"Pam, go back to Ms. Kent's. Ask her for her pajamas she had on just before the attack. Ask for her bed sheets if they haven't been washed yet. Take them to the lab and have them checked for DNA. Take the zip-lock as well and have it tested also."

"Do you have an idea of what this is all about?"

"I'm getting a better picture."

"Care to share it?"

"Not yet. I'll fill you in later."

Officer Trudy took the items to the lab for DNA testing.

Detective Jenkins got on his computer and wrote up his findings. Then he went home. He tried to call Katherine but didn't get an answer at her house. As he was thinking about fixing dinner, his phone rang.

"Frank, what are you doing for dinner?"

"Hi Pam, I was gonna make something here."

"Want to join me?"

"What did you have in mind?"

"How about meeting me at Sundancers in a half hour?"

"I could do that."

"See you in a half hour."

A half hour later, Frank Jenkins walked into Sundancers. He saw Pam sitting at a table away from the bar on the far side, reading a menu, with a glass of red wine in front of her. He walked over, bent over and gave her a kiss on the cheek.

"I'm glad you called. I was about to have cold leftovers."

"And now you don't have to do that."

The waitress came over and he ordered a beer. The two selected dinner items from the menu. After getting his beer from the waitress and taking a pull, he was about to say something when Katherine Sterns approached him from behind.

"Hi Frank. How are you doing?"

"Long day Katherine. Do you know Officer Trudy?"

"We've met. Hello Officer Trudy," she said coldly.

"Ms. Sterns."

The two shook hands. Frank could feel the hostility.

"Discussing business, Detective?" Katherine asked in a condescending tone.

"Nah, just having a bite to eat."

"Just dinner huh?"

"Is there something I can do for you Katherine?"

"Could be, but I see you're occupied tonight."

Pam Trudy shot Frank a glance.

"Don't let me interrupt your evening, Detective," said Katherine smiling. Then she turned and walked away.

"What was that all about Frank?"

"I think she's jealous."

"Of what?"

"I don't know. Sometimes I wonder," said Frank as he looked back watching Katherine go back to the bar.

The two got their dinners. Pam had baked stuffed salmon. Frank had a prime rib dinner. They had an after dinner drink and talked about the case during dinner. Frank told her about the Yarmouth case showing similarities to the Dennis cases. When done, Jenkins saw Katherine still sitting at the bar, alone. He said, "Pam, do you mind staying here for a little while longer to watch Ms. Sterns over there. I want to see if she meets up with anyone else tonight. I'd like to run over to the Bridge Bar to ask the bartender there a question."

"I don't mind. Should I wait for you to come back?"

"No. If you don't mind, I'll go home after talking with the people I want to see at the Bridge Bar. I'll check in with you tomorrow."

"Ok. I'll stay for an hour or so."

"If she does meet up with someone, see if you can get a name or at least a description."

314

"Will do."

Pam picked up her glass and took up an empty stool at the bar. Margarita came over for some chitchat.

"Ms. Trudy, I noticed you and the Detective have been in a few times on a non-business basis. What's the Detective like?"

"He's intense. He is very focused on his work."

"Not like that. What's he like in bed?"

"Why do you ask? Are you interested in him?"

"He's cute. All the cougars are talking about him."

"What are they saying?"

"Well, Katherine and Linda say he is very good."

"How would they know?"

"They both said they have been with him."

"They have?"

"That's what they said."

"And Sue said she wants him for one night."

"What's all this interest?"

"I think it's the authority thing. Me personally, I like a man in uniform."

"But he doesn't wear a uniform."

"Well, maybe I just like men."

"Margarita, I thought you were spoken for?"

"Oh, I am. I'm just fantasizing."

"I guess it's ok to fantasize."

"Maybe I'll get up the nerve to talk to him sometime."

"You should. He's really a nice guy."

"Thanks Ms. Trudy. I might do that."

Pam had just ordered another drink when she saw a man come in and sit next to Katherine. Trudy thought she knew who it was and confirmed it when she asked Margarita if she knew the man Katherine was talking with. She said it was Tom Bowman, so Pam made a note of it, paid her tab and left the bar. Katherine Sterns and Tom Bowman left right after her.

Meanwhile, Detective Jenkins went back to the Bridge Bar and talked with Tim Hurst. He had a few more questions about Tom Bowman.

"Mr. Hurst, do you mind if I ask you a few more questions?"

"I don't mind Detective, but you'll have to bear with me while I work."

"No problem. I'll try not to get in the way."

"Ok, then what do you want to know?"

"Tell me about the relationship between Tom Bowman and Sam Sterns?"

"They used to come in here all the time. They were fishing buddies and would come in after their outings or sometimes for the day if the weather wasn't so good."

"Was there any friction between the two?"

"Not that I can recall, but there would have been if Sam had known about Tom sleeping with his wife."

"What do you know about that?"

"Well, after Sam died, Tom was in here one night right after the funeral and said he didn't think she would ever sleep with him again. He was pretty sauced and depressed."

"And who was he talking about?"

"He was very specific. He said Katherine. Then he went on to tell me about how he had slept with her at the Route 28 motel one night when his fishing partner was away on business."

"So they were having an affair?"

"I don't know about an affair, but Tom said he slept with her." Tim stopped and thought about it for a minute, "Now that I think about it, I've seen the two of them in here together a number of times recently. But I don't understand your interest in Sam. Hasn't that case been closed for awhile?"

"I don't know, but this information is very suspicious. Is there anything else you can tell me?"

"When Ruby Crane left here the other night after the show, Katherine Sterns and Tom Bowman were both in here.

316

Right after Ruby left for the night, Katherine left and then came back."

"Did Tom Bowman leave?"

"No, he stayed until she came back. That was about twenty minutes later."

"Did you see Ed Phillips leave?"

"Yes, he left right before Katherine but after Ruby."

"Did he come back?"

"No."

"Do you know how long Tom and Katherine were here after she came back in?"

"No, I don't. It was a real busy night."

"Anything else?"

"No. I think that's it."

"Thank you Mr. Hurst. If you think of anything else, please call."

"I will. I have your card right here," Tim tapped the card taped to the cash register.

Chapter 36

Later that night, Officer Trudy was at home. She watched a little television and decided to go to bed around nine. She went out to her car to lock it for the night. As she walked back to her house, someone jumped her. Her reaction was to reach down for her service revolver, but she didn't have it. She had taken it off when she changed into sweats for bed. She was knocked down to the ground and scratched across the neck in the process. Then the lights went out. Something struck her head.

When she awoke, it was around eleven. Her sweat pants and underwear were thrown on the back lawn. Her sweatshirt and bra were near the door. She shivered from the coolness of the night. She was just outside her door, naked on her back step. She rose slowly and then went inside and called 911.

"911, please state your emergency."

"This is Officer Trudy," she said in a shaky voice.

"Trudy, this is Sergeant Grimes. Are you ok?"

"I'm a little shaky Sergeant. Someone jumped me when I was locking up my place for the night."

"Do you need help?"

"I don't think so. The attacker might still be in my neighborhood. Can you send a car over to take a look around?"

"Sure."

Trudy could hear Sergeant Grimes talk into the police radio system. He had requested two patrol cars in Trudy's vicinity go to her neighborhood and look for suspicious persons. Then he came back on the phone.

"Trudy, two cars are on their way. What happened?"

"I was just closing things up for the night. When I went outside to get something out of my car and lock it, someone jumped me on the way back in."

"Did you get a look at the attacker?"

"No. I was hit on the head with something. I must have been knocked out completely right away. I woke a few minutes ago and found myself lying on my back porch, naked."

"Were you raped?"

"I don't think so."

"I'm going to call Detective Jenkins. Please hold on."

Sergeant Grimes put her on hold. He called Detective Jenkins who was in his office at the station. "Detective, I have Officer Trudy on hold. She just called in to 911. She was attacked."

"When?"

"A little while ago. She said someone jumped her as she walked back into her house when locking up for the night."

"Is she all right?"

"She says she is. Do you want to talk to her?"

"Tell her I'll be there in a few minutes."

"Will do. I've dispatched two patrol cars to her location as well. I'll call you if they find anything."

"Ok Grimes."

Sergeant Grimes pressed the flashing button on the phone. "Trudy, Detective Jenkins is on his way to your house. He said he would be there in a few minutes."

"Thanks Grimes. I'm going inside to put some ice on my head."

Jenkins didn't waste any time driving to Trudy's home. He was kicking himself for not following up with her earlier, after he left the Bridge Bar. How could he have gotten so distracted? He pulled into her driveway and turned his car off. Pam met him at the door. She was holding an ice pack against her head.

"Are you ok?"

"Just a few scratches and a bump on the head."

"Anything else?"

"If you're asking if I was attacked sexually, I don't think so. The attacker took my clothes off, but I don't think anything else was done."

"How can you be sure?"

"I would know."

"Those are pretty bad scratches?"

"They hurt. I don't know what could have caused them? They look like cat claws when I looked at them in the mirror."

Jenkins looking closely at them, "Or real nails."

"You think someone has real nails with sharp points?"

"I've recently learned of the latest thing in fake nails. They're called Flips. The original nail has to be shaped in order to hold the snap-on nail in place. The original nail is modified to look like a cat's claw kind of. A shape like that could certainly have done this."

"I've never heard of them."

"Look Pam, I'd like you to get checked out."

"I'm not going to the hospital Frank. I'll be fine."

"I'd like you to have a rape test."

"I wasn't raped. I'm not going there."

"You're being stubborn Pam."

"Frank, I was attacked. That should be enough. You know how long it would take to have testing done? I'd rather just go to bed."

"But what if it was our attacker?"

"Then you'd better find him soon if he's attacking cops. That's kind of ballsy."

"Sure is."

Pam noticed a set of headlights shine on her house as another car pulled into her driveway. She and Jenkins went to the door. It was one of the patrol cars Grimes had dispatched to her neighborhood. Jenkins went out on the porch and spoke with the officer. The patrol officer said he and the other patrol car had gone around the immediate neighborhood but found nothing. Jenkins asked them to expand their search a few more streets and then to report back to Sergeant Grimes if they didn't find anything. Jenkins went back into the house.

"Anything?" she asked.

"No. Pam, when you were watching Katherine at Sundancers, did she meet with anyone?"

"Yes. Tom Bowman."

"Why do you ask?"

"No particular reason just yet."

"I left right after the two of them got together at the bar."

"Interesting."

"Then I went home."

"Well I'm going to ask the cruisers to stay visible and in the area for the balance of the night. Double lock your doors. Set your alarm if you have one. Pam, take it easy and call me if you need anything. Then come see me at the station in the morning if you would."

"Ok. I'll see you in the morning."

Jenkins left Trudy's house. He decided to go to Sundancers and see if he could learn anything new. When he got to Sundancers, he talked with Ron Jessup, one of the bartenders.

"Mr. Jessup, do you remember me being here tonight with a blond hair woman?"

"Yes."

"Did you see her leave?"

"Sure did. She left a little while after you did."

"Did anyone else leave around the same time?"

"Yes, Katherine Sterns and Tom Bowman."

"Was it right after the blond hair women left?"

"Right after. I thought it was weird."

"Thanks."

The next morning when Jenkins arrived at the station, Captain Tomlinson called him in to his office.

"Did you learn anything from the Yarmouth case?"

"Definitely another victim with the same pattern. I think our attacker is making the scratches we've seen. Remember the first few attacks? The victims had scratches that looked like a large cat could have done it?"

"Yes, what of it?"

"At first, I had thought the cougar that got loose from the ZooQuarium might have had something to do with the attacks, but these latest attacks can't be tied to the ZooQuarium cougar. It's back in custody. At Sundancers last night the bartender was talking to some folks at the bar about the latest craze. It's a kind of pop on-pop off fingernail. Not acrylic or glue on, so they can be changed rather quickly."

"So what does that have to do with these cases?"

"Well, the real fingernail has to be shaped into a form that the fake nail can snap on to, and is made to look like some kind of pick. Sharp at the end, and rounded on the sides. Then the fake nail can be snapped on and off rather easily."

"You think the attacker has nails like these and is taking the fake nails off when attacking the victims?"

"I think so."

"Does this mean the attacker is a woman?"

"Not necessarily. From what I understand, there are men who have these kinds of nails as well. Course they probably play a guitar, or belong to some weird club."

"Really? So the attacker ends up having something like claws? What about Ms. Crane? Did she have scratches like the others?"

"She had scratches but they looked different and she had them in different places than the others. I have some further investigating to do. When I know more, I'll report back. I have a few suspects I need to check out, especially their fingernails."

"Thanks Frank. Let me know what you find."

"Will do."

Going back to his office, Jenkins got on to his computer and opened up the case file for the attacks. He had developed a theory that the attacker was a woman. He started reading the newer entries most of which identified Tom Bowman's DNA or hair from the materials turned in to the lab. Jenkins thought the focus on Tom Bowman would make his fingernail research a little easier as he could eliminate the other male suspects he had DNA samples on. The one thing that troubled him was how Tom's DNA figured in, if the attacker was a woman. He decided it was time to take a different approach with Katherine Sterns.

When he called Katherine, she told him she was working around her house for the day and he could come over at any time. They agreed on a two o'clock meeting, and Jenkins was ringing the doorbell promptly at that time. Katherine greeted him dressed in jeans and a white t-shirt that was tied tightly in a knot behind her back. Her hair was pulled back into a ponytail. She had a pair of work gloves on her hands. She looked like she had been working in her garden.

"Hello Katherine."

"Hi, Frank."

"Looks like some gardening going on."

"I've been trying to improve the flower gardens around the yard for some time now and today looked like a nice day to attack them. Not too hot, not too cold."

"I have a few things I'd like to run by you if you can give me a little time."

"Sure. Let's sit on the back porch. I'll get us some drinks."

"Ok, but nothing alcoholic."

"I know you're on duty."

"That's right."

"There was another attack recently in Yarmouth. The woman was knocked unconscious like the others. She also had scratches like some of the other victims. When I was at Sundancers, Dee was telling me about a certain kind of fake fingernails that would require the person who has them to have their original nails shaped in a certain way in order to hold the fake nails in place."

"I think I've heard of those nails, they're called Flips I think," Katherine said.

Frank glanced quickly at Katherine's hands but couldn't really tell if her nails were real or fake, and she had left one of the garden gloves on her left hand.

Frank asked if he could use her bathroom for a minute, and while in there, he noticed Katherine had a plastic case on the vanity containing acrylic fingernails. When he came out, he asked her, "Do you have fake fingernails?"

"I have acrylics put on from time to time."

"Do you have the Flips?"

"No, I'm using acrylic nails these days." She held out her hands for him to see. Her nails were acrylics, and Frank held her hands up so that he could see under the nail. There was no sharp tip.

"What are you looking for?" Katherine asked pulling her hand back.

"I wanted to see what your's look like?"

"These nails are glued in place over my own nails. Did you think I had anything to do with those attacks?"

"No. I'm trying to educate myself in fake nails."

Katherine explained the process of getting the acrylics put on and maintained. She talked about how the real nails are typically made very short when the acrylics are first put on, and then once a week or so, she would go back to the salon to have the gaps from nail growth filled in. Katherine also

324

mentioned that having acrylics taken off wasn't a pleasant experience, because the glue was so strong.

"See, it really isn't rocket science."

"But what about the snap on nails, does it require maintenance and appointments too, or is it done at home?"

"That technique is fairly new. I don't want to disfigure my nails so I don't think I would do that. I haven't yet anyway."

"But some women would."

"Probably. Especially someone who wants to be able to change their nails at will."

"Why would someone do that?"

"To have everything match, or to change length quickly, but not permanently."

"You women, it's all about fashion."

"Even some guys use false nails you know Frank."

"For what?"

"There are some guys who are flamboyant and use nails and other female beauty products."

"I can only imagine."

"And I know my former husband used one of my false nails once when one of his had broken really low and he wanted something to cover up the break. And he wanted to keep the rough edge from catching on anything until it grew back in."

"I guess."

"So, having false nails isn't limited to just women."

"Great. I thought I was going to be able to shrink the field of suspects but it doesn't look like it."

"Guess not. Do you mind if I ask you a personal question?"

"What is it?"

"A couple days ago I saw you and Pam Trudy at Sundancers, and it was obviously not business."

"Actually it was. We were trying to look like we were on a date. It's part of the case to find the attacker. We wanted Trudy to look like a potential victim. It must have looked real because you believed it."

"I know faking it when I see it, and that wasn't faking it."

"I don't know what you mean."

"Come on Frank. I saw you two all over each other, and it was hot."

"Katherine, it was all in the line of duty. You seemed to be doing all right at Sundancers as well. Didn't you meet up with Tom Bowman?"

"You know he was a friend of Sam's."

"Yeah, but I thought you told me you never wanted to see him again."

"That was just talk in an emotional state. I know he couldn't help what happened to Sam."

"Maybe yes, maybe no."

"Do you know something I don't?"

"No. I'm just suspicious."

"Tom was a friend of Sam's. That's all it's about."

Detective Jenkins looked at her with squinted eyes. "Are you sure?" Obviously Tom didn't tell Katherine that he had stopped by the house.

"I'm sure."

"Well, that's about all I wanted to talk about."

"Good, now can we get around to business?"

Katherine put her arms around his neck and pulled him to her. She kissed him passionately. He returned the kiss and then said, "I'd like to stay but I have a few things to follow-up on before the day is over."

"Can't it wait?"

"Not really. I'm getting close to cracking these cases and I want to talk to a few other people today."

"Ok, but if you get done, call. I'd like you to come back."

"You go back to your gardening. It's good therapy."

"I don't need therapy."

"You need something to keep you busy."

"Hey, afternoon delight is good."

"I'll bet it is."

326

"Then stay for an hour and I'll show you."

"Can't do it Katherine. I have things to do."

"One more thing before I go. Tom's vehicle was seen in the vicinity of Ms. Kent's home around the time she was attacked. Do you have any idea why he'd be there?" Frank was now very glad Katherine didn't know he had stopped at the house. Not only does she not know that he knows Tom was home while the Jeep was gone, but she doesn't know he knows there's more to their relationship than just the past.

"No. I was at home. How could that be?"

"One of our officers happened to notice the vehicle and took note of the license plate."

Appearing noticeably nervous, Katherine said, "Please excuse me a minute Frank, I need to use the bathroom."

Katherine went into the bathroom. When she did, Detective Jenkins went into her kitchen and opened the freezer compartment of the refrigerator. He took out the box holding zip-lock bags. As he looked through the zip-locks, he noticed some of those he saw before were now missing. He brought the box into the living room and waited for Katherine to return.

"What's this all about?"

"I keep those in case something unfortunate happens."

"Such as?"

"If I end up getting pregnant, it would be easier to resolve a paternity issue than having to go to court. So I'm just protecting myself."

"Are these samples from all of the men you've slept with?"

"Well not all, but most."

There had to be over a dozen zip-lock bags in the tray. He looked at the names written on the bags. He recognized most of the names.

"Any here with the name Jenkins on it?"

"Not yet." She lied. "We could add to the collection."

"I'll have to pass."

"Frank, I'm throwing myself at you. Don't you want me?" She started to undress.

"Katherine, I'm not sure you're going to like how this all turns out."

"What do you mean?"

"You know what I mean. I think you should get yourself an attorney."

"Are you going to arrest me? I didn't do anything wrong."

"We'll see about that."

He went outside, got into his car and left.

After cleaning up from her gardening project, Katherine took a shower and dressed in a short floral skirt that hit at least ten inches above her knees. Her top was a simple peach camisole with some sequins sprinkled around the neckline. With no bra on, her nipples could be seen through the top. She looked like she was dressed to hook up. She went to her kitchen and made a Caesar salad, grilled a few chicken breasts and vegetables. She set the table for two. At six, her doorbell rang. She opened the door and greeted Tom Bowman with a kiss.

The two went to the kitchen, where Katherine mixed up the dressing in a wooden bowl. As she dressed the salad, she asked Tom to open a couple of beers. The two sat and enjoyed their dinner and drinks, and laughed while Katherine ran her foot up Tom's leg under the table. After dinner, Katherine said she would finish cleaning up, if Tom would make her an amaretto on the rocks at the bar. She would join him in a few minutes. Tom left for the living room with the first of the dishes being loaded into the dishwasher. Katherine picked up the kitchen telephone.

"Frank, its Katherine. I didn't like the way we left it when you were here."

"How did we leave it?"

"I think we're growing apart."

"Honestly Katherine, I'm not sure we're together."

"But you're always on duty and I know I have feelings for you."

"Let's skip the double talk. What can I do for you?"

"Not what you can do for me, but what I can do for you."

"What do you mean?"

"I have Tom Bowman here. I think he might be the person you're looking for. I told you I didn't do anything. Now I'm going to help you catch the attacker."

"Why do you say that?"

"I looked at his nails."

"His nails?"

"Yes. I remember what you told me. He has fake nails. When I looked closer, he has sharp tips under the fake nails. I think he's the one you are looking for."

"Katherine, don't do anything foolish. You don't have to put yourself at risk."

"Trust me Frank."

"Katherine, please don't get involved."

"I'm already involved Frank. I just thought I would help you out. After all, I can do some things that you can't. Tom will not be the wiser."

"I'll come see you tomorrow, but you don't have to do anything for me. You and Tom obviously have a thing going, and I don't think you'd want to have to testify against him."

"But I will."

"I'll see you tomorrow." He hung up the phone. What is she doing?

329

Chapter 37

The next night, Detective Jenkins went to Sundancers. He hoped to zero in on the attacker. His suspicion was that Tom Bowman had been committing the crimes but he didn't have enough evidence to positively identify him as the attacker. Everything he had accumulated so far pointed to Tom but Jenkins knew better than to jump to conclusions. Recalling when Sue Kent was attacked, Jenkins knew it couldn't have been Tom Bowman because he was at Katherine's when Jenkins knocked on the door just before Officer Trudy called him to report the attack on Sue Kent.

Tonight, Margarita Ortiz was bartending with Ron Jessup. Dee Crowe had the night off. Jenkins took up a stool at the corner of the bar and asked Margarita for a diet coke.

"Will you be having dinner?" she asked.
"No, I'm just here observing."
"Is there anything I can help you out with?"
"No. I'm here working on a case."

Ron and Margarita went to the far corner of the bar. They spent a few minutes talking about what both knew about the victims, the attacks and the places they occurred. While Ron was interested from a 'mystery to be solved' perspective, Margarita was more concerned as a potential victim.

"Does he think someone from the bar is committing the crimes?"

"I think so," said Ron.

"It makes me nervous thinking someone from here is attacking women."

"It's not just women, it's the cougars."

"I know, but I like to think our customers are friends. Obviously, someone isn't. I'll pay more attention and see if I can come up with anything."

"Margarita, if you hear or see anything, let the Detective know and stay out of it. The boss, Harry, is getting a little concerned that all the bad press will start costing the place some business."

"I understand and I'll avoid the subject if anyone asks."

"Good girl."

Margarita went back to Detective Jenkins. "Detective if I hear or see anything that might help with your case, I'll let you know."

"Thanks Margarita. These cases have been getting to me lately."

"I know what it means to be stressed. If there's anything I can do to help you personally, let me know." She smiled and twirled the ends of her long dirty blond hair as she flirted with Jenkins.

"Again, thanks Margarita. I'll keep that in mind."

Detective Jenkins looked around. He recognized a number of the patrons at the bar. Some were victims in cases he was pursuing, some were suspects and some were bystanders he had interviewed. He walked around the bar and stopped to talk with a few of the patrons.

"Ms. Benard, how are you doing?"

"Detective Jenkins, are you here on business?"

"Yes. And how are you?"

"Good. Thanks for asking."

Detective Jenkins looked at her from the floor up. She had on a pair of high heels, short black skirt with a low cut tank exposing more than it should.

"I'm glad to hear you're well. I hope to get your case, along with the others, resolved very soon."

"That'll be good. It seems the attacker is still at work."

"Why do you say that?"

"A friend of mine, Ruby Crane, was attacked over in Yarmouth the other night."

"I'm aware of the attack. The department was called in to consult on it."

"Do you think the attacks are linked?"

"I can't comment on it right now, but our department is working with both the Barnstable and Yarmouth police departments just in case."

"I sure hope you catch this guy soon."

"Has someone made a threat or advance on you recently?"

"Not a hostile advance."

"That's good. If anyone threatens you, call the police immediately."

"I will."

Detective Jenkins turned and walked further down the bar to where Tina Fletcher was sitting talking to Linda Sage.

"Well, well, well. If it isn't Detective Jenkins."

"Hello Ms. Fletcher and Ms. Sage."

"How are things with you Frank?" Tina said as she checked Frank out.

"I'm still working the cases, but I hope to have a breakthrough soon."

"Say Detective, you're working so hard on our behalf. How about we do something for you?"

Detective Jenkins was afraid where the line of talking was headed. There he was with two cougars wanting to repay him. What could they have in mind?

"I'm taken care of already, thank you. It's my job."

"Detective, Linda's told me all about how hard you work. I'm impressed."

"Thanks Ms. Fletcher, I'm flattered."

Tina picked up her cosmopolitan martini from the bar. "Well, if you change your mind about further reward, you know where we are."

"Thanks again," said Jenkins and he continued around the bar.

As Jenkins neared the door, he approached Tommy Anderson, Paul Bremmer, Bobby Jones and Kenny Brown. Tommy and Paul were seated at the bar. Bobby and Kenny were standing behind them. The four were having a conversation about the Sundancers baseball team with Ron Jessup.

"Gentlemen," said Jenkins.

"Any of you know where I can find Ed Phillips?"

"I thought he was in here a little while ago," said Tommy Anderson.

"He said he was going surf-fishing up at Chapin's tonight," Ron said.

"He was leaving when I came in," said Kenny Brown.

"What do you want with him?" asked Bobby Jones.

"Just some routine questioning," replied Jenkins. "If you see him, tell him I have a few questions for him."

"I will," replied Ron.

Detective Jenkins neared the door. The last person at the end of the bar was Easy Sue. She had been at the bar for a while and had already had too many drinks. Sue was dressed in a pair of jean shorts with a tiger print t-shirt that had a slogan on it, "Save the Cougars".

"Detective Jenkins," Sue slurred.

"Ms. Kent."

"On your way out?"

"Yes."

"Care for company?"

"No thank you. I'm on duty."

"So am I. We can be on duty together."

"I don't think we are in the same line of work."

"Oh we are. I'm looking for pricks and so are you."

"You have a point there."

She pointed at her chest, "I have two points here."

"Thanks anyway Ms. Kent. I like to work on my own."

"That's not what Katherine says."

"What does Katherine say?"

"She says you were in here a few nights ago working with a partner. Just like what I do."

"She said that, did she?"

"Sure did. She said you hooked up with that partner of yours after you left the bar."

Jenkins turned a little red. "I don't know what you're talking about."

"Oh yes you do. Don't be shy Detective. You were detecting. Your job carried over into the wee hours of the morning."

"As I said, I don't know what you're talking about."

"Ok. Have it your way, but we have more in common than you might think."

"Good bye Ms. Kent."

Detective Jenkins turned and walked out the door. As he walked away, he thought about his night with Pam Trudy. Apparently everyone knew about it. Jenkins started his car. He put it in gear and was pulling out when he spotted Ed Phillips coming down the driveway, so he circled the lot and parked again. Ed had already gone into the bar. Jenkins walked back in. Sue saw him. "So you rethinking my offer?"

"No. I remembered something I need to follow-up on."

Ron and Margarita were both standing in front of Sue on the other side of the bar. Detective Jenkins asked them where Ed went. Ron pointed to the men's room.

"You wanted to talk with him Detective?" said Ron.

"He'll be right out. I just poured him a beer. He'll be sitting over there." Ron pointed to a set of keys and a newly poured beer on the opposite side of the bar. Jenkins went over to Ed's seat, and took up the stool next to it. Margarita went over to him and asked if he wanted anything. He asked for another diet coke. When she brought it over, Jenkins noticed she had elaborately decorated fingernails.

"You have fake nails Ms. Ortiz?"

"Yea. They break quite a bit in this line of work. My hands are wet all the time, and my real nails get so soft."

"Are they the glue on or snap on kind?"

"Glue."

"Why not the snap on Flips?"

"I don't want to get my own nails shaped in order to accommodate the Flips"

"Know anyone who wears them?"

"Sure. Matter of fact, Ed does."

"He does?"

Ed was coming out of the bathroom. He came up to the stool where he had left his keys. He saw Jenkins sitting at the next stool, "I hear you were looking for me."

"Mr. Phillips, I would like to talk to you for a few minutes if you don't mind?"

Ed sat and took a sip of his beer. "What would you like to know?"

"I understand you use women's fake fingernails?"

"Who says they're women's?"

"Let me rephrase that. I understand you use fake fingernails?"

"So?"

"Can I see your hands?"

Ed held out his hands in front of Jenkins. Jenkins took hold of the hands and held them up so he could see under the nails.

"Flips?"

"What about them?"

"Can you snap one off for me?"

335

Ed grabbed the end of the nail and made a slight turn to one side. The nail snapped off. His own fingernail underneath the fake nail was shaped in a cylinder shape coming to a point.

"Can you grip my arm for me with the fake nail removed?"

"Sure."

Ed gripped Jenkins' arm.

"Turn your hand up so that you might scratch my arm."

Ed did as instructed. Ed didn't apply much pressure but the tip of his own nail left a line on Jenkins' arm.

"How many of your nails are fake?"

"Only three. I break them when I'm fishing and have found these fake nails work pretty well. I shake a lot of hands in my business, and it looks more professional."

"Why not just let your own nails grow out?"

"That takes too long. A friend of mine told me about these fake nails some time ago and I've used them ever since."

"Who told you about the nails?"

"Tom Bowman. Tom has fake nails on both his hands. Not all of his nails are fake you understand, but he said he had broken a few on each hand fishing and has started using the Flips. He learned about fake nails from Sam. I think Sam learned about it from his wife." Ed took a sip of his beer. Then he continued. "Tom said Katherine uses fake nails."

"She uses glue on acrylic fake nails. I've checked her," Jenkins said with a frown on his face.

"Maybe she grew her own nails back after Sam died."

"Did she ever have Flips that you know of?"

"I don't know. I only know what Tom told me."

"Well thank you Mr. Phillips for talking with me."

"Any time Detective."

Jenkins didn't finish his soda. He got up and left the bar with a sick feeling that his list of suspects just got bigger, again.

Margarita came over to Ed, "What was that all about?"

"The detective is interested in fake fingernails. He looked at mine. He made a few notes in that notepad of his and then left."

"Ed, you might have helped him with the lead he needs to solve the recent attacks."

"Really?"

"Really. That would make you a hero. Better watch out for the cougars."

"They're just pussy cats." He scanned the bar.

"Oh you think so?"

"I know so."

Chapter 38

Detective Jenkins went back to the station. He asked Officer Trudy to join him in Captain Tomlinson's office. When the three were seated, Jenkins said, "I think I have a good idea as to how these attacks have played out."

Captain Tomlinson took a sip of his coffee. "Let's hear it."

"Some of the attacks have involved sexual assaults and some have not. We have DNA samples from those involving sexual assault. The lab has been able to identify all of those samples. Ms. Sterns has never forgiven Mr. Bowman for the loss of her husband, Sam Sterns. As you recall, he died in a freak accident a few years ago while ice fishing with Mr. Bowman."

"You think she held Mr. Bowman responsible for her husband's death?" asked Officer Trudy.

"I do. To show how far she would go to get revenge, she would sleep with him. She also would get him to meet with her at certain locations that would put Mr. Bowman in the vicinity of the attacks."

"But that doesn't explain the DNA that was recovered."

"Here it gets interesting," said Jenkins.

"I can't wait to hear this," exclaimed Captain Tomlinson.

"Ms. Sterns would have the men she had sex with use a condom. Then she would save the condom, spread the semen on some of the victims, implicating one of her lovers."

"Didn't she turn a condom over to you Frank?" asked Officer Trudy.

"Yes, but she only gave me one condom and that was the one I had you take to the lab to be tested."

"Pretty creative if I do say so," said Captain Tomlinson.

"Sure was," said Detective Jenkins.

"So she used Bowman's DNA to implicate him?" asked Trudy.

"That's what I think. What I'm not sure of is how I actually prove this theory and that's not the end of the DNA story. She has condoms in her freezer from other men she slept with."

Jenkins looked at Trudy and continued. "When you saw the attacker squeezing something out of a zip-lock marked 'T. Bowman' onto Ms. Kent, I believe it was Ms. Sterns. She had a condom from Bowman and was using his semen to mislead us. She used the saved condoms to place semen on some of the other victims as well."

"And what about the scratches?" Asked Captain Tomlinson.

"As it turns out, Ms. Sterns used to have those snap-on fingernails, Flips. She went back to using the acrylic version after her husband died. I was pursing leads for suspects who have Flips because the real nails are shaped like claws with fairly sharp tips. One of the suspects, Ed Phillips, has nails as I described. When interviewed, Mr. Phillips said he learned of the technique from Tom Bowman who had learned of it from Sam Sterns."

"And Sam Sterns was Ms. Sterns husband," said Officer Trudy.

"That's right. According to Mr. Phillips, Ms. Sterns might have used those fake snap-on nails in the past and he said Bowman has a few fake nails on his hands now."

Captain Tomlinson stood and walked around his desk. "So let me get this right, the scratches were done by someone who has fake fingernails, the snap-on kind?"

"That's what she wanted us to think. In actuality, Ms. Sterns inflicted some of the scratches on her victims as a result of wearing her gardening gloves during the attacks. A few of the attacks were actually carried out by Bowman himself. In those attacks, Bowman did the scratching with his nails," Jenkins said as he turned to speak to a pacing Captain Tomlinson.

"How were the scratches created?" asked Tomlinson.

"Her gardening gloves have grips on them. They're rather abrasive. The grips leave a pattern that looks like fingernails did the scratches. I didn't think much of it, but she actually scratched me with them one day when I was at her house. Granted the scratches on my arm were not as pronounced as those on some of the victims, but then again, she only touched my arm lightly."

"How did she knock some of the victims out?" asked Officer Trudy.

"The women who were knocked out were attacked by Bowman, but he wasn't present at all of the attacks and he didn't spread all of the semen. Katherine followed him on a few of the attacks and deposited it after Bowman left the scene. He didn't even know she was there. I think if we check out her garage, we'll find her gardening gloves with DNA from a few victims on them, and maybe even something she used to hit some of the victims. I've seen the zip-locks in her freezer containing condoms and they all had names written on them."

"Then get a warrant and search her place. I'd like to get this wrapped up," ordered Captain Tomlinson. "And take Trudy with you. If you find evidence, send it to the lab and have Trudy arrest the woman."

"Ok Captain. We'll get right on it."

As Detective Jenkins and Officer Trudy were walking out, Captain Tomlinson whispered to Jenkins, "And thanks Frank for keeping me out of it."

"No need to whisper Captain, Trudy knows of your indiscretions."

"How?" Captain Tomlinson asked in an angry tone.

"She saw you at the Route 28 Motel with Ms. Fletcher."

"She did? When?"

"It really doesn't matter Captain. She was watching the place as part of our investigation when she saw you there leaving a room. When you came out, Ms. Fletcher came to the door and gave you a kiss."

"So?"

"She was wearing only a bath towel."

"Trudy told you that?"

"Actually, she has it on video. We were taking video of the cougars coming and going. You're on it."

"Have it destroyed."

"Already done. We didn't need it so I had Trudy dispose of it."

"If my wife ever saw that..."

"Or the Town Council."

"Them too."

"No worry Captain."

"Thanks Jenkins."

Officer Trudy and Detective Jenkins went back to his office. They requested a search warrant. Jenkins told Trudy to pick it up and then they would go check out Ms. Stern's residence.

"Ms. Sterns sure went out of her way to implicate Mr. Bowman."

"I guess she just couldn't get over her husband dying."

"I think about the planning and execution. She must have really worked at this for some time."

"I'd say. She got me to confide in her. She got Bowman to sleep with her and provide the DNA. She used the garden gloves to scratch the victims so it looked like someone with those false-nails did it, knowing that would lead us to Tom. She pretended to cooperate with us in providing leads and evidence."

"She must be crazy," said Pam.

"This is more than crazy Pam. She knew all of the victims. She knew where they would be and when. She had the knowledge, the means, the tools and the nerve."

"I'll get the search warrant and be back in twenty minutes."

"See you then."

Detective Jenkins and Officer Trudy went to Katherine Stern's residence. When they pulled up, Katherine was working in one of her flower gardens. She stopped tending to her flowers and stood up. She was wearing sneakers, a bathing suit, and a beach cover up. Her hair was pulled up in a twisted bun. Detective Jenkins walked up to her.

"Ms. Sterns. We have a search warrant to search your residence."

"Frank, you've been here numerous times, why do you want to search my home?"

Officer Trudy reached out and presented Katherine Sterns with the search warrant. "We're looking for evidence."

"Evidence of what?"

"The recent attacks that have taken place on some of your friends," said Officer Trudy.

"Frank, some of the women were raped. How could I have done that?"

"It will all come out later. Now, can I see those gardening gloves you have on?"

Katherine took off the gardening gloves. Jenkins put on a pair of plastic gloves and took Katherine's gardening gloves from her. He put them in a plastic zip-lock bag. As he did, he turned them over to look at the palms. "New gloves." He exclaimed.

342

"Do you have more of these in your garage?" asked Officer Trudy.

"Why do you want my gardening gloves?" Katherine asked in a tone of exasperation.

Officer Trudy went into the garage and found a shoebox stuffed behind some paint cans. Inside the box were two pair of used gardening gloves. Trudy bagged the gloves. Looking around more, she found what looked like a handle for a maul. The metal maul was missing. She picked it up and came out of the garage with the maul handle and the bagged gloves.

"I think I have something here Detective."

She held up the items. "Ok. Take them to the lab and we'll see if we have a match."

"Frank, why are you doing this to me?"

"Ms. Sterns, you did this to yourself."

Officer Trudy took a set of handcuffs off her service belt and approached Ms. Sterns.

"Ms. Sterns, we're taking you to station for questioning in the cases of the attacks on Ann Benard, Tina Fletcher, Linda Sage, Carrie Morgan, Ruby Crane and myself."

Officer Trudy read Katherine her rights and made sure she understood them. Jenkins took Katherine Sterns into custody and put her into the back seat of the cruiser. On the way back to the station, he told Pam to get the evidence they found tested and he would take her in for the questioning. Pam dropped them off at the station and continued on to the lab.

As Detective Jenkins and Katherine Sterns were walking into the station, her in handcuffs, she said, "Frank, I can make you happy. Just make this go away."

"Katherine, there's nothing you can do that can get you out of this mess you've created."

"But Frank. He had to be held accountable for Sam's death."

"You attacked your friends. You went through all that trouble to implicate Mr. Bowman. Why didn't you just go after him directly? You had him in your bed. You could have done things to him that would have made him regret having ever known your husband."

She was quiet. She didn't say another word.

"And what about all those zip-lock bags? You slept with all those men just to be able to plant evidence. What were you thinking?"

After the booking process was complete, Jenkins walked her to a holding cell. As he did, Officer Trudy was just coming back from the lab.

"I waited until the lab technician did some preliminary test on the things I turned in."

"What did they find?"

"The maul handle contained hair samples matching Ms. Benard and me. One of the pair of gloves had DNA on it matching Mr. Bowman and Ms. Fletcher. The other pair of gloves, the ones that looked like they had blood stains on them, matched up with Ms. Sage. I think we have what we need."

Katherine didn't say a word. She went into the holding cell without a protest.

Detective Jenkins went to Captain Tomlinson's office.

"The search warrant produced enough evidence for us to solidify our case against Ms. Sterns," said Jenkins.

"Good. Go find Bowman and arrest him. The two of them were in this together. First get her and take her in to see Judge Benson. If she doesn't have an attorney, get a Public Defender assigned. Get her to plead and then it's out of our hands."

"Sure. She has her own attorney coming down to represent her. As soon as the attorney is here, I'll get her into the court."

344

"Thanks Jenkins."

Katherine's attorney arrived within a half hour. Detective Jenkins was notified. He had Katherine brought from the cell and into the court. The DA had already been briefed and was ready for the charge. The bailiff announced for all to rise.

Katherine had tears in her eyes and had been whispering something to her attorney. When Katherine saw the Judge, the tears stopped and she smiled.

The bailiff announced, "the Honorable Michael Benson presiding."

Detective Jenkins who was seated behind the Prosecutor looked at Katherine and wondered why her expression had changed from despondent to a smile.

Then it hit him. She knew Michael Benson. This couldn't be good.

The Judge ordered a bond of fifty thousand dollars. Katherine's attorney indicated she would post the bail. A court date was set for three months from then. The attacks on the cougars were over for now.

Chapter 39

A few days after wrapping up the case, Detective Jenkins and Officer Trudy went to the ZooQuarium. They went into Mr. Carson's office.

"Detective Jenkins, I read in the paper where there was an arrest in the attacks."

"Yes, we have someone in custody."

"I'm sure glad the investigation vindicated Charlie."

"As it turned out, the suspect had read about Charlie's escape in the paper and used the information to set clues to mislead the police."

"Still, I'm glad we didn't have to put Charlie down. Come follow me. The show is about to begin and you two are our special guests of honor today."

Jenkins and Trudy followed Mr. Carson into the amphitheater. Joe Mains was up front of a large crowd. He motioned for Mr. Carson to come up front with the two guests. Joe Mains had a headset on and spoke to the audience.

"Ladies and Gentlemen. Let me introduce our special guests to you. This is Detective Jenkins and Officer Trudy of the Dennis Police Department. Thanks to their good work we still have Charlie."

The crowd gave a loud applause. Joe Mains raised his right arm high and everyone turned to look at a small side door just off the stage. Charlie ran out. He approached Joe

Mains. Joe motioned with his hands to Jenkins and Trudy. Joe held one hand to his cheek and with the other pointed directly at Officer Trudy. Charlie turned and went right to Trudy. He sat in front of Pam Trudy and then gently put a paw on her knee and reached up with his head. He gave her a lick on the cheek. Everyone in the audience cheered. Then Joe Mains made a hand shaking motion with his hands and Charlie turned to Jenkins and held out his paw. Jenkins shook it. The crowd roared and clapped. Joe Mains snapped his fingers and Charlie returned to the stage.

Joe and Charlie entertained the audience for the next forty-five minutes. When the show was over, everyone cheered. Jenkins and Trudy were standing and clapping with the rest of the guests.

After the show, Joe Mains and Mr. Carson thanked Frank Jenkins and Pam Trudy again for their help. As the two left the ZooQuarium, Frank said, "Want to get some lunch?"
"Sure."
"How about Sundancers?"
"Sounds good to me."
"Plus, we might get to see another cougar show."
"You think?"
The two left the ZooQuarium heading east on Route 28. Pulling into Sundancers nearly full parking lot, Trudy commented, "Looks like Sundancers is pretty busy."
As they entered, Frank Jenkins looked past the bar and saw all of the cougars sitting around a table having drinks and talking. Kat was at the head of the table. He and Pam took up seats on the corner of the bar within earshot of the group. They ordered drinks from Dee Crowe. As Dee was making the drinks, Ron came over to her and whispered, "This should be interesting."
"You think?" said Dee.
She took the drinks back to Jenkins and Trudy. As she did, Dee could overhear the conversation taking place amongst the cougars.

347

"But Kat, why didn't you just come to us? We would have helped you," said Ann.

Tina added, "We women have to stick together. If we had known, we would have helped you."

"Kat, why did you get so involved with this Tom guy just to get revenge? We could have gotten some of the guys here to take care of things for us," added Sue.

"I wanted to make sure he paid for what he did. I think the officials think there's more to Sam's death than what was told."

"Really?" said Linda. "Did a certain Detective tell you that?"

Linda motioned with her head in the direction of Detective Jenkins.

"Not in so many words. I just know there's more to it than Tom Bowman has told."

Kat bowed her head. When she looked up again, she had tears in her eyes. In a broken voice she said, "I'm so sorry. You're all my friends and I didn't mean to hurt any of you and I had no idea Tom was....."

Ann stood and came around to Kat. She put her arms around her. "I forgive you Kat. You don't have to worry. I'm sure we'll all support you."

Katherine looked at each of them. "Thank you. I don't deserve you as friends."

"We've all been there Kat," said Sue.

"I'm just sorry you'll have to get involved with the police and the court case as it comes up."

"Don't worry about us Kat. We're with you," Linda said looking around at the other cougars. "We're not pressing any charges and I don't think any of us will be helpful to the authorities if they come after you."

"Thank you again. All of you."

They all stood and gathered around her. They had a group hug.

Ron said to Dee and Margarita, "Look at that. The cougars are banding together. I didn't think they acted as a pack. Who would have guessed?"

Frank Jenkins turned to Pam Trudy. "Now isn't that interesting?"

Pam Trudy added, "There is no other place like Sundancers."

Made in the USA
Charleston, SC
11 May 2010